PRAISE FOR ANDREW KNOTT

"I thoroughly enjoyed Andrew Knott's delightful debut! This quirky, second-chance romance explores the complexities of love in all its disastrous forms, with a cast of unforgettable characters and an unlikely romantic hero you can't help but root for. Knott's background as a humorist is evident, as his signature, self-deprecating humor and hilarious one-liners light up every page. Charming, witty, and heartfelt, *Love's a Disaster* will remind even the most cynical of readers that sometimes second chances do exist (and also that there's never a bad time to quote Green Day). Knott is a true talent and one to watch!

- LINDSAY HAMEROFF, AUTHOR OF TILL THERE WAS YOU
AND NEVER PLANNED ON YOU

"*Love's a Disaster* is laugh-out-loud funny in places and then breaks your heart a page later. And it is all very, very real."

- GARY M. ALMETER, AUTHOR OF KISSING THE ROADKILL
BACK TO LIFE AND THE EMPEROR OF ICE-CREAM

"Andrew Knott's *Love's A Disaster* is a witty and wonderful second-chance romance perfect for fans of *About A Boy* and 'Gilmore Girls.' In addition to lots of lighthearted moments, this novel's complex characters provide emotional depth that stays with you well beyond the final page. Complete with a swoon-worthy ending, *Love's a Disaster* serves as a beacon of hope for anyone yearning for another shot with the one who got away."

- LIZ ALTERMAN, AUTHOR OF THE PERFECT
NEIGHBORHOOD AND SAD SACKED

LOVE'S A DISASTER

ANDREW KNOTT

Copyright © 2024 by Andrew Knott and Bayou Rose Press, an imprint of Bayou Wolf Press

All rights reserved.

No part of this book may be reproduced in any form or by any electronic or mechanical means, including information storage and retrieval systems, without written permission from the author, except for the use of brief quotations in a book review.

Paperback ISBN: 9798988635437

Ebook ISBN: 9798988635444

❀ Created with Vellum

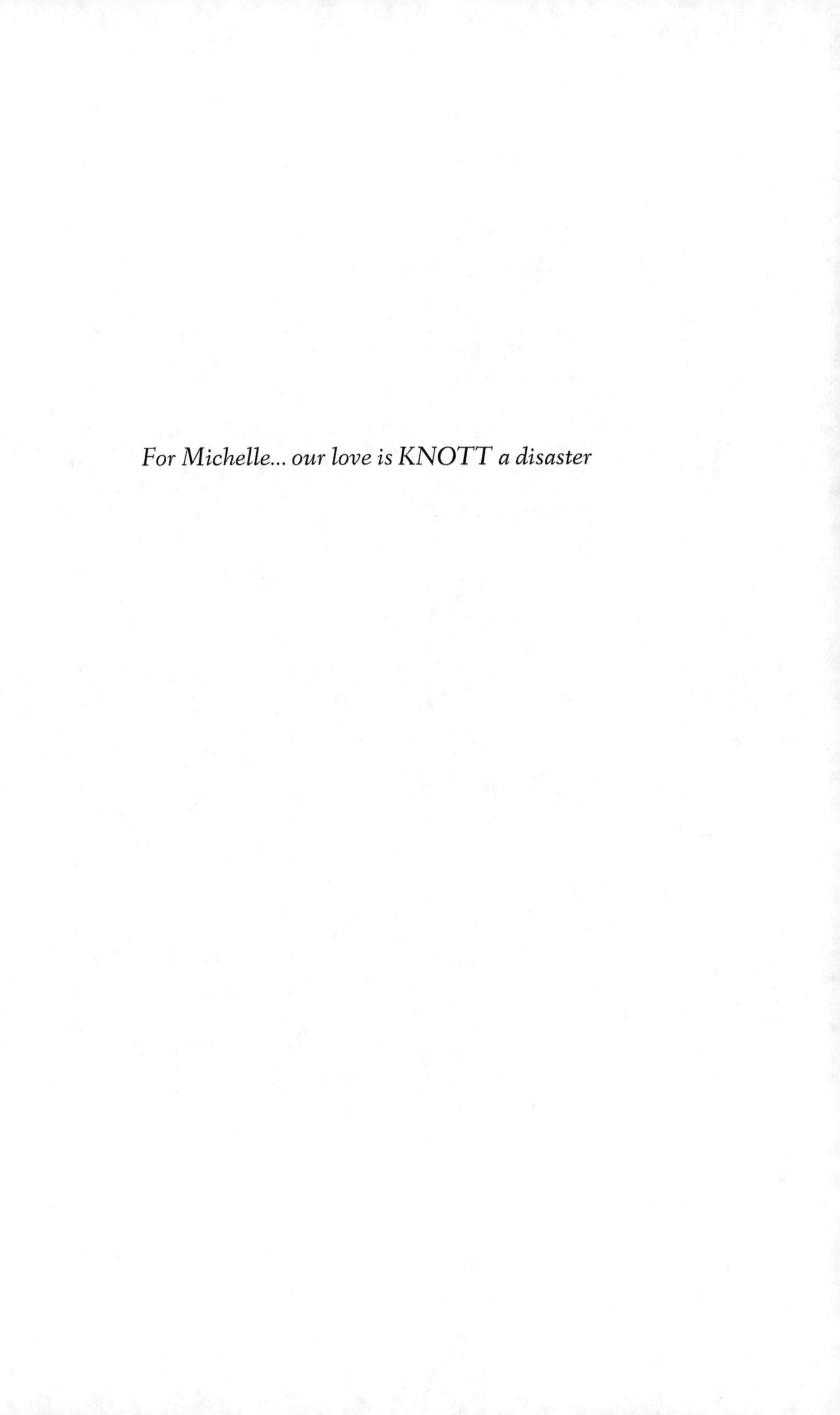

For Michelle... our love is KNOTT a disaster

"Being in love is totally punk rock."

– Joey Comeau, *A Softer World: Truth and Beauty Bombs*

...

"Maybe love is just about finding the person you can be your weird self with."

– Matt Haig, *Reasons to Stay Alive*

September 3, 1999

A BOLT of lightning creases the Florida night sky, illuminating the bedroom of an eleven-year-old boy. The boy leaves the blinds that cover his bedroom window open so the early dawn light can slip in to wake him. He loves having a few extra minutes before school to spend with his dad. Sometimes they play a card game or sit side-by-side on the couch watching TV. A cataclysmic clap of thunder resonates through the bedroom a split second after the lightning flashes across the wall. A small metal statue of a knight in armor rattles on the shelf above the boy's bed, nearly toppling off.

The boy sits up. He'd been asleep, barely, but the light and the noise startled him awake. Thunderstorms are an inescapable feature of a Florida childhood, but for some reason, this storm, this bolt, seems different. He can almost feel the electricity penetrating his body, traveling straight through to his core. The boy shivers. He lies back down and pulls the covers over his head. It takes him nearly an hour to fall back asleep. When he wakes up in the morning, his life will have changed forever.

PART 1

CHAPTER 1

September 3, 2010

If Caleb Monroe could give all the guys out there just one piece of advice, it would be this. If you're planning to propose to the love of your life at an outdoor punk rock concert during summer in Florida, do not, and this can't be emphasized enough, wear black eyeliner. No matter how cool you think you look, it's not worth the risk. Because if things go south, your would-be fiancée panics and runs out while you're down on one knee, and the tears start welling up from somewhere deep inside, the waterfall of emotion will have your make-up running faster than, well, the person who just broke your heart into a zillion pieces. Getting rejected is hard enough. But having to jostle your way out of a mosh pit with black smudges on your cheeks *after* getting rejected? That's even more humiliating. Because between the smudges and the damp, sweaty hair and the black tattered jeans and the leather choker with spikes, you'll probably look like a bedraggled coal miner who shops at Hot Topic.

Now, this might seem like extremely specific advice. You might be asking yourself: *Is it very likely that this advice will come in handy in my life?* Well, it's hard to say, but one thing is certain. Caleb Monroe wishes someone would've given him a heads-up about this particular possibility before it all went down.

Sometimes extremely specific advice is the best kind.

...

"Hey, I'm going to grab a drink before The Pigeontoes come on," Caleb shouts over the thrashing of guitars and primal screams produced by the concert's opening act. It's Labor Day Weekend in the heart of Florida, so the air is thick with humidity and the smell of weed and sweat. "I've always wanted to try one of those Smirnoff things! Maybe something with pomegranate in it. I'm feeling a little crazy tonight!"

"Um, can you just get me a bottle of water?" Sadie replies.

"Okay! One bottle of water for M'lady!" Caleb gives a little bow like he's a medieval knight at court. He thinks it's kind of their thing. It's unclear whether Sadie agrees.

...

Caleb and Sadie are positioned close to the stage and the crowd has filled in some since they arrived a half hour before. They are two small dots floating in an undulating, buzzing mass of exposed flesh, piercings, green hair, tattoos, and body odor. The sun is finally starting to dip behind the tree line, silhouetting the palm trees and tall pines on the horizon. The sweltering heat doesn't diminish, it just changes shape.

Caleb takes a moment to get his bearings, identifying the path of least resistance to the concessions area. One path is blocked by a guy and girl who have been making out for so long that Caleb wouldn't be surprised if their tongues are knotted together, perhaps requiring medical intervention. He leaves them to it, because sometimes people have to learn the hard way, and slides past an older man with a wild look in his eyes and a leather backpack looped over one shoulder.

While it's true that Caleb is "feeling a little crazy tonight," the prospect of a pomegranate-flavored alcoholic beverage is probably not what's causing his stomach to churn relentlessly. His thoughts are scattered and completely lacking organization. Caleb's mom would be very disappointed.

Where is the ring? It's gotta be in one of these pockets, right? Will it even be possible for Sadie to hear my proposal over all the noise? Am I doing the right thing? At this particular moment in time and, you know, in general?

At last, the mass of humanity recedes, and the concession stand beckons. Caleb falls into line behind an extremely tall, lanky man who seems even taller because of his heavily shellacked, spiky mohawk that juts out at least six inches from his closely shaved scalp. The man orders three cans of Bud Light. After he collects his drinks, he gives Caleb a nod, his mohawk trembling menacingly, before moving aside to clear the way.

"Do you have any drinks with pomegranate?" Caleb shouts to the concessions worker so she can hear him above the din of the concert crowd.

"What?" she replies. She looks at Caleb as if he has two heads, maybe three.

"POM-E-GRANATE!" Caleb shouts a bit louder, enunciating the syllables.

"Um, I don't think so? We have Mike's Hard Lemonade?"

"That will do! And let me get a bottle of water and a beer. Actually, make it a double!"

"A double what? Two beers?"

"Sure! It's a big night!"

"Oh yeah?"

"Yeah! I'm proposing to my girlfriend!"

"Wow. That is big. Here, the lemonade is on me then. For good luck. And since we didn't have the pome... whatever."

"Thanks! That's really cool of you!"

Caleb gathers up the bottles and two cups of beer. A small rivulet of foam sloshes over the edge and drips down the side of the plastic onto his fingers. He belatedly realizes he ordered way too many drinks for two people. Especially since one of the people only asked for water. He's not sure what he's going to do with all the drinks now that he has them in his possession, but he has more important things to worry about.

"Hey," the girl says as Caleb turns to leave. He looks back. She looks pensive. Maybe a bit sad. "Don't mess it up," she says.

Caleb flashes a nervous smile, "That's the plan," he replies. "I mean, trying *not* to mess it up is the plan."

He leans down to take a sip from one of the beers to stop it from leaking all over him. Then he turns toward the crowd, ready to brave the maelstrom with way too many drinks in hand, one ring in his pocket (hopefully), and a destiny to fulfill. If he doesn't mess it up.

...

The concert feels like it goes on forever. Has it been seven hours? Eight? Forty-five minutes? Caleb has lived his entire life in Florida, so he knows it is always hot in early September, of course, but is it usually *this* hot? The heat feels different somehow. Like it's emanating from inside of him. He thinks back to summertime when he was in high school, and his Society for Creative Anachronism troupe used to suit up for medieval battles at the park beside the middle school. Wearing chainmail on a late-July afternoon before the daily thunderstorms descended was pretty damn uncomfortable, but this heat was even more all-encompassing. Maybe it's the Mike's Hard Lemonade? Honestly, the drink is a delight, but it does seem to be pretty potent. And perhaps pairing it with two beers wasn't the smartest decision Caleb has ever made.

He begins to feel lightheaded and dazed. When he looks around at Sadie, the crowd, the stage, it seems like there is a film covering the world. Like someone unraveled a gigantic roll of Saran Wrap and covered everyone and everything except for Caleb. Maybe the gods did it? If gods existed, Caleb wouldn't be surprised if this was how they chose to spend their time and utilize their powers. Messing with him specifically. And based on Caleb's personal history, it certainly seemed like the gods did enjoy toying with him. Like bored house cats torturing an innocent mouse.

The Pigeontoes have been rocking out for quite some time now, but honestly, Caleb's barely noticed. He's been focusing on staying upright and keeping an eye on Sadie to see if she's giving off any particular vibes he should be aware of. He studies Sadie's face and his heart almost stops. She has a way of doing this to him. In fact, she has since the first time they met. Her black eyeliner makes her piercing blue eyes stand out even more. Just one look with those eyes can turn Caleb's whole world upside down. He becomes so captivated he can't think straight. Sadie looks in Caleb's direction now and gives him a small smile. He gives her a big goofy smile back and he's certain he looks like a complete moron.

From what Caleb can tell, Sadie is having a good time. She's bobbing her head a fair amount, singing along sometimes, throwing her hands in the air when the lead singer says she should. Everything seems normal enough. She was a little distracted when they stopped for pizza on the way to the concert. She was on her phone most of the time and she didn't eat much, but she falls into those moods some-times. It's like her mind slips away into another dimension for a few minutes or hours or days, leaving her body behind to steer the ship. And then suddenly, she's back. Happy Sadie returns. Well, not Happy Sadie so much as caustic, sarcastic, and whip-smart Sadie. When she starts to poke fun at him for making puns instead of letting the puns slide by, Caleb knows she's back to her normal self.

Oh god, the song is coming up. For weeks, Caleb has been obses-sively checking online for information about The Pigeontoes' shows. He has memorized their standard setlist, and the song they're on now, "All My Favorite Hearts are Broken," comes right before the song he's been waiting for. Where is the damn ring?

While he's searching the pockets of his jeans, Caleb pulls out his phone. A notification on the lock screen indicates a text message from Mom. He glances at it quickly and sees

need to talk

and

it's important.

He doesn't think much of it. Something is always important to Mom. She probably found an error in the Excel spreadsheet he emailed her this morning that they use to track sale prices at the local grocery stores.

No time for coupons now! It's go time. Time to focus and land this plane. Maybe his preparation hasn't been flawless, but what matters most is the moment. That's what his high school robotics team coach, Ms. Farragut, used to tell Caleb when he got nervous before regionals. She would say, "Robotics stars aren't made in the lab or classroom. They are made at that moment when the gymnasium lights are burning bright, and the first bits of metal begin to clash and clang."

A different type of metallic clashing and clanging brings Caleb's attention back to the present. The Pigeontoes have just wrapped up "All My Favorite Hearts are Broken" and the crowd is delirious. The drummer, shirtless and apparently enraged by something (maybe the heat?), has just put his foot through his base drum and tossed a cymbal stand across the stage. The spectacle, the clattering of the crashing cymbals, and the squawking of the pummeled stage mic only make the crowd more frenzied. In the pit, it feels like standing in the ocean when a hurricane is churning way out in the Atlantic. Waves of bouncing bodies undulate and crash around and against each other. Their brains are all melting, but goddammit, they are having the time of their lives.

For a terrifying few seconds, Caleb thinks he might die before his big moment. What a shame that would be, but also a bit of a relief, maybe? However, things settle down as the lead singer, his black hair damp with sweat and sticking out in every direction, steps up to the mic, stretches his arms to the side, and rasps, "Whoa, whoa, whoa," while making the calm down motion with his hands. During the lull, Caleb gathers himself, slipping the ring out of his back pocket–that's right! He had moved it to the back pocket so it wouldn't fall out when he was messing about with his wallet or phone. He clenches the ring tightly in his sweaty palm, hiding it from the world.

From here it's a blur. The song starts. The crowd quiets. Raising their cell phones in the air, illuminating the night sky with the flashlights. From above, it probably looks like the world has turned upside down. The sky with its twinkling stars has somehow switched positions with the muddy earth. From Caleb's perspective, it feels like one million cars have directed their headlights straight into his eyes all at once. Is the world upside down? Right-side up? It's impossible to say. With his last remaining thread of conscious thought, Caleb recognizes that the song's bridge is coming up. It's now or never.

He hurriedly grabs Sadie's wrists. She is quite obviously startled. He turns her toward him, gazes into her ocean blue eyes, and begins to sing along. Sadie is clearly uncomfortable now, her eyes wide, like a cartoon character who has just seen an anvil hurtling toward her head. The music fades away. The crowd seems to recede. All that's left is Caleb down on one knee with a ring in his hand, saying something that Sadie may or may not be able to hear.

She pulls her hands away. Recognition in her eyes. And something else. Perhaps a twinge of... horror? She takes a quick look around to find a way out. Her eyes are watering. She races away, grasping, pushing, and shoving through anyone and anything blocking her escape.

Caleb is still down on one knee, one hand outstretched, the ring still clenched between his thumb and index finger. The light from cell phone flashlights glints off the small diamond. All that's left in front of him are the shoe-shaped indentations in the mud where Sadie had been standing. And what feels like a billion strangers surrounding him. He looks up and catches a glimpse of Sadie disappearing into the crowd. One moment she's there and the next she's gone. It's funny how that can happen.

...

Sadie doesn't look back. To her, it feels like everything all at once. Sadness. Regret. Shame. All of it washes over her. A movie montage of the past few months plays in her mind. The fun moments with Caleb are there, of course, but so are the canceled dates, the unreturned texts, and most vividly, that night. *That* night. Caleb pacing in the living room, agitated and upset. The text messages she wasn't supposed to see. The crowded bar. The tequila. The dark bedroom. The pulsing headache the morning after. It's all too much. It's everything. All at once. Sadie doesn't know where she should go, but she knows she has to get out of here. She runs... fast.

...

Of course, Caleb knows what just transpired is a big deal. How could he not? In fact, it was probably the biggest of deals. A deal so big that if his mom had found it at their favorite grocery store, she would've texted him immediately just so he wouldn't miss out on it.

He knows that he has blown it. But in his mind, what exactly *it* is remains to be determined. In the immediate aftermath, after he has fought his way out of the concert pit, made his way to a bathroom, and cleaned up his face, he thinks maybe things will just blow over. He tries to text Sadie, but she doesn't answer. No surprise there. She was clearly upset and not ready for the whole marriage thing. But that doesn't mean their relationship is over, right?

In the past when they had disagreements, they would spend a few days apart and then reconnect. Sure, they had never had a failed marriage proposal before, but still. Like all couples, they had ups and downs. Bumps in the road. They had actually been traversing a bit of a rough patch over the last couple of months. There was that one night that it all went wrong, and it seemed like they might be over. The night that Caleb made a huge mistake that almost cost him everything. But he reconnected with Sadie the next day and they talked things out. They even talked about forever. Things seemed better after that. Almost normal. Caleb never even considered the possibility that this was the end. The final bump. The bump that would toss them from the car and leave them broken on the side of the road.

Caleb sets his phone down on the edge of the bathroom sink while he cleans up. A notification illuminates his screen. A message, but not from Sadie. It's his mom, again.

CALL ME NOW! It's about Lauren.

Whatever. It can wait. Everyone else can wait.

Staring at his reflection in the bathroom mirror, the music still pulsing from outside making the walls vibrate, Caleb thinks about the soles of Sadie's Converse sneakers. The last trace of her he saw as she ran away. They were worn, almost threadbare around the edges. Caleb hadn't realized their relationship was even more tenuous than her worn-out shoes, but it turns out it was.

...

Sadie was gone for good.

CHAPTER 2

September 3, 2022

A LOT CAN CHANGE in twelve years. Is that a particularly profound statement? Probably not. After all, 4,380 days is a lot of days. It feels like a vast expanse of time even before you start tallying up the hours, minutes, and seconds. But the passage of time really hits extra hard on certain days of the year. It's funny how a day on a calendar, a little number in a square, can awaken memories. It can make it feel like twelve years have passed in the blink of an eye. On the other hand, it can make it feel like twelve years ago happened in a different lifetime. Maybe even in a different universe.

Caleb sits uncomfortably in the middle seat of the most budget of airplanes. It's just past nine in the evening and it just so happens to be the same day on the calendar that he unsuccessfully proposed to a girl he once loved. At a punk rock concert of all places. What had he been thinking?

As is often the case during his more contemplative moments, particularly on this particular day of the year, Caleb's mind wanders.

Mostly in the back-in-time direction. He glances to his left. The man seated beside him is dressed in a white dress shirt, the top button is undone, and his tie is pulled down, so it hangs sloppily around his neck. The man is fast asleep, his head resting against the side of the plane next to the window. Caleb doesn't know how the man possibly fell asleep so fast considering that the plane hasn't even completed its ascent.

Caleb looks across the sleeping man out the window. He sees the twinkling lights of the city below, illuminating the September night sky. All those pinpricks of light look familiar. He knows why, but then again, he doesn't.

Twelve years ago, at almost this exact time, everything changed. He checks his watch to confirm. Yes, 105,192 hours have passed. Almost to the minute. And 23 years ago—or approximately 201,480 hours ago—at almost this exact time, well, Caleb chooses not to think about what happened then. All of it is ancient history. None of it can be undone. Decisions that were made, actions that were taken or not taken, none of it really matters.

Caleb's ruminations about past failures are suddenly interrupted by the urgency of his current failures, as is often the case these days. The five-year-old child seated to Caleb's right begins to methodically, and with unmistakable intention, kick the back of the seat in front of her.

Thump, thump, thump.

This is just Caleb's luck. Of all the seatmates he could possibly have on this flight, he ends up wedged between a snoring busi-nessman and an annoying five-year-old. Outrageous. Maybe there is someone he can complain to? An airplane seat-assignment czar, perhaps?

Even if there was some sort of emergency hotline he could call, it is unlikely that Caleb's complaints would be taken seriously. Primarily because his seat assignment wasn't some random act of the airline gods. He was assigned this particular seat because the five-year-old girl (who he has to admit, if not for the seat-kicking thing, is rather adorable with her curly brown hair and headphones with a Minnie Mouse bow on top) kind of belongs to him.

When it comes to children, Caleb thinks that possession is a bit of a funny concept. "Your little girl is so cute," strangers will say to him at the grocery store or the library. "Which one is yours?" a mom will ask anywhere there is a pack of children with no defined attachments to adults. Like at the playground.

Caleb understands such statements and questions are innocent and trivial. People toss them out into conversation reflexively without thinking. Yet he still pauses to think each time, if only for a split second, before he responds.

"Thank you," he says. Or, "The girl over there with the curly brown hair is mine. The one who, well, apparently she's not wearing shoes anymore. Sorry about that."

The truth is, Emily, the curly-haired five-year-old in question, is not *his* in the way most people would assume. But he supposes that she is *his* in most of the ways that matter.

First off, she lives in his house without paying rent. The house is small and sits on a busy, four-lane road that cars drive much too fast on in Caleb's opinion. There are no neighbors. This house sits alone. Caleb always assumed it was the stubborn one. All the other houses that sat on this road when it was less busy must've picked up and left in search of more peaceful locations on quiet cul-de-sacs. Or alternatively, this little house plopped down in between a brick wall, which blocks out a small strip of offices and shops, and a clump of unruly palmetto bushes, which partially hides a salvage yard. Maybe the little yellow house managed to wedge itself into this unlikely location, like a weed growing from a crack in the concrete.

Caleb was obsessed with this house for years. He knew it had to have many stories to tell. It is also remarkably cute with an almost perfectly square shape, a facade that gives off a Spanish vibe, a tiny driveway, and a yellow shed tucked behind and off to the side that matches the color of the house. The brown awnings that jut out above the two square windows on the front of the house are like hooded eyelids. Two small palm trees stand in front near the road, leaning in toward each other like lovers about to kiss. Finally, one day when Caleb was driving by, a "For Sale" sign appeared behind the chain link fence that rings the front of the house to keep strangers out and children and pets in. Caleb put in an offer that day and moved in two months later. It was extremely affordable, because, well, who else would want to live there? Located in the heart of suburban Florida in a town called Oakwood, the house affords none of the perks of suburban life and none of the conveniences of city living. Objectively, it is the worst of both worlds. Caleb loves it without reservation.

However, Caleb will concede that it is far from a perfect home for a child. It is certainly more suited for a bachelor in his thirties who has learned not to wander out into traffic or dig through piles of metal in a salvage yard.

That was what it was supposed to be. A home for Caleb. By himself. He could sit by the front window, sipping coffee while working on his morning spreadsheets, and watch the cars zipping past at scandalous speeds. The cars would be just twenty feet away, maybe less. He could literally touch them if he opened his window and stuck a pole out that was half as long as the one you might use to touch the Grinch.

But now there is Emily, and everything is different.

At Caleb's little home on the street that is much too dangerous for a small child, his vinyl record player has been relocated to the shed to make way for a Barbie Dream House. And the second bedroom he once used as an office, which is about as big as a medium-sized walk-in closet, is now painted pink and filled with American Girl dolls, stuffed animals, picture books, and a collection of Emily's favorite scraps of paper, rocks, and pinecones.

"Emily. Please stop kicking the seat," Caleb says, resting his hand on top of Emily's wrist so she will notice that he is talking. It's unlikely she can hear him over the din of whatever inane children's show is currently streaming directly into her ear canals.

"WHY?" Emily says in a much-too-loud voice.

Caleb slides a headphone off of Emily's left ear.

"Because it's rude. And you were shouting, by the way."

"It's not rude. I'm just bored!"

"Bored? I downloaded basically every piece of content available on the internet that contains dolls, princesses, unicorns, or farting cartoon animals onto your iPad. The one you're holding right now. How could you possibly be bored ten minutes into the flight?"

"It's boring!" Emily replies, making what she clearly feels is an unimpeachable point. "But this is fun!" She looks directly into Caleb's eyes. Her gaze penetrates straight through to the back of his skull. She begins to methodically kick the seat again.

Thump, thump, thump.

(PAUSE).

Thump, thump, thump.

"Stop that NOW," Caleb says in an angry hiss. Returning Emily's gaze, attempting to make his look even more withering than hers. "If you don't stop by the time I count to three, I'm taking away your iPad for the rest of the flight! One..." Emily continues kicking the seat. "Two..." At this point, Caleb does his best to keep his countenance composed with just a subtle tinge of menace. He doesn't want Emily to know that inside he is panicking. By starting this count to three nonsense, he has effectively painted himself into a corner. He has pushed all his chips into the center of the table with no good cards in his hand. He is bluffing and if/when she calls his bluff, he is busted. The house always wins.

What is he supposed to do? Carry through with the threat and take away her iPad? That would undoubtedly result in screaming, crying, and perhaps even more chair kicking. Punishing himself and all the passengers on the flight for a child's misbehavior seems a little silly when you really think about it. Oh well, here goes nothing.

"Three!"

At this moment, a head peeks around the seat in front of Emily. It belongs to a girl who appears to be eleven or twelve years old. She has deep blue eyes, straight black hair, and freckles across the bridge of her nose and under her eyes.

"Hey, there," the girl says to Emily. She doesn't look Caleb's way. "I don't mind if you kick my seat. It's kind of like a little massage."

Emily giggles.

"I understand," the girl continues, glancing at Caleb now and giving him a knowing look. "I get bored on planes, too. I'm actually flying home by myself and I'm a little lonely. Can we be friends?"

Emily beams back at the girl. Her whole demeanor has transformed in a matter of seconds. She nods eagerly, saying nothing, suddenly shy now that she has gained the attention of a "big girl."

Caleb smiles at the girl and mouths "thank you." He is completely floored. Is it possible that in just five or six years, 1,825 to 2,190 days, the little girl sitting beside him, the one who lives in his house rent-free, the one who has upended his world with her dolls, toys, and need for attention, will turn into this other thing? This self-assured and mature person who looks like a child but carries herself like an adult. It seems impossible. Perhaps this other girl is exceptional in some way. Caleb thinks he'll have to do some research on the subject when he gets home. Maybe figure out a way to create a child maturity predictive algorithm.

The remainder of the flight proceeds largely without incident. Emily slowly sheds her shyness, leaning forward to whisper to the girl and show her funny parts of her favorite Netflix shows. By the time the plane is about to touch down in Orlando, Emily's only complaint is that the flight can't go on any longer. It's already way past her bedtime, and now that she has a new friend, well, it feels like anything is possible.

Caleb hopes to find the girl's parents at baggage claim, so he can compliment them on raising such an outstanding child, but between the crush of people trying to get off the plane, double-checking to make sure none of Emily's precious stuffed animals or sacred bits of paper were left behind, and traversing the sprawling airport with a tired five-year-old who insists on being carried, Caleb loses track of her.

By the time Caleb and Emily ride the monorail across to the baggage claim area, all the passengers from their flight are gone. Caleb and Emily's suitcases stand watch by the vacant conveyor belt.

Caleb guesses this girl will be one of the thousands of people you randomly cross paths with, share a few meaningful moments with, and never see again. He will simply remember her as the girl who saved his neck that one time on an airplane. He's always thought it's weird how that happens.

One moment someone is in your life and the next they're gone. Sometimes forever.

CHAPTER 3

I'M DEFINITELY GOING to cut a finger off and end up in the emergency room. That would be just what I need, Sadie thinks as she chops an onion in the kitchen of her townhouse on Sunday morning of Labor Day weekend, trying her best to avoid severing any appendages. She grabbed the first knife she could find amidst the jumble of boxes, which seem to be growing in number despite her best efforts to unpack. She is now paying for her unwillingness to embark on a search and rescue mission for the fancy knife set she bought when she moved into her flat in Brooklyn years ago and then never used. In her New York neighborhood, there were professionals on nearly every corner ready and willing to prepare food for her. As an amateur, cooking seemed like a silly and presumptuous thing to do. And a waste of time. Time she never had.

The knife she found was dull, unwieldy, and had likely been most recently used to make a car out of a cardboard box. *When was the last time we did that?* Sadie thinks. *Five years ago?*

Sadie remembers Scarlett sitting on the tattered hardwood floor of their tiny living room, her black hair tangled and messy. It would've been around 5:45 in the morning, of course. And although

Sadie had been awakened at an ungodly hour almost every morning by her child for five or six whole years at this point, she never could get used to it. She was doing her best to wake herself up to face yet another day of Sadie against the world. Meanwhile, Scarlett was fully charged. Each morning she went from dead asleep to full throttle in seconds. It was still pitch black, the New York skyline illuminated outside the window; Sadie hadn't had the chance to make coffee yet (or even better, go to the coffee shop and buy it), and yet, Scarlett was already demanding that Sadie create a car out of a cardboard box. One that "looks like a real car" and "I can drive!"

Sadie saws her way through the onion, keeping a close eye on the fingertips of her left hand to make sure they're all still accounted for. The knife was never very good at cutting cardboard either, but despite the early wake-up calls and the sheer intensity of raising a child on her own, they did have fun. Even if to Sadie it felt like fun in a secondhand, detached sort of way. Like if she were a ghost floating around in the apartment watching from above not having to do all the miserable cardboard cutting and playing with dolls, she would think that looked like a fun time for a mother and daughter.

Sadie is making omelets this morning because, well, why not? It's not like she has anything else to do at the moment. Sure, she could unpack these boxes that have been sitting around for six weeks since she moved in, but what's the rush? The boxes are kind of like her roommates now. If only she could teach them to order pizza on her behalf or maybe do the laundry.

Scarlett has finally joined her at their new home and is still asleep upstairs. Even though the quiet mornings are the norm now, they still feel like little miracles. It also feels like something is amiss. It happened so fast. One day, the tide came in and washed the cardboard creations, dolls, and glitter out to sea. All that it left behind were headphones, iPhones, jeans with holes in them, and moodiness.

Despite the fact that Sadie has felt increasingly disconnected in recent years, as Scarlett has grown from precocious child to sullen tween, she is still happy that they are physically together again. She had left Scarlett behind in New York so she could enjoy her summer doing fun things with Sadie's aunt while Sadie set up their new life in the land of humidity, apocalyptic afternoon thunderstorms, and alligators. Like the one that is crawling out of the lake in front of Sadie's eyes as she stares out the kitchen window. *Florida is such a ridiculous place to live*, Sadie thinks, tossing the chopped-up onions into a frying pan on the stove. The hot oil sizzles and pops. Their townhouse backs up to a small pond filled with all types of Florida wildlife. Turtles, frogs, large white birds that wade daintily through the water, and of course, alligators. The HOA gets the city to "rehome" the gators when they reach a certain size, but new ones always crop back up. There seems to be an endless supply.

When the summer storms roll in with their pulsing lightning, raucous thunder, and torrential rain, the pond swells beyond its edges, often rising to within feet of Sadie's screened back porch. The first thing she did when she moved in was place a cinder block against the metal door on the porch. As if *that* is what would keep the alligators, lizards, and heaven forbid, snakes out of her house and out in the pond where they belong.

While she waits for the onions to "become tender and translucent" as the omelet recipe she found online directed, she picks up her phone and calls her best friend, Paige. Sadie and Paige have been best friends since fourth grade. Paige thought Sadie was cool and mysterious because instead of rainbows or ponies, she had stickers of rock band logos on the outside of her binder. One day during the first week of school, the outgoing and bubbly Paige appointed the shy and sarcastic Sadie as her bff. And that was that.

Paige answers the call immediately as if she had been staring at her phone willing it to ring.

"Just the person I wanted to talk to this morning!" Paige says.

Who needs coffee when you have Paige?

"I hope I'm not calling too early," Sadie says.

Through the phone, Sadie hears what sounds like an entire

cymbal stand and drum set clattering to the ground. Paige shouts, "Come on, guys! Give me five minutes!"

"Sorry, Sadie," Paige says, back into the phone now. "It's a little deafening here at the moment... and, well, pretty much every other moment. The kids are practicing slamming baking pans together right now, apparently. What were you saying?"

"I said I hoped I didn't wake you, but I forgot your... um, house-hold situation."

"You mean my four-ring circus? Or is it a three-ring circus? Whatever. Mine has four rings. On a good day. And no worries about calling early because I've been up for hours. Maybe days? It's hard to know at this point."

"Mine is still sleeping if you can believe that," Sadie says.

Paige sighs wistfully. "That. Sounds. Like. Heaven. What does the other side feel like?"

"It's," Sadie hesitates, trying to think of a word for what *it* is. "It's nice. Very quiet."

"Quiet sounds fantastic to me," Paige says as another crash detonates in the background. This time punctuated with a child's wailing. "For fuck's sake," Paige whispers, then shouts away from the phone, "You're fine! You probably didn't need all those fingers anyway! Be more careful with the box cutters, my darlings!"

"Just kidding on that last part, of course," Paige says into the phone. "They're just bashing each other with couch cushions. So, tell me, how are *you*?"

"I'm good," Sadie says. "I think? I honestly don't know anymore."

"You seem down. I can always tell, you know. Are you still hung up on Asshole?"

"His name is Ashford," Sadie replies. "And no, I'm not hung up on him. It's just, when you trust someone, love someone maybe. It takes time."

"I get it," Paige says. "But to be honest, the fact that his name is Ashford was always a huge red flag."

"It was New York, Paige. All the guys there are named Ashford."

They both laugh and settle into a comfortable silence. The type of silence that only friends who have been through it all together can easily embrace. Finally, Paige picks the conversation up again.

"You know I always said: you were the Skater Boi in that relationship, and he was the snooty girl with a pretty face."

"I know. You told me many, many times over the past three years. And I think you even told Ashford once when you visited. I think he was mostly confused by the weird analogy."

"Definitely more than once! And let's face it: Asshole was easy to confuse."

"I'll be fine," she says, ignoring Paige. "I'm just in a bad place right now... Florida."

"Hey! It's not that bad. You'll feel better about it when it's 75 degrees in January and we're sunning ourselves like lizards by the pool instead of trudging through snow. I can be at your house in like ten minutes, and trust me, anytime you ask me to come over, I will be there!" There's another loud clattering and crashing on Paige's end of the call. "By myself, to be clear," she adds.

"If you say so. I am literally watching an alligator crawl into the pond behind my house at this very moment. Have you ever watched one of those things move? It's just not right. It's like a crime against nature."

"See. Every day is an adventure! And remember all the good times we had here as kids? Flashlight tag on summer nights when we were in what, middle school, maybe? The weekend beach trips in high school. And *all* of the stuff we did in college. The parts I remember from that time period were pretty cool. Admittedly, there's a lot I don't remember, but we mostly had fun, right?"

"I guess so," Sadie replies with a soft sigh. She pauses for a moment before continuing. "You know what yesterday was?"

"I don't think I do," Paige says. She hesitates and the line goes silent for a few moments. "Wait! It was your weird anniversary day, wasn't it? Caleb Canceled Day!"

"Sure was. I actually haven't thought about much the last few years, but this year I remembered."

"Of course you did. You're in a bit of a dark spiral and if there's one thing I know about Sadie it's that she loves to dive headfirst into a dark spiral and ride that thing down into the abyss."

"You do know me," Sadie says with a little laugh, attempting to sound cheerful.

"I've never understood why you do this to yourself. You and Caleb dated for what—a year? We had just finished college when you dipped out on him. It's not *that* big of a deal. Definitely not something to commemorate like it's Dia De Los Muertos for Christ's sake! So help me, if you've set up a little shrine to Caleb—anything at all that involves framed pictures, skeletons, or skulls, I'm coming over there right now!"

"Don't worry," Sadie says. "There's no shrine. Just regret."

"No regrets, Sadie. Come on! What you need is a night out! A few drinks, dancing, karaoke! Maybe find someone tall, dark, and handsome to use and set loose?"

"Jesus, that sounds miserable."

"Fine. How about we watch stupid TV shows and drink wine? Suburban mom style."

"That's more like it," Sadie replies. "Oh, I think I hear movement upstairs. Guess I should finish up these omelets."

"Sadie Warren is cooking? Will miracles never cease?" Paige teases.

"Shut up. I'll talk to you later."

"Love ya, girl!"

Sadie dumps the mixture of beaten eggs and milk into the frying pan as Scarlett emerges from the stairwell, eyes bleary.

"Hey, Scar," Sadie says. "Omelets?"

"You're cooking?" Scarlett asks, eyes clearer now. The shock of the scene she's walked in on acts like a jolt of caffeine, waking her up instantly.

"Yep. Turning over a new leaf," Sadie replies brightly. "When in

Florida, do what the Floridians do. Which is cook omelets, I think? I'm not sure. It's been a while."

"Who are you and what have you done with my mom?" Scarlett says, a mischievous gleam in her eye as she pushes a few cardboard boxes aside and pulls up a chair at the kitchen table.

CHAPTER 4

May 2009

Sadie and Caleb met the old-fashioned way. There was no swiping left or right. No witty profiles or staged pictures with fish or exotic wildlife. None of the shouting "Can I buy you a drink?" in a crowded bar and pointing to the ears to say, "I can't hear you over this music that is rattling my teeth!"

They met in a coffee shop. A small, locally owned coffee shop because when you're in college and your every move speaks volumes about your level of independence and grown-up-ness, you can't be seen at one of those corporate coffee joints.

Sadie was carrying a guitar in a black guitar case and Caleb was dressed in body armor made mostly of foam, pvc plastic, and duct tape. It was a classic boy meets girl situation.

...

. . .

"Oh, god. I'm sorry!" Sadie exclaims as the front end of her guitar case clatters into Caleb's stomach. He had just left the bathroom and was rounding the corner at breakneck speed.

"No, no," Caleb says, clearly flustered but attempting to appear unperturbed. "It's my fault for not checking for guitars before turning the corner. Luckily, I was wearing armor, or you might've run me through." He laughs nervously, gesturing at his unexpected ensemble.

"Yes, that is very fortunate," Sadie says. When she looks into Caleb's eyes for the first time, she feels something unusual. His eyes are a deep chocolate brown with small flecks of faint yellow. His gaze makes Sadie's stomach flutter. "Do you always wear armor or just when you're getting coffee?"

"You can never be too careful, that's what I always say," Caleb replies with a little laugh. "But seriously, I'm on my way to sword fighting practice."

"Of course," Sadie says. "I should've guessed. All the signs were there."

There's an awkward pause now. Sadie tucks a strand of black hair behind her ear and looks to the side, suddenly taking a great interest in the leg of a nearby table.

"Well–" Caleb breaks the silence. This is the moment when these two should part. Likely forever. This chance encounter should be a slightly amusing anecdote they can tell their friends later that night. It should be one of those stories their friends will pretend to be interested in, but really won't be.

But instead, a flash of lightning creases the afternoon sky and a crash of thunder makes almost everyone in the small coffee shop jump, especially Caleb. The thunder is so sudden and unexpected that Caleb reaches out and grabs Sadie's elbow. Sadie pulls back reflexively.

"I'm... I'm sorry," Caleb says, clearly shaken. "That caught me by surprise."

Sadie relaxes, disarmed by the fear on Caleb's face. "I'm guessing you're not used to Florida?" she asks.

"Actually, I am. I grew up here," Caleb replies. "But lightning is not my favorite thing about this place."

The rain is pouring down outside the shop now, pounding against the pavement and cars parked along the narrow street.

"That one seemed to come out of nowhere," Caleb continues. "Anyway, I guess sword fighting practice is out."

"Well, you know what they say," Sadie says. "If you don't like the Florida weather, just wait five minutes." Sadie is mortified the second the words slip out of her mouth. *Who am I*, she thinks, *my dad?*

"So, would you like to have a... coffee?" Caleb asks.

"Sure," Sadie replies. "That does seem like the thing to do considering the location."

While they are waiting to place their orders, Sadie and Caleb make their formal introductions. When Sadie gives her name, Caleb's eyes light up.

"Oh, Sadie. Like Sadie Hawkins?"

Sadie blinks a couple times quickly. Her big blue eyes trained on Caleb like she's searching his face for signs that he is wearing a mask that can be peeled off. Perhaps he isn't who he claims to be.

"How did you know that?" she says, her voice skeptical, guarded. "Who told you?"

"How did I know about Sadie Hawkins?" Caleb says with a little laugh. "Because I watched a lot of legacy TV when I was a kid. I had a very cool childhood."

"No," Sadie says, rolling her eyes. "I meant how did you know I was named after Sadie Hawkins?"

Caleb looks at her closely. He notices she has a few faint freckles under her eyes and across the bridge of her nose. They are unequivocally adorable. "Well, I didn't," he says. "But now I do, and I will never forget it. Why were you named after Sadie Hawkins?"

Sadie sighs, her shoulders slumping slightly. "Ugh, well, my parents met at a Sadie Hawkins dance in high school."

"Ohhh," Caleb says, lifting one hand to his face, feigning astonishment. "So, they didn't just watch old TV shows, they lived in one of them! That explains a lot, to be honest."

"Excuse me?" Sadie says indignantly. "What exactly does it explain?"

"Well, everything. The disinterested affect. The skater girl look. The urge to embrace darkness. Classic signs that you're the child of perfect parents who grew up in Mayberry and attended Sadie Hawkins dances in high school. Mayberry is a fictional town in *The Andy Griffith Show*, in case you haven't–"

"I know what Mayberry is," Sadie snaps, a small smirk forming on her lips despite herself. She wants him to be wrong because he is annoying her to no end, but truthfully, he is absolutely right.

Sadie and Caleb sit in the coffee shop together for hours, long after the storm passes. Long enough for two or three more small storms to sweep through, in fact. You know what they say about Florida weather. They drink cappuccinos one after another like chain smokers. The conversation grows more open and animated as day turns to night.

They talk about Sadie's love of music (hence the guitar) and Caleb's hobbies, most notably sword fighting. They determine they both have one year left at Murphy College, the small liberal arts school they both attend which is located in an upscale suburb of Orlando. They even find out that they grew up in the same suburban town less than ten miles away. They had gone to different high schools but knew of or about some of the same people and many of the same places.

The last glimmers of light are fading outside the coffee shop windows, the sky is clear now, the air heavy and wet. Neither Caleb nor Sadie wants this encounter to end, but they are the last customers in the shop and the remaining barista is growing impatient, wiping down the counter with increasing vigor and clattering chairs on top of tables.

Caleb or Sadie or maybe both of them at the same time suggest that they should be heading out. To go back home and study or work on a paper or eat dinner. Caleb offers to carry Sadie's guitar because it seems like a thing he should do. Carry it to the door where they will... go their separate ways? It seems unnecessary but Sadie doesn't object.

As they exit onto the sidewalk, night has fully arrived and the bugs or frogs or whatever it is that chirp in the trees as night falls are singing their screeching song. The May night air is cooler now after the storms, almost welcoming. After hours and hours of easy conversation, Caleb and Sadie again share an awkward moment. Both are uncertain of what comes next. Do they shake hands? No, that would be weirdly sterile. Do they kiss?

The insane amounts of caffeine from a day spent meticulously consuming who knows how many cappuccinos courses through both of their veins.

"Well, that was fun," Caleb says to fill the silence.

A couple cars flit past, their tires squishing along the wet asphalt, headlights dancing across the glass-fronted shops.

"It was," Sadie says. "I guess I should be heading home. I've got a paper to finish tonight."

"Yes, right," Caleb answers. "I have some studying to do, too."

"Ok," Sadie says, lingering one moment longer.

"Ok, I'll see you," Caleb says, turning and walking away into the night.

...

Sadie watches him. She's not sure what that was all about. It felt different. Important.

...

After Caleb takes exactly 122 steps along the sidewalk, he stops and glances back over his shoulder. There is no trace of Sadie. He continues on until he arrives at his apartment building. He climbs two flights of stairs, pulls his key from his pocket, and unlocks the door.

His roommate, Blaise, is sitting on the couch in their tiny living room watching TV while smoking a blunt. Many people have remarked on how ironic it is that Blaise's name sounds exactly like the word "blaze," so there's no need to mention it, really. We all have our personal destinies to fulfill.

"Yo, man," Blaise says, his eyes unfocused like a labradoodle trying to track a hundred squirrels at once. "You've been gone a long time."

"Yeah," Caleb says. "I was having coffee with a... friend. Kind of all day."

"Hell yeah, man," Blaise says, taking another hit from his blunt. "That's what it's all about! That must've been some kind of friend to keep you there that long."

"She was," Blaise replies. "She was definitely... some kind of friend."

...

Sadie arrives at her ground floor apartment a few minutes later. Her roommate, Paige, is on the couch, watching one of those dating reality shows that Sadie can't stand.

"And where have you been, ma'am?" Paige says with mock exasperation.

Sadie quickly recounts the story of her chance encounter with Caleb, from the initial collision to the slow burn of the coffee and conversation. Paige's eyes light up as the story unfolds.

"Uh-oh," Paige says in a lilting voice. "I think Sadie has found her knight in not-so-shiny armor! This could be just what you need to get back on the... wait for it... horse!"

Sadie punches Paige in the arm. It's probably harder than she's ever hit anyone in her life. She didn't have siblings to fight with after all. It probably hurt, but Sadie thinks Paige had it coming. Sadie has been down the relationship road before, and frankly, it's not all it's cracked up to be. In Sadie's experience, it doesn't end well. It's definitely not worth the trouble.

And suggesting that Sadie of all people was falling for a guy she just met? A guy who wears plastic armor in public and practices sword fighting? Preposterous. Completely and utterly preposterous.

CHAPTER 5

September 2022

"ARE you sure you got all the supplies?" Caleb's mom, Helen, asks for what seems like the hundredth time from the passenger's seat in Caleb's car.

Caleb is enrolling Emily in kindergarten today. It is the Tuesday after Labor Day Weekend, so Emily is starting school about three weeks late. Less than ideal, Caleb concedes, but some things can't be helped.

"Yes, Mom," Caleb answers flatly.

"One backpack, twenty-four pencils, one box of crayons, four folders, one binder, one container of antimicrobial wipes, one box of colored pencils, one box of Ziploc bags, two erasers, four glue sticks, and one pair of scissors," Helen rattles off the list without hesitation. Lists are what she does best. She understands lists. Lists are orderly and not the slightest bit messy or painful.

"All of it," Caleb says. "Every single thing."

"Just double checking," Helen says. "There's no harm in being sure."

"Are we going to school or not?" Emily pipes up from the backseat.

"We're here!" Caleb says. "Stonewall Jackson Elementary School! Just kidding. They changed the name from that at least a year or two ago. Very progressive. Anyway, welcome to Swamp Crest Elementary!"

"I still can't believe they renamed it Swamp Crest," Helen says.

"I think it has a lovely ring to it," Caleb replies. "Really captures the essence of the place."

"I don't know what you are talking about, but can we go to school now?" Emily asks.

"Let's do it!" Caleb enthuses.

Caleb woke up this morning feeling like he had just gone ten rounds on the fiercest rollercoaster at Universal Studios. His stomach seemed to be slightly out of place, like it needed a little nudge to return to its rightful position after an extended freefall. Not only did he have to worry about Emily's first day of school and how she would handle the separation, and well, all of it, but he also had to explain his family's rather unique situation to the school personnel.

He hesitates for a moment after exiting the car, contemplating the possibility of taking Emily home and never coming back here again. But then he shakes his head and retrieves Emily's shiny new rainbow sparkle backpack from the trunk. The one that is definitely filled with every school supply on the list, thank you very much. Emily walks between Caleb and Helen, holding each of their hands as they make their way toward the squat and sprawling school building made of mustard-colored bricks.

There are children everywhere. Rushing around with their backpacks bouncing on their little backs, shouting, laughing, creating a cacophony of sound that Caleb finds overwhelming. Emily, on the other hand, seems energized, her eyes wide taking everything in. After a short wait in the office while the front desk staff tends to the morning emergencies, a flustered-looking woman with curly red hair beckons Caleb forward.

"Hi," Caleb says. "I called last week to register my niece Emily Monroe for kindergarten. We had some... logistical issues, which is why she's starting late."

"That does sound vaguely familiar," the woman says. "Excuse me one second." She looks to the side where a little boy is seated in a chair, leafing through a binder.

"Alex," the woman says sternly. "It's time to put away the Pokémon cards and head to class, dear." She returns her attention to Caleb and taps away on her computer keyboard. "Sorry about that. Okay, I've got Emily's record here. Let's make sure everything looks good." She turns the computer screen to face Caleb.

"Yeah, that looks right," Caleb says after reviewing the information on the screen. "Except it has my relation to Emily listed as father and I'm actually her uncle."

"Oh, no problem," the woman says. "So, is this mom?" She asks, gesturing toward Helen who is standing beside Caleb now. Emily has gravitated over toward the little boy who is still seated in the chair, leafing through his binder of Pokémon cards.

"This is *my* mom," Caleb clarifies. "Emily's grandmother. My sister is Emily's mom."

"Oh, no problem," the woman says. Clearly nothing is a problem around here. "Is her mom... *dead?*" The woman leans forward and drops her voice to a whisper while saying the last word.

Caleb and Helen hesitate. Caleb opens his mouth to speak but before he can, Helen cuts across him and says, "Yes." Caleb gives her a pointed sidelong glance.

"Oh, I'm so sorry," the woman says earnestly.

"Thank you," Caleb replies solemnly, regaining his composure. "We are doing our best considering the circumstances."

"Yes," the woman says. "Well, I will update Emily's record. It's no problem! I will call her teacher right now and have someone come up to take her back to her classroom." She directs her attention toward Emily, "Are you ready for school, dear?"

Emily nods her head eagerly.

"And Alex, dear. I believe I said to put away the Pokémon cards and get to class. Please and thank you!" Grudgingly, Alex stuffs his binder into his Pokémon backpack and trudges away.

A few minutes later, two little girls arrive in the office, giggling with each other as they enter.

"Great, here they are!" the woman at the desk says. "Miss Emily, you can go with your new friends here. They will take you to Ms. Johnston's classroom."

Caleb crouches down to give Emily a hug, straightening the backpack straps on her shoulders. "Are you good?" he asks. She doesn't say anything, only nods. He looks in her eyes and sees a mixture of excitement and nerves. "You've got this! I'll be here to pick you up after school."

Emily nods again, then walks slowly over to the two girls, and they leave the office together. Caleb and Helen stare after the girls until they disappear around the corner, their footsteps echoing off the tile floor.

"Well," Caleb says after a moment. "I suppose they'll make it to the classroom."

"Certainly," Helen replies. "It's a school. Where else could they go?"

"What do we do now?" Caleb asks.

"We go to work, of course," Helen replies. "We follow our routine. Life isn't worth living without routines. I've told you this before."

"Only two million times, Mom."

"Well, now it's two million one then."

...

On the way back to the car, Caleb decides to ask Helen a question even though he's pretty sure he doesn't want to know the answer. All around them, harried parents are rushing to and from cars. Cajoling children, tying shoes, clutching tightly to little hands as cars and minivans dart in and out of the parking lot. A blue Honda Odyssey honks impatiently when the car in front of it rudely decides to linger when the stoplight turns green instead of plowing through a geriatric crossing guard who is struggling to make his way back to the curb. The crossing guard glares over his shoulder as he clears the road, takes a deep, cleansing breath, and begins to jab methodically and relentlessly at the pedestrian crossing button. Life goes on.

"Mom," Caleb begins hesitantly. "Why did you tell the school that Lauren is dead?"

Helen continues walking, looking straight ahead. They walk another thirty seconds in silence before reaching the car. Caleb is beginning to think his mom is going to ignore his question when she says, "It's just easier that way. And it's really nobody's business. I know how school people are and it's better to keep things simple."

Helen opens the car door and slides into the passenger seat. Caleb stares across the roof of the car, examining the empty space she left behind. He shakes his head, runs a hand through his hair, and says quietly to himself, "Yeah, sure. Why not? It's not like lying about Lauren has ever caused problems before."

CHAPTER 6

SADIE SITS ON HER COUCH, legs outstretched and resting on the ottoman, wine glass in hand. Paige is here, as promised, seated sideways in the recliner, legs draped over one arm of the chair. Scarlett is hunched up in the corner of the room on a bean bag chair, hoodie pulled up over her head, eyes fixed on her phone.

"Well, this is fantastic," Paige says, bringing the energy as she always does. "It's been way too long since we've done this!" They are watching one of those real estate reality shows that bear no semblance to any reality that Sadie has ever experienced. "And I still can't get over our little Scarlett," Paige continues, looking in Scarlett's direction. "You seem so much older than eleven!"

Scarlett gives a small smile and an ambivalent shrug.

"When you ride the subway to kindergarten and start picking up bagels by yourself at the corner shop for breakfast on Sunday mornings when you're eight, you kind of grow up faster," Sadie says.

"So, growing up in New York City ages you in dog years?" Paige asks.

Scarlett snorts and shakes her head without taking her eyes off her phone.

"Exactly like that, yes," Sadie replies. "We'll probably have to put her down soon, sadly."

"Mom!" Scarlett cries.

"Just making sure you're listening," Sadie says.

"How could I not?" Scarlett says. "I just texted you something, by the way."

"Texted me?" Sadie asks, faux incredulity in her voice. "We're in the same room."

"And what I sent you is on the internet," Scarlett shoots back.

Sadie can't think of a comeback for that one, so she sighs and lets it go. The daughter takes this round. Sadie pulls up the link that Scarlett has sent her while Paige chatters about the design choices of the people on the real estate show. "Wait," Sadie says, looking toward Scarlett. "Did you mean to send me a link to a community sword fighting club signup form?"

"Yeah," Scarlett says dully.

"Why?"

"You always say I should find new things to try. Meet people or whatever."

"Well, yes, but I don't really mean it." Scarlett rolls her eyes. "And why a sword fighting club," Sadie continues. "I was thinking more like tennis or piano or something."

"I've seen it on YouTube. It looks interesting."

"Hey," Paige cuts in, her eyes lighting up. "Isn't that what You-Know-Who used to do?"

"Not now, Paige," Sadie says.

"Who is You-Know-Who?" Scarlett asks, suddenly interested.

"No one," Sadie replies.

"Uh, definitely someone," Paige says playfully.

"No. One," Sadie affirms emphatically, glaring at Paige now.

Scarlett's eyes flick back and forth, attempting to determine what is happening between her mom and best friend. After a few seconds, she gives a little shrug and returns her attention to her phone.

"Anyway," Sadie says in Scarlett's direction, "it says this sword fighting thing happens every Saturday morning at Greenbrier Park. I guess I can take you."

"Cool," Scarlett says, unwrapping a granola bar and taking a bite.

Sadie has no idea where the granola bar came from or how and when Scarlett procured it. They sure do grow up fast. Dog years.

...

Scarlett has retreated to her room, leaving the old people downstairs to swap stories about their aching backs and miserable lives or whatever it is that old people do at night when there are no kids around. Sadie and Paige are sitting at the kitchen table drinking wine and playing Uno Attack. As old people tend to do.

"So, now what?" Paige says as she deals the black and white cards.

"One of us plays a card?" Sadie replies. "What do you mean?"

Paige has an annoying habit of starting up a conversation with a question one could only understand by reading Paige's mind. Unfortunately, Sadie can typically read Paige's mind pretty well. So, as is often the case, she knows what Paige is asking even though she pretends not to.

"You know what I mean," Paige says, exasperated. "What are you going to do with your life now?"

Sadie scoffs. "Sure, let's dive right in. Why not?"

"My thoughts exactly."

"You're impossible," Sadie says, laying down a wild card.

"That's why you couldn't live without me," Paige says. She taps the button on the red contraption that randomly dispenses cards. The little machine squawks and spurts out a stream of cards. "My god!" Paige exclaims. "That is frankly obscene! They let children play this game?"

"Thankfully, most children aren't perverted like you."

"I suppose," Paige concedes. She heaves a dramatic sigh, "But seeing that thing do its business does make me miss Matt. I should text him."

Sadie laughs, "Oh my, you've clearly had too much wine."

"No, I'm fine! And back to the topic at hand... Sadie's future!"

Sadie stays quiet for a few moments, studying her cards carefully. "I don't know. We're settling in," she says while playing a red two. "Uno. Scarlett is here now. I'm starting to get some students at the studio. We'll figure it out as we go from there, I guess?"

"Okay," Paige says, laying down a red seven. "But hear me out. Just a few months ago you were booking gigs for mega music stars and managing tours. Now you've given that up to achieve some sort of work-life balance, whatever that means. You gave up New York. You're back living in bumblefuck Florida teaching guitar to ten-year-olds. I'm just worried it's not going to be enough for you."

"I win," Sadie says, playing the last card in her hand. "And I'm going to be fine. Remember, I wanted to do all this. I loved my life, but it was getting to be too much. I missed out on so much of Scarlett's childhood because I wanted to prove I could be the mom who had it all. We needed a change."

"All right," Paige says. "If you say so. But I'm going to keep my eye on you. I'll be on the lookout for Sadie Sadness."

"Oh, I know you will. And I've also got my parents close by now, so that's nice. They get to see Scarlett more. Maybe they can come cheer her on at sword fighting practice."

Paige laughs knowingly. "You know they will be there if you ask them. Waving a banner, probably! The Warrens. The world's most supportive parents... and now grandparents!"

"You know it," Sadie says. "I mean, I complained about my mom and dad a lot when I was younger, but I'm really lucky to have parents like them."

"Oh, I know," Paige says. "Remember when you did that cracking eggs on your head thing during your, um, artistic phase in high school?"

"Jesus, don't remind me!" Sadie exclaims. "One of the most mortifying moments of my life!"

"But looking back on it now," Paige says. "It's sweet, right? We're both parents. We know what it's like to love your kids so much you just don't know how or where to direct that emotion. So, you do ridiculous things to prove how big your love is."

"Yeah, I know." Sadie sighs. "Look at me. Reconfiguring my whole life so I can try to be a better mom. Having kids makes us do the dumbest things. Like, can you believe I'm going to take Scarlett to a sword fighting club of all places? What are the odds?"

"Truly astronomical," Paige replies. "Like, what are the chances that the two people you've loved most in your life are such complete nerds? It's almost as if they share DNA!"

Sadie slaps Paige's arm playfully. "Stop that," she scolds. "Scarlett is *not* a nerd, and while the other sword fighting person you speak of certainly is a nerd, he is *not* one of the two people I've loved most."

"Mm-hmm," Paige taunts. "You've said that for over a decade now, but I still don't believe it."

Sadie busies herself packing up the card game and adjusting her wine glass on the table.

"Why did you give up on him?" Paige continues, gazing at Sadie with a concerned expression. "I'm not sure I'll ever understand that one."

"I know," Sadie replies. "But some mistakes just can't be undone."

CHAPTER 7

CALEB AND SADIE'S first official, pre-planned date is at a Renaissance faire. Seriously. The day after they literally ran into each other at the coffee shop, they both happened to return to the same location at the very same time. They would both tell you it was quite a coincidence. They have coffee together again, sitting at the same small table in the corner. Caleb is dressed in 21st-century garb this time with no extra layers of protection, completely exposed to any guitar attacks that might come his way. After browsing through his selection of clothing more thoroughly than he typically does, Caleb chose black athletic shorts and his extra special dri-fit polo shirt that several random people had complimented him on over the years. His untamable wavy hair is cropped short, and it sticks out in several different directions.

As they talk, Caleb leans forward, resting his elbows on the table, hands cupping a white porcelain mug. Sadie notices that even though Caleb is tall and lean, his face isn't sharp and angular. It is a little soft around the edges, kind, comfortable. He is so clean shaven that Sadie wonders if he even has to shave. As she takes a sip of her coffee, she imagines it would feel nice to have Caleb's head resting on her shoulder, his warm breath tickling her neck. Her face grows hot, and she attempts to tamp down this thought as quickly as it arrives. As if the thought were an ant invading a picnic.

Before they part ways, Caleb asks Sadie if she'd like to meet up on Saturday at a local park. He says there's an event he's planning to attend. He doesn't go into the details. No need to complicate matters, he thinks. Sadie accepts. She doesn't have plans, so what's the harm? She certainly wouldn't mind seeing those chocolatey brown eyes again. And that soft, inviting face that is already beginning to invade her dreams at night.

...

As Sadie approaches the park on Saturday, she notices that it is much, much more active than she's ever seen it. She walks by this park regularly while going to and from the college, and there are typically no more than a handful of people there–usually, tired-looking parents with young children playing on the small playground.

But today, the park is buzzing with activity and life. And everyone here seems to be, well, from another time and place. Of course. Caleb had said he was going to an event. The realization dawns on Sadie that what he meant by 'event' was a Renaissance faire. She uses her supreme powers of deductive reasoning to arrive at this conclusion. It also doesn't hurt that a man walks past wearing a chain mail vest with a live falcon perched on his shoulder. Then, a white horse wearing a little mask clops by carrying a knight decked out in bright red and yellow armor, lance in hand. It is a bit unusual to see horses roaming around this part of town.

Before Sadie can run away, she hears Caleb call out from off to her right. Caleb is standing by a canopy where a small group of people are playing some sort of game with colorful wooden balls. They are all dressed in a range of medieval attire from full-fledged metal armor to more understated frocks and kilts. Sadie notices that no one is dressed in black shorts and a black tank top except for her. She hugs her arms to her chest self-consciously.

Caleb trots across the grass to greet her. He is wearing a bright green tunic which is cinched in at the waist. The padding or armor or whatever it is he is wearing under the tunic bounces as he jogs. He also has a long silver sword on his hip, hanging from a belt-like contraption that is looped around his waist. As he approaches, the sun illuminates the subtle purple streaks in Sadie's black hair that is pulled back revealing multiple piercings in each of her ears. Caleb thinks she looks stunning.

"Hey," Caleb says as he comes to a stop in front of Sadie, a bit out of breath. "You made it!"

"I did," Sadie says hesitantly. "I feel a little underdressed, though?"

"Oh," Caleb says, registering Sadie's discomfort. "No, you look great!" Caleb's face reddens. He looks around at his surroundings to avoid having to make eye contact with Sadie. Inviting a girl he likes *here* of all places is not something Caleb would typically do. Certainly not so soon. Many years of being the nerdy guy who plays with swords has taught him that this part of himself is something that should stay hidden. It's funny. The same people who complain that chivalry is dead will turn around and call sword fighting, a sport that focuses on literal chivalry, a dorky hobby. People just don't make any sense.

For some reason Caleb can't quite pinpoint, however, Sadie immediately made him feel like he didn't have to hide. But now that she's standing in front of him, her icy blue eyes completely unreadable, the doubts return. His palms begin to feel clammy.

"Well," Sadie says with a small smile, running a hand through her hair nervously. "You look nice as well. Very... regal?"

"Thanks," Caleb says, exhaling. "Yeah, I guess I didn't mention this was a Renaissance faire, did I?"

"You did not."

"Sorry. I guess I'm a bit embarrassed by it." He hesitates, fidgeting with his wide black belt. "A lot of people don't really get it. It has a very nerdy reputation, if you didn't know."

Caleb looks down, poking at a tuft of grass with the toe of his shoe. He thinks about the pretty girl named Ashley he had a hopeless crush on in high school. He changed his entire personality to seek her approval, feigning interest in sports and fashion. It almost worked, or at least he thought it did, until she found out about his favorite hobby and mockingly called him Caleb the Conqueror in front of a tableful of cool kids in the school cafeteria.

"I'm aware, yes," Sadie says, smiling. "But it's cool with me. I'm not dressed for any jousting, unfortunately, but next time I'll bring my spear and horse."

Caleb laughs, finally relaxing. "Your lance." Sadie looks at him questioningly. "For jousting. It's called a lance, not a spear."

Sadie shakes her head, looking down toward the ground to feign embarrassment. "I can't believe I did that again. I always mix up my jousting terms. You really can't take me anywhere."

Caleb laughs. "We all have our weaknesses," he says with faux sincerity. "How about I show you around so you can see what we have to offer here?"

They walk through and around the stalls and canopies where men and women of all ages are cooking hunks of meat over open flames, playing games that Sadie has never seen before, making crafts, and admiring each other's swords. Thankfully, it is an overcast day, so the heat isn't quite so oppressive. The air is wet and heavy, and the horse stench adds a layer of authenticity to the proceedings.

"Do you ever wonder what it smelled like?" Sadie asks suddenly. When Sadie gets nervous, she gets weird. And she's nervous now, even if she's not exactly sure why.

"What do you mean?" Caleb replies.

"Like, in medieval times, what was the smell?"

"Oh, right, no. I hadn't really thought about it. I mean, I assume it smelled bad, right?"

"Yes, but specifically. I need details. What kind of stench are we talking about here?"

"Like animals and raw sewage, I suppose?"

"And disease, or rather, pestilence as you would say, I'm sure," Sadie adds with a little smile.

"Of course."

"I wonder if they got used to it," Sadie continues. "Like, if a medieval person time traveled forward to our time–hopefully not to this exact time and place because they'd be like, 'wow, nothing has changed,' you know, because this is so authentic." A boy of about twelve zooms past them riding an electric scooter. Sadie and Caleb both laugh before Sadie continues. "But, say they time traveled to a normal place and time in our present day. Would they notice the difference in smell immediately? Would they think it smelled bad here or would they be excited about being free from the relentless odor that defined their wretched existence?"

Caleb hesitates, rubbing his chin. "Wow, that's a lot to unpack. I can't say I've thought about the history of odors much. Honestly, I'm not big into the historical side of all this," he gestures vaguely with his hands. "I guess that seems kind of weird, doesn't it?"

"I mean, it all seems weird," Sadie says. "But why did you get into it if you didn't dream of being a knight in shining armor?"

Caleb runs a hand through his hair that is damp with sweat. He exhales and begins to speak at a faster pace as if he's racing to get the words out before he loses his nerve. "So, I got into sword fighting when I was in middle school," Caleb explains. "My dad was a big sports guy—he played everything when he was a kid—so he got me into different sports when I was little. I never really enjoyed any of them, but I always tried because my dad loved watching me play so much, even when I was objectively terrible."

Caleb is startled to hear these words come out of his mouth. He doesn't like to talk about his family, particularly not his dad, and he definitely wouldn't volunteer something like this on a first date. At least not on a normal first date. But with Sadie, nothing feels normal. Talking openly with her feels natural and easy.

"Yeah, I know how that is," Sadie says. "Not so much the sports but the doing things to please your parents part."

"Oh yeah? Your parents pushed you into stuff?"

"Not exactly." Sadie hesitates, trying to find the right words. Sadie has spent much of her life running away from her parents' smothering presence, but it is very difficult to explain why. Most people don't understand what it's like to be loved too much. "It was more that they were *so* supportive of everything it became over-whelming. Suffocating even. It made me want to do nothing at all or do weird things to see how far I could push their, like, almost toxic level of positivity?"

"Did you ever find the limit?"

"I did not," Sadie replies with a little smirk. "And I certainly tried. Big time."

"This sounds like a story." Caleb raises his eyebrows, and Sadie notices a glint in his dark brown eyes that makes her insides do a little somersault. "Tell me."

"I walked right into this one," Sadie laments. "Fine. I'm definitely going to regret this, but fine. You invited me to a Renaissance faire, so I feel like I have some ground to make up. So, one time in high school, God, this is going to sound outrageously dumb." Caleb's armor clinks a little as he kicks a broken tree branch out of their path. "I joined this performance art group," Sadie continues. "Well, it wasn't exactly a group because we weren't allowed to talk to each other or acknowledge each other's exis-tence, so more of a loose association I guess you could call it. Anyway, we met up at a street corner one afternoon at rush hour. We each brought a metal folding chair, sat down on the sidewalk, and started breaking eggs on our heads. Like, really slowly and methodically because we didn't have that many eggs. We're sitting there, cracking eggs on our heads every few minutes and like rubbing the goo into our hair and on our faces. Yeah..." Sadie trails off, making sure to look anywhere except in Caleb's direction.

"Huh," Caleb says. "That is really... something. Wish I could've seen that."

Sadie laughs. "That's not the best part."

"What could be better?"

"My parents were there," Sadie continues. "And not only were they there, they brought their own folding chairs and sat across the street. They literally cheered each time I cracked an egg like I had just made a three-pointer at a basketball game or something."

"Aw, that's sweet," Caleb says.

"I don't think you're understanding me. They *cheered*–and I'm talking like whooping and hollering–when I cracked an egg over my head and smeared it all over my head and face."

"Okay, so my mom *definitely* would not have done that, but maybe my dad would have," Caleb says. "I'm not sure. But it's good to have parents like that on your side, isn't it?"

"I guess it is," Sadie admits, noticing her nervousness has eased. Telling the stupid story about her parents provided a strange release. A heaviness has lifted. "Even if it does make me a little crazy some-times. But hey, at least I know they'll think it's fine if I tell them I got asked on a date to a Renaissance faire."

"Great news," Caleb enthuses. "I'm so glad I'm at least on equal footing with The Egg Cracking Society."

"I wouldn't say equal," Sadie says. "But maybe you'll get there."

"I mean," Caleb says, "it's something to aspire to, right? Who knows what the future holds for us?"

Us is a small word but it can be as powerful as a nuclear bomb when deployed at certain moments. This was one of those moments. Caleb and Sadie go quiet, both retreating into their thoughts. Caleb thinks about how nice it feels not having to hide. Being his authentic nerdy self is freeing, like riding a galloping horse (he's never actually ridden a horse, but it must be exhilarating). Sadie thinks about how running away from the saccharine perfection and cheesy love of her parents has resulted in so many wrong turns. She spent so much time looking for the storm, and she found it. It turns out edginess and angst and anger masquerading as passion aren't all they're cracked up to be. Now, she's feeling this weird pull toward what feels like home.

"Anyway," Caleb says, clapping his hands, snapping them both back to attention. "I got into all this for the sword fighting. There's so much strategy to it, like boxing. And it's a surprisingly good workout. I've never really gotten into the role-playing and all the nerdier aspects of all this."

At that moment, a man passing by, dressed like Caleb in green regalia, stops, drops to one knee in front of Caleb, bows his head and says, "Lord Dagwyn! I pledge fealty to you and the House of Dagwyn!"

Unsheathing his sword, Caleb taps the man on each shoulder and says, "Rise." They nod at each other solemnly, Caleb gives the man a hearty clap on the shoulder, and the man continues on his way.

Caleb slowly turns toward Sadie, knowing what's coming.

"As you were saying," Sadie smirks, her ocean-blue eyes lighting up.

"Well," Caleb says. "I guess sometimes I dabble in the role-playing aspects."

Sadie gives a little curtsy. "Whatever you say, Lord Dagwyn."

There's a very specific gleam in her eye that Caleb finds intoxicating. He noticed it before at the coffee shop. Whenever she delivers a witty barb or sarcastic comment she's particularly proud of, one that really delivers a body blow, her eyes sparkle. It's even more noticeable and captivating outside under the late evening sun.

"I deserved that," Caleb admits. "But there's one thing we kind of glossed over amidst all the excitement and I'd like to circle back."

"And what would that be?"

"You said this was a date," Caleb says.

"Yes, and...?"

"So, you do think this is a date, huh?" Caleb does his best to deliver this line with swagger, but inside, his stomach is churning. Is jokey confidence the way to go? He's not sure, but there's no going back now. He sucks in a deep breath. "A little presumptuous, M'lady," he teases as he gives a small bow.

"I don't think it's a date," Sadie says, closing the distance between them. "I know."

She rests her hands on Caleb's chest. They lean into each other and kiss. Softly at first and then deeper, more urgent. As they embrace, the white horse clops by and the rider shouts in a faux British accent, "Well done, Lord Dagwyn!"

Caleb and Sadie both laugh. Spluttering, genuine laughs that disrupt their kiss. It doesn't matter, though. The moment is still perfect.

...

Caleb and Sadie sit side by side on a park bench, their thighs touching. The Renaissance faire is wrapping up as the sun sinks below the tree line. The last rays of sunlight illuminate the few remaining people packing items into boxes and taking down canopies. Caleb rests his head on Sadie's shoulder. She ruffles his hair with her hand. His breath is warm on her neck. It tickles a little, but in a pleasant way. Sadie was right. It does feel nice.

CHAPTER 8

GETTING ready for sword fighting club practice on a Saturday morning is much more difficult when you have a five-year-old. Caleb is discovering this universal truth for the first time today. The club takes a break over the summer because sword fighting in 95-degree weather and 100 percent humidity is simply medieval. And not in the good way. Today is the first practice of the fall season. The weather isn't any cooler, but once the calendar turns the page to September, everyone tries to pretend that fall has arrived. That it's time to emerge from the heavily air-conditioned bunkers they've been hiding in since June.

Waking up early for the 9 a.m. practice was easy enough. Caleb will concede that. In the past, he would hit the snooze on his phone alarm four or five times before finally dragging himself out of bed. Sitting at his kitchen table all week moving numbers around in an Excel spreadsheet can be extremely exhausting. By the time Saturday morning rolls around, Caleb feels like a man who has trudged many miles through a desert without drinking water. This morning, however, Caleb was up and out of bed by 5:43 a.m., leaving him ample time to prepare. Well, in theory he should've had ample time to prepare if not for the insatiable needs of the aforementioned five-year-old. Several months into this new reality, Caleb is still adjusting.

On Saturday morning, Caleb used to throw on his sparring gear, fill up his water bottle, and grab a granola bar before rushing out of the house. He went from out of bed to out the door in about eight minutes. But fortunately, because of the pre-6 a.m. wake-up call, during which Emily practically pried Caleb's eyes open with her little fingers, Caleb had plenty of time to fill the bathtub with water, dump the entire contents of a large plastic toy bin on the bathmat in front of the toilet, and create a luxurious resort experience for Emily's dolls. Of course, Emily refused to actually get into the bathtub like a normal person to play with the dolls, so now, at 8:15 a.m. the clothes Caleb wrangled her into a couple hours earlier are almost completely soaked.

"Caleb! Caleb! Caleb!" Emily has called his name so many times in the however many hours Caleb has been awake now—four? seven?—that he has almost completely blocked out her voice. It's like she's a persistent troll on Twitter and Caleb has muted her so Emily is now just screaming into the void.

"Cayyyy-lebbbb!" Emily calls one final time.

This new, extremely irritating cadence finally does the job. Startling Caleb out of his dissociative state of being. "Yes, right," he says, attempting to buy time while he gets his bearings. "Chelsea over here is having the time of her life in the... lazy river?"

"Wrong," Emily replies flatly. "That's not Chelsea and I already told you that there is NO WATER at this hotel." Emily punctuates her pronouncement by splashing the water in the tub with her hand. It splatters up onto her shirt, but who cares? That was a lost cause hours ago.

"Oh, right," Caleb says. "I don't know why I keep forgetting that there is no water at this hotel in the bathtub that is filled with water. I can be a bit dense. I apologize."

Emily gives a little nod as if to indicate, *yes, you certainly can be a complete idiot,* before returning her attention to playing God, making the dolls, all of which are in various states of undress, talk, move, dive, and tumble during their extremely confounding resort-style rave that contains absolutely no water, thank you very much.

"However," Caleb continues. "One thing I do know is that we need to get cleaned up and change clothes so we can head out. We have to be at the park by nine."

"Yay, the park!" Emily exclaims.

"And remember," Caleb says, "like we talked about last night, you'll have to sit and play on your own for a bit while I'm busy. After that, we can go over to the playground."

"I know," Emily says. "Can I use your phone?"

"Um, maybe bring a few dolls and we'll see how things go." Caleb makes a mental note to download the Netflix app so Emily can use his phone. Early and often.

...

After much cajoling and promises of many things he will regret later, Caleb manages to wrangle Emily into the car, and they arrive at the park more or less on time. As Caleb had expected, the turnout for practice is sparse. It typically takes a few weeks each new season for everyone to get back in the swing of things, both figuratively and literally. Walking from the parking lot to the grassy field in the back corner of the park next to the utility shed, Caleb notices that a teenage boy is down on his knees clutching the side of his head with both hands. Gavin. The first casualty of the day. Another teenage boy stands over him, laughing while waving a wooden longsword around gleefully. Garrett.

Gavin and Garrett are fourteen-year-old identical twins. They joined the sword fighting club a few years ago as short and scrawny pre-teens. Now, they are tall and scrawny young men. Their voices have deepened, their Adam's apples jut from their thin necks, and they stand six-feet tall, almost all stringy arms and legs. They remain completely identical. They even wear their rusty brown hair in the same style, long and shaggy, covering their ears and the backs of their necks. The only way Caleb can tell them apart is that Gavin is almost always injured, and Garrett is almost always taunting him after inflicting an injury. The club spars mostly with wooden swords, but they can still do plenty of damage. Gavin and Garrett's parents presumably signed them up for the club to provide them with an outlet for their unbridled energy and so they could learn to eviscerate each other more efficiently in hand-to-hand combat when their daily arguments inevitably descend into violence. If that was indeed their parents' goal, it was working at least halfway. And Gavin was learning to take a thrashing and get back up, so Caleb figures that both boys are learning valuable lessons.

"Ahh, my eye!" Gavin cries out, still clutching his face as Caleb and Emily approach.

"Come on, Gavin!" Caleb says encouragingly. "I'm sure you've taken worse hits. And Garrett, stop dancing over your brother."

Standing next to Caleb, holding a naked Barbie doll in each hand, Emily giggles as Garrett continues his awkward shimmy. He holds his hand in the shape of an L and places it on his forehead, mimicking a celebratory Fortnite emote. Revitalized, Gavin swipes across the ground with his sword in the direction of Garrett's feet. Garrett deftly hops over it like he's skipping rope.

"You'll have to do better than that, bro!" Garrett croaks, his voice deep but still cracking a little. Gavin just grumbles as he uses his hands to push himself up off the ground.

The only other two people in attendance are Harold, a big beefy man in his fifties who, despite being a club regular for years, no one really knows much about, and Tonya. Harold has a bushy black beard with streaks of gray and thick, curly hair that makes it almost impossible to tell where the beard ends and hair begins. He is standing off to the side brandishing a gleaming metal sword working his way through a series of fighting positions. Tonya, an athletic-looking woman in her late twenties, is crouched down rifling through her gym bag. She is in the process of putting on her protective gear. She currently has one glove and wrist guard on and appears to be looking for the other. Tonya is extremely fit and powerful, respected and envied by all the club members.

Caleb is the group's de facto leader, not just because he's arguably the most skilled, but also because he's been around the longest. He started coming to practice and meet-ups when he was about the same age as the twins are now. Harold is the only member with a longer history, but if he were in charge, very little would get done. Communication is not Harold's strong suit.

"Hi, Harold," Caleb calls out, waving in the large man's direction. Harold grunts a gruff "hey" without looking in Caleb's direction or taking even the slightest break from his warm-up routine.

"How's it going, Coach?" Tonya says heartily.

"Tonya!" Caleb calls back. "I've missed you! And for the last time, please don't call me Coach. Even though I have a master-level HEMA instructor certification, we're all equals here!"

They both laugh. HEMA stands for Historical European Martial Arts and Caleb is in fact a certified instructor, though he tries not to get a big head about it.

"All right!" Caleb says loudly. "Let's pair up and start working on technique! Remember, even though we're just shaking off the rust, we do have the big exhibition at the high school football game coming up in just a few weeks!"

Tonya bangs her sword against her small metal shield excitedly. "Let's go!" The twins look a bit nervous and unusually subdued as they contemplate the idea of sword fighting in front of a crowd, and Harold stares at a fixed point in the distance, as if he's keeping an eye out for enemy combatants who might be popping out from under the big slide on the playground at any moment.

Caleb has managed to pull some strings to secure a halftime performance slot for the sword fighting club during the annual clash between cross-town rival high schools Bear Lake and Riverside. In other words, he asked his mom who works as the school bookkeeper at Riverside to see if the band director would let them do a sword fighting exhibition off to the side while the band played. The band director said he guessed that was fine as long as they stayed way down in the end zone and didn't make too much noise. They were in!

The Riverside High School mascot is the Raiders, so thematically the whole thing makes at least a little bit of sense. Or at least as much sense as is necessary to secure a halftime performance slot at one of the saddest events of the year. Despite the rivalry, the game tends to draw a rather small crowd because both teams are historically terrible at football. They are so hapless, in fact, that if both teams manage to break through the busting sign on the first try when entering the field, everyone considers it to be a successful night. Fortunately, Riverside and Bear Lake play each other every season so at least one team can chalk up a win, except for a few years back when the game ended in a 0-0 tie, so each school finished the season with zero wins, nine losses, and one tie.

Caleb knows that this exhibition means he'll have to return to *the* high school football stadium where it all happened on a game night, which he hasn't done in more than a decade, but it will be worth it. He wants to give his clubmates a reward for all their hard work and training, and this is the perfect opportunity. Besides, facing down old demons is an adventure, a challenge. Kind of like trying to slay a dragon in battle. Which, to be clear, has nothing to do with what Caleb and his teammates do. HEMA is a real sport requiring skill and athleticism, unlike the cosplay silliness that Caleb used to dabble in a little but left behind many years ago. But still, the point stands. Facing fears is an important part of life.

Caleb is thinking about all this until Tonya, his sparring partner, thunks him in the ribs with the flat of her sword. "Wake up, Coach! You're just going through the motions."

"Sorry," Caleb replies. "My mind wandered. I'll focus now."

Before they can start back up, Emily leaps up from her spot on the sidelines where she'd been seated playing with her dolls, and races over to Caleb. "I'm so bored," she whines. It's been about six minutes.

"Grab my phone out of the bag," Caleb says. "You know the passcode, obviously. Just don't break it. And if you're good for the whole hour, I'll take you for ice cream after. It'll be like ten a.m., but we'll figure something out."

Emily cheers and runs back to the side to retrieve the phone. Parenting is easy.

As the five swordspeople begin to progress through their practice routine, a girl hesitantly walks up and stands about ten yards away. She stands with her arms crossed and her shoulders hunched. She tries to watch the sword fighters without watching. The girl appears to be about eleven or twelve years old with deep blue eyes, straight black hair, and freckles across the bridge of her nose and under her eyes.

...

Emily is the first to recognize the newcomer. She gives a little squeal of excitement, leaps up and tosses Caleb's phone to the ground. Caleb looks over just in time to see the phone bounce once on its edge before settling into a clump of grass. He winces a little, then looks around to find Emily. She is hugging the girl who just walked up, nearly tackling her to the ground.

Caleb does a quick double take. It's the girl from the plane. His savior. Caleb walks toward where the girl and Emily are standing, lifting up his protective head gear and resting it on the top of his head to show his face. Practice has only been going on for about ten minutes, but he is already soaked with sweat. His face is flushed.

"Hey." Caleb gives a little wave as he approaches. "Emily, you found our friend from the plane!"

"I knew I would see her again!" Emily claps her hands excitedly.

"I'm Caleb, by the way. I don't think we officially met before."

"I'm Scarlett." She shifts from foot to foot nervously, uncomfortable suddenly being the center of attention. "Um, it's good to see you guys again." It comes out sounding almost like a question.

"Great to see you!" Caleb enthuses, sensing Scarlett's discomfort. He claps his hands together, putting on what he hopes is his most positive and welcoming face. "I wanted to thank you for helping me out on the plane, but we couldn't find you when we arrived. You *really* saved me." He whispers this last part, trying to avoid drawing Emily's attention.

"Can you play?" Emily asks eagerly.

"Well, I'm actually here to see about trying the sword fighting thing," Scarlett replies.

"Really?" Caleb says. "I mean, that's great! You're more than welcome, of course. Have you ever done sword fighting before?"

"No," Scarlett looks around at the other participants. "And I don't have any swords or equipment."

"No worries!" Caleb says. "I always bring extra gear in case we have newcomers. And it looks like you are our newcomer of the day!"

"Yay, me," Scarlett says flatly. Caleb laughs.

"Did your parents bring you or did you come on your own?" Caleb looks around to see if any parents are lurking nearby.

"My mom is in the car," Scarlett jerks her thumb up, pointing backwards over her shoulder. "Over there in the parking lot."

Caleb thinks he can make out the silhouette of a woman behind the steering wheel of a dark blue Toyota, but the parking lot is a couple hundred yards away, so he can't say for sure.

"Okay, well, if your mom is good with it, you're welcome to join!"

"She is. I just told her to stay in the car and work. I'm eleven. I don't need her around all the time anymore."

"Right," Caleb says. "That makes sense. And once you master the ancient art of sword fighting, you probably won't need her around at all!" Scarlett snickers. "But don't tell her I said that." He cups his hand to one side of his mouth to indicate the secretive nature of this final bit of information.

Caleb is often uncertain—how to be a good parent to a young child tops his current list of things he's perpetually confused about—but on the fake battlefield, he always feels in control. He becomes his most authentic self. Scarlett's presence energizes Caleb, and he does all he can to make her experience a positive one. He takes the lead confidently and rearranges the pairings so he can teach Scarlett the basics. He pairs Tonya up with Gavin and Garrett up with Harold. He figures Garrett could use a little humbling.

It turns out Scarlett is a natural with the sword. She takes to it easily and by the time the hour is over, she is quite adept at carrying out basic longsword attacks and parries. She is clearly enjoying herself and so is Caleb. He hasn't spent much time with children besides Emily. Unless you count the twins, who are more feral beasts than children. He is surprised how enjoyable it is to teach someone so young. Perhaps because Scarlett is such a quick learner. At one point toward the end of the session, Scarlett executes a perfect attacking maneuver, avoiding Caleb's attempted block and thumping the side of Caleb's torso with the flat of her sword. A clean body blow. Caleb notices an elated gleam in her eye. He knows that look. She is hooked.

"Okay." Caleb removes his head gear and drops his sword to his side. "That's probably enough for today. You did really amazing, Scarlett. You're a natural!"

Scarlett smiles, avoiding eye contact. She's both embarrassed by the attention and thrilled. "Cool, thanks," she says, trying to appear nonchalant. "I guess I'll see you next week?"

"For sure! And if you ever want to do some extra sessions to build up your skills, I'd be happy to help," Caleb says. "If it's okay with your mom and dad, of course."

"My dad's not around," Scarlett says casually, "but yeah, I'll ask my mom."

"Awesome! Tell her I said hi!" Caleb pauses. "I mean, we've never met, so that might be weird, but you know what I mean."

"I'll tell her," Scarlett says. "She's weird too, so it's fine."

"Well, weird people are my people. That's what I always say." Caleb looks around at his teammates and notices they are all listening in on the conversation. "I mean, weird people are *our* people. Right, everyone?"

There are a few rumbles of assent or confusion. It's hard to say which. Scarlett walks away toward the parking lot. Caleb watches after her. It may be his imagination, but he thinks he notices a bit of bounce in her step. Scarlett opens the passenger side door and climbs into her mom's car. They drive away.

Caleb can't help feeling that there is something familiar about this girl. He can't quite put his finger on what it is, but it feels like... something. Maybe it's simply the memories from their encounter on the airplane. Memories can be funny that way. They can make you imagine things that aren't there. They can leave you grasping at ghosts.

CHAPTER 9

"How DID IT GO?" Sadie asks as Scarlett climbs into the car.

"It was fine," Sadie says, untying her hair that is damp with sweat and letting it down.

"Did you like it?"

"I said it was fine, Mom."

Sadie sighs, checking the rear camera on the dashboard before backing out of the parking space.

"Okay, that's good, I guess," she says. "So, are you going to do it again?"

"Yeah," Scarlett replies. "The one guy said he could give me extra lessons if I wanted. He's like a teacher or something, I think."

"Hmm," Sadie looks both ways before making a right turn out of the park onto the main road. "Sounds a little weird to me."

"He said you would say that."

"That honestly makes it even weirder."

Sadie flicks on the turn signal as they approach a large intersection, pulling to a stop at the traffic light.

"We're going to stop by Grandma and Grandpa's for a little bit, by the way," Sadie says.

"Okay," Scarlett replies, moving to put her headphones on and beginning to scroll through her phone.

"Back to this man at sword fighting," Sadie says, testing out the water before diving in. Scarlett doesn't show any signs of irritation, so Sadie continues. "What's his deal? How old is he? What does he do for a living?"

"I didn't ask his life story. He fights with swords at the park on Saturdays? I don't know," Scarlett says, looking down at her phone. "And I don't know how old he is, exactly. Old, I guess. Probably your age."

"Well, thanks for that," Sadie replies, bemused. "But what have I told you about becoming too familiar with strange men?"

"He's not a strange man. He's in the sword fighting club. It seems like he's kind of the leader. And he said he sometimes gives private sword fighting lessons. Like, he has a certification or something."

"You're kidding me, right?" Sadie drums the steering wheel with her fingers as she sometimes does when she gets worked up. "I say, 'don't get too familiar with strange men,' and your response is, 'he's not strange, he dresses up like a knight and teaches children to sword fight in private at his home?'"

"Come on. He doesn't teach lessons at his house. Just at the park... way off in the back behind the shed where they store all the maintenance equipment. You know, really sharp or heavy stuff like metal rakes and shovels and all the best murder tools." Scarlett smirks, running a hand through her hair and tucking the still damp strands behind her ear.

"Very funny," Sadie says flatly. "That location is so much better. Does he drive his large unmarked white van to these lessons?" Sadie can't imagine parenting a tween without employing a healthy dose of dark humor.

"I'm done here," Scarlett says. "You're just trying to pick a fight over nothing. Anyway, he's also not a stranger because I met him on the airplane last week."

"Really?" Sadie asks. "That's weird. Do you think he's following you?"

"Mom! I picked this sword fighting thing out, remember? And I didn't even really talk to him on the plane, only his daughter. She's like five, so unless he's trained her to be an accomplice, I don't think you have anything to worry about."

"Maybe you're right," Sadie admits, swerving across the midline of the winding road to avoid a gray-haired man riding a bit erratically on a bicycle. "I just worry about you, you know. And with the new places and new people... well, I'm still getting adjusted. But, I'm glad you had fun."

Sadie pulls the car into the driveway at her parents' house—a modest, ranch-style home made of white stucco. The yard is neat and well-maintained with crisp green grass and a strip of small bushes under the windows at the front of the house. A large hibiscus bush dominates the corner of the house by the garage.

Sadie turns off the car and takes a deep breath, collecting her thoughts. Spending time with her parents requires a great deal of energy and focus. She opens the car door, quietly steeling herself for the onslaught.

...

"SADIE! SCARLETT!"

Within a half second of the front door opening, Sadie's mom's voice echoes around the small entryway, bouncing off the cream-colored walls and porcelain tile floor. A small, wiry woman appears. Jessica, or Jess as everyone calls her, has dark brown hair with subtle streaks of gray and a kind, welcoming face. She can be a lot, but Sadie has always felt a profound sense of home when she looks into her mom's blue eyes.

Jess wraps Scarlett in a big hug. Scarlett pats her grandmother's back with one hand, her other arm hanging limply at her side, trapped by Jess's vise grip. After Jess releases Scarlett, she moves on to Sadie. "You look a little tired, dear," she says, resting her hands on Sadie's upper arms, studying her face carefully. "Are you sleeping?"

"Every chance I get, mom," Sadie replies.

Every time Sadie and Scarlett see Jess and Sadie's dad, Tom, their reunion is treated as a colossal event. It's as if Sadie and Scarlett are Odysseus and they have been away from Ithaca for twenty years. Except, in this case, twenty years is typically two to three days and Ithaca is this small house in an Orlando suburb where many of the yards have little cloth signs that say things like "Tonight's Forecast: 90% Chance of Wine" and (perhaps somewhat incongruously) "Put the Christ Back in Christmas" during the holiday season. Sadie supposes her parents are still making up for all the time they feel like they lost while she was living in New York. Sadie knows she didn't get home enough to see them. She was busy and maybe a little selfish.

But when you're a single mom, particularly a young single mom trying to create a new life in a new place, sometimes you have to be a little selfish. Sadie loves her parents, but she always yearned to be different. She wanted to create a life of her own, a big life, one that didn't follow the typical path that so many of her peers from Orlando walked down. High school, college, a regular job, marriage, kids, and maybe one day, a house with a swimming pool. Sadie didn't want any of that. Except when Caleb swept into her life, and for a brief moment in time, she could picture herself being happy with normal. Well, maybe normal plus Renaissance faires. Of course, that particular flirtation with the expected did not turn out so great. In fact, it ended in disaster.

"Where's Dad?" Sadie asks, subtly giving her mom the slip and walking into the living room.

"Oh!" Jess's eyes light up and Sadie braces for what might come next. "Since we heard about Scarlett's new passion," she gives Scarlett a knowing glance, "he's been working on something special. He's in the garage. I'll go check to see if he's ready!"

Sadie and Scarlett both cringe as Jessica rushes into the kitchen and flings open the door to the garage.

"Whatever this turns out to be," Sadie whispers to Scarlett. "Just be nice, okay?"

"I know the drill, Mom."

Sadie sits down on a recliner and Scarlett sits on the light blue couch. They both pull out their phones, as loud metallic clanking sounds emanate from the garage. Always a good sign. As Sadie scrolls through her phone, hoping to find a suitable distraction, she thinks back to when she was seven or eight and Tom spent the entire summer building her a tree fort in the backyard. Or, at least, attempting to build one. Every evening, Tom would come home looking slightly downtrodden, his thinning hair messy, his tie hanging loose around his neck, after a long day spent sitting at a small desk being yelled at by unhappy insurance customers. But the moment little Sadie wrapped him in a hug and Jess kissed him on the cheek, he transformed, his signature smile returning. He quickly changed into a t-shirt and baggy gym shorts so he could get to work in the yard, nailing pieces of wood to other pieces of wood. If you squinted a little and turned your head the right way, it *almost* looked like a tree fort. Sadie pretended to like it; she'd never asked for a tree fort anyway, so it was fine.

"Any bets on what they made?" Sadie asks.

"Definitely a ballista," Scarlett says matter-of-factly.

Sadie laughs. "I don't even know what that is."

"Like an old-school missile launcher or something."

"Why do you know that?"

"I'm a medieval weaponry expert now. Don't you remember?" Scarlett says sardonically.

"Ah, right." Sadie is secretly delighted to be bonding with Scarlett in their sarcastic way. Kids grow up and change so quickly, but there are upsides. Like having someone to roast your parents with.

"And they mention ballistae in, like, all the fantasy books I read, so I had to look it up finally because it came up so much."

"Yeah, you're probably right," Sadie says. "What do you plan to do with your new ballista?" She's eager to keep their banter going. It sure beats worrying about how exactly her parents are about to mortify her.

"Get revenge on my enemies, mostly."

"Smart," Sadie says, nodding her head. "You can never have enough revenge."

"But," Scarlett says, "with Grandpa's track record on crafting projects, I'm probably more likely to blow myself up."

"Accurate."

The door to the garage squelches open and Jess calls out, "Girls? Are you ready?"

"Sure, Mom," Sadie answers. "We're in here."

"Perfect." Jess enters the living room. "Stay right there and close your eyes. You used to *love* making us close our eyes for the surprises you cooked up when you were little. It was so much fun!"

"Some of us progressed forward from the peek-a-boo stage, but–" Sadie mutters under her breath.

"What was that, Sadie?" Jess asks.

"Nothing."

"We're ready, Grandma," Scarlett chimes in, putting on her most granddaughterly smile.

"That's my girl!" Jess beams, clapping her hands together once. "Tom! Come on in!"

The door to the garage opens again and Sadie and Scarlett hear the clattering of metal, heavy footsteps in the kitchen, and Tom's low voice: "Whoa there, easy."

They didn't buy a horse... did they?

"Did you do the trumpet fanfare yet, honey?" Tom calls out from the kitchen.

"Oh, shoot," Jess says. "I totally forgot to download the app. Do you want to wait?"

"We do *not* need a trumpet fanfare," Sadie says sharply. "Let's go, Dad. We don't have all day here!"

The heavy footsteps approach the living room and Tom emerges from the kitchen. Or, Sadie and Scarlett assume it's Tom. It's impossible to tell for sure because his head and the majority of his upper body is obscured by a large metallic object he is carrying. The metal monstrosity has what appears to be a colorful peacock feather jutting out of the top. It looks a bit like the top half of a silver, vaguely humanoid statue that has begun to melt.

"Is that you, Dad?" Sadie asks, standing up from the chair.

"Yep!" Tom calls out, clearly straining. "This thing is a bit hard to carry, but it's more because it's awkward, not because it's that... heeaavy." As he gasps out the last word, he stumbles forward and dumps the metal contraption onto one end of the couch, nearly collapsing on top of it. Scarlett leaps up and dives to the side to avoid being squashed. The evasive sword fighting defenses she learned this morning may have already saved her life.

Scarlett gets up off the floor after her brush with death. "Wow, Grandpa!"

"Isn't it something!" Jess says brightly.

Tom and Jess both look back and forth between Sadie and Scarlett, big smiles on their faces. Sadie and Scarlett share a confused look. They always expect the unexpected at Jess and Tom's house, but they can apparently still be surprised.

"So," Tom says, breaking the silence. "What do you think?"

"It's...," Scarlett begins, struggling to come up with the right words. It's hard to know what exactly one is supposed to say when your grandparents present you with a hulking mass of metal adorned with a peacock feather.

"What is it?" Sadie asks, abandoning pretense.

Tom looks a little surprised. "It's body armor and a helmet, of course!"

Sadie tilts her head to the side to change her point of view. "Oh," she says. "I see it now."

"Of course! It's beautiful, Tom. Some of your best work!" Jess gives him a congratulatory pat on the back. Her hand lingers for a moment, rubbing his back affectionately.

"It wasn't easy, that's for sure," Tom explains. "But thanks to hard work and a little help from my friends over at YouTube, I got the job done! Anyway, the important thing is that now Scarlett has the gear she needs for her, well, knight games? Knight-ess games?" Tom hesitates, his eyes looking upward, deep in thought. "Anyway, whatever you call it. We know that Scar is going to be amazing at it!"

"That's right!" Jess adds, giving a little fist pump. "Come over here, Scarlett, and get a closer look. We, and I say we because your grandpa calls me his muse," she flutters her eyelids as she says this, "*we* came up with a lot of neat little details!"

Sadie massages her temples with her hands and considers, for at least the ten millionth time, how these two people produced her. Perhaps there was a mix-up at the hospital? Of course, Sadie knows the real story. She knows her parents always dreamed of having a big family, but as fate would have it, they ended up with only Sadie. So, Sadie received all the love and devotion that should've been parceled out to five or six children. Honestly, Tom and Jess offered enough love and attention to sustain twenty kids, probably more.

Scarlett joins Tom and Jess beside the mass of metal. "Look here," Tom says excitedly pointing toward what appears to be the head area. "I made a retractable visor so when you close it to cover your eyes, your opponent will see *this*!" With a bit of effort on Tom's part and some grating of metal, the visor crunches down revealing sparkly pink lettering on the top of the helmet. The lettering is rather small, sloppy, and scrunched together to allow the message to fit in the relatively small space. It reads "Prepare to Be Scar-red!"

Tom and Jess both look at Scarlett expectantly.

"Wow," Scarlett says. "That's... pretty cool?"

"I have a few questions." Sadie moves in for a closer inspection. "First, what's with the hyphen?"

"See, Tom, I knew the hyphen was going to be an issue," Jess says.

"You did, honey," Tom replies. "It was a very tough call. We agonized over it for several hours, didn't we?"

"We did," Jess confirms. "We even called up our friends Isabel and David because they have a really good eye for these types of things."

"To be clear. When you say, 'these types of things,' you mean messages scrawled on medieval armor?" Sadie asks. Scarlett tries her best to stifle a giggle.

"Of course, you know Isabel and David," Jess continues, unperturbed. "We play rummy with them every Thursday night."

"Sometimes Wednesday if either of us have something else to do on Thursday," Tom adds.

"Yes, sometimes Wednesday, but we shoot for Thursday and–"

"And sometimes *gin* rummy if we're feeling a little wild," Tom cuts in.

"Oh, Tom," Jess gives Tom a playful slap on the arm. "There are children present! Anyway, Sadie, you definitely know Isabel and David, right?"

"I have never heard of these people in my life," Sadie replies flatly. She shakes her head and runs a hand through her hair. "Anyway, what about the peacock feather?"

"Oh, right!" Tom exclaims. "That is the *piece de resistance* in my opinion! It is a peacock feather and I stuck it into the top of the helmet."

There's a pause as Sadie waits for more elaboration, her will to live dangling by the thinnest of threads.

"Like the plume," Tom adds helpfully. "It's a genuine peacock feather, too! Preston the Peacock dropped it in our yard."

"Preston the Peacock?" Sadie asks.

"You know," Jess says. "Preston. The peacock that hangs around the neighborhood? We feed him and give him water."

"And we started an Instagram account for him," Tom adds, winking at Scarlett. "At PrestonThePeacock is the name, Scarlett, if you want to give us a subscribe! Don't look at the replies, though. Sometimes they get a little salacious."

"My god," Sadie says.

"So now you'll have a little piece of Preston with you when you go into battle, Scarlett," Jess says brightly. "For good luck!"

"We hope you love it, Scarlett," Tom says earnestly. "We're so happy you've found a new passion!"

"Thanks, Grandpa, it's great," Scarlett says, "and Grandma! I'm sure it'll be very... useful for me." Jess and Tom both beam at Scarlett. Jessica wraps her in a tight hug.

"Well." Sadie tries to keep her voice light. "I guess we should get going. Do you have a forklift we can use to get the armor to the car?"

"Don't be silly!" Tom says brightly. "I'll carry it. Unlock your car for me."

"Dad, I don't think...," Sadie begins, but Tom has already started lifting the armor with much heaving and grunting. He staggers toward the door, Jess opens it for him, and he exits, banging the helmet on the door jamb. Preston's feather catches on a curtain beside the door, nearly coming loose, but ultimately remaining in place. The feather brushes against the door frame as Tom disappears from view.

"Well, it was great seeing you girls, as always!" Jess hugs Sadie. "Don't be strangers! And we can't wait to see this one in action with that sword!" She pats Scarlett on the arm. "Sadie, do you remember when you were in high school and you joined that art group and your dad and I came to–"

Sadie grabs Scarlett by the arm and tugs her away.

"Bye, Mom!" she calls over her shoulder as they storm out the front door.

CHAPTER 10

Sadie and Caleb are lying side by side in the single bed that is shoved into the corner of Caleb's small room. There isn't enough space for two people to rest comfortably but neither of them seems to care. Their bodies are nearly melded together. Leg to leg, hip to hip, shoulder to shoulder. The gray sheets are twisted around legs and torsos and various other body parts. The early morning sun filters in through the slats of the blinds covering the window, bathing the room in soft, sleepy light.

"Hey," Caleb whispers loudly. "Are you awake?"

"I am now," Sadie answers.

Caleb's hand finds hers, their fingers lacing together. "Do you want to go play minigolf?"

Sadie laughs. "Minigolf? Are you serious?"

"Yeah, it's fun. And I haven't played in years, a decade, maybe."

"Sorry, but goths don't play minigolf." Sadie rolls over away from Caleb, pulling his arm with her so it wraps around her waist.

"Well, it's good that you're not a goth, then. Your disposition is way too sunny, despite the black and purple hair."

Sadie flips over to face Caleb, locking eyes. "I'm offended! Don't you insinuate that I have a sunny disposition ever again!"

Smiling, she cups his soft cheek in the palm of her hand and kisses him.

...

The first thing Sadie notices at the minigolf course is the baby alligators. They are lounging in piles, sunning themselves on the rocks surrounding the artificial pond inside a rope enclosure. It seems like a sad existence, but perhaps, Sadie thinks, the little alligators feel the same way as they watch the humans batting colorful balls around on artificial grass.

The first thing Caleb notices is that the minigolf course sure has changed since the last time he was here more than a decade ago. The alligators are new, the pirate-themed decor is new, and instead of orange metal rails, the golf holes are lined with jagged rocks. Ridiculous. It's like no one even cares about skill and accuracy anymore and all they want is a fun time. Pretty typical of the way society is heading these days.

The last time Caleb came to this minigolf course on the corner of a busy intersection by the mall, his life was very different. Mainly because he was about ten years old. Also, he was with his father who was very much still alive at the time and his older sister who was, well, still the person he recognized. The sister he grew up with. The sister who used to pick on him until he cried, and then play board games and LEGO with him for so long he would forget what he was upset about.

Caleb's dad was passionate about minigolf, as he was about most everything he did. He also had stringent beliefs about how the game should be played. For example, he only frequented courses that had traditional metal rails enclosing the holes because the consistent and predictable bounces the rails provided allowed for strategic maneuvering. This commitment to predictability and analysis was one way his worldview overlapped with that of Caleb's mom. However, unlike Helen who believed order and reason were ends in themself, Caleb's dad used predictability as a means to have even more fun.

"This, this is what it's all about, Caleb!" his dad would say, spreading his arms wide as they approached the first hole, which was always a straight-on hole with few obstacles. An easy start. "Lauren, remember, sometimes it's more effective to use the bounce off the rail even when the straight shot is available."

Lauren, Caleb's sister, rolled her eyes. She was fourteen. That age when rolling your eyes at everything your dad says and does is like a full-time job. She lined up her putt, taking dead aim, of course. She gave it a good roll, but it carried a little too much speed when it reached the hole. It bounced off the back lip and settled a few inches away from the cup. Caleb's dad aimed toward the side railing, delivered a smooth stroke, and the ball ricocheted perfectly. It toppled over the side edge of the cup into the hole. A hole-in-one. Caleb's dad didn't rub it in or say, "I told you so." That wasn't his style. He acted surprised, as if he had just had a stroke of beginner's luck.

"Would you look at that," he said jovially. "A lucky start for the old man!"

Caleb smiled before stepping up to take his shot. He tried to emulate the path his dad took, but he couldn't quite find the perfect angle. His shot bounced off the railing and slid past the hole on the low side.

"Great start, Lauren and Caleb!" their dad said encouragingly. "We're looking like pros out here tonight!"

As a ten-year-old, Caleb was completely enraptured by his dad's infectious charisma. His dad was his hero. Even Lauren, who did her best to maintain an aura of teenage jadedness, was not immune. By the end of the night, they were all cheering each other on, laughing, high-fiving, and generally having the time of their lives. To this day, Caleb can't remember ever being happier.

Well, until now.

"Do you think they drug the alligators?" Sadie asks. She's leaning against the wood railing, staring down at the piled-up reptiles. They do seem pretty relaxed, only becoming somewhat lively when a guest drops food pellets into the water.

"I hadn't thought about it," Caleb replies. "But, maybe? I guess they wouldn't want them eating people."

"What do you think they do with them when they get too big? Or are they like a miniature strain of alligator?"

"Again, I hadn't thought of that." Caleb smiles. "I guess if they get too big, they rehome them in the swamp or something?"

"Or they kill them," Sadie whispers, her eyebrows raised. "Or, and I'm very much hoping for this one, the guy behind the counter over there takes them home and keeps them. So, by now he's got like fifty alligators that live with him in his little bungalow. I think alligators live like a hundred years, so they will all outlive him. We won't talk about what they'll do with his body when he passes away."

"You are so strange," Caleb says, his eyes bright. He looks over at the guy behind the counter and almost loses it. The man is older with a bushy white beard and matching bushy white eyebrows. He has a safari hat perched on the top of his head and eyeglasses with thick black frames. Caleb can't explain it, but for some reason he *does* look like a man who might just go home at night to a house filled with fifty alligators of various sizes and ages. He has definitely named all of them and considers them his children.

"Yes, but that's why you like me." Sadie pulls Caleb close and kisses him on his cheek.

Caleb tucks a strand of hair behind Sadie's ear. "So, are we going to play or discuss alligator theory all day?"

"I was just buying you some time. I know once I destroy you at your own game, you're going to be sad. Figured I'd let you enjoy the time you have left before the beat down commences."

"Ha! We'll see about that. However, I should note that this course has changed a lot since I was last here. Most notably, they replaced the orange side rails with jagged rocks, which frankly is an abomination."

"You read my mind," Sadie says dryly. "I'm like, my god, would you look at these damn rocks lining the holes of this miniature golf course? What type of philistines could do something like this?"

"I'm just saying. If my game isn't sharp, that's probably the reason. This course used to be pure, but now it's gone all commercial like the rest of them!"

"I have bad news for you, Caleb," Sadie says seriously. "Your game is never sharp."

Caleb shakes his head and rolls his eyes before grabbing Sadie around the waist and pulling her in for a kiss. "It seemed like my game was sharp enough last night."

"Eh, I was feeling generous."

The day proceeds generally in this manner. Caleb and Sadie take turns hitting putts on the minigolf course with maddeningly rocky, jagged perimeters that provide no consistent or predictable bounces. They also take turns trading verbal barbs and playful insults. They can hardly keep their hands off each other. The course is nearly empty because it's the middle of the day and the heat is overpowering. But the few people who are there, like the tired couple in their late thirties who are being dragged around the course by three small children, can't help but notice how in love these two young people are. Even if they haven't admitted it to themselves yet, it's plain for all the world to see.

Caleb ends up winning the match by two strokes. He's kept the little pencil tucked behind his ear, removing it after each hole to carefully mark their scores on the scorecard, filling in the neat squares with numbers. Sadie makes fun of him for his meticulousness multiple times. It's possible that she misjudges the speed of her putt on the last hole intentionally, to avoid the possibility of beating Caleb at his own game, but she'll never admit it. They are both damp with sweat and red-faced by the time they return their putters to the rack in the thatched-roof hut and wish the alligator man well with his reptilian family. They hold hands as they walk to the car and Caleb opens the passenger side door for Sadie like a gentleman.

Back at Caleb's apartment, they take turns showering and fall into his small bed exhausted from the fierce competition and a day spent in the Florida sun. Not too exhausted, though. Their bodies find each other. It's like one of those holes at minigolf that is placed at the bottom of a funnel. It doesn't matter where you aim, the ball will end up in the hole. It doesn't matter what path they take; Caleb and Sadie will end up together.

...

At least, it's beginning to feel that way.

CHAPTER 11

A PINK GOLF ball ricochets off a rock and bounces into a concrete pond, landing with a dramatic splash. A lizard sitting on the edge of the water looks on, unperturbed. Shrieking with outrage or possibly glee, a small child races toward the water, looking more than willing to dive in to rescue her golf ball.

"Emily, stop!" Caleb shouts.

By the grace of some higher power–perhaps Soteria, the goddess of salvation–Emily stops and does not tromp into the water with her sparkly Skechers.

"I'll get it," Caleb says calmly. He uses his putter to rake the ball back to the edge of the small pond, plucks it out with his fingers, and dries it off on the bottom of his shirt before handing it back to Emily. "So, maybe try hitting it just a little bit softer next time. You don't have to take a huge sw—"

Caleb stops short because Emily has already flitted away, the rubber head of her small putter bouncing along the ground behind her. Well, this certainly is a new and exciting minigolf experience. One with which Caleb is completely unfamiliar. He hasn't been here since, well, since Sadie. That round was quite different. He remembers that he won, which was nice even though he always suspected that Sadie might have let him win. And the rest of the day was pretty perfect. Much like a lot of the days during that year as far as he can remember.

By the time Caleb awakes from his daydream, Emily is about three holes ahead. She slaps the ball with her club, runs after it, and hits it again before it stops rolling. When she gets close to the hole, she rakes the ball into the cup with a scooping motion before racing off to the next hole. The way things are progressing, Caleb thinks, they will complete this round in about seven minutes. He takes the tiny pencil he had tucked behind his ear and tosses it into the trash can. There will clearly be no time for scorekeeping, or anything else really, on this day. He had hoped this outing would kill off an entire afternoon, but as always, Emily manages to take a wrecking ball to his plans. Filling the after-school time when he's technically supposed to be working from home, but pretty much never does, has proved to be a challenge.

Caleb has to console Emily when her ball disappears into the final hole. It takes longer to convince her that the ball is gone for good than it did to play eighteen holes. Eventually, he is able to get her off the course and back to the car without much further damage. He did have to spend ten dollars on the claw machine in the arcade so Emily could win a small stuffed cat. Retail value: fifty cents. As they ride home slowly in early rush hour traffic, Emily cradles the stuffed cat under her chin. She looks happy, content, and possibly a little sleepy, so Caleb guesses the effort and expense were worth it.

Caleb whips into the driveway at his small yellow house. He always feels compelled to turn in quickly without slowing down too much. There is no turn lane, and no one expects a car to turn off the busy road at this nearly hidden driveway of all places, so Caleb lives in constant fear of being plowed into from behind by a car driving much too fast. Caleb's mom's car is in the driveway. This is unexpected and it can't be good. Mom showing up unannounced means she definitely has an agenda.

"Grandma's here!" Emily shouts from the back seat, perking up as she sees Helen's black car. Surely Emily knows by now, Caleb thinks, that she's not going to receive an enthusiastic reception from her grandmother, but she remains steadfastly optimistic. Emily unbuckles her seatbelt, bolts out the door, and bounds inside the house. Caleb, on the other hand, takes his time. He sees no reason to rush things. After checking the mail, Caleb opens the front door and finds his mom seated at the small table that separates the kitchen from the living room area. She has her laptop open in front of her, eying the screen carefully. Emily is talking to her, or at her, rather, regaling her grandmother with details about her minigolf adventure. Helen nods her head and looks in Emily's direction every few sentences, occasionally tossing out a disinterested "ah yes" or "that sounds fun." Eventually, Emily wraps up her story time and migrates toward the loveseat where her iPad is plugged into the wall charging. Caleb gets a Sprite from the refrigerator and pops the top on the can.

"Hi, Mom," he says.

"Hi," Helen says without looking up from her computer. Caleb thought she might explain her presence in his house, but then again, he really didn't think that. He knows he will have to pry it out of her. It will take more skill and luck than trying to win a stuffed animal from a claw machine.

"Nice to see you," Caleb says, testing the waters.

"Yes, thanks." Helen closes a tab on her browser and switches over to an Excel spreadsheet filled with numbers and cells highlighted with a rainbow of colors.

"Is there any particular reason for your visit?"

"Yes."

"And that would be...?"

"I wanted to see my granddaughter, of course."

"Is she inside the laptop?" Caleb asks, sitting down on the small rug in front of the TV where Emily is playing with Barbies. He makes a point of doing this as often as possible. It's not that he enjoys playing with dolls or is particularly good at it–Emily routinely reminds him that he is, in fact, terrible at it–but it seems like something a parent should do. An attentive and caring parent, that is.

"We need to talk about something," Helen says, her eyes still fixed on the computer screen.

The claw has grabbed the stuffed animal. Now it's just a matter of maneuvering it to the drop zone without fumbling it. "Okay." Caleb pretends to play with Emily until she swats his hand away.

They sit in silence for several minutes. The only sounds are the clicking of the keys on Helen's laptop keyboard and Emily's ongoing chatter.

Helen finally breaks the silence. "I don't know where she is."

"Who is 'she'?"

"You know."

"But we never know where she is." Caleb looks toward Emily to see if she is paying attention to their conversation. She doesn't seem to be. "Not really. She's still in rehab as far as we know."

"But I can't get in touch with her. Not at all."

"That's how it goes though with her, isn't it?"

"It's different this time."

"How do you know it's different?"

"I can feel it," Helen says.

Caleb lets that pronouncement settle. Perhaps if he leaves it unanswered, it will evaporate like a puddle on a hot summer day. He fiddles with a small, fuzzy dog that presumably belongs to one of the Barbie dolls. A real parent would know the pedigree and ownership of all the toy pets in the bin, Caleb thinks. His dad would know. Or, if he didn't know, he'd make up a story about the dog that Emily would actually enjoy.

"That's not very analytical, Mom. Sounds like something I would say." Caleb hesitates before continuing, "Or Dad."

Helen doesn't visibly react. Her face remains composed as she continues to type. Her attention never wavers as she stares at the computer screen, as if the answers she's looking for are there somewhere in the spreadsheet. She just needs to find the right search term to enter so she can find them.

"It'll be okay." Caleb stands up and walks over to the table. Hoping that Emily can't hear, he leans over and whispers, "I don't know if Lauren will ever come back, but we have to focus on Emily for now. We've got this... *I've* got this."

Helen closes her laptop gently and begins to place it into her computer bag. "I should probably be going," she says, as if she and Caleb had been making small talk about the weather. "It's getting late. You'll make sure Emily gets to bed at a decent time?"

"Yes, Mom," Caleb says patiently. "I always do."

...

After Emily is asleep in bed at a time that is mostly decent, Caleb settles on the couch and flicks on the TV. He has to keep the volume low because Emily's room is just a few paces away, but he likes having the closed captions on anyway so he can follow along more easily. After choosing a show on Netflix, he almost immediately loses interest.

He slips his phone out of his pocket and opens several social media apps one after the other. In each, he types "Sadie Warren" into the search bar. As always, he finds nothing of interest. Sadie has never been on social media as far as he can tell. Not that he's obsessed or anything. He checks in maybe once a week at most. For the past twelve years or so. That's approximately 624 fruitless searches. It doesn't seem like too big of a number considering the circumstances. He has found her on Google several times through the years. He may or may not have a Google alert set up for her name. Nothing he's found has been particularly illuminating, however. He knew she moved to New York shortly after everything happened. He doesn't remember exactly how he found that out, but they did have a few common friends and acquaintances at the time, so he assumes somebody told him. Google indicates that she works for some sort of music promotion and marketing company. He noticed that her job title on the website switched from Publicist to Senior Publicist about four years ago. He recognizes a few of the artist names on the website, but not many. He looks at her headshot on the website approximately once every two to three days. The photo hasn't changed since he first found it, so it was probably taken only a few years after she left Florida. The photo is black and white. In it, Sadie sits with her elbow on the desk in front of her. Her head is tilted to the side, resting on her right hand. It appears that she's looking slightly to the right of where the camera must be positioned. Her features are mostly neutral, perhaps one corner of her mouth is turned up in the slightest of smiles, but Caleb has never been able to tell for sure. To this day, every time he looks at the picture, his heart beats just a little faster.

Thump, thump, thump.

A banner indicating a text message from Blaise appears at the top of Caleb's screen and he navigates to it.

> Hey man i'm in town tomorrow…you want
> to catch up,

Caleb thinks for a moment and then types back:

> sure, let me see if my mom can babysit.

Blaise immediately replies:

> what?

Caleb writes:

I'll explain tomorrow…let's meet at our
normal place at around 8?

Blaise likes the last message and Caleb sets his phone down on the couch.

It'll be nice to get out, Caleb thinks. His life has been very kid-centric these last few months. It's funny how that happens.

CHAPTER 12

SADIE LIES IN BED. The pre-dawn light pushes against the sheer drapes covering her windows. She hears the soft beep-beep of one of her neighbors unlocking their car with a remote. The parking lot is located right outside her bedroom window, which is one of the less appealing aspects of townhouse living. Sadie finds it odd that this superficial level of closeness with strangers somehow annoys her here in Florida when years of living shoved up against and piled on top of strangers in New York never phased her.

It's too early to be up and about but too late to go back to sleep, so Sadie opens Instagram on her phone. She's been meaning to check something; she types "Preston the peacock" in the search bar and taps on the first result that pops up. She glances at the profile and her mouth drops open due to a combination of shock and pure horror. The account has fifty thousand followers, which is appalling in its own right, but her eyes gravitate immediately to the bio. Under the picture of Preston posing with his tail feathers fanned open regally in front of what appears to be her parents' house, the bio reads "Preston The Peacock: Jess and Tom's Favorite Cock."

Sadie rests her phone face down on her chest for a moment,

closes her eyes, and tries to think of a way to lobotomize herself quickly and efficiently. Failing to come up with any good options, she picks the phone back up and scrolls down to the pictures on Preston's profile. There are... many of them. Preston eating from a plastic dish. Preston lying down under a bush. Preston standing beside a plastic four-leaf clover yard sign (the caption for that one says, "Even if I'm Irish, you can't kiss me because I don't have lips"; probably not their best work, Sadie thinks). Sadie browses through the comments on a few of the pictures and is, frankly, horrified. Tom wasn't kidding. The internet can be a scary and confusing place. Particularly when your parents are using it.

...

Sadie wakes Scarlett up to get ready for school. As is the case most mornings, Scarlett is slow to rise. She mutters complaints and pulls the covers up over her head to try to get her mom to leave her alone. Things sure do change fast, Sadie thinks. How is this almost teen the same child who just a few short years ago used to wake her every morning and demand that Sadie create magic with a pair of scissors and some cardboard? It's not so much that Sadie misses the little girl Scarlett once was, but rather, she misses the simplicity of that time in their lives. It certainly did not feel simple then, when she was really in the thick of it, with the sleepless nights and early-morning wake-up calls, but now, looking back, it seems like it must have been so easy. When Sadie wasn't working, she played with Scarlett, fed her, read to her, watched TV with her, gave her a bath, and helped her brush her teeth. There was no need to worry about screen time limits and structured activities and school and everything else that comes along with growing up.

"You need to leave in like twenty minutes," Sadie says, finally giving up and leaving Scarlett's room. This is how she ends most mornings now, by giving up.

A few minutes later, Scarlett emerges, bleary eyed and sullen. Despite the predictable back and forth, Sadie knows she can count on Scarlett to do what she's supposed to do and be where she's supposed to be. It's just that the journey is sometimes more stressful than she would like. Scarlett is a good kid. Exceptional in many ways. Smart, perceptive, and kind. Sadie knows that she is lucky to have her. Things could be so much more difficult.

"Want me to make you breakfast?" Sadie asks.

"You mean pour the cereal?" Scarlett replies.

"Yes."

"Sure."

Sadie pours cereal and milk into a blue plastic bowl—the same bowls she's used since Scarlett was little. They are sturdy, utilitarian, made to stand up to hundreds if not thousands of falls to the floor from tables, counters, or highchairs. Sadie thinks that it might be time to move on to grown-up glass bowls, but why toss aside something that is so reliable and unbreakable? Things you know you can count on are hard to find in this life. Sadie slides the cereal bowl across the counter to Scarlett and pours herself a cup of coffee.

"So, we didn't really talk much after Grandma and Grandpa's," Sadie says. "What did you think of all that?"

Scarlett gives an amused snort and scoops cereal into her mouth.

"I guess we need to figure out what to do with the suit of armor?" Sadie continues.

"I've heard it's really hard to find someone to take care of suits of armor these days," Scarlett says between bites. "Think I saw a video about it on TikTok."

"Yeah, maybe there's a non-profit or something that specializes in rehoming armor? Like the ones that find homes for elderly pets."

"The ads would say 'our body is protected, but our hearts are wide open' with really sad music playing in the background."

"Exactly that, yes," Sadie says, smiling. "But seriously, you should probably start working out so you won't topple over when you have to model it for them. I believe in you. You've got this." They both laugh. "And you might want to hit the gym after school today, because you're hanging out for a bit with Jess and Tom tonight."

"Why?"

"I'm going out with Paige."

"You're going out?" Scarlett asks skeptically. "You don't go out."

"I know, but Paige convinced me. She said she needed to get away from her children for a night or she would literally die."

"Hope you don't talk about me like that."

"Never. At least not unless you have your headphones on."

...

Sadie has never really understood the concept of going out. On a theoretical level, she gets the idea of it and sees why it might hold some sort of vague appeal. She went to bars and clubs and events in college, but typically spent most of her time skulking around the periphery, plotting an early exit. When she was with Caleb, they had fun doing things, but it was more because they were together, not because of any particular location. In New York, she worked in an industry that many would consider glamorous–even if her work was decidedly not–but because she was a single mom to a small child at the time, she was able to beg off most afterwork events and the debauchery that came with them. Later, when she and Ashford were together, he was completely content going out on his own with friends while Sadie stayed home with Scarlett. In retrospect, that probably should've served as a bit of a red flag, but she mostly enjoyed those solo nights when she could watch TV or read a book and drink a glass of wine alone in the apartment while Scarlett slept.

No pressure to interact or perform a relationship after the demands of the day.

Of course, going out in suburban central Florida is a completely different experience than going out in New York City. When the bar you're going to is tucked into the nearly forgotten corner of an L-shaped shopping plaza flanked by a Publix on one side and a nail salon on the other, passing through the glass door with tinted film that is peeling around the edges feels completely chaotic. Like going through a portal from one dimension to another.

It's still intensely bright outside, the sunlight bounces off the windshields of the cars in the parking lot. Sadie's eyes take a few moments to adjust to the dim light of the bar. Through the haze she catches sight of Paige at a high-top table in the corner waving at her frantically. She carefully maneuvers around the two pool tables in the middle of the room–she's always felt like giving drunk people easy access to long pointy sticks and heavy balls is not the smartest idea–and slides into the chair across the table from Paige. Paige has a fruity drink in front of her. She stirs it with a small cocktail straw before taking a sip.

"Ah, freedom," Paige says in an exaggerated tone.

"Freedom to sit in the dark in a loud, crowded room?"

"Yes, it's loud and crowded... with adults! Simply beautiful."

"Sometimes I forget that we are very different people," Sadie says. A waitress sets a drink down in front of her. Apparently, Paige has ordered on her behalf. "How did we ever become friends?"

"Oh, you know," Paige replies. "I forced you. It was the best decision I ever made for you. And this drink I picked out might be the second-best decision I've made for you. You're going to love it!"

Sadie shakes her head and smiles. When she's with Paige, she tends to find herself shaking her head and smiling quite a lot. It's been that way for decades now. It's nice that some things never change.

"So, tell me," Paige says as Sadie tastes her drink (it is very good, of course). Amidst the laughter and clinking glasses, Sadie braces herself. She knows what's coming and she feels a subtle undercurrent of anxiety. Paige's questions rain down as fiercely as a cloudburst on a summer afternoon, and with each query, a range of emotion ripples through Sadie—amusement, nostalgia, a tinge of discomfort.

"How are things going? You're getting adjusted to Florida life, I hope?" Paige's words hang in the air, and Sadie takes a moment to process them. Adjusting, she realizes, is an ongoing process. Paige continues with her interrogation. "Getting used to the humidity? The crazy drivers? Finding that work-life balance or whatever it is you were looking for? How's Scarlett doing? Is school going okay? Any love interests for you on the horizon yet?"

Suddenly, the downpour of stream-of-conscious thoughts stops. Sadie takes a moment to collect herself. She is momentarily distracted by a man and woman, both hammered, who have begun to make out passionately about fifteen feet away from Sadie's chair. The woman is seated on the edge of the pool table, and the man has pressed his body between her legs. It's possible they are doing more than making out, but Sadie decides not to go in for a closer inspection. She returns her attention to Paige. "Um, which of those twenty questions would you like me to answer first, or do I get to choose?"

"Be my guest!" Paige replies cheerily. "I'm very accommodating... particularly since this is my second drink already!"

"You better take it easy," Sadie says. "We know you're not twenty-one anymore. Even though I clearly still am."

"Very funny," Paige says flatly. "You sound like *such* a mom."

"Remind me. How many children have you given birth to?"

"Exactly. That's why I refuse to sound like a mom when I don't have to. You can learn so much from me, Sadie. I'm very wise." Paige nods knowingly, as if she's just delivered a death blow in a high school debating contest.

"And *very* drunk," Sadie says.

"What? Do you expect me to be out here rawdogging reality?"

Sadie shakes her head and covers her eyes with her fingers.

"Rawdogging reality? Is that what those two are doing?" Sadie cuts her eyes toward the couple groping each other by the pool table.

"No," Paige replies, after following Sadie's subtle head nod and locating the objects of her attention. "To describe what they are doing, I think you can just drop the word 'reality' from my description."

Paige and Sadie laugh and take sips of their drinks.

"Annnyway..." Paige expectantly, props her elbow on the table, resting her chin in the palm of her hand and giving Sadie a slight smile. "I'm ready for the latest gossip. Ready, go!"

Sadie laughs. "No pressure, right?" She stirs her drink and takes a sip. Conflicting emotions course through her veins. She feels like, more than anything, her world has flattened. In some ways she's finding what she was looking for when she left New York–a slower pace, more time with family, and less stress. But at the same time, she can't help but feel a little let down by it all. Despite their long friendship, she's not sure Paige will understand. "Let's see. I'm doing fine. Booking a few more students for lessons here and there, so that's good. My parents are still nuts–apparently, they are peacock influencers now, by the way–but it's good to be closer to them. I mean, they are hanging out with Scarlett tonight so I can be here with you."

"Hold up," Paige cuts in. "Can you tell me more about the peacock influencer thing, please?"

"No. I can't bear it, sorry."

"Unacceptable! You can't leave me hanging on that one! Spill it or... and this is another great option... tell me about your love life!" Sadie doesn't respond immediately. "Well...?" Paige prompts.

"I'm thinking," Sadie is genuinely conflicted. "Both bad options, but I'm going to go with my love life because I really have nothing to share on that front anyway."

"Oh, goodie!" Paige exclaims. She set the trap and Sadie walked right into it. "I have specific questions prepared!"

"Of course you do. Go ahead. But I promise you there's nothing to tell."

"Actually, it's just one question." Paige pauses for dramatic effect. "What happens when you run into Caleb again?"

"Why in the world would I run into Caleb again?" Sadie snorts. As well as she knows Paige, she didn't predict this line of questioning. "And even if I randomly did, so what? It's been twelve years. It's ancient history."

"So, let me explain my theory here," Paige says. "I've had lots of time to think about this while pushing my kids on the swings. Literally the most boring of parenting activities by the way. But, silver lining, it does give me time to think about Sadie love scenarios." Sadie shakes her head and smiles again. Undeterred, Paige continues. "First, Caleb seems like the type of guy who would stick around where he grew up. I don't mean that in a bad way, to be clear. I just mean he seems super loyal."

At this, Sadie's eyes widen ever so slightly, and her eyebrows raise. She thinks about what it means to be loyal and considers whether that's the right word to describe Caleb. She composes herself quickly before Paige can notice her reaction. "Also, he was big into the sword fighting thing, right? Like, if I remember correctly, your first kiss was at a renaissance faire?"

"Yes, I was there, thanks."

"No judgment! Here's my point. Caleb probably still lives somewhere in the general central Florida area, *and* he probably still does his jousting or whatever." Paige pauses, waiting for Sadie to catch on.

"Yes, and..."

"And... Scarlett does sword fighting now. I believe you said she likes it. If she continues doing it, I feel like the odds are pretty high that you'll run into Caleb sooner rather than later. I mean, how many people around here possibly do that? Like ten?"

Sadie rolls her eyes. "I guess it's theoretically possible, but it also seems pretty likely that Caleb is married with a kid or three by now, right?"

"I have considered this." Paige thrusts a finger into the air. "But let's examine the evidence. First, you broke this man's heart. Like, completely shattered it into a million pieces in front of men, women, maybe children, the gods, and The Pigeontoes."

"I feel like you're exaggerating a bit here, but–"

"Whatever." Paige waves a hand dismissively. "The point is, he might not have recovered. He might still be completely broken to this day–"

"You're painting a very rosy picture here," Sadie interrupts.

"And, let's face it," Paige continues, ignoring Sadie's comment. "The man is into sword fighting as we have already discussed. There is zero chance he found a damsel even half as fetching as you."

"Thanks?"

"The point is, this could be your second chance at love, Sadie! It could be like a fairy tale. Quite literally in your particular case! Oh..." Paige's eyes brighten even more, and she squeezes her hands together like she just can't contain her excitement. "What if you run into Caleb at some sword fighting battle and he's wearing a helmet or whatever it is they wear so you can't tell it's him. But, you know, because your energies are cosmically aligned, your body kind of feels it. Like the air suddenly feels charged and electric. The hairs on the back of your neck stand up because you just know."

Sadie scoffs. "How many drinks have you had?"

"So, you feel this unexplainable energy and then he sees you. Presumably you won't be wearing any headgear, so he recognizes you right away. Then, he slowly removes his helmet, you lock eyes, and you let out a little involuntary gasp. A gasp that you've been holding inside for over a decade without even knowing it. My God, I'm going to make myself cry." Paige dabs at her eyes dramatically and gives a little sniffle. "You move toward each other, like you have a magnet attached to your body and it's pulling you toward Caleb who is, as it turns out, conveniently dressed in metal armor. Then you kiss like it's dusk at the renaissance faire again and no time has passed. And you live happily ever after."

Paige is almost breathless now. Sadie remains silent. She looks away as if suddenly interested in the game of pool that is taking place across the room. She focuses on the clattering sound of the pool balls colliding to steady herself. When Paige started with her fairytale nonsense, Sadie was nothing more than slightly amused. However, as Paige picked up steam and the clearly impossible situation heightened, as she layered the details on top of each other, the hair on the back of Sadie's neck did begin to tingle. It felt like Paige was describing a scene that Sadie had encountered before but did not remember. Like she had dreamed it, maybe more than a few times over the past twelve years, but it was always the type of dream that remained lost in the land of sleep. But now, here it was. Her best friend was attempting to speak it into existence.

"Hello," Paige says. "Are you still with me?"

Sadie looks across the table at Paige. "You have quite the imagination, Paige," she says finally. "But again, it's ancient history. If I was going to reconnect with Caleb to explain myself or try to make amends or whatever, I should've done that years ago. I have a child who is eleven years old now! And, anyway, who knows what his life is like."

"Um, the eleven-year-old child part of this isn't exactly coincidental to the current conversation though, is it?"

Sadie shakes her head, looks down at the table, and swirls her glass in her palm. "The weird thing is," she says without looking up. "Since I moved back, I have started thinking about him again. I really didn't for many years, but now... I don't know. I think it's, like... being back here in this godforsaken state is dredging up old memories. And almost all my most recent memories of Florida involve Caleb in one way or another. Anyway..."

"Anyway," Paige fills in as Sadie trails off. She claps her hands together. "I think it's time to lighten the mood! We've had enough drinks, so it's karaoke time!"

"Ha! Too many drinks make you do things you regret. Trust me on that one."

"Ah," Paige says with a knowing expression, raising a finger and wagging it. "Your attitude is about to change, my dear Sadie. Because we *won't* regret this. Well, you might, and I probably won't remember it, but that's not important. Only this moment matters!"

Sadie laughs knowing that she has already lost. Paige always wins.

"Fine," Sadie says. "But only one song, and I get to pick."

"It's a deal!"

Sadie and Paige make their way toward the back corner of the dark bar where there is a mostly forgotten karaoke set up with a small TV screen and microphones. Sadie maneuvers through the room with relative ease while Paige moves more hesitantly, measuring her steps carefully like she's stepping from stone to stone across a stream where the water is moving at a rapid pace. No one is using the karaoke system, so Paige grabs a microphone, taps it, and says in an exaggerated voice, "Hey hey, everyone. Who's ready for a show?"

Sadie covers her eyes with one hand. She is not prepared for how mortifying this is going to be.

"I've got my girl here and she's ready to sing for you incredible people," Paige continues. A few people hunched over nearby tables glance in her direction, but most don't even turn their heads.

"What song do you want?" Paige asks, covering the microphone with her hand.

"I've got it covered," Sadie replies. "It's loading up now. Let's get this over with."

An electric guitar with tremolo emanates from the speakers and Paige lets out a groan. "Of course," she says in an exasperated tone. "You pick your favorite depression song. If only you had brought the sadness sweater you used to wear around the apartment for weeks at a time while you thought about being chronically misunderstood."

Sadie smiles. If Paige was going to make her do this, Sadie was going to make her pay. Sadie begins singing the opening lines of *Boulevard of Broken Dreams* by Green Day. Her voice is soft, but pure. When she reaches the chorus, Paige joins in. She is terribly off key, Sadie thinks, but she loves her for trying. As the song reaches its final crescendo, Sadie and Paige toss their mics aside, stand back-to-back, and jam out on their air guitars as the final, pulsing, distorted notes reverberate off the walls in the corner of the bar. When the music stops, they turn to face each other, and they hug. Paige rests her head on Sadie's shoulder.

"You know you'll never walk alone as long as I'm around, right?" Paige says.

"I know," Sadie replies. "Thanks for asking me out tonight. Even if I am depressing."

"You really are, but I love you for it."

...

Meanwhile, in the same bar, a man sits across the table from his old college roommate. They can't see the karaoke area from where they are sitting, but they are just within earshot. The man is so enamored by the story his friend is telling him about the time a mid-level celebrity showed up for the launch party of his friend's new line of CBD that he doesn't notice the music until the final thrashing notes ring out.

That's an unusual karaoke choice, the man thinks. *I haven't heard that song in, well, about twelve years or so.* He excuses himself, stands up, and makes his way toward the corner of the bar where the music is playing. For some reason, he feels like he needs to know who chose this song. But, by the time he makes his way through the crowded room, the karaoke area is empty. There are two microphones resting on a small table under the TV screen, their cords dangling and brushing against the floor.

...

Life doesn't usually give second chances.

CHAPTER 13

"So, um, would you maybe want to come watch me play at the coffee shop later today?"

Sadie and Caleb are in bed on a Saturday morning, her place this time. Her room is small and haphazard. There are a few band posters on the cream-colored walls, a small desk pushed into one corner that is piled with books, papers, and a laptop. A guitar in a black case is propped against the wall in the other corner, and one window is covered with yellowing plastic blinds. One slat in the middle of the blinds has a piece broken off on one end, leaving a jagged edge and about a three-inch hole where the morning light penetrates. The beam of sunlight lands on Sadie's foot. She is sitting up on her side of the double bed, wearing a purple t-shirt, her back resting against the dark wooden headboard, cradling her phone in her lap with both hands, staring at it.

Caleb is reclining on his side of the bed, shirtless, the bedsheets tangled about him at the waist, one foot sticking out from under the covers. "Wow, yeah, of course," he says, rubbing the sleep from his eyes with one hand. "I've always wanted to go to one of your gigs, but I didn't want to intrude, you know? Make you uncomfortable or anything."

"Cool," Sadie says, still staring at her phone. "I would've asked you before, but it seemed weird. Like, too personal or something."

"Yeah, I get it. It feels, like, really intimate, right? And vulnerable. I mean, not that all this isn't, but—" Caleb trails off, moving a hand around vaguely in the air to indicate *all this*.

"Exactly," Sadie says, looking toward Caleb now. "Sex is one thing, but singing? *That* is some sick, deeply personal shit."

She smirks and Caleb laughs, covering his face with his hands. Sadie slides down from her seated position and turns toward Caleb, draping her arm across his chest. She rests her head against his shoulder, and they stay like that for quite some time.

...

Caleb learned later that Sadie sometimes played guitar at the coffee shop where they first met, which explained why she was carrying the guitar case that nearly impaled him. Now, he's back where it all began, this time with his roommate Blaise, who is predictably stoned. They sit at a small table along the wall of windows at the front of the shop. It's late afternoon and the crowd is sparse. There are a few college-aged people scattered about at various tables with laptops open in front of them.

An older couple sits in the corner with coffees. The man is reading a newspaper, the woman is looking at him with a pinched expression on her face. They don't talk to each other. The two baristas, a young man and woman, are standing behind the counter trying to look busy while engaging in an ongoing conversation that is possibly flirtatious in nature.

Sadie has set up in a corner. She is seated on a stool with her guitar resting on her lap. She is dressed in dark jeans that are ripped at the knees and a long-sleeved black shirt. Her dark hair is pulled back. There is no need for a microphone because the shop is small. Sadie begins to work her way through a series of songs, mostly acoustic versions of rock songs and a few others that Caleb doesn't recognize. He wonders if they are originals. Sadie plays and sings softly and gently, as if she's trying to blend into the background. After each song ends, there is a smattering of applause, from the mostly disinterested patrons. Caleb applauds eagerly, but not loudly. He doesn't want to make a spectacle of himself. Sadie looks his way and gives him a small smile every now and then, but otherwise doesn't pay him any special attention. After the first few songs, the crowd begins to fill in a little. Most of the tables are taken now and there is a sustained low buzz of conversation. Sadie continues to play.

"This is amazing, right?" Caleb says to Blaise during a break between songs. "I mean, I knew Sadie was good, but I didn't know she was this good."

"Yeah man," Blaise replies, his eyes unfocused. His paper coffee cup sits on the table in front of him with the lid off. He stares into the cup as if it might contain all the galaxy's most closely guarded secrets.

"I've heard Sadie messing around on her guitar before, but this... this is something else entirely," Caleb gushes, catching Sadie's eye from across the room and giving her a little thumbs up as she takes a sip from her water bottle.

"Are you going to marry this girl or something?" Blaise asks. He floats in and out of lucidity so capriciously that Caleb is slightly taken aback by this surprisingly relevant question.

"Um," Caleb stammers, "it's kind of early to think about stuff like that, I think. She's great, of course, but we haven't even finished college yet."

"You will soon." Blaise stares intently at Caleb now. "Then what? She moves to some big city, and you never see her again?"

Caleb looks away, unable to match Blaise's intensity. "I don't know. I guess I have to figure that out before the end of the year. Just trying to take things slow for now."

"Love doesn't follow a calendar, man. It wants what it wants. It has its own timeline." Sometimes stoned Blaise is unexpectedly insightful.

About an hour after she started, Sadie clears her throat and says tentatively, "Ok, I have one more song for you. Thanks for coming out today."

She positions her guitar on her lap and begins to strum, slowly at first and then with increasing urgency. The intro sounds familiar to Caleb, but he doesn't recognize Sadie's acoustic arrangement until she begins to sing the opening line. Ah, of course, "Boulevard of Broken Dreams." Caleb is completely captivated from the first note all the way to the dramatic finish. He can't take his eyes off Sadie. She has her eyes closed throughout most of the song, completely immersed. Caleb gets the feeling that the rest of the people in the coffee shop can't take their eyes off Sadie either. The mood has palpably shifted from disinterested to fully engaged and energized. The room is quiet and still except for the guitar and Sadie's soft yet piercing voice.

When the song ends, Sadie opens her eyes and sees a room full of faces staring at her. She gives a sheepish smile, lifts her hand to give a small wave in acknowledgment of the applause, and looks to find Caleb. He is standing at his table clapping, a big grin on his face. She smiles back, almost laughing now. Caleb motions toward the door and mouths, "meet you outside." He gestures around with his hand as if to say, "after you deal with all this." Sadie nods.

Caleb gathers his things and walks outside. Blaise disappears somewhere as Blaise tends to do. Sadie accepts compliments from a few coffee shop customers who approach her as she packs up her guitar, shaking hands and engaging in idle conversation. The older couple passes by on their way to the door and the man says, "I didn't know any of the songs, but I sure enjoyed your pretty voice." His wife scowls, swats him on the arm, and tugs him toward the door.

...

.   .   .

Outside, Caleb stands on the sidewalk leaning casually against the white brick wall of the Italian restaurant beside the coffee shop. He studies the large crack in the sidewalk at his feet where sprigs of grass or weeds with yellowish-green briars on the end are growing. He removes a pack of cigarettes from the back pocket of his jeans. He stopped at 7-Eleven on the way to the coffee shop and bought the cigarettes because it seemed like the appropriate thing to do. It was the first time he had ever purchased cigarettes and he was extremely nervous during the entire transaction. The man at the register, however, barely noticed Caleb was there, wordlessly retrieving a pack of Camels from the display behind him and plopping it down on the counter. Caleb chose the Camels because the name started with C, and he therefore felt a cosmic connection with it. That and he used to love looking at old cigarette commercials on YouTube and the Joe Camel character did seem pretty cool.

Now, he shakes a cigarette out of the pack and examines it for a moment, rolling it around between his fingers. He puts it between his lips just to see how it feels and leaves it dangling there. He stares off into the distance pensively. Not because he's feeling particularly pensive, but because the cigarette is already having an effect on him. He can feel the coolness and insouciance coursing through his veins. If he keeps this up then soon, he imagines, he won't care whether he lives or dies. He considers the possibility that buying a leather jacket might not be such a bad idea, even though it is early November, and the outside temperature is 80 degrees shortly after sunset.

Sadie pushes her way out of the door of the coffee shop, holding it open with her hip while maneuvering her guitar through the opening with her free arm. She swings the guitar around, letting the door fall shut as she turns in Caleb's direction. She takes a few steps toward him and as she approaches, she is clearly suppressing a smile. Caleb is wearing a lime green golf shirt. All three buttons are buttoned up, so the collar lays flat and even across his neck. The light coming from the restaurant window makes him appear a little fuzzy around the edges.

"Hey, there, superstar," Caleb says earnestly, steadying the cigarette with his hand while he talks and then replacing it between his lips.

Sadie doesn't respond. She moves toward him in one smooth motion, stopping in front of him. Setting her guitar case down on the cracked pavement beside her, she reaches up to Caleb's neck. She deftly unbuttons the top button of his shirt, presses up on her toes, and kisses him on the cheek. The end of the unlit cigarette brushes against the side of her face.

"There, that's better," she says, her hands resting on Caleb's chest as she studies his face. "Now you don't look like the son of a venture capitalist waiting for the deckhands to finish washing your boat."

He laughs, almost dropping the cigarette.

"I didn't know you smoked," Sadie says.

"I actually don't." Caleb removes the cigarette from his mouth and holds it loosely at his side. "I thought it would make me look cool enough that maybe the rockstar would notice me after her concert."

"Do you want a tip?"

"Sure."

"You have to light it."

Caleb laughs again. "My mom always said don't play with fire. I'm actually not joking. Fire was one of her big hang-ups."

Sadie laughs, shaking her head. "Such a rebel, you are. Parading around with an unlit cigarette. Your mom must be rolling over in her grave."

"Well, that would be my dad, actually," Caleb says, surprising himself with his candor. "In the grave, I mean."

"Oh, God." Sadie covers her mouth with one hand. "I'm so sorry. We haven't talked much about our families, I guess. Or, at least not in much detail. I really didn't mean anything by it."

"I know." Caleb is still a little stunned that the word "dad" slipped out so easily, almost like his body believed he was ready to say it even if his mind had other thoughts on the matter. His mind takes control of the wheel again as he blinks away the momentary lapse. Walling off that part of himself is safer. Smarter. He tries his best to speak with a breezy tone. "It's no problem. He died when I was a kid. An accident. I don't really like talking about it."

"Of course, I understand."

"Actually, while we're talking about this, I should probably mention that my big sister died as well." This lie arrives fully formed in Caleb's brain, and the words are out of his mouth before he can think twice. His sister isn't dead, but she sometimes seems so far gone that Caleb feels like he's already lost her. Just a few days ago, she knocked on his door at one in the morning, strung out beyond belief. Caleb couldn't look her in the eye. He couldn't bear to see the emptiness where there used to be so much life.

Almost immediately, Caleb wishes he could take this lie back. It's a big one, he knows, and he hates lying to Sadie. But the lie came so easily, Caleb can't help but wonder if his subconscious has been preparing for this moment for quite some time. And he also can't help but wonder if his subconscious is right. Maybe this lie about Lauren is necessary? Caleb has already fallen for Sadie; there's no denying it. He started falling for her the first time she rounded the corner in the café with her guitar, and he hasn't stopped. Seeing her perform tonight makes Caleb realize that Sadie is even cooler than he thought, and that is really saying something because he already thought she was the coolest girl he's ever met. Girls like that don't go for dorks who dress up like knights. It's an immutable law of the universe. And girls like that *definitely* don't go for dorks who dress up as knights *and* have serious personal baggage. In Caleb's experience, the best guys like that can hope for is pity. Like that time in high school when the head cheerleader and her cool girl clique found out about Caleb's dad and adopted him as their pet project for about a week and a half. Caleb doesn't want pity; he wants Sadie.

"I'm so sorry, Caleb," Sadie says finally. "I'm glad you told me."

She pulls Caleb into a tight hug, and he rests his head on her shoulder for a moment. After the embrace, an awkward silence settles over them. Sadie tucks a strand of hair behind her ear and looks across the street, watching an older woman walking past pushing a stroller in which a small dog is seated, its tongue lolling. The woman, stroller, and dog pass out of the cone of light emanating from the overhead streetlamp, disappearing back into the darkness.

"If you ever need to talk..." Sadie begins before trailing off.

"Thanks," Caleb replies. "I usually just try to leave the past in the past. You know, bury things deep down and pretend everything is cool and normal. It's the American way." He smiles sheepishly and Sadie lets out a small laugh. "Anyway, enough of that!" He claps his hands once, trying his best to sound upbeat. "You... you were amazing! I was telling Blaise that I knew you were good, but I didn't know you could do *that*. Did you see how into it the crowd was at the end? You totally won them over!"

"Thanks. Well, there was nowhere to go but up. I think you were the only one paying attention for the first half hour. But that's how these things are. Random coffeeshop isn't exactly the Hard Rock Cafe."

"You have the talent to play anywhere, Sadie! And when you play Hard Rock Cafe or the arena downtown, I want a backstage pass."

"You've got it, Lord Dagwyn," Sadie says with a mischievous gleam in her eye.

"Can I walk you home?" Caleb asks. "We can grab something to eat on the way. If you want?"

"Sure. I'd like that."

Sadie reaches down to pick up her guitar case, but Caleb beats her to it. He takes Sadie's hand with his free hand, and they begin to walk. A few of the shops and storefronts have strands of multi-colored lights ringing their windows. It feels a bit early for holiday decorations, but sometimes these things follow their own timeline.

CHAPTER 14

CALEB AND BLAISE are seated together at a small table in their "normal place." Their normal place happens to be a small bar located in an L-shaped shopping plaza between a Publix and a nail salon. There are a couple of pool tables, dim lighting that gives the whole place an eerie, hazy feel, and a mostly forgotten karaoke setup shoved into one corner. Blaise is wearing tight-fitting, tapered black jeans and a button-up shirt with the collar splayed open. The shirt has a shiny metallic sheen, almost like a salmon's scales. His hair is shaved tight on the sides and pushed up on top, locked in place with sticky gel. He is also wearing aviator sunglasses, so Caleb is unsure if Blaise can even see him from across the table.

"So, yeah, I am really loving where my life is right now," Blaise is saying. They are on their second drinks at this point and Blaise hasn't stopped talking about himself yet. "Don't get me wrong, it can be a grind with all the travel, long hours, and hot women throwing themselves at me, but it's all part of the game, you know?"

Caleb has zoned out a bit. He is moving his glass around on the wooden table from place to place so the circles of condensation the bottom of the glass leaves behind form what looks like the interlocking Olympic rings. He's pretty sure it's supposed to be three rings on top and two on the bottom, but he makes a mental note to look it up later to confirm.

"You know?" Blaise prompts, finally noticing that Caleb isn't completely with him.

"Oh, yeah," Caleb mumbles, trying to remember what Blaise was talking about. "I'm sure that is a challenge."

Blaise nods and gives a little shrug. This acknowledgment apparently appeases him sufficiently, because he continues talking about himself some more. While he pontificates, Caleb returns to his glass, creating long rows of interlocking condensation rings on the table now. Seven, eight, nine. He thinks about Emily and wonders if she is giving his mom much trouble about bedtime. She can be very particular. Bossy, some might say. Then he admonishes himself for worrying. He's supposed to be having a night off, and yet, he's still thinking about kid stuff. He supposes that's just what parents do, even ersatz parents.

"I mean, honestly, sometimes I can't even believe it," Blaise continues as Caleb tunes back in, and it's like he's flicked the dial on an old car radio; the static dissipates, and the station comes in loud and clear. "I know my reputation in college wasn't the best. I was always 'the stoner' or 'the pothead' or 'the loser' or 'the guy you wouldn't let your sister near,'" he makes air quotes with his fingers while listing off all his illustrious titles. "And now, well, I haven't really changed much at all. I'm a bit humbler, maybe, but otherwise I just take my cannabis in a slightly different form and do a little yoga and the occasional juice cleanse, and suddenly I'm considered to be a health and wellness influencer! An icon. Someone that people look up to. Aspire to be. It's pretty heady stuff, man."

Caleb exhales heavily, as if he's been holding his breath during Blaise's entire soliloquy. "That's great," he says after a short pause. "Really... great. Awesome, actually. I'm glad you're doing so well!"

"Thanks," Blaise says cheerily. "That means a lot coming from you. And look at me. I got so caught up in telling you about myself I forgot to ask about you. How are things going? How are your mom and... sister, right? You have a sister? Oh, yes," he says, snapping his fingers and pointing across the table at Caleb, "you definitely have a sister, and if I remember correctly, she was... well, never mind, I don't want to make things weird since she is your sister and all."

"Uh, thanks?" Caleb says. "Well, my mom is babysitting right now so I can be here with you."

"Whoa, congrats!" Blaise exclaims. "I didn't know you had a kid!"

"I mean, I said when you texted that I had to get my mom to babysit, so..."

"Right, right. I forgot about that. I remember being surprised, but I had a girl over at the time, so I kind of immediately forgot about it, if you get my drift. Anyway, who's the mom?"

"Well, that brings us back to my sister."

"You lost me. What does it have to do with your sister?"

"My sister is the mom."

"Your sister is the mom? Dude!" Blaise's mouth tightens into a grimace.

"She is," Caleb continues. "I'm not the father, of course."

Blaise sits forward and slaps the table with both hands. "Wow, that is a huge relief, my man. Things were about to get *really* uncomfortable. I was already planning my exit strategy. I was going to be like, 'very cool, Caleb, I'll leave you to that while I head over to the bar and talk to the girl who has been staring at me all night and is not my sister.'"

"My sister has major addiction problems, depression, anxiety, you name it," Caleb says, undeterred. "She's been in and out of rehab for, well, years now, I guess. She fell off the wagon again earlier this year."

An uncomfortable quiet settles over the table, then Blaise sits back in his chair and says, "Whoa, well, things just got really uncomfortable anyway."

Caleb waves a hand dismissively. "No, we're old friends. I'm comfortable telling you anything."

"Cool, cool," Blaise says, clearly agitated now. "Um, I hope you don't blame me and, you know, my people for your sister's problems."

"No, no, not at all. I mean, I haven't really thought about it too much, but she's more into pills, alcohol, those sorts of things. Not weed or whatever it is you do."

"Cannabis," Blaise says quickly. "We like to keep things official. In fact, and this might be interesting to you, my R and D team has been looking into the possibility of using some of our products to help people struggling with addiction and mental health problems. If you want me to send along some information so you can have a—"

"Please don't," Caleb cuts in. "I love you and all, but I can't take advice when it comes to Lauren. Actually, it's like, my mom and I have decided that we don't talk about Lauren, no, no, no."

Caleb sings the last three words to the tune of the hit song from the movie *Encanto*. Blaise tilts his head to indicate confusion.

"You know," Caleb says. "Like the song in the movie?"

"I don't know it."

"I guess since you don't have kids, you probably wouldn't know about it."

"Oh, yeah," Blaise says. "If it's a kid thing, you can count me all the way out! I really can't stand those little creatures." Caleb stares at him blankly. "But I'm sure your daughter, I mean, niece or whatever, is great. Very cute and all that."

"Nice save," Caleb says flatly. "So, yeah, that's pretty much my story. As far as I know, Lauren is in rehab up in New York. I'm in charge of my niece Emily, indefinitely, it would seem. Lauren wanted me to take her. Even though she was completely messed up, she still had enough sense to know that our mom couldn't handle it. There's not a whole lot she's been able to handle lately, to be honest. It's like she just slipped away after my dad died and never fully came back. I mean, she does okay taking care of herself for the most part, she still works at the school and everything, but she just gets absorbed in her little world of spreadsheets and lists and numbers. It's like she thinks if she studies hard enough or discovers the perfect macro or something she'll be able to, well, bring him back, I guess?"

"That is seriously crazy what happened with your dad, bro,"

Blaise says. "I honestly still can't believe it's real. Like, when you told me about it back in college, I was probably a little stoned at the time, so I definitely thought you were messing with me. And even now, I'm literally the founder and CEO of a cannabis company that is about to have an IPO next month, not sure I mentioned that yet, but here I am, tons of things on my plate every day, people pulling me in every direction, but when I'm hitting the lotus pose during yoga, just honing in on my goddamn center, Caleb," he pauses and looks directly into Caleb's eyes, "I still think about your dad. And, obviously, I didn't even know him! Never even met the guy. But the way you talked about him, I feel like I knew him and that he's still alive, still right here with us. It's wild that a spirit like his, or the way you described him at least, could just be snuffed out like that." Blaise snaps his fingers and Caleb winces almost imperceptibly.

They sit in silence. Blaise takes off his sunglasses and wipes down the lenses with the bottom of his salmon shirt. Caleb repositions his glass and swipes his hand slowly across the table, turning the interlocking rings of condensation into a long smear of dampness. Blaise puts his glasses back on and launches into another story about his weed business. He talks about a launch party he hosted at his house for their new line of CBD. A mid-level celebrity actor was there, and Blaise says despite being "crazy short" the man has hands the size of baseball gloves. Despite himself, Caleb becomes interested, primarily because, as is the case with most of Blaise's stories, it seems completely outlandish, but knowing Blaise, it probably somehow contains more truth than fiction.

As the anecdote begins to wind down, Caleb notices for the first time there is music playing. It must be coming from the karaoke setup. He can tell the song is winding down, because he doesn't hear any singing, just slightly distorted electric guitars. He recognizes it. "Boulevard of Broken Dreams." He considers this to be a relatively odd karaoke choice. He also remembers the last time he heard the song. A very vivid image of himself standing against a brick wall with an unlit cigarette in his mouth forms in his mind. It feels like he's looking at his old self from outside his body. From above. He sees Sadie emerge from the door of the coffee shop and walk toward him, guitar case in hand. She unbuttons the top button on his shirt and kisses him on the cheek.

Caleb rises from his seat at the table. Blaise continues talking; perhaps he doesn't notice Caleb has left. Caleb walks toward where the music was coming from, but it has already faded away. When he gets close enough to see the karaoke station, the only things there are two microphones resting on a small table under the TV screen, their cords dangling and brushing against the floor.

CHAPTER 15

Sadie wakes up the following morning with a pulsing headache. Her bedroom feels as bright as the face of the sun even though only a soft schmear of morning light pushes in through the window. She moves her hand to her face, pinching her eyebrows between her thumb and index finger, massaging gently. She's only had a hangover headache this bad one other time in her life. She has made a point of avoiding hangovers so she would never be reminded, yet here she is.

The big mistake was letting Paige convince her to go to the wine bar *after* the regular bar. Paige wasn't ready to go back to reality, primarily because if she got home around eleven, her youngest would just be waking up for his nightly bout of insomnia. She couldn't face the prospect of lying on the floor beside his bed for an hour as he poured forth the entire contents of his brain. Enjoying just one or two more drinks and adult conversation at the fancy wine bar before Ubering home was a much better option. Well, it was a better option for Paige, but perhaps unsurprisingly, it was not such a great choice for Sadie. Particularly since she has a Friday afternoon filled with beginner guitar lessons to look forward to. She can already hear the screeching chords reverberating in her head, bouncing off the inside of her skull, caroming in every direction like bowling pins blasted by an expertly-rolled bowling ball.

On the plus side, not having a traditional day job anymore means she can curl up in bed all morning even though it's a weekday. Once she gets Scarlett up and off to school, it will be straight back to her comfortable cocoon.

...

Of course, best-laid plans and all that.

...

Sadie hears the knob on her bedroom door rattle and turn, then Scarlett enters, a bit more gently than when she was three years old and scared in the middle of the night, but still with enough force to announce her presence.

"Hey," she says. "You remember you said you'd pick up the sword from that guy on Facebook, right? For my exhibition tonight."

"Yes, of course," Sadie replies, turning toward the door and sitting up halfway to give the impression that she was just on the verge of getting up. "I've got it covered."

Sadie, in fact, did not remember. Now that Scarlett has mentioned it, a vague recollection begins to form in her mind, but the details remain fuzzy. Fuzzy enough that she needs to unearth more information before she lets Scarlett leave to catch the bus to school.

"Make sure you send me the guy's address before you head out," Sadie says briskly.

Scarlett leans against the doorframe and rolls her eyes. "Come on, Mom," she says. "I sent you the info yesterday. It's a screenshot from the Facebook message. You told me to stop messaging with strangers."

"Right," Sadie says. "That sounds like something I would say. And definitely don't meet up with them in real life."

Scarlett sighs. "That's why you said you would do it. The sword is twenty-five dollars. Cash only."

"Sure. All the good swords are cash only."

"What does that mean?"

"I don't know, really. Just felt like I needed to say something."

"You're so weird," Scarlett says. She turns and leaves the room, letting the door fall closed softly behind her.

Sadie lies back down. "The things we do for our children," she says quietly to herself and immediately wonders if Jess ever felt put upon by her when she was growing up. She had to have, right? Sadie knows she never really showed gratitude for all the things her parents did for her, and yet, they always maintained their sunny, relentlessly optimistic exterior. At least as far as she knew or can remember. Maybe Jess and Tom were crying behind their closed bedroom door at night, but somehow Sadie doesn't think so. One thing she does know is that growing up with parents who seem to enjoy *everything*, who are like the walking embodiment of those "Cherish Every Moment" decorative canvases, can certainly skew the lens through which you evaluate your own parenting experience. Through the painfully long days and surprisingly short years, there was never a moment where she thought she was doing enough. Enjoying her daughter enough. Having enough fun and making enough memories while pushing four-year-old Scarlett on the swing again and again and again at the little park around the corner from their tiny apartment.

And now, lying in bed on an early October Friday morning, back in central Florida of all places, Sadie somehow feels *less* on top of things than she ever has. It doesn't make any sense. She spent years juggling single parenthood and a high-powered career in the entertainment industry where everyone is expected to perform, to always wear a mask and play a role. She did it all while living in a big city far from home with no family support. Maybe it was a massive mistake moving back here, she thinks. She had told herself she wanted to slow down, to be closer to her parents, to spend more time with Scarlett and less time at her office at eleven p.m. on a Friday night. But what if what she was really doing was giving up? Or giving in? Letting go of the real, authentic life she worked so hard to build just so she could chase an ideal of parenthood and work-life balance that doesn't exist. One that she cobbled together by reading too much nonsense on the internet and watching her parents be perfect parent cyborgs for decades.

In the past few weeks, Sadie has begun to suspect that having objectively less to do opens up way too much time for being sad. Scarlett growing from an extension of her body to a slightly less needy early elementary school student to an obstinately independent and somewhat aloof tween was okay when Sadie had work to occupy her mind, but with only beginner music lessons to teach in the afternoons and evenings, she has too much time to think about all the things she doesn't have to do or get to do anymore. No more playing in imaginary worlds and doing it all wrong. No more spreading peanut butter and jelly on bread three times a day. No more bedtime stories and lying on the uncomfortable wood floor while Scarlett fell asleep at night. She does, however, have to pick up a medieval weapon of war from a random man on Facebook, so she guesses that is at least something.

Speaking of weaponry, Scarlett has been quite diligent in wielding her sword every Saturday morning for more than a month now. Sadie still doesn't know much about it because Scarlett has made sure to keep her mom out of her space. Sadie remains strictly banned from even setting foot out of the car at practice. Sometimes she stays, reading a book or looking through her phone, but most of the time now she leaves and comes back after an hour to pick Scarlett up. She doesn't feel great about it since these people are strangers and heavily armed, but Scarlett reminds her that prior to this summer, she had been running short errands in New York City on her own. Sadie can concede that she does have a point.

It's certainly nice that Scarlett has found something to connect her to her new home. Sadie knows it can't be easy for a sixth grader to start over so completely. To be picked up and dumped onto what must feel like a foreign planet. Surrounded by palm trees, lizards, and strip malls instead of skyscrapers, subways, and art museums. She seems to be doing remarkably well, all things considered. She has few complaints about school, and she does like that there is a Chipotle on almost every corner. And tonight, Sadie will get to see Scarlett in action, showing off her new skills. She's legitimately excited. As a parent, there's nothing better than watching your kids do things. Soccer, ballet, piano, karate, longsword death matches. It doesn't matter what. Seeing your child, the one you feed, nurture, and argue with for hours every day about the necessity of maintaining basic hygiene, participating in an activity that you have absolutely nothing to do with is a purely magical experience. Will tonight be magical? Sadie isn't sure, but she's more than ready to find out.

...

Caleb is ready. Or at least that's what he keeps telling himself over and over again as he drives from his little yellow house on the busy road to the football field that the two rival high schools share. The field is not located at either school; it sits on county property next to the large dirt parking lot where the school buses live at night, their hulking bodies lifeless and still. A single lamp jutting out from an old wooden pole covers half of the lot in a pale yellow light, the buses' shadows loom, reaching out for the darkness. On the other side is a large, boxy building that used to be a dog track, and then a church, and is now abandoned, the parking lot overgrown with weeds, a few shattered windows marring the facade. A lot of praying no doubt happened in that building during all its iterations, but apparently none of the prayers were answered.

Caleb's mom is riding in the passenger seat. She pushes her glasses up her nose with one finger as she studies the screen of her phone. Emily is in the back seat, giddy, the heels of her feet bouncing excitedly against the car seat. She's asked so many questions about this night from the time she arrived home from school a few hours ago that Caleb assumes she must be compiling some sort of almanac.

"So, we're playing football?" Emily asks from the back seat. One last question. Well, almost certainly not the last, so one *more* question.

"No," Caleb answers patiently. "It's high school kids playing football. We're just watching."

"Do we know them?"

"No."

"Then why would we watch them and not play ourselves?"

"Well, it's just something people do. And, more importantly, my sword fighting club is doing an exhibition at halftime. Halftime is the break at the middle of the football game when the band goes on the field and plays music, but we don't have to get deep in the weeds here, it's kind of complicated. What matters is that we'll be doing a short performance."

"Can I have cotton candy?" Emily asks.

"Yes, sure," Caleb says.

"It's kind of late at night for so much sugar, don't you think?" Helen says without looking up from her phone.

"It'll be fine, Mom. It's a special night." Caleb's mom gives a soft "hmm" and doesn't say anything more.

As they approach the field, traffic begins to pick up. A skinny high school boy in a ROTC uniform signals for Caleb to turn into a grassy parking lot, but Caleb waves him off and continues creeping forward as pedestrians clad in school colors weave in and around the line of cars. Caleb hasn't been to this place on a game night in years, but he still remembers where to park. The designated parking lot is much too crowded and a nightmare to get out of after the game. Caleb knows the smart play is to drive past the field, turn onto a side street, and park beside the road next to the ditch. The terrain is a bit treacherous, the grass is always unkempt, there is a significant risk of tumbling down into the rainwater that always pools at the bottom of the ditch, and the walk to the field is a bit longer, but it is totally worth it to avoid the chaotic traffic jam that is certain to ensue after the high school football game concludes. Caleb is adamant about this. It is the only way.

"We're here," Caleb announces as he eases the car into park, tilted at nearly a forty-five-degree angle downward.

"Where?" his mom asks. "On the side of a mountain?"

"This is the best place to park," Caleb says. "Trust me."

Caleb steps out of the car onto the road and quickly jogs around to make sure his mom and Emily get out safely and don't topple over, roll down the hill, and splash into the unseen water below. Everything goes off without a hitch. This is going to be an exceptional night. Caleb walks hand-in-hand with Emily as she skips along beside him. His mom trails a few steps behind. As they walk, Emily keeps up a meandering chatter, commenting on things she sees, clutching one scraggly doll in her hand, another tucked under her arm. Caleb marvels at how small and delicate Emily's hand is. It feels good to hold it. It makes him feel important, like he's her protector.

The last time he walked toward this football field holding someone's hand, things felt much different. Everything seemed bigger, more chaotic, more magical. The roles were reversed then. He was the one who needed protecting. He went to countless high school football games just like this one when he was little. He didn't particularly like football—it seemed very chaotic and carnal—but he still loved those nights. He liked it best when the air had finally turned cool and there was a little drizzle. Walking from the car toward the field huddled close under a large golf umbrella. His small hand nestled in his dad's large palm. He liked to run his fingers across the pads at the base of his dad's fingers to feel the rough calluses–vestiges of years of baseball, golf, yard work, a life lived with purpose and energy.

The rain drops felt gentle and fleeting as they tap-tap-tapped softly on the umbrella over their heads. However, those same raindrops looked much more tangible and menacing as they slanted through the glowing light cascading from the gleaming bulbs atop the high poles surrounding the football field. It's funny how two things you know are the same can look so much different. Perspective changes everything.

Just as there are now, there were clumps of teens roaming around then. Different teens, of course, but teens nonetheless. Caleb remembers he felt like he was catching a glimpse of a life he might have one day. It was both exhilarating and terrifying, so he gripped his dad's hand a little tighter and cast his eyes down toward the muddy ground hoping to avoid being noticed. As if any teenager would care about an eight-year-old boy when there were potential boyfriends or girlfriends to impress and position in the social hierarchy was hanging in the balance each and every Friday night under the bright lights.

Caleb and his dad sat on the cold metal bleachers, slowly getting more and more soaked as the night wore on, but it never dampened their spirits. Luke Monroe wouldn't let it. Caleb's dad was not the type of man who grumbled when things didn't go perfectly or raged against a world that had treated him unfairly. He was a magnet for joy. He didn't just look for a silver lining in a dark cloud, he gave the cloud a hearty slap on the back, told it a dumb joke, offered it a beer, and sat with it until the whole darn cloud was glowing. And he always brought a towel to the football field on rainy Friday nights. Most people don't even think of bringing a towel, but Luke always remembered. He was the towel guy. And he was more than happy to share it with anyone sitting nearby so their backsides wouldn't get quite so wet.

Luke cheered and whistled throughout the entire game, shouting encouragement to the players no matter how badly the team was losing. And, honestly, the team was almost always losing. It was the school's oldest and most steadfast tradition. Caleb always wondered if the players could hear his dad shouting "Great effort, boys" or "Next play, get 'em on the next play!" He assumed they could. They always sat directly behind the team bench about halfway up the bleachers. Right in the center of the action. Some of the players' moms made noisemakers by putting small rocks inside old milk jugs. The moms always made sure to offer one to Luke. He was, after all, very popular amongst the mom set because of his cheery demeanor and the way he made everyone feel like a friend. Of course, the chiseled jawline and large biceps that strained against the sleeves of his royal blue golf shirt probably didn't hurt. Luke passed the noisemaker along to young Caleb, patting him on the back and saying, "All right, shake, shake, shake, Senora!" Caleb never understood what that was supposed to mean, but he laughed anyway because his dad seemed to think it was funny. From start to finish, Luke made every Friday night under the lights fun, like it was one long celebration of life. Caleb's sister Lauren came along sometimes, too, but she was a few years older and cooler and took any opportunity to escape her dad's earnestness. It's not that she wasn't captivated by his energy, but she had to pretend that she wasn't. She snuck away quietly, huddling with her tween friends under the bleachers, hoodies or rain jackets pulled up over their heads to obscure the edges of their faces, feeling devious and daring because they were hidden from their parents' vigilant eyes, if only for a few moments.

When the game ended, Luke would sometimes give Caleb a piggyback ride back to the car. Luke knew the best place to park, of course, so they never had to worry about getting stuck in a postgame traffic jam. They drove home easily, wet and tired, listening to the crackling voice on the local AM radio station recapping the game. There were many long pauses, unusual background sounds, and plenty of static. It wasn't the most professional production, but it was an integral part of the Friday night experience. Even though the drive home wasn't a long one, Caleb often fell asleep, pushing his seat belt down and pulling his feet up so he could curl into an awkward sleeping position on the backseat of the car. When they arrived home, he kept his eyes shut tight. He was getting too big to be carried, but he still loved it. He felt safe in his dad's strong arms, resting his head on his dad's shoulder. He knew his dad could handle his weight. Nothing was too heavy for him. He was invincible.

Looking back on it now with his limited experience as this weird sort of pseudo parent, Caleb has no clue how his dad did it. He assumes it must be natural, innate. His dad had the lively, fun, exuberant gene and he simply doesn't. Not really. Sure, he likes to laugh and all that, and he plays with swords as a grown adult for God's sake, but when he's taking care of Emily, he always feels like he's checking items off a list rather than reveling in her company. Play dolls, check. Read a book, check. Feed, check. Bathe, check. Put to bed, check. Repeat. His approach to parenting is definitely more in line with his mom's approach, but with at least a dash of humanity and tenderness.

As they approach the entrance to the football field, Caleb's senses are flooded. He sees, smells, feels everything all at once. The earthy aroma of grass. The still-damp air that has softened a bit but is still far from crisp. The clear night sky, deep and black, stars twinkling. A lone towering pine tree standing just outside the fence that loops the field. It seems lonely, out of place, its upper branches dipping over the fence line, its lower branches bending as they push against the chain link fence, needles poking through the holes. A violent black slash runs down the trunk.

Caleb grips Emily's hand, keeping the pine tree in his periphery, never looking directly at it. The ticket booth is just to the tree's right. A small crowd of people queue up to buy paper tickets which are torn in half moments later by the mom and dad volunteers standing a few feet further to the right at the gate where the crowd enters. Lights buzz on top of tall polls. Cones of light cascade down onto the field. Feet clomp and rattle the metal bleachers as people move to and from their seats. The marching band is already playing the same droning songs they will repeat over and over for the duration of the game, providing a constant background soundtrack, almost like a white noise machine that is heavy on the brass. Cheerleaders shout their staccato cheers.

Teenagers and pre-teens mill around, some watching the game, most watching each other. A crackling voice over the PA system reads off a list of sponsors. Caleb buys three tickets from the middle-aged man in the ticket booth who is wearing a blue baseball cap. When they proceed through the gate, Emily lets go of Caleb's hand and skips ahead. Caleb calls out, gesturing with his hand toward the end of the field where a few of his clubmates are gathered. Caleb's mom says she's going to see how things are going at the concession stand. As the school bookkeeper, she feels like anything monetary falls under her purview. Parents are seated sullenly under the press box in the bleachers, watching their children either in the stands or on the field, worried and anxious either way. Always worried, always watching. The teams enter the field to raucous applause and the game starts. Whistles chirping, popping of pads, grunts of effort, coaches shouting instructions, a kicker thumping a ball into a net again and again on the sidelines. Fans stomping their feet against the metal bleachers creating a roaring rumbling noise meant to urge on the defense on third down.

Few notice the small group of men, women, and children in armor gathered by the north end zone where the light doesn't quite reach. Up close, they can see each other well enough, but from a distance it's mostly outlines and angles. Caleb had dropped off supplies and equipment earlier in the day, so he rummages through the pile of gear laying on the grass, fishing out his armor and sword.

The twins are there, sweaty, unusually subdued, twirling their weapons nervously, eyeing the crowd in the stands suspiciously. Burly and mysterious Harold is all business, ignoring the game and everything around him, focusing only on his blade and his warm-up exercises. Tonya is amped up, bouncing on her toes as she talks with Emily, who is holding a stick of puffy pink cotton candy. Like there was ever any doubt. Her mouth is already outlined by a ring of pink sugar.

A handful of the other club members who have returned to practices since Scarlett first joined are milling about. They range in age from high school to somewhere less than Harold. Caleb slips on his helmet to test the fit, and as he puts on his first glove, tugging at the wrist to get his fingers in all the way, he stops suddenly. He sees Scarlett approaching, longsword in hand. There is someone else with her. Caleb thinks his eyes must be playing tricks on him. Maybe it's the obstructed view through the eyeholes of his helmet or the dim light. That must be it. He makes a move to lift his helmet to take a better look, but then he stops, uncertain. Frozen.

...

It feels like everything all at once.

...

Sadie's rendezvous with the sword man from Facebook went surprisingly well mainly in that she didn't die. As one might expect, that was her primary concern going in. She handed over cash and a slim young man with glasses, a pasty complexion, and slightly greasy hair handed over the sword. It looked quite nice as far as swords go.

"Are you ready yet, Mom?" Scarlett asks in a slightly exasperated tone while leaning against the kitchen counter, new sword gleaming at her side.

"Just about," Sadie replies. "Pretty ungrateful tone you're using toward the person who risked her life to get you that sword you're holding. The guy made me pull it out of a stone!"

Scarlett rolls her eyes.

"Before we go," Sadie continues, "we probably need to address the armor situation."

"I mean, I can't wear it," Scarlett says. "I think our car almost broke down from carrying it in the trunk. I would literally die."

"Yeah, I know, but your grandparents will be there, so if they ask, maybe say that you're saving it for the big competition or something? I don't know. Whatever you think."

"Okay."

"They said they are bringing signs, by the way, so be prepared."

"Do you think Grandpa will go shirtless and paint his chest?"

"We can hope!" Sadie says.

...

"Do you know where this place is?" Scarlett asks, sitting in the passenger seat of the car as Sadie drives.

"Do I ever," Sadie returns with a little laugh.

"Okay," Scarlett says flatly, clearly not seeking any further explanation.

"It's just that I've been to this field a few times. Many years ago." Sadie didn't realize where Scarlett's event was taking place until this morning. But of course, it would be this place, this high school football field. The thing about moving back to the place where your past happened is that you have to face all of it again. There's no escape. Nowhere to hide. So many streets and stores and restaurants and schools and football fields of all places contain ghosts that no one else can see.

Sadie is completely out of her element. She has still not reacclimated to the suburban, car-driving lifestyle and navigating crowds and tight spaces makes her extremely anxious. She spots a teenager in a ROTC uniform directing traffic near the field and she whips her car into the parking lot, grateful to have someone make the decision for her. Even if the someone is a boy with acne. She carefully maneuvers her car into a parking space and exhales a sigh of relief. The cars are crowded together like New York commuters at rush hour waiting for the subway door to open.

Scarlett bolts out of the car and heads toward the field. She carries her sword awkwardly, as if she could hide it from judgmental eyes if she positions it just right. Sadie scrambles to catch up. She's always trying to catch up these days. Always a step behind. The days of tugging a little girl by the hand, cajoling her to walk just a little faster to catch the bus are long gone.

They make it through the gate without incident leading Sadie to question if the school has the proper safety and security measures in place. A girl wielding a longsword did not seem to set off any alarms or draw any attention at all, really.

"Can you slow down just a little?" Sadie asks as Scarlett races away again, inside the fence now.

"SCARLETT! SADIE!"

Both Scarlett and Sadie pause, looking around for the source of the shouting voices. After their names are shouted one more time, they find Tom and Jess. They are standing at the bottom corner of the bleachers on the home side, about thirty yards from the entrance. They are each holding a piece of white cardboard, on the cardboard there are hand drawn bubble letters, royal blue in color. The sign Tom is holding says "Scar 'Em" and the sign Jess is holding says simply "Scarlett!" Again, probably not their best work, Sadie thinks, but the "Scar" pun isn't bad. Scarlett gives a little wave in their direction and Sadie gestures toward the sword fighting group, indicating that she's going to get Scarlett settled before joining Tom and Jess in the stands.

Sadie walks toward the north end zone trailing Scarlett by a few steps. She's seen this ragtag group of medieval enthusiasts from a distance on multiple occasions, but she's eager to get a closer look and find out who exactly her daughter has been hanging out with. The excitement of the night has apparently gotten to Scarlett, because she hasn't questioned Sadie's presence or attempted to shoo her away. Scarlett approaches the group slowly, as if she's planning a sneak attack. A few of the group members greet her. When Sadie catches up and arrives by Scarlett's side, Scarlett clears her throat and says in a quiet voice, "Well, this is everybody. And, um, this is my mom."

Emily gives a little squeal and rushes forward, wrapping her arms around Scarlett's waist, doing her best to keep the cotton candy from sticking to Scarlett's shirt. "And this is Emily," Scarlett says.

"Hi, Emily." Sadie smiles at the little girl. "And hi... everyone. Good luck with the performance!" Everyone except Harold acknowledges Sadie with a wave or a nod or a mumbled "thank you."

"I don't have a mom!" Emily chimes in, eager to redirect the conversation and the attention back to her, where it belongs. "I just have a grandma," she continues as most of the eyes in the group shift in her direction, "and a Caleb."

"That's not true, Emily," Caleb says reflexively, lifting the helmet off his head without thinking.

No one is talking now. The game continues, of course, but it feels like it's suddenly far away. The crowd noise fades, the sound of the referee's whistle dampens, the popping of pads is more distant, less violent somehow. Caleb's eyes flick to Emily first, but quickly move to Sadie. Again, it is Caleb and Sadie. Nothing else matters. They lock eyes for two seconds? Three? Caleb is still holding his helmet atop his head almost like he is doffing a metallic baseball cap. Sadie moves a hand to her face, covers her mouth partially, and begins to laugh. It's not a deep laugh, but it's a laugh, nonetheless. Under her breath she mutters, "Of course."

Caleb knits his brow, tilting his head slightly, clearly confused. Neither of them knows what to do. It is a unique situation. When you randomly run into an ex twelve years later at a sword fighting club exhibition taking place at a high school football game, the behavioral protocols are not well established. There are few if any guidelines to follow. And when it's not just any ex, it's *the* ex? Well, the territory is even more uncharted.

All eyes are on Sadie and Caleb now. Scarlett looks from her mom to Caleb and back again. Measuring them carefully. Trying to get a read on the situation. Sadie can tell Scarlett is trying to put the pieces together, but then she gives a little shrug as if to say, "if it involves my mom, it must be something extremely boring."

"Hi, Sadie." Caleb finally breaks the silence, his voice is shaky, uncertain. "So, you're Scarlett's mom?"

"Yeah, I am." Sadie tucks a strand of hair behind her ear nervously. "I guess you guys have a bit of a history already. Of course, I didn't realize... maybe I should've paid closer attention."

"No, no, it's all good," Caleb says, scrambling to regain his composure. "Scarlett is such a great kid! We love having her in the group. Don't we?" Caleb looks around to the group who are all observing closely, even Harold. Several murmur their agreement.

"You two know each other?" Harold asks in a deep gruff voice, his dark eyes peering out from between his bushy eyebrows and even bushier beard and mustache. Everyone is stunned. This is the most words anyone has heard Harold string together in... well, ever.

"Yeah, this seems awkward and juicy!" Tanya adds excitedly. "Dish!"

Sadie doesn't know what to say. All she can do is look at Scarlett, sadness in her eyes. Scarlett stares back, searching for answers.

"Uh, no, it's nothing really," Caleb says. "Old friends! We haven't seen each other in twelve years, so it's unexpected, that's all. Anyway, look. The game clock is down to three minutes in the second quarter, so it's almost showtime! Final preparations, everyone!"

Caleb's words seem to break the trance the group has been under. They all begin to gather up equipment, make adjustments to their clothing and protective gear, and talk to each other again. Caleb is doing his best to remain casual and nonchalant, but when he said the words "twelve years" out loud, a shockwave coursed through his whole body. The color drained from his face. It was like he saw a ghost and turned into one at the same time.

Twelve years. Twelve years. Twelve years!

He looks around to see if anyone has noticed his discomfort. He looks toward Sadie, who is standing angled away from the group now, staring out across the football field, arms folded across her chest, an unreadable expression on her face. Scarlett is kneeling down, adjusting her shoelaces. Looking at it from a strictly mathematical perspective, the fact that Caleb last saw Sadie about twelve years ago *and* her daughter, Scarlett, is eleven years old is fascinating. However, looking at it through a more personal or emotional lens makes the numbers seem... Caleb isn't sure what it makes them seem. Horrifying? Invigorating? Rage-inducing? Earth shattering? Maybe a bit of all of those mixed together with a side of confusion and desperation? Dates on a calendar. Years. Months. Days. Hours. They don't mean anything, really.

...

Until they do. Until they mean *everything*.

CHAPTER 16

ONE WEEK. Seven days. 168 hours. Sadie is late, and she knows. She just knows. She doesn't need to see the two lines peeking out at her from the little window in the piece of plastic, but she checks anyway. Might as well make it official.

It's been three weeks since that night. The one night in her life she would take back if she could. The night that gave way to a morning that was overcast, damp, and depressing. Sadie hid under the covers, her head felt like it was splitting open. It was the worst hangover she'd ever had, and she welcomed the pain. Relished it. She would've taken her brain out of her head and drop kicked it out the window if that was physically possible. She thought the splat of the spongy tissue landing on the wet pavement would be satisfying. And she wanted the memories gone. She had hoped the alcohol would take care of that, but it didn't. They were still there, ready to pounce on her when she woke up from a fitful few hours of sleep. And pounce they did.

...

. . .

The night started at Caleb's apartment. Sadie and Caleb are hanging out like they do so often, even if their meet-ups have been a bit more sporadic in the last few weeks. They have a vague discussion about maybe going to see a movie if they can find anything good, but Caleb is agitated. Sadie has never seen him like this. He's pacing back and forth across the small living room, running his hands through his hair. Every few minutes, he pulls his cell phone out of the pocket of his jeans, looks at it expectantly, then glances at Sadie nervously before shoving the phone away again. Sadie asks him if something is wrong, but he waves her off. Finally, he stops his pacing and stands at the kitchen counter, drumming his fingers against the Formica, making one of Blaise's glass bongs tremble.

"Sadie, we have to talk," Caleb blurts out, looking in the opposite direction from where Sadie is seated. "I'm not sure if I can do this anymore."

Sadie's heart begins to pound. She can feel it in her ears. "Do what?"

"This." Caleb begins to pace again. "Maybe it's time for a little space. So... I don't know... we can figure things out. So... *I* can figure things out."

"Wait," Sadie says, standing up now. She moves toward Caleb, trying to corral him, to make him wake up and come to his senses. She grabs his arm and turns him toward her. He still won't look her in the eyes. "Are we breaking up?"

Caleb pulls away and returns to the kitchen counter. He picks up his car keys and then plops them back down with a clatter. "No, no," he says, looking toward Sadie now with wet eyes. "That's the last thing I want." He runs his hand through his hair. "I mean... I don't think we're breaking up."

Sadie's confusion quickly turns to anger. "You don't *think* we're breaking up? Well, let me know when you decide, I guess!" She grabs her phone and looks around the room quickly, her eyes darting back and forth like a frightened animal. She's been here before. She's felt this before. She's had this conversation before. She can't believe it's happening again. The room feels like it's shrinking, and she has to get out. Now.

"Wait," Caleb says, reaching for Sadie. "Please don't go. Let me get us a drink and we can talk."

Sadie hesitates and Caleb walks into the kitchen. She hears the clinking of ice in a glass. Then, she sees something else. Something she doesn't want to see. Something she almost can't believe. Caleb has left his cellphone resting face up on a TV tray in the living room. Text messages light up the screen and Sadie looks down.

From here, it's a blur. Shock. Despair. The jangling of car keys. A door slamming. Hurried footsteps on concrete. Driving on slick roads. Windshield wipers flicking away small rain drops. Smears of yellow light dotting the periphery. Thoughts and memories rushing toward her relentlessly, blurring her vision like oncoming headlights. Disconnected snippets from different times and places assembling into a grisly mosaic.

Caleb doesn't know if they're still together or if they're breaking up? As far as Sadie's concerned, if you don't know, you know. Sadie lived in the in-between space before and she promised herself she would never exist in that sort of wretched limbo again. The unexplained absences, the elusiveness, the assurances that everything's okay, that this other girl is "just a friend." Promises of the stars and the moon that turn out to be airplanes passing through the sky or a yellowing, cracked streetlight about to die out.

Before there was Caleb, there was another boy who wanted to be a man but didn't know how. He looked like the star of a CW teen drama with effortless blonde hair and a dimple on his chin. Sadie was shocked that a boy who looked like that would go for her, but he was so persistent that she finally let him in. Eventually, though, as so often happens with young romances, their relationship went sideways. The boy grew distant and weird, and Sadie remembers vividly that he started protecting his phone like it was the nuclear football. "Don't you trust me?" the boy said before flying into an unexplained rage, leaving a fist-sized hole in the drywall. He made her feel stupid and ungrateful. She doubted herself up until the very last moment. He couldn't be cheating, Sadie thought. He was too beautiful, too caring, too kind... until he wasn't.

But Caleb? Caleb could never be like that boy. Sadie just knew it. But then again, did she?

Sadie drives past her apartment without thinking. She keeps driving and driving, growing sadder and angrier with every mile. It's done. All of it. She was so stupid for doing this all over again, for letting herself feel.

Her car takes her to a dark, dingy parking lot lit by amber-colored lights that buzz and hum like a million mosquitos. She doesn't know how she got here, and she doesn't care. She wants to forget. Forget Caleb, forget the other boy, forget that she exists.

Her world that felt so big for the last year is reduced to almost nothing. A tiny speck on a dying planet in a vast universe that is complete and utter bullshit. All that's left is a dirty, crowded bar. Gritty floors. Pulsing music. Sweaty bodies dancing, moving against each other in the darkness. Colored lights flashing on the ceiling. Shots of tequila sloshed into small glasses on the lacquered bar marred with scuffs and scratches. The burn of the liquor in her mouth, the stinging of the lime, her tongue licking salt from her hand. Licking someone else's hand? Strong hands on her waist, pulling her closer on the dance floor. More shots. Enough shots to make her forget the hands pressing into her aren't Caleb's. That they will never be Caleb's again. Because, according to the text messages she saw, some girl named Lauren needs Caleb now. It's no wonder that he doesn't know if they're breaking up or not. He may not know, but Sadie does. It's over. Finished. She should've known it was all too good to be true. The other boy's deceit and betrayal hurt, but this time it hurts so much more. Because it's Caleb. The person who made her believe that forever was possible. Stupid.

Submitting, letting go, abandoning everything. His mouth on

hers. Salty, sour, eager. Tongues swirling, moving against each other. His arms around her now, their bodies pressed together, swaying slowly to the music.

Do you want to go to my place?

Yes.

In a car again. Hers? His? Driving through dark streets that are quiet, spectral, empty. In the parking lot of an apartment complex. Kissing again, pressed against the side of the car. No turning back now. No more minds, just two bodies existing in space. Up one flight of concrete stairs, him fumbling with keys, the clicking of the lock, through the door and straight to the small bedroom. Blank walls, lights off, light from a much-too-bright bulb in the hallway pushing through the half-closed door. Clothes taken off, pulled up, pushed aside. On the bed. His weight on her, pressing her down, it feels good. Eyes closed tight. Bodies moving against each other, both wanting more. She puts her head back and moans softly.

Is this okay?

Don't stop.

He doesn't.

...

And now, three weeks later, there are two lines. And a pulsing headache that has nothing to do with alcohol or bad decisions. It's an existential pain. Like being stabbed over and over and over again. Probably with a longsword.

CHAPTER 17

THE HORN SOUNDS on the scoreboard indicating halftime. It sounds distant, faint, completely unimposing, almost like it's a horn on a boat that's sunk about 100 feet underwater. That scoreboard *is* pretty old, Caleb thinks as he stares at the black board with the weathered, fading Coca-Cola placard on one end that is more pink than red now. The scoreboard feels kind of like an old acquaintance to Caleb–an unchanging background character in his life. Like the old man who rides the bike with the fat tires along the sidewalk near his house. It's unclear where the man comes from, but he just always seems to be there. This scoreboard always seems to just be there, too. The clock shows all zeros, and the score indicates two points for the home team and zero points for the visitors. It's an unusual score for most football games, but this annual tiff between two hapless squads is not like most football games.

Caleb does his best to slow the tsunami of thoughts that has crashed into his brain. He tries to focus on the task at hand, which is organizing a group of kids and adults into formation in the end zone of a high school football field so they can attack each other with swords while a high school marching band plays "O Fortuna" from *Carmina Burana* with squeaking horns and a fair amount of notes that are just far enough off to make the hairs on your arms stand up. It's a difficult job, but someone has to do it.

Caleb shouts directions and gestures with his arms to move the group into the right positions. At practices leading up to today, they developed an exhibition routine that involves a sequence of choreographed moves. The group pairs off into sparring partners and spends most of the three-minute routine dueling. The grand finale involves a rotation in which one member of each pair shifts counterclockwise to finish the duel against a new partner. One person in each pair is supposed to fall to the ground as the music ends. At least one person has been injured or nearly injured during every partner swap grand finale at practice, but Caleb has decided to stick with it. Fortune favors the brave... hopefully.

The members of the group are dressed in a wide range of attire for the big event. Some like Caleb have authentic-looking armor or chainmail with neat paint jobs and insignias. Some wear a patchwork of homemade gear that makes them look like a cross between a person who is ready to serve as bait for police dog training and an honorable mention award winner at a medieval cosplay contest. They take their positions in the gloomy end zone and the band begins to play. Swords swing, shields rise, metal clashes on metal. A few *oohs* and *aahs* emanate from the bleachers where more and more people are beginning to pay attention to the spectacle. The onlookers include Sadie, who has made her way up to the stands to join her parents and their poster board signs, and Caleb's mom and Emily, who are seated only a few rows higher up.

Caleb is paired up with Scarlett and as the sparring begins, and she almost takes his head off with her opening swipe. It was a part of the choreography they had practiced, but Caleb is distracted and unprepared. He is too busy staring at Scarlett's face. Unlike Caleb, she is not wearing any protective gear on her head. It's not really necessary; Caleb and some of the others wear helmets but it's primarily to enhance the aesthetics. Caleb can't help but wonder if the familiarity he sees in Scarlett's face is because she looks like

Sadie, and now that he knows she is Sadie's daughter, he can see the resemblance more clearly; or if she looks like, well, the face he sees every morning in the mirror. Is there something in the curve of her chin? The shape of her nose? The eyes are all Sadie's, that much is clear, but the rest of the face? Caleb doesn't know what to think. He tries to regain his focus, clearing his mind of everything except his sword, his technique, and the girl across from him who may be his daughter. Ah, well, perhaps the clearing the mind part is not quite working to perfection.

Meanwhile in the stands, Sadie is transfixed. Her past and her present are literally doing battle right in front of her eyes. Medieval hand-to-hand combat. Swords clashing against swords. *I am possibly the first person in history to experience a moment like this*, she thinks. This thought gives her a few seconds of peace. It calms her racing mind. The situation is so completely absurd that it can't possibly have real stakes, can it? It seems impossible. So impossible, in fact, that she almost begins to believe that everything is going to be fine. Almost. Until Emily spots her and rushes over to say hello again.

"Hey," Emily says excitedly, her feet clomping on the metal steps of the aisle. "You're Scarlett's mom!"

"That's right," Sadie says. "You see Scarlett and Caleb out there?"

"Yeah," Emily says, eyes wide. "They are really good!"

"They are," Sadie agrees. Emily isn't wrong. Sadie is legitimately impressed by Scarlett's skill. She moves effortlessly with the fluidity of a dancer. She's only been sword fighting for weeks, but the sword already seems to be an extension of her body. It moves with her, almost floating through the air as if it were weightless. It's not, Sadie knows. The sword is actually quite heavy. She struggled just to carry it comfortably after picking it up from the Facebook arms dealer. She ended up carrying it with two hands like a barbell she was getting ready to curl.

"Emily," Helen says, approaching now. "Who are you bothering?" She stops short as Sadie turns in her direction. "Oh, it's you."

"Uh, yeah," Sadie stammers. "How are you?"

"Why are you here?" Helen asks, ignoring Sadie's question.

"My daughter, Scarlett, is sword fighting," Sadie replies. "She's, um, battling Caleb, I guess."

"Daughter?" Helen looks toward the field again, pursing her lips. "Hmm."

As the marching band plays the final notes of "O Fortuna," the sword fighting brigade executes its grand finale. Everything appears to go smoothly except that one boy ends up injured, writhing on the ground. It is relatively obvious to anyone who knows their history which of the twins has been mortally injured and which is standing over the fallen body, sword raised, pointing at the sky triumphantly.

"GARRETT! STOP CELEBRATING AND HELP YOUR BROTHER UP," a slender woman with red hair and freckles shouts down toward the field while a smattering of applause and a few appreciative whoops fill the air.

"WAY TO GO, SCARLETT!" Jess shouts, bouncing up and down on her toes and thrusting her cardboard sign into the air.

"THAT'S OUR GIRL!" Tom adds in a booming voice. To Sadie, he raises his hand to his mouth in a conspiratorial gesture. "Too bad she didn't wear her armor. That would've been a real showstopper."

"It literally would have been, yes," Sadie says. She can't help but smile.

...

On the field, as the band music and clashing of metal stop, Caleb awakens from the trance he fell into for about four minutes. He blinks a couple of times and his vision clears. He notices that he is looking directly at Scarlett. She switched sparring partners during the finale, so she is a few paces away, squared up to Harold, who gives her a formal nod as they lower their swords to their sides. Tonya is across from Caleb, and she gives a fist pump and exclaims, "Let's go!" She moves toward Caleb and claps him on the back, a big smile on her face. "We did it, Coach."

Caleb still can't take his eyes off Scarlett. She is trying to hide it, but she can't stop smiling. Caleb knows that look. She has the bug. The sword fighting bug, that is. This particular bug is, thankfully, not nearly as dangerous as a medieval plague, but it can be life-changing, nonetheless. It's almost like sword fighting is in her blood. That thought brings Caleb back to the torrent of thoughts he had tabled during the exhibition. They have returned now. All of them. Poking and prodding like a swordfighter probing for a weakness in her opponent's defense. Caleb gives his head a little shake, trying to clear things out in there.

"Um, great job, everyone," Caleb says finally, removing his helmet. His gaze lingers on Scarlett. She returns his look momentarily, blue eyes sparkling, before quickly looking away.

The band marches off the field and Caleb gestures for his group to retreat to their meeting spot by the end zone. A skinny football player trots out onto the field holding a football. He slows down, attempts a punt, and the ball flies off the side of his foot, nearly hitting Garrett in the head. Garrett growls and raises his sword menacingly before Caleb intervenes and shoos him away toward the edges of the field. "Easy, Garrett," he says. "Our battle is already won."

...

One battle may have been won, but the silent battle that Sadie and Caleb have been waging, mostly with themselves, since they first laid eyes on each other about an hour ago is just beginning. Honestly, it's been simmering for about twelve years, it's just that no one really knew about it because the combatants had left the battlefield. Even the participants didn't know. Not really.

There were periodic reminders, sure, but it was easy for both of them to shrug those off. Sadie had a child, a career, a real life she had built. Caleb had his little yellow house, his hobbies, and a few relationships from time to time that allowed him to feel happiness, at least for a little while. And now, of course, he had Emily. They had both decided that thinking about that admittedly magical time when they were young was pointless. That period of their lives was over. Done. People don't get second chances. And who's to say things would've ended differently had the proposal not happened the way it did. They burned bright and burned out fast. Maybe that was better than a slow decline toward disinterest that would eventually end with mutual disdain. But, as much as they both tried to forget, they couldn't. Not completely.

For Sadie, big storms always reminded her of Caleb. Both because of their first meeting at the coffee shop and because of the two days they spent together hiding out in her apartment as a tropical storm swept across the state. It was just two weeks after they met. They watched TV to calm Caleb's nerves until the power flickered out early in the morning hours. Then, they lay side-by-side in her bed with no covers on for what seemed like hours. No parts of their bodies were touching. It was almost becoming awkward how long they had been lying there together, maintaining a rigid adherence to personal space, listening to the tree branches clawing at the windows as they were buffeted about by the wind. Finally, *finally*, Caleb ran his finger softly along her wrist and Sadie immediately laced her fingers with his. They didn't get out of bed at all that day. Sadie has a vivid memory of Caleb getting up, what seemed like days later but must have been that evening, his body silhouetted against the pale window as he pulled on his shorts. He had strong arms and a slim waist and somehow seemed completely irresistible as he stood there, scratching the back of his head, his shoulders hunched almost shyly as he peeked out the blinds to get a look at the outside world.

She didn't know how all *this* had happened so fast. Lying there on her back with one hand resting on her bare stomach and the other tucked behind her head on the pillow, just watching Caleb, she felt inexplicably happy, almost joyous. *Oh*, she thought, *this is what falling for someone feels like?* She never felt this swept away before, not even with the last boy who eventually broke her heart. Falling for someone was as stupid as she always suspected it would be. Love is a disaster waiting to happen. Sadie knew it.

When Sadie descends the metal stairs of the bleachers, her whole body vibrating with each step, all the time and space that separated then from now disappears. She tucks her hair behind her ear as she walks along the concrete path toward the north end zone. Teens and adults and children pass by her, completely oblivious as everyone always seems to be. Monumental moments are meaningless to all those who aren't participating in them.

Sadie approaches the group as they are taking off armor and gear, packing away items into large duffle bags, and standing around chattering about their epic exhibition performance. "That was something else, wasn't it Harold?" Tonya says excitedly, clapping Harold on the back. Harold avoids making eye contact and gives a half-hearted grunt. He seems to be back to normal now after the earlier burst of loquaciousness. Caleb and Scarlett are standing just a few feet apart. Scarlett is kneeling down, retying her tennis shoe. Caleb is pretending to look through his bag. Sadie hesitates, gathering herself, before walking up to Scarlett and patting her gently on the shoulder. "Good job, Scar. That was impressive," she says. Scarlett looks up and mumbles something that Sadie can't make out. "Do you want to talk?" Sadie says, still looking at Scarlett.

"What?" Scarlett replies, confused.

"Not you, sorry." Sadie slowly shifts her gaze toward Caleb. Caleb is staring at her with a slightly bewildered look on his face.

"Um, yeah, sure. That would be... nice? Do you mean now or,"

Caleb trails off, looking in Sadie's direction now but not exactly at her.

"Let me get Scarlett to my parents and then we can, you know," Scarlett trails off now.

"Yeah," Caleb says with a little nod. "I'll wait here."

Sadie walks Scarlett over to Tom and Jess, who greet her like she's a conquering hero who left home seven years ago to wage war with an enemy force across the sea. They head off toward the parking lot and Sadie makes her way slowly back to Caleb. Perhaps it's the culmination of a twelve-year journey, but who's to say? Sadie greets Caleb again awkwardly and says, "Where do you want to sit?"

"Our usual spot?" Caleb gestures toward the large pine tree a few yards away.

"Sure," Sadie replies.

They walk over to the tree and sit down on the grass side-by-side a few feet apart. Just like they have before.

CHAPTER 18

THE AFTERNOON AFTER THE NIGHT, *that* night, Sadie finally gets out of bed, her head still fuzzy. Her bedroom feels like it's tilting when she stands up. Like her apartment was somehow relocated to a cruise ship at sea. Her eyes are scratchy, and her tongue feels like it's tripled in size. The morning rain has passed, and despite the best efforts of the air conditioner that is whirring constantly, she can feel the midday heat pushing in from outside. She walks slowly to the bathroom, grabbing the doorframe to steady herself, pausing for a moment before completing her journey to the shower.

She turns the water scalding hot, undresses, and steps into the shower carefully. She lets the water run over her, burning her skin. It feels good, cleansing. She washes every inch of her body meticulously until her skin is pink both from the heat of water and the scrubbing. After she towels off and dries her hair, she lies on the bed wrapped in the towel for at least thirty minutes, staring at the blades of the ceiling fan as they rotate slowly. She focuses on one blade, following its path with her eyes until it makes a couple of revolutions, then chooses another blade and repeats the process. When she tires of the ceiling fan, she gets dressed, picks up her car keys and wallet, and leaves.

Outside, the sun is blinding. The afternoon thunderstorms

haven't descended yet, but the sky is threatening, a patchwork of blue and gray. Sadie makes the short drive to Caleb's apartment complex, parks, and walks directly to his door before she can lose her nerve. Caleb is the last person she wants to see right now, but in her haste to leave his apartment last night, she left her backpack behind. She knocks and takes a step back. The door doesn't open, so she steps forward and knocks again, this time more forcefully. She hears the doorknob rattling and the door opens inward a couple of inches. One eye peeks out through the crack. It's Blaise. Sadie lets out a sigh of relief.

"Is Caleb here?" Sadie asks.

"Uh, no. I don't think so." Blaise opens the door a little more so Sadie can see both of his eyes. His black hair is greasy and long, framing his face. His pupils are large and unfocused. He appears to be shirtless from what Sadie can see.

"Good," Sadie says. "I just need my backpack from the living room. Can you get it for me?"

Blaise nods quickly and pushes the door closed. Sadie hears his footsteps retreating and then growing closer again. The door creaks open slightly, and he thrusts the backpack through the crack.

"Wait." Sadie takes the backpack and stops Blaise from closing the door on her face. "Do you know where he is?"

"I think he's at his sadness spot, but I'm not sure."

"His what?"

"You know."

"No, I don't."

"The football field or whatever. Where he goes when he's sad."

"Is he sad?" Sadie asks.

"I guess so if he's at his sadness spot."

"Okay."

They stand there in silence for a few moments, Blaise's eyes shifting from side to side, as if he's expecting someone or something to attack from the periphery. Sadie examines her fingernails carefully and thinks about what Blaise might look like as a corpse. Finally, she asks for more details about this "sadness spot" and Blaise is able to supply enough information that Sadie is at least fifty percent sure she'll be able to find it.

Sadie gets back in her car and sits for several minutes. If Caleb was cheating on her and he was ready to break up, sadness doesn't seem like it would be his first emotion. She drums her fingers on the steering wheel, thinking, and starts the car. Last night, the whole situation seemed cut and dried, but now beneath the glare of the Florida afternoon sun, Sadie isn't so sure. She decides what she must do. It might hurt her even more, but she has to know. She has to make Caleb tell her why he ended things. She needs to hear it from his mouth so she can have some sense of closure.

Sadie drives, unsure of where she's going. She tries to organize the clues that Blaise gave her in her mind and arrives at the conclusion that Caleb is probably at the field where his high school's football team played. This doesn't make any real sense to her because Caleb never mentioned football before or this particular field, but she does have a vague recollection from her own high school days that there was a shared field where a couple schools played games. As she navigates using a combination of distant memories and Blaise's equally hazy landmarks like "near that one store with some kind of animal statue outside," Sadie thinks about what would happen if her parents were killed in a car accident. The thought arrives completely without invitation, as it always does. Sadie tends to imagine such macabre things when she is stressed and anxious. It soothes her somehow. It's like her brain is saying, "here's the worst thing that could happen, this other thing you're worrying about doesn't seem so bad now does it?" It's a neat trick.

The only drawback is that she rather routinely visualizes her parents' deaths or the deaths of other people in her life in great detail. She sees their bodies still and lifeless, seatbelts holding them up, their heads lolling to the side with blood trickling from various body parts. She imagines a knock on the door or a phone call from a police officer delivering the news. For some reason, she's convinced she would feel cold, empty, unable to cry or react in any appropriate way. The police officer would feel a bit awkward because Sadie would just say something ridiculously bland like "thanks for letting me know." She suspects she's so blasé about the matter because she's been anticipating it for years, ever since she was a child.

When she was eleven or twelve years old, the mom of a boy at Sadie's school died of some sort of illness, probably cancer. Sadie knew who the boy was, he always seemed to have red eyes and often wore a rather vacant expression, but she didn't really know him. She observed him quietly at lunch and recess, thinking "yes, that will be me one day." Sadie knew her life was too easy. She never had anything substantial to worry about. No tragedies or losses to overcome. Surely, she couldn't keep on living such a charmed existence forever.

Perhaps last night was the beginning of a tragedy. One that Sadie has been anticipating for so long. Finally, something in her life isn't going the way it's supposed to. If this thing with Caleb that inexplicably felt so easy and natural and right turns out to all be an illusion, then, well, maybe that will be good. She'll have something to push against, something to overcome.

After a few wrong turns and a bit of backtracking, Sadie pulls into the grassy parking lot at the football field. She immediately knows she's in the right place because Caleb's car is there. It is the only car in the lot. Sadie parks, leaving enough room for one car to fit between her car and Caleb's. It feels like the appropriate thing to do. She can see through the windshield that Caleb is sitting on the ground with his back resting against the metal fence that rings the football field. A tall pine tree towers over him, making him look small and insignificant.

Sadie wonders one final time if this is a huge mistake. What is she supposed to say to him after his suggestion that they were breaking up? Or after what she saw on his phone's lock screen? Or after what she did? Three text messages from someone named Lauren. That's what she saw.

Are you there?

Please call me.

I need you.

Nine words. That's all it took to make her lose her mind. It wasn't just the text messages, but those were certainly the tipping point. Caleb had seemed distant and sullen the last couple of weeks, unlike his normal happy self. He'd canceled dates with vague excuses about headaches or needing to study for exams. And finally, when they did hang out at his place like they used to always do, Caleb suddenly said that he needs space and maybe they should end things? It didn't add up. But when Sadie saw the string of text messages while Caleb was in the kitchen, the puzzle pieces clicked into place. That's all it took. When you're standing on the edge of a cliff, even a slight breeze can make you topple over. It's just a matter of how much damage the fall does, if you can even survive it.

Sadie takes a deep breath before getting out of the car and walking toward Caleb. When she's about halfway there, he looks up. He does look sad; Blaise was right. His expression changes slightly when he sees her, but Sadie can't tell what it indicates. Bemusement would be her best guess.

"Hey," she says, sitting down with her back against the fence, leaving enough room for another person to sit between her and Caleb. It seems like the appropriate thing to do.

"Hi," Caleb says. "How did you find me here?"

"Blaise. He said you were at your sadness spot."

Caleb laughs. "I guess he's right."

They sit in silence for a few moments. Caleb plucks a blade of grass out of the ground and begins to peel away the strands. Sadie rests her elbows on her knees and looks off to the side, toward the parking lot where the school buses are parked.

"Is everything okay?" Caleb asks finally.

"I don't think it is, but you tell me," Sadie replies, still looking away. "You're the one who said we were breaking up."

"Yeah... I don't know. I don't know what got into me last night. I was stressed about... things." Caleb is calmer than he was last night, less manic, but Sadie can still sense a strange energy buzzing beneath the surface of his placid exterior.

"Things?" she asks, growing agitated herself now. She runs a hand through her hair and looks down to study the laces of her shoes.

"It's complicated and I don't know how to..." Caleb begins, but Sadie cuts him off. She's ready to take control. She's not going to twist in a non-existent breeze on this muggy, still afternoon.

"Who's Lauren?" Sadie looks in Caleb's direction now, not making eye contact.

"Lauren?" Caleb's eyebrows lifted when she said the name. It was slight, but Sadie saw it.

"I saw some texts on your phone last night. Right after the whole 'let's maybe break up' thing, coincidentally."

"Oh."

"It seemed like she really needed you," Sadie says with more than a hint of malice in her voice.

She looks toward Caleb, and he meets her gaze. He can see the fire in her eyes.

"It's not what you think," he says.

"Okay."

"Lauren's my sister."

Sadie has a sudden sensation of being squeezed, as if the gravity on the small patch of earth her body is occupying has increased by one hundred times. She will be completely flattened soon and then there will be relief. "Sister?" It's all she can manage to say.

"Yeah, I know I said that she was..."

"Wait, stop," Sadie says emphatically, cutting in again. "You're telling me now that Lauren is your dead sister? Really? I'm supposed to believe that?"

"It's true. Well, obviously she's not dead. But yes, Lauren is my undead sister."

Despite it all, Sadie can't help but laugh. It's all so ridiculous. Caleb is ridiculous. She's ridiculous. Existing is ridiculous.

"Wait," Caleb continues. "Not undead. She's not a zombie or anything... more like a ghost, I guess."

"Well, that's a relief," Sadie's stomach is churning and her head is spinning so she reverts to her comfortable default setting: sarcastic defensiveness.

"Ghost in a metaphorical sense."

"Yes, thanks. I get the idea."

"I'm sorry I lied," Caleb says. He pauses for a moment, thinking about how dumb he felt when he made up the lie in the first place and how even dumber he feels now. He feels like a colossal idiot. An idiot who has just ruined the one thing he cares about most. "It's just... I don't really talk about my family much. It's typically easier that way." Sadie says nothing. "I should've told you the truth, of course. The moment I said she was dead I wanted to take it back."

A downpour of thoughts flood Sadie's brain like a Florida afternoon thunderstorm. The blond-haired boy and the fist-sized hole in the wall. Secret text messages. Lies. Half-truths. Caleb and his unlit cigarette. The dark and dirty dance floor. The unfamiliar body pressing into hers. Reckless abandon. The feeling of being on stage, immersed in the music, and the only things in the world that exist are a guitar and a microphone.

"That's a *huge lie*, Caleb," Sadie says finally, her voice breaking. "Huge. It's not like you added an inch to your height or something. How am I supposed to trust you when you can lie about something that big?"

"I don't know." Caleb runs a hand through his hair. "But trust is a dirty word, right?"

Sadie smiles despite herself. "Are you quoting Green Day at me? At a time like this?"

"Is there a bad time to quote Green Day?"

"No."

They sit in silence for several moments, the distant rumble of a school bus engine the only sound.

"Can you tell me the truth now?" Sadie asks finally, breaking the silence.

"Yes."

"Everything?"

"Okay." Caleb runs his hand over his face, inhales deeply, and exhales. "Okay, so, my dad died when I was eleven. I kind of told you about that."

"Yeah, you told me, but you didn't tell me much." Sadie looks at Caleb now. "You said 'accident,' so I assumed he and Lauren died in a car accident or something. But now I know that's not right."

"No." Caleb pauses, looking everywhere but at Sadie. "He was struck by lightning."

Sadie scoffs. "Come on. Be serious. How did he really die?"

"I am being serious. Actually," Caleb pauses, considering, "he kind of died here. Under this tree."

Without thinking, Sadie tilts her body away from the tree slightly. "You can't be serious."

"I am. Is it shocking to you?"

Sadie can't help but laugh. "Caleb!"

"Because it certainly was to Dad."

"Jesus Christ, you're terrible!"

"As a child who lost a parent to a lightning strike, I'm one of the few people on earth allowed to make that joke. And, honestly, Dad would love it."

"Your dad was a good guy?" Sadie asks.

"The best. Like I mean that literally. Everyone loved him. And he was my hero. That sounds dumb, but I was eleven."

"I think it's nice." Sadie feels herself relaxing just a little, her guts unwinding from the knots they've been tied in. Everything is still a mess, but she's able to push the disaster that was last night to the background, at least for a moment, because she's caught up in Caleb's story. What can she say? She is a sucker for a morbid tale. "How did your family get through it?"

Caleb laughs. "We clearly didn't. My mom basically disappeared. It was always an opposites attract kind of thing with her and my dad. She was proper, buttoned up, and analytical, while he was, like, bold and joyful. But, when he died, she just became like a caricature of who she was already. She wouldn't let anyone in. She buried herself in her account balances and spreadsheets and rules. And Lauren, she uh," Caleb hesitates, looking toward the tree for a moment then staring blankly into the distance. "She thinks she... caused our dad's death, so she was completely shattered."

"Caused it?" Sadie asks. "Is she Zeus or something? Does she control lightning and the heavens?"

Caleb laughs a little. "No, that would probably be easier." He pauses, looking at Sadie before looking away toward the bus depot. "She was here with a boy. It was late. After the football game was over on a Friday night. Dad got worried because she missed curfew and wasn't home, so he came looking for her. It was raining on and off all night, but when he got here, a thunderstorm swept through suddenly. He got out of the car to find Lauren who was over there under the bleachers apparently." Caleb gestures with his hand over his shoulder toward the bleachers. "And when he got to this tree, lightning struck it."

Caleb stares at his shoes and Sadie looks away.

"Did Lauren see it happen?" she asks.

"Yeah," Caleb answers.

"Jesus."

"Yeah. I was home in bed. Like your typical 11-year-old. Anyway, that's the story. That's why I come here. Or... it's one of the reasons."

"Sadness spot," Sadie says.

"Yep."

They sit in silence for a few minutes. The sky grows darker.

There's a soft rumble of thunder in the distance, but it's not even close enough to bother Caleb yet. The air begins to smell wet.

"Lauren's been a disaster ever since," Caleb says, breaking the silence. "Alcohol, drugs, you name it. And, like, she has these periods where she's okay and life seems kind of normal and then suddenly everything changes and she's all I can think about. It feels like she's here and then she's gone, and I can try to forget everything that's happened for a few days or weeks, but she's never *really* gone, if that makes sense? Like she's always with me."

"Like a ghost," Sadie interjects.

"Yeah." Caleb nods his head slowly in agreement. "Like a ghost. And these last few weeks have been particularly bad. She's using again and she keeps begging me for help." Caleb looks Sadie in the eyes, and she meets his gaze. "But it's not real help she wants. That I would give her. There's nothing I wouldn't do to get my sister back the way she used to be. What she wants, though, is money. And she plays on my emotions to try to get what she wants. She manipulates and manipulates and then she gets mad when I won't give in. She whines about me not trusting her." Caleb lets out a rueful laugh. "There's that dirty word again: trust. And, well... I was texting with her yesterday, and it wasn't going well. She seemed even more untethered than normal. Angrier, more desperate. I thought she was about to show up at my door, and I didn't want you to find out that way. My lie was haunting me as much as Lauren was, I think, and I panicked. I didn't want to disappoint you."

Sadie moves closer to Caleb now so they are seated side by side, their thighs touching. Caleb takes Sadie's hand and squeezes it.

"And you know what the worst part is?" Caleb asks, staring into Sadie's blue eyes urgently, like he knows that's where he'll find the answers he's looking for. "I was upset about Lauren, of course, but what really made me lose it was that I felt like I was on the verge of losing you." Caleb sits forward and takes both of Sadie's hands, turning toward her. "You're the best thing that's ever happened to me, Sadie. I *can't* lose you. My dad's never coming back, and the real

Lauren might never come back, and my mom will probably never be the same again, but if I lose you, Sadie..." He trails off and lets go of Sadie's hands so he can wipe a tear away from his eye.

"Caleb, I..." Sadie begins, her eyes wet, too.

"Wait," Caleb cuts in. "I'm sorry I lied to you. I have to say that again. And I know it's no excuse, but the reason I lied is that I didn't want to weigh you down with my baggage. You've got a big life ahead of you. You're going to do huge things once you get out of here." He hesitates, gesturing with his hands to indicate "here."

"And I want to be there with you more than anything, Sadie," Caleb continues. "I do. But I want to be there because you want me, not because you feel sorry for me, or you feel obligated to keep me around because of my messed-up family."

"You don't have to carry all this weight by yourself, Caleb," Sadie says, her eyes glistening. "I want to help you carry it. That's part of the deal. You're nerdy and weird and goofy and absolutely... the person I love more than anything in this world. I've tried to convince myself that isn't true because I was afraid I'd get hurt. I've been hurt before and it *really* sucks, but I'm willing to take the risk. Because you're worth it."

Caleb moves toward Sadie, and they kiss. She cups his face in her hands.

"And the internet told me that girls don't want guys with baggage," Caleb says with a wry smile, his face just inches from Sadie's.

"The internet isn't always right," Sadie replies, the corners of her mouth turning up.

"Now you've gone too far," Caleb says, and they both laugh, holding each other tightly.

...

"Can you picture us lasting forever?" Sadie asks as she and Caleb walk hand in hand back to the parking lot.

"You mean if neither of us have any more undead siblings lurking in our closets?" Caleb replies with a smile that doesn't quite reach his eyes.

"Obviously," Sadie says. "You never know one of those might pop up, but like, assuming all the key people in our lives remain above ground and non-zombified, *and...*" She hesitates, tucking a strand of hair behind her ear and glancing at Caleb out of the corner of her eye. "And if neither of us... hypothetically, of course... dashes off into the night the moment things start to go wrong." She gives Caleb's hand a little squeeze. "Can you see us, you know, one day... taking our kids to Disney World or whatever? Having grandkids, maybe? Sitting on rocking chairs on the front porch watching the sun drop below the horizon?"

"More like rocking out on the front porch, am I right?" Caleb says, letting go of Sadie's hand to play air guitar. Sadie rolls her eyes and smiles. "But yes, I can picture it. Honestly, I think I started picturing forever from the first time you rounded that corner and ran me through with your guitar."

"For the last time," Sadie says, feigning an exasperated sigh. "I did *not* run you through with my guitar!"

"It was close. I could've died that day."

"But you survived," Sadie says, taking Caleb's hand again. "Both of us did. We're still here."

...

They say what doesn't kill you makes you stronger. Is that true of relationships, too? If the difficult times, the mistakes, the misunderstandings, and the insecurities don't kill a relationship, can they make it stronger in the end? If two people are meant to be together, can they overcome any obstacle? Even obstacles that seem bigger than life itself?

Of course, it's not dying that you have to worry about. Death is easy; life is hard. Death is uncomplicated; life is unpredictable. Life is full of messes and mistakes. So many mistakes.

...

When Sadie slides into her car and settles into the driver's seat, the headiness of the last hour immediately disappears, and it's replaced by a gnawing dread. She and Caleb covered a lot of ground, but they didn't discuss *everything*. Some things were left unsaid. At least one big secret was kept locked up tight.

It was one night. One mistake. A mistake caused by a misunderstanding and complicated life histories and repressed insecurities and tequila. A mistake driven by a breakup that Sadie knew she could never truly recover from. It didn't mean anything. Telling Caleb would just hurt him and that's the last thing he needs right now. This is a secret Sadie can keep. She can carry this weight by herself.

What other choice does she have?

CHAPTER 19

Caleb and Sadie are sitting side by side a few feet apart under a tall pine tree with an ugly black scar running down the trunk. It's not nearly as quiet and empty as it was the last time they were here together. The football game is still going on and one of the teams has just scored a touchdown. It was a bit of a fluke play that involved a forward pass caroming off the helmet of an unsuspecting tight end, but frankly almost all the plays are flukes when Bear Lake and Riverside square off.

"Well, here we are," Caleb says, smiling at Sadie.

"Again," Sadie says.

"Scarlett is great, by the way," Caleb says, not knowing where to start even though he's dreamed about the possibility of this conversation for a decade. "She's a real natural at sword fighting. And she saved me big time on the airplane. Emily was about to lose it... or I was, I don't remember which. Probably both of us were."

"I get it, trust me. Flying with kids is a complete nightmare," Sadie says. An air horn sounds indicating that someone has done something noteworthy on the field. The metal bleachers rumble with the stomping of feet. "That was a crazy coincidence that you ended up on the same plane."

"I know! Kind of spooky almost. But Scarlett was so great. She was friendly and understanding. Emily idolizes her now."

Sadie laughs. "Are we talking about my Scarlett?"

"Yep. I guess it's different when they're not with you," Caleb says, smiling. "I mean, I guess the kids are different."

"Apparently so," Sadie says. She is nervous but does her best to hide her discomfort with idle chatter. She clasps her hands together tightly to stop them from shaking. "She's transformed from a cute little girl to sullen teen in like the last three months. Or so it seems, I guess."

"She's... how old?" Caleb asks tentatively, looking toward the football field.

"Eleven."

"So," Caleb says, still not looking at Sadie. He stares at the scoreboard, trying to make the blurry numbers come into focus. His thoughts drift back to those days and weeks in September so long ago that seemed to stretch on forever. The unanswered texts and calls. The times he stopped by her apartment and knocked on her door only to find no trace of her. It was like she had disappeared from the planet.

"She's not yours," Sadie says, her eyes welling up.

"Okay," Caleb says, still staring off into the distance.

"If that's what you were wondering."

Caleb laughs, feeling empty, hollowed out like a jack-o-lantern. "It was."

"Look, I made a huge mistake, and for whatever reason, I could never bring myself to tell you." Sadie pauses, running her hands through her hair. "Remember that day I found you here and you told me about your dad and your sister?"

"Of course."

"The night before, when you were acting so weird and suddenly talking about breaking up, I saw the text messages from Lauren. I was shocked. Hurt. Angry. I don't know what I was. You had been distant and strange for a few weeks because of Lauren, who was alive, as I found out the next day." Caleb grimaces, looking at Sadie now with sad eyes. "I thought we were done, and I was devastated. The guy I was with before you cheated on me, and it seriously messed me up. And, like, I wasn't going to be strung along again." Sadie hesitates, takes a deep breath, exhales slowly. "So... I went to a bar... and drank way too much... and ended up hooking up with some guy. And, of course, I got pregnant. It was the dumbest thing I've ever done. I thought we were over, but that's no excuse."

After this, they sit in silence. The clock on the scoreboard ticks down, the seconds dripping by. 8:23, 8:22, 8:21...

"That's why the proposal went so disastrously," Caleb says finally. "Even after we talked things out the next day and talked about forever."

"Well, yeah," Sadie says. "That was one reason. The main reason, obviously."

"What were the other reasons?" Caleb asks.

"I don't know. I mean, even if things had been going perfectly, it all seemed a bit rushed. Like you were racing toward some imaginary finish line."

An extremely short running back whose helmet looks about three sizes too big for his body breaks free from the clump of players at around midfield and scampers toward the end of the field where Caleb and Sadie are sitting. One of the opposing players chases after him and eventually drags him down. One half of the crowd cheers, the other half groans.

"I was," Caleb says after the crowd quiets down. "The concert was on September third."

Sadie stares at him blankly.

"My dad died on September third."

"Oh."

"Yeah, I had some grand vision that I could reclaim the day." Caleb raises his hand like a speaker delivering an important oration. "That did not work out at all."

"Yes, I know. I was there."

"It was even worse than what you know."

Sadie looks toward Caleb now. He is still looking away, toward the action on the field. "How could it be worse?"

"Lauren tried to kill herself that night." Caleb runs his hand across the side of his head, ruffling his hair. Sadie closes her eyes like she's in physical pain. "My mom was texting me during the concert, but I ignored her. Then I find out after all the proposal mess that Lauren is in the hospital. She survived, obviously. She's also Emily's mom, if you hadn't figured that out yet."

"Oh," Sadie says. "Right. God, I'm so sorry."

"Yeah, I'm just taking care of Emily for as long as Lauren is, well, incapable of taking care of a child. So, none of the children in question tonight are mine, as it turns out." He looks toward Sadie. "But by some stroke of luck they met on an airplane on yet another September third."

"Is that like some sort of twisted serendipity?" Sadie asks.

"Maybe," Caleb says. "Or a twisted practical joke."

The game is winding down and fans are starting to meander toward the exits as another silence settles over Caleb and Sadie.

"Are you mad at me?" Sadie asks finally. "I mean, you should be. I should've told you, but I was too much of a coward. Running away was... easier, I guess."

Caleb takes a moment to consider his answer. "No, I'm not mad at you. Not anymore," Caleb says. "I was, I guess? I was mostly really confused though. Like, I didn't know exactly how it went wrong *that* spectacularly. I think finding out the details is more of a relief than anything. And I thought I might be Scarlett's dad for the past couple of hours, so I can breathe again now, which is nice."

"I would've never kept her from you if she were yours," Sadie says.

"I just don't get why you didn't tell me, though." Caleb has a pained expression on his face. "Obviously it would've been extremely awkward, but just running away and hiding... that sucked."

"I know," Sadie says, thinking about the panic that washed over here that September. How she shut out the world and got away as fast as she could. "I'm sorry. I regretted that decision every day, but at some point, it was just like... there was no going back."

Caleb watches a father walk by holding the hands of his two children, a little girl with blonde hair pulled back in a ponytail on his left and a boy with short spiky blonde hair on his right.

"I forgive you," he says finally. "And I'm sorry again for lying about Lauren. And trying to break up with you to cover that stupid lie. I was so dumb."

"That seems pretty small now."

"Everything kind of does," Caleb says. "Even the big stuff... I guess time does that."

"Shrinks things?"

"Sure," Caleb laughs. "Let's go with that."

A group of high school students pass by, a mixture of boys and girls. Most are dressed in school colors, but a few are decidedly not. A pair of girls walking side by side are dressed in tattered black jeans and black t-shirts. Sadie smiles to herself.

"I thought about the proposal last month." Sadie leans her head back against the fence and looks up at the night sky. "I hadn't for a few years, but I thought about it on the date this time around. The day you met Scarlett as it turns out."

"Yeah?"

"Do you remember the song you proposed during? Because I don't and it was driving me crazy."

"Yeah," Caleb says. "I do actually remember. I mean, it was a banger."

"What was it called?"

Caleb hesitates, checks his watch. "Uh, it was called...'Love's a Disaster.'"

Sadie's eyes light up. "Oh my god." She places the palm of her hand on her forehead. "I think I had blocked that out. I honestly don't know how the moment could've been any more perfect." She sits up a little straighter and looks toward Caleb. "Maybe if the 45-year-old dude dressed in a banana costume hadn't bumped into me and splashed me with beer. But you can't have it all, I guess."

"In retrospect," Caleb says, "maybe I should've put more thought into my plan, but I knew 'Love's a Disaster' had that cool break toward the end where it would get quiet, so you could hear me tell you how *our* love would never, uh... be a disaster?" His face takes on a slightly puzzled expression. "In fact, I made that clear right from the jump. You remember how the song goes." He begins to sing softly now, a little offkey, "There's no need to ask her, I know I'm a bastard, My mind's racing faster, Love's a disaster!"

"Well, damn," Sadie replies, shaking her head, a wry smile on her face. "I did not remember that but now that you've reminded me, I am feeling much better about the setup. Continue, please..."

"Right. So, after I sang along to the 'love's a disaster' line, before I got started with the proposal proper, I yelled, 'except ours!'"

"Oh, so that's what you shouted. Honestly, I was extremely confused in that moment because you had just taken my hands, looked deep into my eyes, and said 'love's a disaster.' I thought maybe you were shouting for me to watch out for the Banana Man sloshing beer." Sadie looks toward Caleb, who is looking in her direction now. "And did you not feel the need to negate the 'I know I'm a bastard' line?"

"I figured that was implied," Caleb replies.

Sadie laughs. "It was quite the plan."

"It was maybe a bit... rushed?"

"We were twenty-two years old, Caleb."

"And you were, well, pregnant," Caleb says, seemingly without any malice. "Which explains why you asked for a bottle of water that night and left me to drink like seven beers and a Mike's Hard Lemonade."

"There is that, too, yes," Sadie says. "We had only been dating for, what, a year and a half? And for three of those months, you had the made-up girlfriend from high school you still talked about a lot."

"She was completely real! I am friends with her on Facebook to this day!"

Sadie raises both hands, palms up, acknowledging the brilliance of Caleb's statement. "Wow. That is pretty convincing evidence. More ironclad than a TikTok follow."

Caleb pretends to look dejected. "You always had to turn everything into a joke."

"No joke! I'm just glad you're on such good terms with the first and perhaps greatest love of your life."

"Well, that last part definitely isn't true."

Caleb looks toward Sadie. She is staring back at him, her eyes penetrating and intense. She closes the distance between them and tilts her head to kiss him on the mouth. His lips remain closed, impenetrable. Sadie pulls away.

"I'm sorry," she says. "Did I misread that?"

"No," Caleb replies before changing his mind. "I mean, yeah, you did. I'm... I can't."

"Right, yeah," Sadie says briskly, standing up now, wishing she could evaporate away like a puddle in the sun. "I should go. I need to pick up Scarlett."

"Okay, sure," Caleb says, trying to regain his footing. "I need to go rescue Emily from my mom."

"It was good seeing you."

"Yes."

Sadie walks away hurriedly. Caleb stands up and watches her. She moves in and out of the faint yellow light coming from the parking lot lamp posts, almost flickering. One moment she's there, the next moment she's gone.

...

It's funny how that happens with people.

PART 2

CHAPTER 20

May 2023

EVEN THOUGH MORE THAN six months have passed since that night at the football field, Caleb can't seem to put it behind him. Rebuffing Sadie's advance was the right decision—he's about 95 percent sure of that—but that doesn't mean it was an easy one. It took every ounce of discipline and willpower he had. For twelve years, the girl who got away was gone and then suddenly she was there again. Her lips pressed against his. It was like a dream. Or a nightmare? Sometimes it's difficult to tell the difference.

The revelations about Scarlett were a lot to take in, of course, but getting a sense of closure had been a relief. Sadie hadn't disappeared because of the stupid proposal and there was really nothing he could have done differently. Well, he guesses he could've done some things differently, like telling the truth about his sister or choosing a different song to propose to or forgoing the whole proposal thing altogether since his and Sadie's relationship hadn't been on the most solid of footing. However, 22-year-olds do dumb things. Especially when they're in love and the intensity of the love they feel terrifies them.

Caleb thinks about all this while he's sitting in a restaurant on a late-spring evening across the table from a woman. The woman is not Sadie. Caleb and this woman, Penelope, did not meet the old-fashioned way. Instead of a guitar to the chest, there were rightward swipes on phones and a few weeks of textual banter. And now, Caleb sits with his elbow on the table, his chin resting in the palm of his hand, thinking about a kiss that happened half a year ago while a different woman he's on a date with talks about her love of the British royal family.

"That's kind of funny, right?" Penelope says, and after not getting an immediate response adds, "Right, Caleb?"

"Oh, uh, yes." Caleb blinks a couple of times quickly and sits back in his seat. "That's definitely right. You really can't beat Buckingham Palace."

Penelope stares at Caleb with a confused look on her face. "I stopped talking about the Royals like two minutes ago. I said I've been playing on my company's softball team and isn't it kind of funny how softballs aren't really soft, they're hard."

"Yeah, sorry about that," Caleb says. "I kind of zoned out for a minute, it's been a long week. But yes, that is funny... I guess? I mean, I think they call it softball because the ball used to be soft, so it's more of an anachronism."

Penelope stares at Caleb blankly.

"Anyway, I've been talking my face off! What do you like to do in your free time, Caleb?"

"Well, the past eight months or so my main leisure time activity has been helping a little girl learn letters and numbers so she can pass kindergarten. It's honestly much more time-consuming than I thought it would be."

"Oh, you have a kid?" Penelope asks, a look of alarm on her face.

"Well, she's not mine exactly, but she does live at my house."

"Okay?"

"Emily is my niece and it's a bit complicated."

"Well, I guess these things can be. I do have to say, though, I'm not really much of a kid person."

"Me either!" Caleb says with a laugh. "But you get used to it."

"Are you saying I'd get used to it if we start dating and get married?"

"Uh, no." Caleb desperately searches for an off-ramp now. "I mean, theoretically yes, you probably would get used to it. There's not much to it, really, just menial tasks every minute of every day and night. And noise, lots of noise. The noise never really stops unless you get them a good pair of headphones." Caleb notices he's taken a wrong turn somewhere, so he hesitates, taking a moment to recalculate. "But no, I mean, we're obviously not dating, so I don't think it matters what—"

"Um, obviously?" Penelope cuts in, her eyes a little wild now. "Why obviously?"

"You know what else I like?" Caleb tries to keep his demeanor breezy. "Sword fighting! Some people used to call me Lord Dagwyn!"

This pronouncement quiets things down very quickly. Penelope gives a thin smile and her eyes dart to her phone that is resting on the table in front of her like she's considering making an emergency call. Caleb has been on several first dates in the past few months, and it might be hard to believe, but this one is probably the best of the bunch. It's exceeding his expectations. Their food arrives at an opportune moment and Caleb begins to eat quickly, minimizing the need for further conversation. He spends the rest of the evening imagining Penelope is Sadie and they're sitting in a coffee shop. Drinking cappuccinos one after another.

Caleb thinks again about the kiss he rejected. He was originally 95 percent sure he did the right thing, but that number has been steadily dropping. Usually, a few percentage points at a time, so he doesn't really notice. But sometimes, on evenings like this, it drops ten or twenty points. A few more dating app encounters and the certainty percentage could be down to zero. It might even dip into the negatives depending on how things go.

...

Meanwhile, Sadie has a very different type of date. It's 7:00 p.m. on a Friday evening and she is ready to suffer through her last beginner guitar lesson of the work week. She sits on a stool in a cramped, windowless room with a piano shoved against one wall. An eight-year-old girl sits on a chair as far away from Sadie as is possible in the small space, but there is nowhere to hide. Sadie could reach out and touch the girl's knee without even leaning forward. This is the first lesson for the girl named Bryn. Her mom called Sadie earlier in the week, and when Sadie answered, she instinctively jerked the phone away from her ear. The mom's aggressively chipper voice made it feel like she was poised to leap through the cell phone and wrap Sadie in a big hug. Sadie felt physically attacked just by a bit of idle small talk, and when she hung up the phone call a few minutes later, she immediately collapsed onto her bed and lay there with her eyes closed tight for several minutes. Needless to say, she didn't gather a great deal of information about Bryn, but she did manage to set a time and day for a trial guitar lesson.

Sadie's expectations were extremely low. She anticipated she would be meeting a mini version of the maniacally merry mom, but instead what she got was a little girl with luminous black hair, penetrating brown eyes, and a quiet intensity. When Bryn sits down and looks Sadie squarely in the eye, Sadie feels the need to sit up just a bit straighter.

"Okay," Sadie says a bit hesitantly, caught off guard by the fact that she finds herself in the presence of an eight-year-old girl who looks ready to pass judgment on souls at the gates of Hell. "So, before we get started, why don't you tell me why you want to learn to play the guitar?"

Bryn shrugs her shoulders, maintaining eye contact with Sadie. "When I listen to guitar, it makes me feel... something. I want to figure out what that feeling is."

Sadie nods her head, a small smile on her lips. She hasn't figured out what Bryn's deal is yet, but she is certainly intrigued. After another long afternoon spent trying to teach guitar to students with very little talent and even less interest, any type of peculiarity is welcome. And this eight-year-old sure is peculiar. Sadie's first impression is that Bryn is much like she was as a girl. Young Sadie had exuberant parents and a somber intensity much beyond her years. And what drew Sadie to music from the very first time she picked up a guitar, and even before that, the first time she heard a frantic, pulsing The Donnas guitar riff on the radio, was that it made her realize there was a whole big world out there beyond her cozy yet oppressive suburban street filled with helicopter parents. Music made her feel like anything was possible, and that she could be anyone she wanted to be. If she could just unlock the secret.

"We can work with that," Sadie says.

The lesson proceeds as most first lessons do except that Bryn is much more attentive than Sadie's typical students, even students twice her age. She is a quick learner and holds the guitar effortlessly. Working with a student who clearly gets it energizes Sadie and the hour flies by. When it's over, Sadie actually feels disappointed. She needs more of this in her life. More energy. More excitement. Running into Caleb again was certainly exciting, but that was six months ago, and it did not end well. Since then, her world has felt flat. Like she's had the same boring playlist stuck on repeat.

"Can you play something?" Bryn asks as the lesson wraps up. She hasn't asked any questions until now or said much at all.

"I don't really play anymore," Sadie says with a little laugh.

"Why not?" Bryn asks.

"Um, I don't know. I guess I just haven't been feeling it lately."

Sadie is standing up now and looks down at Bryn who is still seated. Bryn doesn't say anything. She looks back at Sadie impassively.

"But, uh, I'll practice and try to play something for you next time," Sadie continues. "If you want to do more lessons?"

Bryn gives a small nod and stands up to leave. She walks out the door without looking back. As Sadie watches the girl walk away, she definitely feels something. She wouldn't mind finding out what that feeling is.

CHAPTER 21

SCARLETT IS WORRIED about her mom. She's twelve years old now, practically an adult, so she feels like it's her responsibility to make sure Sadie is okay. If she doesn't, who will? Her mom has been acting weird for the last several months. Even weirder than normal. Ever since she met Caleb at the football game about six months ago, she's seemed sad. When she's not teaching music, she's usually at home, looking at her phone with the TV on. Sometimes she even goes back to bed after Sadie goes to school in the morning. Scarlett found this out because she had a headache one morning and when she called her mom from the school clinic, she sounded like she had just woken up. The holidays have come and gone, and even though they did all the normal things, Sadie wasn't totally present. She totally mailed it in on the gift-giving this year; she literally bought Scarlett a Roblox gift card. Something you would buy an eleven-year-old! She excused herself early from family dinners with Grandma and Grandpa and didn't make any jokes at all when they made Sadie and Scarlett stand or kneel around Preston the Peacock so they could take a family holiday picture for Instagram. Her reaction to this last one, or lack thereof, was perhaps the most alarming of all.

There's no two ways about it. It's time for an intervention. That's why Scarlett has called in her best friend, Kaylee. Kaylee is, in fact, the only real friend Scarlett has made since moving to Florida. Kaylee's birthday is in the fall, so she is more like twelve and a half now, one of the oldest kids in their grade. Those extra six months of experience are vital when it comes to love and relationships and all that. Kaylee is also very much into boys. She loves to talk about the boys they know at school, analyzing their facial features and haircuts, comparing and contrasting their levels of cuteness. She sometimes even writes fanfiction about her crush of the week in big loopy hand-writing in her notebook with the sparkly pink cover. Scarlett finds all of this behavior to be completely mortifying, and frankly ridiculous, but she feels like Kaylee's single-minded focus and wealth of knowl-edge are exactly what she needs to help her navigate her current situation.

The way Scarlett figures it, she needs to find a way to get her mom and Caleb together. She's seen enough Netflix movies that Kaylee has forced her to watch during their sleepovers to know that when an adult is sad, it's likely because they're not with their soul-mate, who happens to be nearby. Scarlett has pieced together enough information from strategic eavesdropping to determine that Caleb must be her mom's soulmate. It's incredible the things you can hear when you sit on the couch, acting disinterested and sullen, wearing headphones that aren't turned on. Caleb and her mom seem like an improbable match, but Kaylee does always say that opposites attract. Kaylee typically says this in reference to the one-week fling she had with Cameron, an extremely skinny boy with a pointy nose who is obsessed with anime.

It's a Friday afternoon in early May and the two girls are in Scar-lett's bedroom. Scarlett is lying down across the foot of her double bed on top of the dark purple comforter, staring at the ceiling. Kaylee is sitting on the floor, her back resting against the bed. A small desk sits on one side of the room piled with books and papers. Scarlett's sword fighting gear takes up one corner of the room. Her sword is standing against the wall and the hulking half-suit of armor her grandparents made sits in a heap, the helmet resting on top crookedly with the peacock feather jutting out, tickling the wall.

"Okay, so where should we start?" Kaylee asks. She has her notebook out and has opened it to a blank page. Scarlett told her about the project at school today and she is extremely excited. "Should I sketch out a map of all the key players?"

Scarlett sits up on the bed, crossing her legs in front of her. "I'm not sure how that will help, but okay."

"Great." Kaylee begins to scratch away furiously with her pen, writing, underlining, and circling. When she's done, she holds up the notebook so Scarlett can see her work. Kaylee seems very pleased with herself. "There."

Scarlett stares at the notebook for a few moments, taking it all in. Kaylee has written "Sadie" on the top of the page, "Caleb" on the bottom, circled both names, and drawn a few squiggly lines between with arrows pointing in both directions. There is also a big heart in the middle and "Scarlett (+ Kaylee)" written on one side and "Emily" written on the other.

Scarlett makes a small noise like "hmm" and continues to look at the paper. It seems so obvious now. Why didn't she think of it before? Kaylee was totally right about the need for a map of the key characters. Seeing it there on paper makes everything so clear. Sometimes age, wisdom, and quality penmanship do pay off.

"You're a genius, Kay," Scarlett says.

"I know." Kaylee smiles coyly and places the notebook on the floor by her side. "Why am I a genius now, exactly?"

"You figured out what our plan of attack should be. It's right there on your map."

"Oh, yes." Kaylee picks the notebook back up, tapping her pen against the paper, and studies the diagram carefully. "And the plan of attack would be?"

"Emily," Scarlett says simply. She looks toward Kaylee and sees that it hasn't quite clicked for her yet. "Emily is the key. So, I see Caleb at sword fighting practice each week, right? Emily is usually there, and she loves me. If I tell Caleb that I'm available to babysit, *and* I make sure to tell him this when Emily can hear me..."

"He'll have to say yes," Kaylee cuts in excitedly, her eyes lighting up.

"Yep," Scarlett says. "Emily will make him. I think he's a little scared of her."

Kaylee gets up and jumps onto the bed beside Scarlett. "That is an OP plan!"

"When did you start saying OP?" Scarlett asks.

"Oh, I forgot to tell you. I'm kind of dating Brayden from our math class. He's a huge gamer and says OP a lot. It means overpowered."

"I know what it means."

"Anyway, he's really cute, right? I love the way he covers his face with his hair when he gets embarrassed."

"Sure," Scarlett says noncommittally. "But back to the plan real quick. Will you babysit with me? I don't really want to be in a house by myself."

"Of course!" Kaylee says, practically glowing now. "It will be so O...," She stops, looking at Scarlett. "I mean, it will be so cool!"

"Cool." Scarlett examines her fingernails. "Do you think we need to do anything else, or will this be enough to get my mom together with Caleb?"

Kaylee considers this for a moment. "I think it should be enough, right? Your mom will have to drop us off at Caleb's house, so they'll have to see each other. Oh." Her eyes widen. "Maybe I can casually ask Caleb what he has planned and that will get things going?"

"Maybe," Scarlett says, picking up her phone and checking the lock screen. "Just don't be obvious about it."

"Duh." Kaylee slaps Scarlett's arm playfully. "I'm, like, super cool about these kinds of things."

...

. . .

The next morning, Sadie drops Kaylee off at her house on the way to Scarlett's sword fighting club practice. When they pull in the driveway, Kaylee opens the door and mouths to Scarlett "good luck, text me." Scarlett nods. Kaylee thanks Sadie and bounces off toward her front door, backpack slung over one shoulder. Sadie then drops Scarlett off at the park and leaves, offering a quick goodbye and saying she'll see Scarlett in an hour. Scarlett gathers up her gear and her thoughts and walks toward the grassy field where Caleb, the twins, and a few others are gathered.

Emily is sitting down, picking the small white flowers that grow on the weedy grasses. Spotting Scarlett, she jumps up, hustling over, her face beaming. "I picked these for you," she says excitedly, thrusting a small bunch of flowers toward Scarlett.

"Thanks, Emily," Scarlett says, smiling. "They're beautiful."

Caleb approaches and greets Scarlett. "Ready to start?"

"Uh..." Scarlett hesitates. "Can I ask you something first?" She knows she needs to act now before she loses her nerve.

Caleb lets his sword hang down by his side. "Sure."

Scarlett checks to make sure Emily is still close by and listening. "I was wondering if you might need me to babysit sometime. For Emily."

Emily perks up at the sound of her voice like a puppy responding to the crinkling of the bag of treats.

"My friend Kaylee and I are trying to start a babysitting business," Scarlett continues. "But we need some customers to get experience."

Caleb looks toward Emily. "Oh, okay..."

Emily races toward him. "Can we? Can we? We have to!"

Caleb rests his hand on Emily's shoulder and looks back toward Scarlett. "Yeah. I think that would be fine. Obviously, Emily would love it. And I guess it would be good to have a reliable babysitter in case I ever need one."

"Great," Scarlett says. "How about tonight?"

"Tonight?" Caleb looks a little flustered.

"Yes! Tonight! Tonight!" Emily practically screeches.

"Um, I don't really have any plans for tonight, but..."

"I was thinking maybe we could do a practice run," Scarlett cuts in. "For a couple hours just to see how things go. I could come to your house and Kaylee would come with me so we wouldn't be alone. She's twelve and a half."

"Oh, right." Caleb raises his hand to his face and cups his chin as if he's deep in thought. "Well, if it's okay with your mom, then sure. Let's give it a try."

"Perfect," Scarlett says, smiling. "We won't even charge for the first time. Like a free trial."

"Well, I can't pass up a deal like that," Caleb returns, smiling too. "But... please make sure it's okay with your mom?"

Scarlett's eyes shift. "Oh, it is. She already said she could bring us to your house tonight." This is a small lie, but Scarlett believes it is a necessary one.

"Scarlett is coming to my house tonight!" Emily announces to the group in a very loud voice. There is a smattering of applause in response.

The group begins practice, working through their standard warm-ups and exercises. Scarlett is paired up with one of the twins and she has to keep reminding herself to focus. Thoughts about babysitting and her potential career as a matchmaker are swirling in her head, but the last thing she needs is to get distracted and end up with a concussion caused by a clumsy headshot by Garrett.

Tonight is definitely not the night she wants to be concussed. She needs to be on top of her game.

CHAPTER 22

Sadie can feel it in the air and she's not happy about it: Summer is coming. Florida summers are the worst because they contain the worst of everything. The worst heat and humidity. The worst mosquitoes. The worst thunderstorms. And the worst people because everyone is delirious from all of the other worst things. It's also way too bright. Even early May mornings like this one are excruciatingly upbeat. With the sun shining like this, making everything glow and shimmer, Sadie feels compelled to be happy. It feels like nature is reprimanding her for being sad and introspective. She much prefers being inside in the air conditioning with the blinds drawn, but she also knows that going outside every once in a while to move her body is probably required to maintain some semblance of mental and physical health.

After she dropped Scarlett off, she drove just down the road to another small park that is quiet, mostly empty, and has a small pond with a walking trail around it. Now, she is trudging around the pond, shading her eyes from the blinding sun because she left her sunglasses in the car. She doesn't feel like going back for them because that would be a bit too much exercise for one day. At one end of the pond, she sees two turtles standing on a concrete beam that runs along the edge of the water. They are facing each other about six feet apart, their necks outstretched, soaking up the morning sun. Sadie thinks the turtles look like they are about to joust. All they need are little spears. Wait, no, lances. That's it, lances.

She shakes her head; it seems like she's seeing Caleb everywhere these days. It's silly, really, but she can't escape the feeling that their story is still unfinished. Even though she vividly remembers the October night half a year ago when Caleb made it clear that he believed their relationship was very much complete. She can still feel her lips on his, unyielding, unwelcoming. It's dumb. She's a grown woman, not a teenager or college student who doesn't have more important things to worry about. Like raising a child and paying outrageous rent on a townhouse with a view of a pond that's bound to hold the remains of at least one dead body.

Sadie checks her watch and makes one more revolution around the pond. She feels a bit like a hamster on a wheel when she walks here, but it's better than nothing. And at least there are no people today. Sadie walks back to her car and slides into the driver's seat. She is significantly sweaty just from walking, which never ceases to be annoying. She starts the car and tunes the radio to the '90s alternative station. There's a Pigeontoes song on. Of course. She presses the button to turn the radio off and makes the short drive back to the other park in silence. She'll pick up Scarlett and then, well, she will do whatever it is one is supposed to do on a Saturday. Whatever she does today, it certainly won't be interesting. That much she knows for sure.

...

Scarlett tosses her equipment into the trunk of Sadie's car and climbs into the passenger seat.

"Hey." Scarlett settles into the seat and pulls the seatbelt across her body to buckle it.

"Hey?" Sadie says hesitantly. In the more than half a year that Sadie has been driving Scarlett to these practices, Scarlett has never once initiated conversation upon entering the car. Even a simple "hey" has been, until this moment, completely unheard of.

"What do we have to do today?" Scarlett asks. She seems downright chipper, which Sadie finds very suspicious.

"Um, I don't know." Sadie turns right out of the parking lot onto the main road. "I don't have any plans. Anything you want to do?"

"Well, this is pretty crazy," Scarlett says, tucking her hair behind her ear, "but Caleb asked if I could babysit Emily tonight." This is another small lie, but Scarlett believes once again that is a necessary one.

"Oh." Sadie pulls the car to a stop at a red light. "What did you say?"

"I said I could do it as long as Kaylee came with me. He said that was fine."

The light turns green and Sadie drives forward, flicking on her blinker as they approach the turnoff for their neighborhood. "Okay," she says, keeping her eyes squarely on the road, trying her best to play it cool and normal. "I guess you'll need me to drop you off?"

"Please?" Scarlett says.

"Sure," Sadie replies as she maneuvers the car into their driveway. "Like I said. I don't have any plans."

Sadie doesn't notice as Scarlett turns her head toward the window and smiles.

...

"Is that what you're wearing?" Scarlett asks, emerging from her room at 6:40 that evening.

Sadie is standing in the kitchen slouched over the counter holding her phone in front of her with both hands. She is wearing black leggings and a Nirvana t-shirt with the smiley face on it. Her hair is pulled back into a ponytail. "Uh, yeah," she says, looking up with a quizzical expression on her face. "Why?"

"You don't want to wear something, I don't know, nicer?"

"To drop you off to babysit?"

"Yeah." Sadie takes her small backpack off her back, setting it down on a chair, and looking through it.

"You're not exactly dressed up," Sadie notes. Scarlett is wearing black athletic shorts and a baggy sweatshirt that doesn't seem particularly stylish or climate appropriate.

"I'm just babysitting," Scarlett says flatly. "It doesn't matter what I wear."

"And again, I'm just dropping you and Kaylee off, so it definitely doesn't matter what I wear."

"Whatever," Scarlett says, rolling her eyes.

...

After picking up Kaylee, Sadie navigates to the address that Caleb gave Scarlett. Luckily, the May days are long, and the sun is still hanging just above the horizon when they arrive. Sadie would not have been able to locate this place in the dark. Or, if she had, she wouldn't have believed it was a residential house and not part of the salvage yard. But in the late evening light, Sadie can clearly see the small yellow house as she swings her car off the busy road into the driveway and pulls past the chain link fence to park behind Caleb's car.

The house is rather charming, it's just so oddly positioned. When she opens the car door, she immediately notices the noise. The buzz of cars passing by is constant, visceral. It reminds her of living in New York. She kind of digs it.

"All right, girls," Sadie says, closing her car door. "I'll walk you up and then head out."

Scarlett and Kaylee are huddled together, whispering to each other, and their eyes dart toward Sadie in unison.

Scarlett hefts her backpack over her shoulder. "Okay."

"You look great, Ms. Warren," Kaylee adds brightly. "I love the vintage shirt."

Sadie eyes the girls warily. "She told you to say that, didn't she?" She points at Scarlett while directing her words to Kaylee. "I don't know why my wardrobe is so fascinating to everyone tonight."

The girls share a look and a few stifled giggles. Then, Emily bursts out of the front door and races up to the girls, wrapping her arms around Scarlett's waist.

"I have sleeping bags!" she squeals in delight.

"Oh, okay." Scarlett pats Emily on the head. "This is Kaylee, by the way." She gestures toward Kaylee.

"I know." Emily hugs Kaylee around the waist now. It is unclear how she knows, but no one questions it.

Sadie is standing just in front of her car when Caleb walks out of the front door that Emily has left partially open. He looks a bit flustered and also frustratingly handsome. Sadie thinks this would be so much easier if the physical attraction was gone, but alas. She runs a hand through her hair before moving toward the girls.

"Hi... everyone," Caleb says, looking at Scarlett and Kaylee first. His eyes drift toward Sadie and he quickly looks away when he meets her eyes. "Scarlett, Kaylee, I can show you around the house real quick and then I'll get out of your way." He looks toward Sadie again. "Sadie, you can come in, too."

"I'm good," Sadie says quickly, smiling politely.

Once everyone goes inside, she exhales. She hasn't had a cigarette in years, but she suddenly thinks that's exactly what she needs right now. A lit one. She almost bursts out laughing as this very random memory floats to the front of her mind: Caleb's younger, charming face looking utterly ridiculous with an unlit cigarette clenched between his teeth. She raises a hand to her face to cover her eyes just as Caleb emerges again from the front door. He ruffles his hair with his hand and blinks a few times as if he's trying to force his eyes to adjust to the fading light. He notices Sadie.

"Are you okay?" he asks, concern in his voice.

"Oh, yeah." Sadie drops her hand to her side and shifts her weight from foot to foot. She hesitates, then says, "I was just thinking about something funny."

"Hit me with it." Caleb feels the outside of the pockets of his jeans, checking for his phone and keys. His hands move quickly with nervous energy.

"It's about you," Sadie says.

Caleb looks toward Sadie. "Really?"

"I was standing here while you were showing the girls around and it hit me that my little girl is getting ready to babysit for the first time. And at your house of all places." Sadie sees a small smile form on Caleb's face. "I had this intense urge for a cigarette, which is weird since I haven't had one in years, and then I thought about you standing there against the wall outside the coffee shop. With the unlit cigarette in your mouth."

"Oh, wow." Caleb locks eyes with Sadie. "That was probably not one of my greatest hits. But that *was* a great night."

Sadie looks away. The sun has dropped below the horizon and the sky in the west is orange and pink. Two palm trees are silhouetted against the sky.

"I agree," she says finally.

Caleb wants to make this moment last but he's not sure how. "I don't actually know what I'm doing during this babysitting experiment, but I guess I better get going. Emily will probably yell at me if she finds out I'm still here."

"Right." Sadie moves toward her car slowly, lingering, almost willing time to stop just for a moment. "I'll see you."

"Yes, thanks."

Sadie and Caleb get into their cars. Sadie starts hers and sits in her seat for a moment, staring at the back of Caleb's car in front of her. A wave of anxiety sweeps over her as she wonders how she's supposed to get out of this driveway without getting plowed into on the busy street. The taillights on Caleb's car flicker for a moment and then go dark. Then they flicker on and off again. Sadie rolls down her window and hears that his car is making a clicking noise as he tries to start it. Caleb's car door opens, and he steps out, looking around uncertainly. He walks toward Sadie's car and leans down to look in the window.

Caleb winces slightly. "Okay, so this is a little awkward, but I think my battery is dead."

"Yet another death in the family, huh?" Sadie asks, a gleam in her eye.

Caleb places a hand over his chest and feigns an aghast expression. "Ouch! You are still completely savage, I see."

"Sorry. Just instinct. How can I help?"

Caleb thinks. "Um. Well, could you maybe drive me to the auto parts store to grab a new battery?"

"Yeah, sure. No problem." Sadie looks away, surveying the passenger seat of her car which is a bit cluttered but not a complete disaster.

"Thanks," Caleb says. "Let me grab the battery out of the car. Which I assume is something one should do in this situation."

He hurries away, pausing by the car before walking over to the small shed at the top of the driveway. Sadie watches as he retrieves a wrench, pops the hood of the car, and disappears from view behind the hood for a few minutes. He reappears eventually lugging the battery wrapped in an old dirty towel. He asks Sadie if he can put the battery in the trunk and he does before climbing into the passenger seat, which Sadie has cleared off in the intervening minutes.

"Thanks again," Caleb says, smiling warmly. "I didn't have this on my Bingo card for the night, but live and learn, I guess."

"Learn what?" Sadie asks as she begins the slow process of maneuvering the car out of the driveway.

"I don't know. Not to let my battery die when my ex is bringing her daughter over to babysit my niece who is kind of like my daughter?"

"That's a very specific lesson," Sadie laughs, finally giving up on caution and gunning it backwards onto the road when there is a break in the traffic. She shifts to drive, spins the wheel to the left, and stomps on the gas pedal.

Caleb looks out the window at his house as it blurs away. "Sometimes specific lessons are the best ones."

"I don't know how you manage this road every day," Sadie says. "Getting out of the driveway gave me serious anxiety."

"You get used to it," Caleb says. "It just takes time."

As Caleb continues staring out the window, a vivid memory washes over him. A few weeks after the failed proposal, Caleb was driving down this street on a Saturday morning. His sword was resting on the floorboard of the passenger seat and his sparring armor, damp with sweat from a morning spent at sword fighting club practice, was piled up on the back seat. He was distracted, images of Sadie still invading his brain at every opportunity. Out of the corner of his eye, he caught sight of the little yellow house between the salvage yard and the strip mall for the first time. He was so distracted by scenes from his recent past that he almost missed it. He hastily switched lanes and made a U-turn at the next break in the median so he could get a better look. After turning off the road into a doctor's office parking lot, he took a picture of the house from across the street. Without thinking, he opened a text message to Sadie and almost sent the picture to her. She was the person he always wanted to share things with first. He quickly swiped the message away because he remembered he couldn't do that anymore. After tossing his phone on the passenger seat, he smashed the gas pedal and swerved back out onto the street and accelerated quickly to beat the oncoming traffic, his heart beating a little faster.

Caleb and Sadie sit in silence for the rest of the short drive to the auto parts store, the alternative rock station playing softly on the radio. The last of the daylight has faded and the streetlights have switched on. Fast food restaurants, grocery stores with sprawling parking lots illuminated by bright lights, and strip mall shopping centers dot each side of the road. Sadie pulls into one of the shopping centers and parks in front of the auto parts store. Caleb hefts the dead battery from the trunk and goes inside.

Sadie sits in the car with the engine idling. She turns the music up, and lays her head back on the head rest. While Caleb is inside, she has time to think about what would happen if a car swerved off the road and crashed into Caleb's house right now while Scarlett was there. She pictures red and blue lights pulsing, sweeping across the pavement, the small yard, and the yellow stucco walls, casting long shadows that look like demons. She imagines one of those rolling stretchers emerging from the front door, carrying the body of a person that she can't identify from so far away.

Caleb is back. He deposits a fresh new battery into the trunk and gets back into the car.

"Hey, all done," he says, a bit breathlessly. He looks at Sadie. She has her eyes closed; her head is still tilted back against the headrest. "You okay?"

"Yeah." Sadie opens her eyes and sits up straight. "I was just thinking about death and destruction." She's also thinking about why her heart is beating so fast and how she suddenly got herself into such an awkward situation. But, there's no need to get into all that.

"Ah, the usual. Well, on that note, I have some bad news and good news. My old battery has passed away. They tried their best, but they couldn't bring her back." Caleb pauses for a moment and then continues, "The good news is they did have a new one." He does his best to keep his voice and demeanor breezy even though his mind is racing. He's been thinking about that kiss he rejected so many months ago since the moment he slid into the passenger seat of Sadie's car.

"Well, that's good." Sadie shifts the car into reverse. "Gotta love when death has a silver lining." Caleb laughs. Sadie turns out of the parking lot onto the road. "So, back to your house?"

"Uh, let's see." Caleb checks his watch. "We've been gone for about twenty-five minutes, so…"

Sadie keeps her eyes fixed on the road and doesn't say anything. If she ignores the frisson of awkwardness and possibility that fills her car, maybe it will just go away.

"Would you maybe want to grab coffee, or a drink or whatever is appropriate at eight o'clock on a Saturday night?" Caleb is surprised this suggestion slips past his lips so easily. He certainly hadn't planned to ask Sadie out. Or had he? He furrows his brow and gazes out the window at the passing traffic.

"Together?" Sadie asks, her heart beating even faster now. At this point, she suspects Caleb might be able to hear it pounding against her ribcage.

"Yeah. We could catch up or whatever? It's been a while."

That's one way of putting it, Sadie thinks. "So, why exactly did you need a babysitter again?"

"Oh, I honestly didn't." Caleb begins to realize that he was hoping this would happen since Scarlett asked him about babysitting. Not that his car battery would die, necessarily, but that he would somehow end up alone with Sadie. Now that it's happened, he's not at all sure what he wants to happen next. "Scarlett said she and Kaylee were trying to start a babysitting business and they needed to build up their customer base. So, we're doing a trial run. I thought she said she told you all this?"

"She did not," Sadie says, "but that's no surprise." She pauses, thinking about how embarrassing it is to be set up on a date by her twelve-year-old, particularly because it very clearly seems to be working. "Anyway, as far as the having coffee goes… you didn't seem to want to spend time together last time we talked."

Caleb sighs. "I mean, it's not that I didn't want to spend time together. It's more like I wasn't ready to be your boyfriend after not seeing you for twelve years and learning that you have a daughter who was conceived while we were dating. Well, more or less dating. I realize there were extenuating circumstances."

"When you put it like that, it makes me sound like a crazy person," Sadie says.

"Not crazy," Caleb says. "Confused."

"Confused?" The pitch of Sadie's voice rises and her eyes light up.

"I meant me too," Caleb says hastily. "Not just you. I was confused." He ruffles his hair with his hand. "I probably still am."

"You could've attempted to talk again somehow in the last, what, seven months? If you were really confused."

"Yeah, I know." Caleb looks toward Sadie now. "It's kind of hard, right?"

They both sit quietly, looking straight ahead at the road as Sadie pulls the car to a stop at a red light. She looks toward Caleb with a serious expression, he returns her gaze.

"That's what she said," Sadie says.

They both laugh. Real laughs. Cathartic laughter that seems to expel twelve years of pain and unacknowledged suffering. Sadie turns the car into another shopping plaza and parks outside a coffee shop. When she turns the car off, Caleb undoes his seatbelt and leans toward her, still smiling. Sadie's hand is still resting on the gear shift and Caleb covers her hand with his. There is no hesitation. Sadie leans toward Caleb and their mouths meet. This time, his lips are welcoming, warm, eager. Sadie remembers the Renaissance faire and thinks this might be even better. It was worth the wait.

"Coffee?" Sadie asks simply when they move apart. Both their heads are spinning. Caleb says yes.

CHAPTER 23

"Can I ask you one question?" Caleb asks, lifting his paper coffee cup off the table and setting it back down again in a slightly different location. "It's an important one."

The conversation has flowed easily inside the nearly empty and dimly lit coffee shop. It feels like old times. Caleb and Sadie have talked about almost everything in the past twenty minutes. They've caught each other up on their lives, they've talked about kids, parenting, and parents. Sadie nods.

"What do you think your 22-year-old self would say if she found out that, twelve years in the future, she would be having coffee with the one and only Lord Dagwyn?"

Sadie laughs, shaking her head. Caleb tries his best to maintain a serious countenance, but eventually cracks. He reaches across the table and takes Sadie's hand in his. The simple touch feels electric, highly charged.

"Can you believe our first kiss was at a Renaissance faire?" Sadie asks, looking directly into Caleb's eyes.

"I mean, you say that like it's something unusual."

"Oh, you kiss lots of girls at the Renaissance faire, Lord Dagwyn?"

"No," Caleb smiles and squeezes Sadie's hand. "Just one. The only one that ever mattered."

Sadie squeezes Caleb's hand back. Her face and neck flush, turning a very soft pink. A feeling of unexpected elation washes over her. It almost feels like she's been drinking wine instead of coffee because she feels completely uninhibited. A memory forms in her mind. She is lying next to Caleb in his old bed, her head resting against his shoulder, her hand on his bare chest. She remembers feeling his heartbeat against her palm. *Thump, thump, thump.* It was so deep and slow and powerful.

"The sex was good, too, huh?" Sadie says suddenly. The question slips out almost instinctively. Like she doesn't have control of her words anymore.

Caleb is clearly caught off guard. "Um, yeah, sure. I mean, I think it was, right?"

"What?" Sadie exclaims, pulling her hand away, a familiar fire lighting up her eyes. Caleb recognizes that look. It's time to parachute to safety before the whole plane is engulfed in flames.

"I mean," Caleb says hastily, "you were great. Completely fantastic! But I was never sure if I was any good?"

Sadie sits back in her chair, folding her arms across her chest. "Hmm, you were more than adequate."

"Well, that's a relief. I did watch all those videos, so I felt reasonably confident, but you never know."

Sadie snorts out a laugh. "I bet!"

"Not like that, you pervert," Caleb says indignantly.

Sadie throws up her hands. "Come on. What else could 'watch all those videos' possibly mean in this context?"

"You know. How-to videos. Tutorials!"

"Right, right," Sadie says sarcastically. "Sex tutorials. What was I thinking?"

"I don't know," Caleb says, determined not to acknowledge her sarcastic tone. "I used to pick up the VHS tapes from the public library during the summer when I was in high school."

"You're kidding."

"Nope. My mom let me have pretty much unfettered library access my senior year, so I went a little crazy. And luckily, we still had a VHS player. The library didn't exactly rush to convert to DVDs."

"What a life you led," Sadie says, really on a roll now. "But like, what type of videos are we talking about here? I'm having trouble picturing it. Not that I really want to, but..."

"I don't remember exactly." Caleb's eyes wander upward as he tries to recall. He pauses to collect his thoughts, feeling a bit surprised by this turn in the conversation but also relieved. It's fun to chat with Sadie like this. It feels like no time has passed. All the heavy stuff—their past, his family, all the doubts and uncertainties—begins to feel distant. It's nice. "I think it was like the sex-ed videos they show in school but with a little more practical knowledge? They were from the seventies probably, so it was anything goes back then."

"Okay. And you just checked these out from the library?"

Sadie's mind is racing a bit amidst the whirlwind of the last hour, but she does her best to remain cool and composed. She clenches her hands together in her lap.

"Sure," Caleb replies. "Well, I used a bit of subterfuge. I would make a casual comment to the librarian when she was scanning the tape that I just needed it for a research project I was doing on deviant, satanic youths."

"Oh, perfect," Sadie enthuses, clapping her hands together.

"Yeah, I had her pegged as one of those little old ladies who carries a Bible with her to the grocery store. I think I was right."

"Are we talking about the big county library near the Waffle House?" Sadie asks. "Because, if so, I think the librarian there was Ms. Haggerty."

"That's it!" Caleb says excitedly. "She was such a legend."

"She was also a lesbian," Sadie says. "And she had, like, tattoos all over. You could see them under her sleeves and around her ankles."

"Really?" Caleb asks with a quizzical look on his face. "Well, this changes everything. I wonder if she suspected what I was up to?"

"What were you up to?"

"Learning to please my future lady, of course!"

Sadie closes her eyes and squeezes them shut tight. "Please," she says slowly. "Don't ever say that again." With her eyes still closed, she reaches her hand back out across the table like she's feeling for something in the dark. Caleb takes her hand, and they sit there in silence for a few more moments before they both remember they don't have all night to sit together in this coffee shop. Their days of leisure are long past. It's time to return to reality.

...

They kiss again in the parking lot by the car. And again inside the car before they get back on the road. And again at a stoplight while traffic from a cross street creates a blur of white and red light in front of them. They barely notice. They probably wouldn't have noticed if a car plowed into them, tossing their bodies through the windshield, out onto the unassuming asphalt. Neither of them wants to slow down. They feel like if they take their foot off the gas and coast even for a second, they will have to grapple with how stupid they are being. Over the past seven months, there has been next to nothing between them. A few passing "hellos" when Sadie was dropping off or picking up Scarlett from sword fighting practice. Furtive glances over the shoulder. Both of them have had plenty of thoughts, maybe even a daydream or two in idle moments, but nothing more. It all seems so sudden. Like Caleb's battery breaks and the dam that was holding everything in—all the thoughts and dreams and emotions and unspoken words —it just bursts. One moment this impenetrable barrier between them is there and the next it's gone. It's funny how that can happen.

...

Everything all at once. That's what it feels like.

...

When they pull back into Caleb's driveway, Emily is beside the car almost before it pulls to a complete stop, her smiling face nearly pressed against the passenger side window. Caleb worries for a moment that something is wrong but from what he can decipher from the torrent of words that wash over him the second he opens the car door is that everything went fine. Better than fine, actually. It was the best two hours of Emily's life.

Scarlett and Kaylee are standing just outside the open front door, the yellow light from the bulb on the front porch giving their faces a ghostly appearance. Sadie looks toward the girls expecting to detect confusion, but instead she sees something else. The girls look at each other and appear to be smiling. Kaylee clutches Scarlett's wrist with one hand. Both Sadie and Caleb had forgotten that their arrival together in Sadie's car might seem strange. After just a short time together, they felt like this was how things were supposed to be, how things always were. Of course, the outside world doesn't know that yet.

"How did things go, girls?" Caleb asks, draping an arm around Emily's shoulder and subtly guiding her toward the house.

The girls share a look. "It was good," Scarlett says.

"How was your night?" Kaylee adds brightly.

"Uh, it was also good." Caleb glances toward Sadie, seeking guidance. "My car wouldn't start, so Sadie was nice enough to drive me to the auto parts store to pick up a new battery."

"That took a long time," Kaylee says. Scarlett steps on her foot.

Sadie comes to Caleb's rescue. "We also stopped and had coffee."

"Right," Caleb adds. "It had been a while, so we finally got a chance to catch up again."

Kaylee is beaming now. Scarlett does her best to conceal her smile, raising a hand to her mouth, pretending to cover a yawn.

"Well, it's getting late." Caleb takes a wad of cash out of his pocket and holds it out to Scarlett. "Thanks, Scarlett and Kaylee. We'll be sure to do it again if you want!"

"Tomorrow!" Emily shouts, giving both girls a hug.

Scarlett raises a hand. "This was a free trial, remember."

Caleb peels off two bills and holds them out again. "Here. Take a little something, at least."

Scarlett takes the money reluctantly and shoves it into her pocket.

"Okay, girls," Sadie says, gesturing toward the car. "Let's go."

"Oh, my battery," Caleb says. "I almost forgot."

Caleb jogs over to the back of Sadie's car and Sadie meets him there. She lifts up the trunk door and it sits upright, mostly obstructing Scarlett and Kaylee's line of sight. As Caleb carefully lifts the new battery out of the trunk, Sadie runs a finger softly along the back of his hand up to his wrist before letting her hand drop down to her side. A completely insignificant touch, but it still makes the small hairs on Caleb's arm jump to attention. They share a quick look and then Caleb moves away. Sadie shuts the trunk door and Scarlett and Kaylee climb into the car. As Sadie maneuvers the car out of the driveway, Emily and Caleb stand on the front porch waving. Everyone in the car waves back.

CHAPTER 24

"So, any news with you?" Paige's eyes dance mischievously. She sits on Sadie's couch with her legs crossed in front of her, cupping a glass of sauvignon blanc in her hands. It's another PNO–Paige's Night Out–and she is in the mood for gossip. She's heard rumblings and whispers, picked up some vibes, but she's ready to hear it straight from the source.

Sadie looks toward Scarlett, who is sitting behind the couch at the kitchen table, ostensibly doing homework. She has big headphones covering her ears and she is staring intently at the textbook that is splayed open in front of her. Scarlett *is* legitimately doing homework, but she has brought back her signature move of wearing headphones and turning off the sound so she can listen in on her mom's conversation while she works. She's promised Kaylee that she'll report back with any developments about their ongoing matchmaking project. Eavesdropping also makes reading about the Great Depression a little more bearable.

"Not really," Sadie says, keeping her eyes on the TV. This time they are watching a documentary about a serial killer. It was Sadie's turn to choose. They've only been watching for five minutes, and she already wishes she would've chosen the fancy real estate reality show, but she can't turn back now. Paige would never let her hear the end of it.

"Hmm, very suspicious," Paige says.

"What can possibly be suspicious about 'not really'?" Sadie asks.

"It's not the words, Ms. Sadie. It's your actions." Paige gives Sadie a knowing wink. Taking her cue from the documentary, she has gone full detective mode. "It's simple really. Before you answered, you looked over at your daughter, Ms. Scarlett." All Paige needs is one of those plaid detective hats and a pipe and she'd be good to go. "And the only reason you'd do that is because you have something to hide. Something you don't want to talk too loudly about."

Sadie doesn't respond to Paige's little soliloquy. She makes a point to keep her eyes squarely on the TV screen even though this documentary is by far the worst thing she has ever watched. Why would anyone want to learn more about a serial killer? It seems completely demented now that she thinks about it. She certainly knows a thing or two about being morbid, but this is a bridge too far. She picks up the remote and hits the back button. "Fine, let's watch the real estate show," she says, scrolling across the images on the screen and landing on one with a cleanly shaven, extremely attractive man wearing an expensive suit, his arms outstretched, standing in front of an outrageously decadent mansion. She clicks on it.

"Ha, I told you the serial killer thing was too weird, even for you," Paige gloats.

They watch the show for a few minutes without talking. The attractive real estate agent is on the phone, trying to convince his eccentric client that something like fifty million dollars isn't an insulting offer and looking increasingly like he's about to put his fist through a wall. It's all fake, of course, Sadie thinks. No one has that many emotions or feelings about anything, especially not real estate.

Paige appears to be looking at the TV, but Sadie can feel her eyes on her. "I also told you that you and Caleb weren't over," she says slyly.

Scarlett has been listening the whole time, but her focus increases now. She turns her head toward her mom, making sure her movement is subtle to avoid drawing attention. Her phone is laying on the table and she swipes the screen, navigating to her text message with Kaylee. She taps out—

stand by theyre getting to the good stuff

—hits send, and presses the button on the side of her phone to make the screen go dark. Her screen lights up almost immediately indicating a reply from Kaylee that is just a string of exclamation points.

"I don't know," Sadie says finally. "We did have coffee... talked about some things."

"I knew it!" Paige says triumphantly, punching the air with her fist. "Sa-leb is back! Or is it Ca-die? Ca-die might be too confusing, sounds like Katie. Let's go with Sa-leb!"

Sadie shushes her, cutting her eyes toward Scarlett. Scarlett leans in closer to the table and runs her finger across the page of her book to make it look like she's completely absorbed in her studies.

"Did you do anything else? Kiss perhaps?" Paige asks in a much quieter voice. Sadie can't help but smile. "You did!"

Scarlett's eyes go wide. She opens her phone and taps out

they kissed!!!

to Kaylee and sends the message. Kaylee's response is, again, instantaneous. This time it says:

eeeeeekkkkkkk

"So," Paige continues, "is there anything more you might've done or is Caleb pulling his Jesus act like he did when you first met?"

"His Jesus act?" Sadie repeats, perplexed.

"You know," Paige smiles mischievously, "how he rose on the third date."

With this, Scarlett grimaces and does everything she can to suppress her urge to make a gagging motion. She turns the music on and turns the volume up to max so that it pulses through her headphones and straight into her skull, covering up her mom's conversation, all other noise, and her thoughts. She taps out a quick message to Kaylee saying,

> i think that's all.

Meanwhile, Sadie shakes her head and laughs. Only Paige. *Only* Paige. "How long have you been holding on to that one?"

"Twelve years!" Paige exclaims. "Twelve long tortured years. It has literally been killing me."

"I'm very sorry that you had to sacrifice yourself for my sins."

"It's okay. There's nothing I wouldn't do for my Sadie." Paige reaches out and takes her hand, giving it a little squeeze.

Sadie looks toward Scarlett and shouts, "You doing okay, Scar?"

Scarlett pulls her headphones off, letting them rest around her neck. "What?"

"I was just seeing if you're doing okay with the homework. What are you working on?"

"Just reading about The Great Depression," Scarlett says. "It's like reading your diary."

"Very funny." Sadie smiles. "Probably about time to get ready for bed, right?"

Scarlett nods, puts her headphones back on, and begins to pack up her book and papers. Paige and Sadie tell her good night and she heads upstairs.

"So, what comes next?" Paige asks after a few minutes.

"I don't know." Sadie looks down at the palm of her hand as if the answer might be there. "It's complicated, of course, like everything else. We haven't talked about anything yet. With Scarlett and Emily in the picture now, it certainly adds a whole new layer of complexity."

"Sure," Paige says, "but still, it's exciting, right?"

"It is," Sadie agrees. They are both smiling again now.

"I guess we'll see how things go. You'll keep me in the loop?"

"Do I have a choice?" Sadie asks.

"No," Paige says. "You sure don't."

CHAPTER 25

I⊤'s Saturday night at around 8:30 and Sadie is lying in her bed with the cool sheet resting over her, one leg sticking out. *Well, yes,* she thinks, *it turns out I wasn't misremembering. Those tutorials really did do the job.*

Caleb lies beside her on his back, head on her spare pillow. His eyes are closed, and he is breathing a little heavily. He lets out a small sound like "mmm." He opens his eyes and turns his head toward Sadie.

"What are you thinking about?" he asks.

Sadie adjusts the sheet and stares at the ceiling. It's the old-style textured kind of ceiling with flecks of glitter in it that sparkle in the light like tiny stars. "You know when you look at old pictures in a book or newspaper or something? Like pictures with big crowds of people at a theme park or a church or, I don't know, a parade? Do you ever wonder how many people in the picture are dead now? Like, even the ones who are little kids in the photo. Sometimes all of them are likely dead if the picture is old enough." Sadie wasn't thinking about this right now, of course, but she does think about it a lot. It is a small lie, but a necessary one.

"Oh, you mean like in that new Death Cab for Cutie song."

Sadie turns to face Caleb. "I don't think I know it."

"It has a lyric about watching old movies and thinking about how all the actors are dead now."

"Well, yeah." Sadie returns her gaze to the stars on the ceiling. "I guess it is exactly like that then."

"You sound disappointed."

"I just thought maybe I'd had an original thought, but I guess not," Sadie says flatly.

"At least you're on the same page with the Death Cab folks!"

"Super," Sadie says sarcastically. She picks up her phone from the bedside table and checks the time. This isn't like those leisurely mornings twelve years ago when they could stay in bed all day. Scarlett and Kaylee are babysitting Emily again at Caleb's house and Sadie and Caleb have taken the opportunity to, well, reconnect more deeply for the first time. "Anyway, we should probably be getting ready to head back. I'm going to shower off."

"Okay." Caleb turns toward her and kisses her softly on the lips. "I'll be here."

In the shower, Sadie wonders if anything they are doing makes any sense. The hot water releases the tension in her body, but it can't touch the thoughts inside her head. Is she just setting herself up for the same heartbreak? Will she make the same mistakes she made twelve years ago? Run away at the first sign of adversity or conflict. Sabotage herself to make sure she never has the nauseatingly picture-perfect relationship her parents have. She runs her hands through her wet hair, closing her eyes as the jets of hot water massage her scalp. She tries to convince herself that love's a disaster sometimes, but not always. Even if it's the same love, it doesn't have to end the same way.

...

Does it?

...

But is this love between Caleb and Sadie, the love that is unfolding right now, the same love? The people are the same, yes, but then again, they're not. People change and evolve in big ways and small ways. In twelve years, most of the cells that make up their skin and bones have been replaced. Even the cells that make up their hearts are new, different. When they hold hands or kiss or run a finger along the other's wrist, they aren't touching the same cells they touched more than a decade ago. The basic biological material that makes up their bodies is different. So, is their love one continuous love that was placed on pause, that broke off for an intermission? Or is it two separate and distinct loves? Does it even matter? Maybe every morning when we wake up, we decide without even knowing it that we are going to love our person or our people again today. Whether we've been together fifty years or fifty hours, still, we create a new love every morning when we open our eyes. We start fresh. Maybe it's not a conscious choice, but rather, it's automatic. Like a heartbeat.

...

Thump, thump, thump.

...

The next morning, Sadie wakes up feeling determined. Many mornings after eventful nights, she feels untethered, unsure if she's dreaming or awake. It often takes her extra time to get her bearings so she can face a bright new day. But today is different. Today, she is ready to take the proverbial bull by the horns. When she was twenty-one, starting a new relationship was easy. There was no one to worry about except herself. She didn't have to take into consideration how a heartbreak or a misunderstanding could affect other people. But now, things are much more complicated. Primarily because of the existence of a daughter she loves more than the world. A daughter who is on the verge of adolescence and who has taken an unusually keen interest in Sadie's love life the past few weeks. Scarlett probably thinks she has been incredibly stealthy, but Sadie has noticed. Moms always do. And moms always protect their children first, even before they protect themselves. It's relatively easy when the children are babies. Sadie remembers how she held Scarlett close on those interminably long nights during that first year. Even when she felt too tired to move, her body served as a physical barrier, protecting Scarlett from a big scary world. She could hear that world from inside her apartment–the constant whir of traffic, the honking horns, the pulsing music from the downstairs neighbor–but it somehow felt like it was all a million miles away. When she held little Scarlett against her, she knew they were both safe. But now, it's not just Scarlett's body she has to protect, it's her heart, too. And that's a lot harder to manage.

So yes, Sadie is on a mission this morning. She has devised an experiment that will help her determine whether whatever is happening between her and Caleb is real, lasting, solid. It has to be. If she's going to move forward, she has to be as sure as she can be that it's not going to end in disaster. Because this time it's not just her heart on the line, but Scarlett's too. And that's what matters most. Sadie has hidden her heart away for so long that it can't be hurt, not really. No matter what happens, she'll be okay. It's her daughter she has to protect. At least, that's the story she tells herself. It's important to have a story like this, whether it's truth or fiction.

Before she gets out of bed, Sadie reaches for her phone and quickly types a message to Caleb, asking him a question about his plans for today. Her plan is a simple one. It involves two parents, one peacock, and an extremely distinctive suit of armor. The plan is bulletproof. And probably swordproof, too. If that's a thing.

...

Sadie thinks if Caleb can withstand the intensity of her parents, anything is possible. If he isn't scared off by their extraness or put off by their probing questions, maybe there's hope for this second-chance love affair. It will certainly be an interesting social experiment. And if she can rid herself of a monstrous conglomeration of metal while figuring out if her burgeoning relationship is real or imagined? Well, that's just a little added bonus.

When Sadie texts Caleb, he quickly replies that he doesn't have any plans for today. She then asks if he would be able to help her with something. He says sure, no problem. He also might've added

anything for M'lady

but there's no need to get into all that.

Then Sadie proceeds to lay everything out in the open. She tells Caleb that she wants to put on a little exhibition for her parents involving the suit of armor her dad made. She and Scarlett will need help transporting it, so it's best that they drive together from Sadie's house to her parents' place. Then Caleb and Sadie can do their thing with the swords and such in her parents' yard. She says her parents will be thrilled. She also mentions casually that a peacock might be present, and her parents might want them to take pictures with it, but she doesn't provide a deep dive into the backstory. There's only so much one can convey about Instagram-famous peacocks via text message without coming off as deranged.

After Sadie's voluminous text messages, Caleb replies breezily that it sounds like fun, and he is up for it. Well, Sadie assumes that his reply was breezy, but tone is very difficult to determine over text. She imagines him skimming through her messages while pouring cereal for Emily. Perhaps he takes a sip of coffee and smiles before answering.

...

"Why are we doing this?" Scarlett asks. She is standing in the doorway to her room, hands on her hips.

"Because your grandparents will love it," Sadie says. "It will make their entire year."

"And why is Caleb coming?" Scarlett looks away from her mom when she says this. She could be stifling a smile, but it's hard to say.

"Well, we need help getting that thing in the car. And you'll need someone to joust with or whatever."

"Spar with," Scarlett says flatly.

"Right, that's it." The doorbell rings. "Ah, there they are."

Sadie opens the door and greets Caleb with meaningful eye contact, a warm smile, and nothing more. Emily trails behind him, unusually subdued, perhaps because of the new and unfamiliar setting. She says hi to Sadie but remains close to Caleb, holding his hand and positioning herself mostly behind his body.

"The, uh, items in question are in Scarlett's room," Sadie says, gesturing toward the bedroom door. "Scarlett, Caleb is coming your way." There is no response as Caleb heads toward the bedroom. Sadie hears him greet Scarlett and then make a sound that indicates surprise.

"Do you have a cat?" Emily asks. She has remained behind, lingering in the entryway.

"No," Sadie says. "No pets, I'm afraid."

Emily looks disappointed but doesn't say anything else. Meanwhile, a clatter of metal arises from the direction of the bedroom and Caleb emerges clutching a helmet with both arms, hugging it to his chest like a watermelon.

"You weren't kidding," Caleb says to Sadie. "Your parents don't mess around. I'm not sure a nuclear bomb could penetrate this."

After Caleb takes the helmet out to the car, he returns, and together with Sadie and Scarlett, they maneuver the body armor out the door and into the trunk of Sadie's car.

"Okay," Caleb says, dusting off his hands. "You can wear the helmet, Scarlett, and I'll somehow wear the body armor." Everyone laughs like this is a funny joke even though they all know it is the actual plan.

...

When they arrive at Jess and Tom's house, Sadie parks on the street. They've driven only one car to make their arrival less conspicuous. Caleb rode next to Sadie in the passenger seat with Emily and Scarlett in the back.

Sadie turns off the car. "Okay. Caleb and Scarlett, get ready. I'll go up and distract my parents. Emily, you keep a lookout for the peacock."

"Peacock?" Emily says.

"Yes," Sadie replies, "there should be a peacock around here somewhere. He's very famous." Emily looks excited and perhaps a bit overwhelmed at the possibility of spotting a famous fowl. "When you're ready for the exhibition," Sadie continues, "send Emily up to ring the doorbell."

"Got it," Caleb says.

Sadie walks quickly up to the door, knocks, and goes inside. "Mom, Dad, anyone home?" She hears the door to the garage open and close and then footsteps coming in her direction.

"Oh, hi Sadie!" Jess comes out of the kitchen with Tom close behind her. "This is a nice surprise!"

"We were just cleaning up the garage," Tom says, brushing the sleeves of his shirt as if he is trying to remove lint. "Lots of feathers out there."

"Feathers? You didn't have the peacock in the garage, did you?"

"Err, maybe?"

"We did," Jess says in a matter-of-fact tone. "We had an idea for a photo shoot for Preston to celebrate National Peacock Day. That's not for another ten months, but we want to get the backdrop just right, so we figured we better start early."

"Early bird gets the worm, as they say!" Tom adds helpfully. "Anyway, nothing to worry about. Preston got a little flustered and tried to claw our eyes out, but it's fine now. He's in the backyard relaxing."

"Well, I'm glad he's okay," Sadie says.

"Yes, yes," Jess says. "What brings you here, Sadie? It's great to see you!"

"Actually, I have a bit of a surprise for you. I think you're going to like it." Tom and Jess make an "oooh" noise at the same time, then look at each other and laugh. "Let me check and see if it's almost ready."

Sadie walks to the front window of the house and peeks out between the blinds. Emily is crouched down in the yard, examining something in the grass. A person she assumes is Scarlett is standing nearby with the giant helmet on her head, the long peacock feather sticking up from the top and then looping down comically to brush against Scarlett's shoulder. Scarlett is leaning a bit to one side, clutching her sword in the opposite hand, but she is upright which is all that matters. Caleb stands beside the car, doubled over, using his sword as a crutch. He has managed to wriggle into the body armor, but it is clearly weighing him down. And from the way he appears to be gasping for air, it might also be squeezing him like a boa constrictor. Sadie sees him raise an arm languidly and say something to Emily. She hops up and runs toward the front door. "Okay, I think it's ready." Sadie turns away from the window as the doorbell rings.

Opening the door, Sadie steps outside, beckoning for her parents to follow her. "This is Emily," she says to Jess and Tom. "I'll explain who she is in a minute. Emily, these are Scarlett's grandparents." Emily gives them an admiring look, grateful to be in the presence of the grandparents of a legend.

"Wow, what do we have here?" Jess exclaims, her eyes lighting up as she catches sight of the warriors preparing to do battle in the front yard.

Scarlett and Caleb spring into action. They cross swords and begin to spar. Their blades clash and the sound reverberates down the quiet suburban street. They both remain mostly fixed in one spot, unable to move much for fear of toppling over sideways. After a minute or two, Caleb allows Scarlett to land a forceful blow on the side of his torso. The sword clangs against the metal armor and Caleb flops down onto the ground dramatically. It sounds like a metal trash can being kicked over.

"Amazing!" Tom shouts, applauding loudly. "Way to go, Scarlett!"

"You really scarred 'em!" Jess adds. Tom gives her a light punch on the shoulder, congratulating her for the successful callback. Sadie rolls her eyes and smiles.

Scarlett kneels down and carefully removes her helmet, letting it fall to the grass. Caleb manages to roll over onto his stomach and with a little help from Scarlett, wriggles free of the armor, leaving it behind like a snake shedding its skin. He hops up, runs a hand through his hair, and exhales deeply before striding confidently toward Sadie and her parents.

"Hello, Mr. and Mrs. Warren," Caleb says with a big smile. He shakes both their hands. "I'm Caleb!"

"Call us Tom and Jess, please," Tom says. "I'm Jess and she's Tom." Tom and Jess both laugh and Caleb joins in.

"He's such a jokester," Jess says, swatting Tom on the arm. "Do we know you, Caleb? You look very familiar... and handsome." She says the last part in a softer voice, looking at Sadie and raising her eyebrows.

"Mom, please," Sadie says. "Caleb and I used to date back when we were in college. I'm sure you probably met him once or twice."

"That's right!" Tom says, recognition in his eyes now. "Sadie did always like to keep her dating life a secret, so I guess we didn't see too much of you."

"No, probably not. But maybe we'll get to know each other better this time around." Caleb looks toward Sadie, and they share a brief but meaningful look. The conversation moves on from there, but Sadie barely notices. Her plan has succeeded. This little exchange, a special look, and the words "this time around" were all she needed. It isn't proof of anything, but she believes it's enough for now. She feels safe and confident that she can trust her instincts moving forward. Caleb is as charming as ever and he has Sadie's parents eating out of his hand within minutes. Sadie notes this, which reminds her about the last part of her plan.

"Hey," she says to get everyone's attention. "Why don't we see if Preston is around so we can get some pictures? I'm sure Emily would love to see a peacock up close, and, Mom and Dad, I bet you could do something fun with a medieval theme for Preston's next Instagram post?"

"Sadie," Jess grabs Sadie's wrist and looks straight into her eyes, "you read my mind!" She walks off briskly, heading around the house to the backyard.

Sadie moves to position the armor and helmet in a slightly more attractive arrangement. While she struggles with the helmet, she says, "How is this so heavy?"

"Yeah, it's solid, all right," Tom says happily. "Caleb, you'll appreciate this. I took an old football helmet, removed the facemask, and then just layered the heck out of it with papier mache. I mean, I just went to town. Then I let that dry for a few days and covered it up with some scrap metal. Pretty great, right?"

Caleb smiles politely. "That's one way to do it for sure."

"Why in the world did you do that?" Sadie asks. "It seems like the most unnecessarily complicated and unwieldy way to make..." She catches herself. It's not the time for this. Stick to the plan. "Never mind, it's great, Dad," she regains her footing. "Brilliantly executed."

"Thanks!" Tom says.

Emily lets out a shriek as a peacock flutters down and lands on the lawn about ten feet away, seemingly coming from out of nowhere. She scampers over and hides behind Caleb.

"Ah, there he is!" Tom enthuses as Jess comes trotting back around the house carrying a broom.

"He's a little stubborn today," Jess says, a little out of breath. "Maybe because of the photo shoot earlier, but I'm sure he has one more left in him!"

While her parents are fussing about, trying to cajole Preston in various directions, Sadie sneaks over to the armor and takes a small plastic bag out of her pocket. She quickly dumps the contents into the armor and on the ground around it before shoving the empty bag back into her pocket and moving away. Almost immediately, Preston ambles over to the pile of armor and begins pecking at the grass around it. Then he sticks his head all the way inside and remains that way for several moments.

"Would you look at that," Tom says. "Is Preston a bit of a medievalphile?"

"Or a narcissist," Sadie says flatly. "His feather is right there."

"Either way," Jess enthuses, "it's time for some pictures!"

Jess flits about, arranging everyone around Preston as he continues to peck away unperturbed. When Caleb, Sadie, Emily, and Scarlet are all in position, Tom raises his phone, and Jess emits a guttural gobbling cry that makes all humans present except Tom jump. Preston raises his head calmly in response and turns his head toward Tom. Tom snaps several pictures.

"There we go!" Jess says lightly, as if she hasn't just produced a sound that would unnerve a mob of zombies. "Those will turn out great! Preston's fans will be so happy!"

"Mom, Dad," Sadie says as the members of the small group drop their poses and begin to move around again, "it looks like Preston really loves this armor. As much as we'd hate to lose it, maybe you should keep it for him. Kind of like a yard ornament slash peacock palace. We'd be willing to part with it for Preston's sake, right, Scarlett?"

Scarlett has lost interest in the entire outing at this point. "Uh, yeah sure."

"Well, if you don't mind," Tom says.

"Sounds great," Jess adds. "It's so strange that Preston seems to have fallen in love with it so quickly, but sometimes when you know, you know." She gives Sadie a little wink.

CHAPTER 26

In the car on the way back to Sadie's house, Caleb rests his hand on the center console in close proximity to Sadie's hand, which is resting casually on the gear shift. Emily is talking voluminously about the peacock. She didn't have much to say at Jess and Tom's house, but now that she's surrounded only by familiar people, she is trying to catch up. Caleb wonders if maybe she has a daily spoken word count, she has to hit or otherwise she'll explode like that bus in the old movie that has to go a certain speed. He liked that movie. Well, he liked the idea of that movie. He's actually not sure if he ever saw it or if he's just heard it referenced so many times that he feels like he's seen it.

While Emily talks, Caleb drops in the occasional "oh yeah?" or "uh-huh" to prove that he's listening. He then moves his hand a few more inches to the left, closing the distance between his hand and Sadie's. He runs a finger along the back of her hand, tracing a vein, then leaves his hand on top of hers. He tries to stop himself from thinking about the possibility that this could be his entire life. The four people sitting in the car right now could be his family.

Well, it's complicated, of course. Isn't it always? Particularly when it comes to Emily's situation, which always seems like it could change at any second. He shakes his head subtly and stares out the window. Emily is still talking, but he is focused more on the scenery passing by. Calling it scenery is a bit much, perhaps, but the medical offices with gleaming mirrored windows, the giant Walmart the size of some small countries, and the inexplicably large number of car washes that dot the side of the road are the scenery he has to work with in this place he calls home. It feels comfortingly familiar. He could get used to this. All of this.

Sadie spins the steering wheel hard like a sea captain steering a boat, whipping the car across two lanes of oncoming traffic and into Caleb's driveway. "Wow, you're getting good at that," he says as the car bumps to a stop.

"Thanks." Sadie smiles as she puts the car in park. "I'm getting a little more used to it, I guess. It's still complete madness that you live here, though."

Caleb gives her hand a little squeeze. "Do you want to come in?"

"I do," Sadie says quietly, "but we should probably be getting home. Scarlett tends to spoil like milk left out on the counter if she's away from her bedroom for too long."

"Hey!" Scarlett exclaims from the back seat.

"Wow, good ears, Scar. That music you blast all the time hasn't killed your hearing yet, I guess." Sadie pauses for a moment. "God, am I really turning into my parents?"

Caleb laughs. "No, I don't think it's possible for anyone to turn into your parents!"

"You're probably right," Sadie agrees. "But thanks again for doing this. It really did make their day."

"No problem! And nice move with the bird seed by the way. Very smooth," Caleb says.

"You noticed, huh?"

"Well, it wasn't *that* smooth."

"But smooth enough to get the job done." Sadie taps the steering wheel for emphasis.

Caleb opens the car door. "All right, Emily, let's go. We'll see Scarlett and Sadie again soon."

. . .

...

After Caleb and Emily wave goodbye as Sadie and Scarlett pull out of the driveway, they head inside to do—well, Caleb isn't sure what they will do now. It is the eternal question for parents and pseudo-parents of small children. This question is second in urgency and ubiquity only to "what's for dinner?"

"What are we going to do now?" Emily says as Caleb walks into the kitchen and begins to shuffle papers and other miscellaneous items around on the counter. Right on cue.

"Uh, well, we just did a lot of things," Caleb says, "so why don't we just rest for a bit."

"No," Emily says flatly. "Play with me!"

Caleb sighs. He doesn't remember his dad sighing so much, but he thinks that maybe he just didn't notice because he was a kid at the time. Kids aren't great at noticing things or remembering. Caleb doesn't know if that's true, but he hopes it is. Then maybe Emily won't remember him being constantly exasperated and disengaged when he's supposed to be playing with her. As he is mustering the mental energy to embark on another session of doll play, Caleb hears a car pull into the driveway and a car door open and shut. Oh, Sadie must be back, he thinks. Maybe she forgot something? Whatever it is, it's a welcome distraction. It should fill at least two to three minutes of the expansive wasteland of time that is this day.

There's a knock on the door. *Thump, thump, thump.*

Caleb opens it. It's not Sadie.

...

. . .

Back at the townhouse with the picturesque view of the murky alligator pond, Sadie washes some dirty dishes that had been abandoned in the sink earlier in the day. Scarlett is lingering in her general vicinity instead of retreating to her hibernation cave upstairs. It's very unusual behavior, Sadie thinks. She must want something.

"Have you checked on Jess and Tom's favorite, um, peacock yet?" Sadie asks while scrubbing a rectangular baking sheet with a brush.

"Mom," Scarlett says in an exasperated tone.

"We have to joke about these things, Scar, it's the only way. You can't choose your grandparents, but you can make fun of them.".

"Since they are your parents, I guess that goes for parents, too," Scarlett retorts.

Sadie considers that. "Hmm, no. Only my parents, and thus, your grandparents are fair game for ridicule. That's clearly stated in the rule book. Look it up if you don't believe me."

Scarlett rolls her eyes. She looks down at her phone, studying her Instagram feed. "It has nine thousand likes so far," she says flatly.

Sadie shakes her head. "There is no hope for this world. What caption did they go with this time?"

Scarlett looks back at her phone and reads the caption aloud. "Preston the Prince returns from ravaging an enemy kingdom to spend time with his..." she pauses before saying in a softer voice, "family."

"Very profound one today." Sadie places a plate in the dishwasher.

"Is that what we are now?" Scarlett asks.

Sadie turns toward Scarlett and sees confusion and maybe a flicker of hope in her blue eyes. "Are we a family? No, I wouldn't say that, Scar. I mean, Caleb and I are, um, seeing each other again? But I think you knew that already."

Scarlett doesn't say anything. She returns her attention to her phone and starts scrolling. Sadie pauses to gather her thoughts. Her little experiment produced the outcome she was hoping for. Caleb seemed cool with the intensity of her parents and relaxed. Almost eager. Like he had been ready to integrate himself into her world and was just waiting for an opportunity. Things can change quickly, of course, but she didn't see any signs that Caleb was getting cold feet or searching for an exit ramp. She was feeling hopeful. Still cautious, but hopeful.

"Family can be complicated sometimes. Well, when it comes to us, I think it's always complicated. Even when it feels like it shouldn't be."

...

When Caleb opens the door, his heart immediately drops into his stomach. He stands face-to-face with his sister. Smiling back at him shyly, she reaches up and sweeps her bangs off to one side with one hand, then looks into Caleb's eyes. "Hi."

Lauren looks... good, almost normal, Caleb thinks. Her eyes don't look vacant like they often have in the past when she's shown up at his door. She's not fidgety. She stands on his front step calmly, almost like she's returning to pick up Emily after leaving her with Caleb for an hour or so while she went to Target. If she had a Starbucks cup in her hand, she could easily pass for your average suburban mom. She has dark brown hair with maybe a tinge of red in it and a kind-looking face that always reminds Caleb of his dad. She isn't as thin as she sometimes is. She looks healthy.

"Hi, Lauren." Caleb steps forward and wraps his arms around his big sister. He's about five inches taller so the top of her head only reaches his shoulder when they hug. "You're here," he says as he moves back into the house and gestures for Lauren to follow. Caleb knows this is a weird thing to say, but it is a weird situation, after all. His empty words fill the empty space.

"Yeah, um, sorry," Lauren says haltingly. "I would've called or something, but I had to get a new phone and I lost all my contacts."

"Right." Caleb's eyes scanning the room quickly. Emily is nowhere in sight. "Uh, should I get Emily." He lowers his voice. "Or do you want to–"

Emily rushes into the room at this point, making the attempt at subterfuge moot. The house is quite small, so it was pretty much inevitable.

"Mommy?" Emily says softly when she catches sight of Lauren who is standing in the living room area, idly examining some of Emily's scattered toys.

"Baby!" Lauren says in response, reaching out her arms.

Emily hesitates for a moment, looking toward Caleb who gives her a small nod. Then, she launches herself at Lauren. They end up in a thunderous hug. Emily closes her eyes tight and takes a deep breath in through her nose, determined to consume her mother's smell as well as her touch. Caleb turns away. He's surprised to find that his eyes are wet. There are literal tears in there. Weird. He wipes them away with the back of his hand and walks over to the kitchen to act busy.

"Are you back?" Emily asks Lauren, finally releasing her from the hug.

"Yes, baby. I'm back," Lauren says.

"You were gone so long! I'm almost done with kindergarten!"

"I know, sweetie, I'm sorry." Lauren hesitates, looking toward Caleb, who is moving glasses from the dishwasher into the cupboard. "I had to take care of some things, but I'm here now. I *really* missed you."

Emily looks at Lauren, and Caleb can still see the confusion in her eyes. People say kids are resilient. That they can adapt to anything. Whether that's a good thing or bad thing is an open question. Caleb knows that as well as anyone.

When his dad died, Caleb cried for a day and a half. The tears came like sheets of rain during a thunderstorm. He stayed curled up in his bed all weekend, ignoring everyone. He cried and wiped the snot on his sheets and then pressed his face into the comforter where his dad had sat on Friday night. He could still smell him. Wood shavings and freshly mown grass. Then, on Monday, he went back to school. Helen would have it no other way. What is life, after all, without our routines? Helen had always relied on her routines to keep her moving forward, but when Luke died, it was like her commitment to order was dialed up to a thousand. She had to get back to work. The kids had to get back to school. Without routine she would crumble. Everything would fall apart.

The other students gave Caleb a wide berth, as if losing a parent might be contagious. He didn't cry at school. As quickly and ferociously as the tears came, they left. It was like one moment they were there and the next they were gone.

Kids are resilient. They can adapt to anything. But they shouldn't have to.

Caleb's phone buzzes a couple times in his pocket. He takes it out and sees incoming text messages from Sadie. He leaves them unopened and places his phone face down on the kitchen counter.

"Do we have to move back home?" Emily asks. Caleb isn't sure where home is exactly, but he's interested to hear Lauren's answer.

"Well." Lauren takes a deep breath. "I think we'll probably stay around here at least for a little while and then we'll see how things go. We'll talk to Caleb and your grandmother about all that, but why don't you show me your dolls first!" She gestures toward the dollhouse in the corner of the room where several dolls in various states of undress are lounging about like college students after a raucous sorority party. Caleb exhales, his back still turned, busying himself at the kitchen sink, turning the water on and off randomly.

Caleb turns and watches Lauren and Emily playing. They are both fully invested now. Emily's initial hesitance has begun to wear off. They laugh and carry on like the previous however many months never happened. He can immediately tell that Lauren is good at this. Good at playing, good at make-believe. It makes him a little angry. Not angry at Lauren so much as angry at the universe. She would be such a good mom if it weren't for everything else that gets in the way. She is fun. She is full of life. She is his dad. She always has been. That's probably why she tried so hard to push their dad away so violently when she was a teenager. We are always our own worst enemies.

But since these two sides of Lauren are here under this roof right now—the happy, caring, and fun side that Emily sees and the dark and unpredictable side that lurks beneath—where does that leave Caleb? And more importantly, he thinks while leafing through a pile of unopened mail that has built up on the kitchen counter over the course of the week, where does that leave Emily?

Caleb checks his phone again. He runs a hand through his hair as he stares at the screen, examining the most recent message from Sadie:

> Thanks again for today. Maybe Scarlett can babysit next weekend so we can…you know?

What is he supposed to say to that? How is he supposed to make plans now when his whole life has been turned upside down in a matter of minutes? As much as he'd like to have someone he could pass the weight of this moment to, he just can't make himself do it. Not yet. Yeah, he and Sadie talked about sharing the weight before but that was in a different lifetime. So much has happened since those days when forever seemed possible. They've reconnected now, and it's been perfect, but the rest of Caleb's life? It's so far from perfect. Caleb swipes the message away and wipes another tear from his cheek. Then he texts his mom.

…

. . .

Helen is at Caleb's house now. She sits at the dining table, her back extremely straight, not touching the back of the chair. Holding chopsticks in her right hand, she adroitly picks tiny pieces of onion out of the lo mein noodles and drops them into a small pile on the edge of her plate. "Onions," she grumbles under her breath with a mildly disgusted look on her face. "Nasty vegetable."

Caleb ordered Chinese delivery and invited his mother over so they could talk with Lauren about what the plan was for her, Emily, and everyone involved. He sits at the other end of the table, picking up pieces of fried chicken with chopsticks and dipping them in red and sticky sweet and sour sauce.

"You still eat like a little kid," Lauren says from her seat between her mom and Caleb. Emily is watching TV, having already eaten three bites of nothing.

"Well, when in Rome or whatever." Caleb waves a hand toward Emily without looking up from his food. "So, can we talk now? I think she's pretty occupied at the moment." He cuts his eyes toward Emily.

Lauren pushes rice around on her plate with a fork. "Okay." She doesn't say anything more and Helen shows no signs of jumping in, so Caleb assumes he has to get the ball rolling.

"So, I'm guessing you finished your rehab program?" he asks.

"Kind of." Lauren stares straight ahead at the wall instead of looking at any of the other people present.

"Hmm," Helen says, lifting onion-free lo mein to her mouth.

"And what does 'kind of' mean?" Caleb asks.

"You know how those things are," Lauren begins. Caleb and his mom do know, much too well. "They just drag on and on. It becomes a money-making thing at some point. They just want to keep you there forever even when you're already better."

"Okay." Caleb lays his chopsticks down on his plate and runs his hand through his hair. "So, you *are* better then?"

"Yes, absolutely," Lauren says confidently. "I wouldn't be here if I wasn't. I wouldn't put Emily through that."

Caleb wants to believe this. He wants to believe this more than anything in the world. If a genie popped out of a lamp right now and granted him just one wish, his wish would be that what Lauren just said would end up being true. He wouldn't even hesitate. He doesn't know how many times he's wished for this without the genie, but it has to be in the hundreds by now. "But you'll stay here," Caleb says. "At least until school gets out for the year? I'm not going to tell you what to do, but that makes the most sense to me. I think it would be best for Emily."

"Yes, definitely," Lauren says. "Maybe we can stay with Mom... or I can stay with Mom and Emily can continue to stay here? Whatever works best for everyone."

Caleb looks toward his mother, and she looks back at him. She gives a little shrug.

"Why don't you just stay here," Caleb says after a moment. "It would probably be easiest for everyone."

Helen looks relieved but doesn't say anything.

Lauren nods. "Okay," she says, smiling. "Sounds like a plan."

CHAPTER 27

Sadie always wondered what being ghosted would feel like, and now she thinks she is finally finding out. It's Thursday and she hasn't heard anything from Caleb since last weekend. No texts, no calls, no nothing. This wouldn't necessarily be that unusual; they hadn't been back together long enough to establish any communication patterns or protocols, if they were even together at all really, but the fact that Caleb stopped communicating and responding immediately after Sadie's experiment with her parents can't be coincidental. It certainly feels like ghosting.

Of course, Sadie knows what it's like to be on the other side of a ghosting operation. All the signs do seem pretty familiar. She doesn't understand it, but she guesses that's exactly how Caleb felt a dozen years ago. She remembers the text messages she left unanswered. The calls she sent to voicemail. The time before she skipped town for good when Caleb knocked on her door and she sat on the floor in her tiny kitchen, hiding, silent tears streaming down her face. She can still almost feel the cool stickiness of the linoleum against the backs of her legs.

Her confusion is exacerbated by the fact that she felt like everything went so well at her parents' house. Caleb even put his hand on hers on the car ride home, but maybe that was just his way of saying goodbye. Or maybe he got cold feet afterwards. Perhaps their history was just too much to get past.

Scarlett is at school and Sadie doesn't have lessons to teach until the afternoon, so she takes out her guitar and starts strumming randomly. She thinks about her new student Bryn, the little girl with the penetrating eyes and calculating demeanor, and she remembers she promised to practice a song to play for her at the next lesson. After a few minutes, she falls into playing "The Middle" by Jimmy Eat World. It used to be one of her favorite songs to play at her coffee shop gigs. Like many girls of Sadie's particular style and worldview, she always felt like the song was about her. And even though she is trending more toward the middle-aged portion of the ride now, she still loves the song. She plays it now in her empty townhouse as a proper grown-up, singing along softly.

After a verse and a chorus, she stops and laughs to herself. This is all so silly, she thinks. Here she is, the mother of an almost teenager, a career woman, sitting around being emo, waiting for a boy to call her. Maybe she should just get a cat and be done with all of the nonsense. She strums a few chords from "Love's a Disaster" and laughs to herself again. It sure is, she thinks.

...

Sadie showers, gets dressed, and begins to make herself a late breakfast. She closes the blinds on the kitchen window to block out the intense morning sun. As she takes a small plate out of the cabinet and retrieves a butter knife from the drawer, she thinks that perhaps her little experiment with Caleb and her parents and the peacock was a success after all. Not only did she get rid of the hideous armor, a huge win, but she also determined that this was all too much or too fast for Caleb. It's not the answer she wanted, but it is an answer. And she accomplished her primary mission: protecting Scarlett. It would've been much worse for everyone if they had gotten months or years down the road before finding out that it wasn't going to work.

Sadie is finding a bit of closure in this kitchen, and as she places a bagel in the toaster and pops the lid off a container of cream cheese, she suddenly feels the urge to make a new beginning. Well, more like a *new* new beginning. Moving to Florida and changing careers was definitely a new beginning, but it never felt like one she was fully in control of. It was a responsive move. She was playing defense. Against what exactly, she still doesn't know. But whatever the reasons, she has been suppressing a big part of herself in the name of family and fulfilling expectations and being who she is supposed to be. And then Caleb reappeared, and he seemed like a life raft back to her authentic self. The real Sadie was waiting.

Sadie scoops a couple globs of cream cheese out of the container with a knife and smears them on the toasted bagel halves. The real Sadie *is* waiting, but no one else can find her. Only Sadie can. She realizes this before her first bite of bagel. And she knows what she has to do. She texts her mom and asks if Scarlett can hang out with them for a couple hours tonight. Her mom quickly replies **yes** with multiple exclamation points after it.

...

Later that evening, after dropping Scarlett off at her parents' house, Sadie stands alone on a train station platform holding a guitar case. The small train station is entirely outdoors with tall white metal canopies flanking each side of the train tracks. There are several automated ticket purchasing stations and small futuristic-looking ticket validators where riders scan their tickets when getting on or off the train. Sadie stands alone on the platform because there are literally no other people at the station. It is an extremely humid evening, and the sun beats down, making the air above the train tracks shimmer. Sadie reviews the train schedule and purchases a ticket from the machine. She notices that one of the stations at the end of the Southbound line of the commuter train is called Tupperware. She is tempted to scrap her plans and see if there is some magical land of plastic that she's never heard of or if perhaps Disney World has rebranded, but she resists and buys a ticket to her planned destination. She sits down on a black metal bench and stares across the train tracks at a barbecue restaurant. There is a large sign with a neon pig on it. Or rather, three neon pigs that light up in sequence to make it look like one pig is leaping or running. To or from its death, presumably. Sadie thinks the sign is demented, but kind of in a fun way, which pretty much encapsulates the Central Florida vibe.

Sadie had decided what she needed was a dose of public transportation to boost her energy level. Of course, public transportation options being a bit sparser than they are in New York City, Sadie had to drive several miles to the train station beside the demented barbecue restaurant and park in a sprawling and empty parking lot. It was, admittedly, inconvenient, but the point of the ordeal was to ride the train, to be around people, to feel the energy of the city. Unfortunately, as it turns out, there are no people heading toward Orlando from the suburbs late on a Thursday afternoon. It's still nice to be out, Sadie thinks. A few minutes later, the bells at the nearby railroad crossing begin to ring and the small white and yellow train with an upstairs and downstairs pulls into the station, horn blaring. Sadie gets on and decides to lug her guitar up the narrow staircase so she can sit on the top level and get the full experience. There are a few other people on the train. All of them look either very depressed or very confused, as if they are sad their lives turned out this way or perplexed about how they got here.

The train ride is uneventful and relatively short. Sadie's destination is only four stops away from where she started. She steps out of the train into what feels like a different part of the world. Instead of endless parking lots and gas stations, there is an expanse of green space beside the station where people are walking, children are playing, and families are sitting and lounging on picnic blankets. It's like Georges Seurat has repainted one of his scenes, but added in pastel shirts, khaki shorts, and a Spikeball game. The park is bounded on the opposite side by a cobblestone street lined with parked cars. Across the road is a neat row of shops, restaurants, wine bars, and bakeries with outdoor seating areas and handwritten placards outlining the menu options. The vibe is relaxed, but there is still a certain energy to it, Sadie thinks. This is what she needed. Now, for the more nerve-wracking part.

Sadie walks slowly along the footpath in the park, scoping things out, her guitar case in one hand hanging at her side. She watches a few small children as they climb an evergreen tree that has big sprawling branches, the lowest of which droop down and rest on the ground, exhausted. In the middle of the park, a couple of young men in gleaming polo shirts, dark sunglasses perched on the tops of their heads, toss a football back and forth. A small dog on a leash sniffs a neatly manicured shrub before its owner tugs it away. The sun is beginning to drop now; it's all but disappeared behind the low buildings, providing a break from the heat and making the scene feel more intimate. The streetlights and strings of outdoor lights that ring some of the restaurant patios blink on. After making a complete circle around the park, Sadie finds a bench in one mostly empty corner, sits down, and takes out her guitar. She leaves the case propped open at her feet, tunes the instrument quickly, and begins to play.

Sadie works her way through songs she's played thousands of times. Some songs she first started learning and practicing when she was Scarlett's age. Songs from a different lifetime. Other songs she perfected when she used to perform at coffee shops and social events during college. She sits and plays and sings and truly feels alive for one of the first times in months. Well, at least for the first time when she's been alone and not in bed with a ghost from her past. She may not have found the real Sadie yet, but it feels like the process has begun. Each chord, each note, each lyric brings her a little closer.

As Sadie transitions from a folk song to an acoustic cover of a 90s alternative rock song, a man walks up and stands about ten paces away, watching. The man has gray bushy hair and round glasses. He is wearing a tropical-looking button-up shirt that is open at the neck, navy blue shorts, and white tennis shoes–the official uniform of a Central Florida retiree. Sadie pauses in the middle of her song, sensing that the man wants to talk as men tend to do.

"Oh, don't stop on my account," he says congenially. Sadie smiles but doesn't reply. "Is everything okay?"

"What do you mean?" Sadie asks, a quizzical expression on her face.

"It's just..." The man hesitates. "You don't see a lot of people playing music around here. Just out in the park like this."

"Oh, right," Sadie says. "Well, I used to live in New York, so..."

The man raises a hand in the air like, *oh, I get it now.* "Ah, say no more. I've never understood New York people, but the music is nice, I'll give you that."

"Thanks?" Sadie replies.

"I just wanted to make sure you didn't need money or anything. Because if you did, I would've called the police."

Sadie is uneasy now, unsure if the man is joking or serious. Florida's social rules are infamously blurry and capricious.

"Just kidding," the man says jovially, laughing heartily. He looks a bit like Santa Claus on vacation now. "Hey, do you take requests?"

"Sure," Sadie replies.

"Can you play that one song about having the time of your life? I think it says something about tattoos in it?"

Sadie laughs. The man points to a tattoo on the inside of his forearm that Sadie hadn't noticed. It is a faded red heart with script lettering on it, probably a name. "My daughter loved that song." He stops and rubs his face with his hand. "She passed away a while back."

"I'm so sorry," Sadie says genuinely. "Of course I can play it. It's one of my favorites, too."

The man drops a twenty-dollar bill into Sadie's guitar case. "Thanks. It's been nice talking to you."

Sadie gestures toward the money. "You don't have to do that."

"It's all right," the man says. "If I'm being honest, you remind me of my daughter. That's why I came over here in the first place."

Sadie nods and begins to play the song about tattoos and memories. She plays gently, but with an underlying urgency, closing her eyes and singing with real emotion. She gives it everything she has. When she strums the last chord, she opens her eyes and sees that the man is standing a little farther away now. He is holding his glasses at his side in one hand, wiping a tear away from his cheek with the back of his other hand. He nods at Sadie, raises a hand, and walks away into the night.

Sadie places her guitar back in its case and pushes the lid closed. She sits on the bench for another few minutes, checking the time on her phone, trying to remember what time the Northbound train runs next. She lays her head back and looks up at the sky. It is completely dark now, inky black dotted with white pinpricks of light. She got exactly what she wanted and needed out of this night. Even if she didn't know what she wanted and needed until she found it. Isn't that always the way?

It's definitely nice to be alone sometimes, Sadie thinks. But it's also nice to return to the ones you love most. Family feels constant, all-consuming, even overbearing, but ultimately, it's temporary and ephemeral. Just like everything else. Just like *everyone* else. She rides the train back home. Well, back to her car, at least. She sits on the top level of the train again, looking out the window as smears of yellow light race by. The world outside is dark, shadowy, and chaotic from this perspective, but Sadie feels focused. Everything important is happening right in front of her, not on the periphery. She's in control. When the train pulls to a stop at her station, Sadie maneuvers the bulky guitar case along the tight aisle and down the narrow stairs. As she is moving toward the exit, she sees a man seated near the door, his head resting on his folded arms on top of the table that is situated between two sets of seats. He appears to be sleeping. She takes the twenty-dollar bill out of her pocket and places it gently on the table next to the man's elbow. She doesn't know his story, but is it possible to really know anyone's story?

Sadie steps off the train and the automatic doors thunk closed behind her. She walks to her car in the mostly empty parking lot that is flooded with artificial light, gets in, and drives toward her parents' house. She is unmistakably back in suburbia now with the strip malls and fast-food restaurants and pawn shops. But she's heading toward Scarlett. Toward family. Toward home. And that's all that matters at the moment.

CHAPTER 28

CALEB IS PLAYING hopscotch on the driveway with Emily and he is worried. He's not worried about the game, to be clear. It's actually quite easy. He let Emily draw the squares with pink and purple sidewalk chalk, and while they are a bit crooked and cramped in some places, there are only about seven of them. Caleb has above-average leg strength and reasonably good balance for a man in his thirties. When it's his turn to navigate the hopscotch board, he does it effortlessly, sometimes even adding little flourishes like pirouettes. Emily hates when he does this and makes him start over. The game is nothing to worry about and it keeps Emily occupied for an unexpectedly long time. But Lauren... well, Lauren is much more complicated. People do tend to be more complicated than hopscotch, Caleb thinks. Especially sisters.

Caleb is also feeling anxious, and to be honest, a touch devastated. His inability to communicate with Sadie is already taking a toll. He feels terrible that he hasn't responded to her messages, but he just can't make himself do it. This clawing worry about Lauren, and by association, Emily, won't let go of him. Not even for a few minutes. It has won the King of the Mountain game and staked out its place at the top of the heap of misery inside Caleb's brain.

Things went relatively okay for about a day after Lauren's surprise arrival. By now, Caleb is used to Lauren popping in and out of his life seemingly at random. At least that's what he tells himself. It's important to have a story that offers comfort, whether the story is truth or fiction. The reality is you never get used to it. Every appearance and inevitable disappearance rips his heart out. He tries not to build up his expectations or even believe for a second that this time will be different, but he can never help himself. He wants to believe so badly. This time, yes, *this time* is the time he will finally get his sister back. This time she will overcome it all. This time he will be able to save her.

Surprisingly, Caleb isn't pretending right now, because he does know this time will be different. He's not just deluding himself. He knew it from the time he opened the door and saw his big sister's face. This time is going to be different, all right. It's going to be so much worse. It's going to be the worst heartbreak he's ever experienced. And considering Caleb's history, that's saying something.

...

The next morning, Caleb is up and out of the house early. It's Friday and he's going into the office today to make an appearance. He still has to go through the motions every now and then to appease the higher ups who quietly grumble about anyone who works from home. When the old men with stiff white shirts and even stiffer black pants say the words "work from home," it always sounds like there are air quotes specifically around the word "work."

Small puffs of white and gray clouds dot the morning sky as Caleb maneuvers through the busy streets on his way to work. Birds fly overhead in a ragged formation, like they're trying to form a V, but they're not quite executing properly. "Not your best work, birds," he says out loud in the empty car.

When he pulls into the parking lot at work and parks, Caleb checks his phone. There are one, two, three text messages from Lauren. He opens them, his eyes scanning the screen quickly. He shakes his head and hits the button on the side of his phone to darken the screen. Caleb backs his car out of the parking space. Work will have to wait. The old guys in the corner offices will have to grumble. Family comes first. That's what the company always says even if they don't mean it. But family is all Caleb's got. And now, as he drives back toward his little messed up family, he feels sorry for criticizing those birds. They were doing the best they could. Just like he is. But sometimes your best isn't enough.

...

Are you there?

Please call me.

I need you.

...

On his way back home, Caleb drives much faster than he did on the way to the office. He dials Lauren's phone number repeatedly, but it just rings and rings. As he weaves through traffic, he thinks about that night. September 3, 2010. It was the night of the failed proposal, yes, but it was much more than that. It was the night he almost lost Lauren forever. And even though he didn't lose her forever, he did lose her in a different way. Losing someone you love is painful, and the really hard part is, there are just so many varieties of loss. The pain comes in so many flavors.

...

He remembers driving frantically along the dark, empty streets, his vision still a little blurry. He flipped down the mirror on his car's sun visor after he parked in the hospital parking lot, looking at his face that was blotchy and streaked with black mascara tears. He didn't know why he even checked, as if it mattered at all what his face looked like, but ritual and routine are sometimes all we have. He wiped away the black marks as best he could with the towel that was draped across the passenger seat. He pushed a hand through his hair, making it stick up on top. He took a deep breath, got out of the car, and started walking with purpose toward the imposing hospital building with glowing windows. As he walked, he counted. *Eleven years. 132 months. 4,018 days...*

...

"I know you're upset," Caleb's dad says. He is sitting on Caleb's bed. Caleb is curled up under the covers, facing toward the wall. Luke rests his calloused hand on the lump of covers that is Caleb's body. "And that's okay. Getting upset is part of being human."

Caleb doesn't say anything, but he is listening. His dad's voice always calms him down. Caleb had an argument with his mom just before bedtime. Again. She just doesn't understand him. He's not sure if she ever will.

"Your mom loves you so much," Luke continues. "And so do I." They sit in silence for a moment. "I've got to go get your sister, okay. She should've been home by now. But I'll see you in the morning. Everything will be better then." He pats Caleb's leg through the covers. "And if you need help falling asleep, try this little trick. Think of something you're looking forward to and try to figure out how many days are left until it happens. Like, Halloween. Let's see, it's September third, so Halloween will be in about... 58 days? And then try to count how many hours or minutes or seconds."

"That sounds hard," Caleb says, rolling over to face his dad.

"It is," Luke says, "but if you practice enough, you'll get good at it. You'll be a star in math class, too." Caleb can't see his dad's face very well in the dark bedroom, but he knows his dad gave a little wink as he said those last words. "You want to know who taught me that counting trick?"

"Who?"

"Your mom. She's a pretty smart lady." Caleb rolls back over, facing the wall again. "Maybe start with an easier one. Monday you don't have school, so we can think of something fun to do. That's in two days." Luke leans forward and kisses Caleb on the side of the head. "I love you, bud. I'll see you in the morning."

After his dad leaves the room, Caleb rolls over onto his back and stares at the ceiling. *Two days? That's, uh, twenty-four plus twenty-four... 48 hours?* A few minutes later, Caleb drifts off to sleep.

...

Luke used to always count forward. Counting down to the next big day. That's what he taught Caleb to do, too. But now, it seems like Caleb is always counting backwards. It's funny how that happens.

...

Caleb pulls into the driveway, slams the gearshift forward into park, and rushes inside. As he clatters through the front door, he shouts, "Lauren? Emily?" There is no answer. The house is silent. Lauren's car is in the driveway. He walks quickly through the main room of the house to the two small bedrooms. Opening each door, he looks around, calling Lauren and Emily's names again. Nothing. He calls Lauren's phone again. Voicemail. He opens the front door and looks up and down the empty sidewalk in each direction, his heart beating fast now. *Thumpthumpthumpthumpthump.* Lauren has been increasingly erratic and secretive in the last couple of days. Caleb has heard her talking on the phone in the bedroom at all hours of the night. She's been moody, irritable, and withdrawn. And last night when Caleb asked if she was okay, she snapped at him that she was fine. Then she said she was starting to plan for her and Emily to head back up north when school got out for the summer. It was the first time she'd mentioned it and Caleb was caught off guard. He said they should talk about it some more and Lauren said there was nothing to talk about.

Back in the house, Caleb slips his phone out of his pocket and calls his mom. She answers on the third ring.

"Hey, do you know where Lauren is?"

"Yes," Helen says. "She's with me."

Caleb lets out a sigh of relief. "What happened? She texted that she needed me, but then didn't answer her phone."

"Her car wouldn't start, and she needed to get Emily to school. I picked them up," Helen says matter of factly.

"Is Lauren okay?"

"I think so," Helen replies. "Here, talk to her."

Caleb hears the scuffling of a phone being passed and then Lauren's voice saying, "Hello?"

"Hey," Caleb says. "I tried to call you back, but I couldn't get you."

"Oh, yeah," Lauren says. "I had my ringer off and then I left my phone behind in my car, I think. I was rushing around like crazy trying to figure out how to get Emily to school."

"Okay, well, I'm glad Mom could help." There's a pause and Caleb can hear his mom saying something in the background. "You're good, then?"

"Yes," Lauren says brightly. "Sorry for bothering you!"

"It's fine. I'm going to head back to work for a bit. I'll talk to you later."

"Cool, bye." The line goes dead.

Caleb stands in the kitchen still holding the phone up to his ear. He rubs his face with his other hand. Lauren seems fine now, normal. Almost like the last few days, and last night in particular, didn't happen. It's enough to drive him mad. The one thing Lauren has been exceptionally good at through the years is scaring the hell out of Caleb. She's been gone for a long time, but now she's back and she hasn't missed a beat. Caleb pounds his fist on the counter one time. It's a half-hearted gesture but he can feel the sting of the impact on the side of his hand, the vibration runs up his arm.

People can be so confusing, Caleb thinks. As he walks out the front door, the faded hopscotch design catches his eye. He smiles ruefully. So much more complicated than hopscotch.

CHAPTER 29

"So, what did you end up doing last night?" Paige asks. She is lounging on Sadie's couch again, glass of wine in hand. It's another classic PNO.

Sadie points the remote control at the TV screen and scrolls through viewing options."Oh, I took the train down to Park Avenue."

"The train?" Paige asks, confused, taking a sip of her wine. "There's a train here?"

"Yes," Sadie says patiently. "It's like a commuter thing."

"Why would anyone take the train when you could just drive?"

"I mean, based on how few people were on the train, I guess most people agree with you," Sadie replies, "but I love riding trains. And I needed to feel a little of that New York energy. I've missed it. To be clear, the train was a very poor approximation, but it's the best I could do."

"So, you drove to the train station, rode the train, and then rode it back to your car, and drove home?" Paige asks, still perplexed.

"Um, yes, that's kind of how it works."

"Sounds like quite the night, Sadie." Paige raises her wine glass in Sadie's direction. "Cheers to you!"

Sadie shakes her head and rolls her eyes. She hears Scarlett's feet on the staircase. Scarlett enters the room and walks straight to the kitchen without acknowledging anyone's presence. She opens the refrigerator door and stares inside for a few moments.

"I also played some music while I was down at the park," Sadie continues, looking at the TV now.

"Well, that's a little more interesting. I mean, not that interesting since you're single and have a practically grown-up kid." She gestures toward Scarlett, who is now unwrapping some sort of food that is covered in crinkly plastic, her headphones securely in place, covering her ears. "You could've been making some music with you know who, if you know what I mean." Paige gives Sadie a meaningful look.

"Yeah, that's unlikely at this point," Sadie says.

Paige snaps to attention. "And what is that supposed to mean?"

"It means I haven't heard from Caleb in, like, a week."

"Ohh, so that's why you were doing the music playing thing. Being sad and moody and all that. Makes sense."

"No," Sadie scoffs. "I mean, yes, a little bit. But I mainly wanted to actually play music again. Do something for myself. A guy came up to me and asked if I could play a song for him. It was sweet."

"Was he hot?" Paige asks eagerly.

"He looked a little like Santa."

"A hot Santa?"

They both laugh. Scarlett has finished eating now and moves into the living room area. She settles into a chair, keeping her eyes on her phone.

"But back to the Caleb thing." Paige looks into her wine glass as if her gaze could refill it. "You haven't talked to him at all?"

"No," Sadie says, feeling a sudden twang of sadness. She's trying her best to harden her heart, to make herself numb, but it's not working. At least not completely. "He hasn't returned my texts and I even tried to call once to make sure everything was okay. Nothing."

"That seems pretty weird, right?" Paige says. "Like, I know I haven't been on the dating scene for a while, but Caleb isn't a Tinder match you went out with once or something. You have quite a bit of history. He was with your parents last weekend. And the peacock! I saw the Insta post, it did some great numbers."

Sadie laughs and hesitates for a moment. "Yeah, I know. I agree that it's weird and it sucks, but what am I supposed to do about it? I think he's made his intentions pretty clear."

"Well, it could be anything," Paige says, searching for a silver lining. "You know how it is when you have young kids. Things get weird sometimes."

"I guess," Sadie concedes. "Or it's just too much or too fast. We are different people now, after all. It's way more complicated."

"Right, but we're always different people, aren't we? I wouldn't give up on it yet. I have an intuition."

Sadie gestures toward the empty glass in Paige's hand. "Or you've had a lot of wine."

"Yes, that could be it, too." Paige laughs. "Always the optimist, Sadie."

"You know me," Sadie says, shrugging. "But whatever. It's okay. I've made peace with it, and I'm focused on finding myself again. It's been a long few months."

At this, Scarlett sits up straighter in her chair and pulls her headphones off, letting them rest around her neck. "Mom, come on," she says flatly, looking directly at Sadie. "You're not fooling anybody."

Sadie is startled by Scarlett's interjection but she does her best to hide her surprise. "What is that supposed to mean?"

Scarlett shakes her head. It's completely obvious to anyone with half a brain, but apparently, she's the only one with at least half a brain around here. "It's obvious that you're still in love with Caleb. And just because you want to look after yourself or me or whatever, you don't have to just give up on that."

Sadie considers that for a moment. "Okay, first off, have you been listening to us every night or just right now?"

"Every night," Scarlett confirms, "I kind of tune in and out. Most of it is boring."

Paige laughs. An uproarious laugh. Fueled by wine and unbridled elation. "My girl!" she exclaims, sliding along the couch and reaching a closed fist out toward Scarlett. Scarlett tentatively touches her knuckles with Paige's.

"Well, sorry we're not more consistently entertaining," Sadie says. "But eavesdropping is kind of rude."

"It's not my fault you think I don't have ears," Scarlett says. "Or you're too old to know that headphones can be turned off."

"Back in my day," Sadie begins in an exaggerated tone. Scarlett rolls her eyes before Sadie even finishes her sentence. "We actually listened to music with our headphones. On a Walkman with a cassette tape you had to wind up sometimes when the tape broke."

"Yeah," Scarlett says. "I heard you carried a record player around with you, too. In the snow or something."

"Don't be silly," Sadie says. "I lived in Florida. It didn't snow."

The room is quiet for a few moments before Scarlett says, "You're just trying to change the subject."

"Pretty much, yeah," Sadie admits. "I don't really want to take love advice from my twelve-year-old daughter. That's too young to understand."

"But not too young to set you and Caleb back up in the first place," Scarlett says, staring at her phone again now.

"Sure," Sadie says, "that was extremely stealthy of you. You must've had the help of someone older and wiser. Twelve and a half years old, at least."

Scarlett grumbles and puts her headphones back on, securing them carefully over her ears. "I'm still right," she says, a little too loudly. "You know I am."

Sadie shakes her head. Raising daughters is all fun and games until they grow up and start turning into you, she thinks. Is Scarlett right, though? She's not sure, but she certainly can't dismiss it out of hand. Even if she would like to because taking relationship advice from your twelve-year-old daughter is something no mom wants to do. Sword Fighting club practice is tomorrow morning. Sadie guesses there's only one way to find out. She's a grown up, after all. She can stomach a little face-to-face awkwardness. It won't kill her... probably. Who knows? Maybe it will even make her stronger. And one thing is certain, Caleb will definitely be there. He would never miss a sword fighting club practice.

CHAPTER 30

"Why are you up so early?" Lauren complains, wiping the sleep from her eyes as she leans against the door jamb of Emily's bedroom.

"You think this is early?" Caleb says, looking up from his seat on the floor in front of the couch. He has a cardboard box between his knees and a bottle of glue in his hand. He honestly can't remember what he's supposed to be doing, but he knows he's doing it badly. It's hard to forget since Emily keeps reminding him.

Emily sets the iPad down on the floor and jumps up to give Lauren a hug. "Hi, Mommy!"

"Hi, baby." Lauren wraps her arms around Emily's body and squeezes her tightly. "It's not even a school day. I thought we could sleep in."

"You really haven't parented in a long time," Caleb grumbles. He immediately regrets saying this and hopes Lauren didn't hear him. He subtly shifts his gaze in her direction. She isn't looking at him and it's unclear whether she heard him. She says nothing. Emily returns to her spot on the floor next to Caleb, and Lauren moves into the kitchen. Caleb hears a cabinet opening and closing and dishes rattling around.

"Do we have plans for today?" Lauren calls out. She walks into the dining area carrying a bowl of cereal and sets it down on the table.

"I have sword fighting club practice this morning," Caleb says, still not sure what he's doing with the box, exactly, but he's managed to give the box ears, so there's that.

"Sword fighting club?" Lauren asks with a hint of bemusement in her voice. "You still do that?"

"Yes," Caleb says simply. "And Emily usually goes with me. She likes seeing Scarlett, but whatever you want her to do is fine."

Emily taps furiously on the screen of the iPad. "I'm going."

"Who is Scarlett?" Lauren asks, bringing a spoonful of Honey Nut Cheerios to her mouth.

"She's a girl in our club who we happened to meet on the airplane last year," Caleb explains.

"Oh." Lauren studies her cereal bowl. Caleb doesn't need to explain when that particular airplane trip was or why it happened. Lauren knows.

"She's also the daughter of my... friend... um, Sadie from back in college," Caleb continues. "Small world, huh?"

"Sadie?" Lauren seems eager to latch onto anything that will shift the focus from last September. "Isn't she the girl you–"

"Yes," Caleb cuts in, looking at Lauren. She meets his gaze and then smiles.

"She must be something. I remember the way you lost your mind over her... and you don't do that. You're the level-headed one in the family." Lauren scoops up milk and lets it trickle off the spoon back into the bowl. "I mean, not like Mom or anything like that, but more practical than me, at least." She smiles slightly like she knows this is a funny thing to say. As if a lack of practicality is her most famous failing. She taps her spoon on the edge of the bowl repeatedly. It makes a clinking sound that Caleb finds incredibly annoying.

"Can you please stop?"

Lauren freezes, holding the spoon about an inch from the bowl. "Sorry," she mutters, and then tears start streaming down her face.

Her shoulders start to shake as she struggles to hold in the heavy sobs. Stunned, Caleb stands up, checks to confirm that Emily is still engrossed in the video playing on her tablet, slowly walks over to Lauren, and gently places a hand on her shoulder. He's never known what to do when someone starts crying. Even when he was a child and a friend fell and skinned their knee, he always found it extremely awkward. As he stands beside Lauren, he successfully fights the urge to say "there, there" while patting her like a dog.

"Sorry," Lauren says again, inhaling a deep shuddering breath in an attempt to compose herself. "Just feeling a little emotional." She looks up at Caleb and smiles half-heartedly with wet eyes.

"I know it's a lot," Caleb says. "All of it. What can I do to help? Just tell me what you need, and I'll do it."

"You've done more than enough, Caleb. And I'm going to be out of your way soon." Lauren picks up the spoon and starts tapping the side of the bowl again in a rhythmic pattern. She doesn't seem to notice that she's doing it. And despite the tears, Caleb sees for the first time this week, a disconnectedness in her eyes. A chill passes through his body because that emptiness, that lack of... something important, reminds him of the past. How she looked all those times she used to show up at his door. How she looked the day before the failed proposal, just hours before he ended up sitting by her hospital bed, holding her clammy hand, praying to a God he didn't believe in that she would come back to him.

"Like I said," Lauren continues, speaking a little more manically now. "Emily and I will head back home after school ends, and we'll move in with Paolo and everything will be good." She punctuates this pronouncement with one final clink of the bowl.

Caleb furrows his brow. "Paolo? Who is that?"

"Oh, he's my boyfriend." Lauren stirs the milk with her spoon now, scraping it along the bottom of the bowl. "He kind of kicked me out when we had a fight, but we've been talking and it's better now."

Caleb turns away and runs a hand across his face. He looks at Emily who is still watching the iPad, singing along softly to the song that's playing on the screen. He turns back toward Lauren and says with an uncharacteristic harshness in his voice, "You don't have to keep chasing guys, Lauren!"

Lauren looks toward him, a glint of fire in her eyes. He's actually relieved to see that. At least she's still in there. Still capable of caring. Still capable of feeling something.

"No matter how hard you try, you're not going to catch Dad."

Lauren stares at him looking hurt now and defeated instead of angry. She says nothing.

"I'm sorry," Caleb says in a softer tone. "That was over the line."

The room is quiet for several minutes, the sound coming from Emily's iPad the only noise.

"You've always treated me like a child," Lauren mutters finally, staring down at the table. "That's why I can't stay here."

"Fine, if you have to go, then you have to go," Caleb says flatly. "But... you can't take Emily."

"She's my daughter, Caleb, not yours."

Caleb knows he is in a losing position, but he can't give up. Lauren has hit him with a well-timed attack, but the match isn't finished yet. He has to counter. There is no other option. "But you can't take care of her on your own, Lauren." He hesitates. Sometimes the only way forward is through. "Especially not since you're using again."

Lauren cuts her eyes toward Caleb before quickly looking back down at the table. "I'm not using." Caleb doesn't say anything. He pulls a chair out from the table and sits down next to his sister. "I mean, it's not like you think," she continues. "Sometimes I take a pill or two to help me sleep, but that's it. It's not like before."

"I love you," Caleb says. He reaches out and takes Lauren's hand in his. He remembers sitting next to her at their dad's funeral, and later, sitting next to her hospital bed. He also took her hand in his on those occasions. It never seemed to help anything, really, but it always felt like something he should do. Empty gestures are sometimes the most important kind. "And Mom loves you and Emily and...

Dad." Caleb looks at Lauren and she looks toward him with tears in her eyes again. "Especially Dad. And Lauren, you have to believe me. No one blames you for anything." He gives her hand a squeeze and lets go. He stands up and leaves the table quickly. He turns away so she won't see that his eyes are wet now, too. There's no need to make it awkward for everyone.

CHAPTER 31

SADIE WAKES UP FEELING DETERMINED. Again. This is becoming a bit of an epidemic, she thinks. If she doesn't watch out, she's going to end up turning into one of those morning people who jog at six a.m. without anyone or anything chasing them. She stayed up late last night thinking. She sat on her bed with her guitar resting on her lap, quietly moving her fingers across the fretboard, practicing chord progressions for some of her favorite songs without strumming the strings so she wouldn't bother Scarlett.

Scarlett. Sadie knows she's growing up, how could she not, but Scarlett still manages to surprise with her maturity and incisiveness. No one wants to take relationship advice from their twelve-year-old daughter, but what if the advice is good? Parenting books never address questions like this. The internet probably does, Sadie thinks, but there's absolutely no chance she's going to check. She'd rather read comments on Preston the Peacock's Instagram posts or run herself through with Scarlett's sword.

Sadie can't help feeling like she and Caleb aren't over. They are like a half-finished song that needs another verse. She just has to figure out the lyrics and the tune. The first step is finding Caleb, and the best place to do that is at sword fighting club practice in about an hour. If things turn bad and the conversation lags, at least Harold will be there to pick up the slack. This thought makes Sadie smile. Since the big Caleb reveal, she's gotten to know the characters in the club better. She's picked up bits and pieces from Scarlett and Caleb. Harold is her favorite. She likes people who know when to keep quiet. It's an underrated quality in men.

...

In the car on the way to practice, Sadie and Scarlett don't talk much. They don't typically talk that much these days, of course, but the silence during this ride feels different. Instead of waves of angst swallowing up the sound, today's silence feels contented and shared. What needs to be said has already been said.

When Sadie pulls into the gravelly parking lot at the park, she scans the area for Caleb's car but doesn't see it. She was hoping to intercept him before he walked out to the field so they could speak more privately away from prying ears. And where she wouldn't be at risk of being sliced in two by an errant swing of one of the twins' swords. Oh well, love is worth fighting for. Hopefully.

Scarlett gathers up her things from the back of the car and begins to walk toward the small group of club members gathering on the grassy field. Sadie walks a few steps behind, and as they approach the others, she confirms that Caleb is not there. She checks the time on her phone. Five minutes until nine. It's unusual that Caleb isn't early, but maybe he's just running a little behind schedule. Sadie watches as Scarlett fidgets with her protective gear and begins to go through warm-up exercises with Tonya, Harold, the twins, and the other club members present. Several of them ask where Caleb is and no one seems to know. The minutes slip away.

It's ten after nine now and Sadie knows that something is up.

He's not coming. Is he so determined to avoid her or is something wrong? She has to find out. She's not just upset and confused now, she's extremely anxious and worried. She begins to imagine worst-case scenarios but shakes her head to bring herself back.

She gestures for Scarlett to come over to where she is standing. "I'm going to run see if I can track down Caleb, if that's okay?" she says. Scarlett nods and tells her that it's fine, go ahead. The sound of metal crashing against metal grows fainter as she walks back toward the car.

...

When Sadie whips her car into the driveway at Caleb's house a few minutes later, there is a strange car there. It is pulled up to the very end of the pavement close to the small yellow shed. Caleb's car is nowhere in sight. Traffic is light on Saturday mornings, and Sadie can feel the quiet through the closed windows. She walks over to the front door before she can lose her nerve and knocks briskly. *Thump, thump, thump.*

The sound of small feet scuttling across the tile floor, drawing closer. Emily opens the door and looks up at Sadie, eyes big.

"Hi, Emily," Sadie says, smiling. "Is your... is Caleb here?"

A woman with a pretty face and Emily's eyes appears behind the girl. She places a hand on Emily's shoulder and looks at Sadie, who suddenly feels out of place. She has the urge to say she must have the wrong house, but that doesn't make any sense at all, so she fights it off. Instead, she goes on the offensive, doing her best to keep her voice light and airy. "Oh, are you Lauren?"

"Yes," Lauren replies quizzically. "And you are...?"

"Sadie." Sadie immediately sees recognition in Lauren's eyes, but she can't determine if there are any feelings there, positive or negative.

"She's Scarlett's mom," Emily adds helpfully before wriggling away from Lauren and disappearing back inside the house. She clearly has no time to stand around while two women stare at each other.

Sadie breaks the awkward silence. "I guess Caleb's not here? I noticed his car isn't here."

"No, he went out for a bit," Lauren says. Sadie feels like Lauren is looking past her at something over her shoulder. She almost turns to look behind her, but she resists the impulse.

"Do you happen to know where he went?" Sadie asks when it becomes clear that Lauren is not going to elaborate. She immediately regrets adding the "happen to." She thinks it sounds pretentious or even sarcastic.

"Not exactly. He just said he needed to be by himself to think about some things, whatever that means." Lauren waves a hand dismissively. "He said he'd be back by lunchtime, so I can tell him you stopped by?"

"No, that's all right. I think I know where he probably is." Sadie looks down at her phone for no real reason other than she wants to avoid Lauren's gaze. "I, uh, just need to talk to him."

"Well, he certainly likes talking," Lauren returns, her tone cold. She doesn't elaborate and Sadie doesn't follow up. She thanks Lauren and says it was nice to meet her. This is, admittedly, an odd thing to say considering the circumstances and the fact that there were no introductions or explanations of relationships or any of the typical formalities that go along with first meetings. It was more like Lauren and Sadie had known each other forever without fully realizing it. Which, Sadie supposes, is kind of accurate. Either way, Lauren doesn't appear to be bothered by any of it. Sadie doesn't take the time to consider whether that is a good thing or a bad thing. She has more immediate concerns. She knows why Caleb has ignored her all week and she knows where he must be. Now, she just has to get there.

She quickly texts Paige to see if she can pick up Sadie at ten. She adds that it's a Caleb-related emergency. Paige replies:

Say no more. I've got it covered.

Sadie backs out of the driveway and points the car in the direction of the sadness spot.

...

At the field, Caleb's car sits alone in the parking lot. Rows of yellow school buses, even more iridescent in the morning light, are meditating not too far away. The air is still and quiet. The sky is a deep blue with a few streaks of white flat clouds that look like bumpy roads. Sadie parks her car near Caleb's, leaving enough space between them that one car could fit. It still seems like the appropriate thing to do. Sadie looks out the windshield and sees Caleb sitting near the tree, staring out at the football field, his arms across his knees. She remembers another time more than a decade ago when she sat in her car in this very spot looking out at the very same person.

She didn't get out of the car that day.

...

The concert was the last time Caleb saw Sadie, but it wasn't the last time Sadie saw Caleb. She remembers sitting in her car watching him at this field the day after the proposal. Her stomach was upset, and she was taking tiny sips of Coke to try to calm it down. She knew he would be here then. Just like she knew he would be here today. He is the person she knows best. He always has been no matter how far apart they were. There is this undeniable connection that not even time and mistakes and betrayal and complications and family can break.

On that day so many years ago, Sadie sat in her car for several minutes, trying to think of a way to fix the situation. To make things right. She couldn't think of anything. Her mind felt blank. And ten or twenty or fifty minutes after she arrived, she drove away feeling completely empty and slightly nauseous because of the future person who was making her presence known inside her body. If there is one moment in her life she could take back, it would be this one. In some ways, it haunts her more than that night it all went wrong because nothing good came of her decision to drive away. If she could have one second chance, one do-over, this is the one she would choose.

Unfortunately, life usually doesn't give second chances.

For years, Sadie wondered if things would've turned out differently if she'd known what had happened to Lauren the night before. Would she have opened the door and gotten out of the car? It's impossible to say now. It's impossible to know what a past version of herself would have done if the circumstances were different. Hell, it's hard to know what her current self will do.

All that matters? Sadie didn't get out of the car that day. She wiped away a few silent tears, backed out of the parking spot, and drove away.

...

This time it's different. Today, she opens her car door and walks slowly, but purposefully, toward Caleb. This is her second chance.

...

Sadie slows down even more when she gets close to Caleb. She's not sure why she's treating him like a skittish rabbit she has to sneak up on, but the human brain works in mysterious ways. Caleb is facing away from her, so she calls his name softly. He turns toward her.

"Oh, hey," Caleb says. "You found me."

Sadie isn't sure what to say to that. A thought flickers into her head that maybe this whole week was some sort of strange treasure hunt with Caleb as the final prize. Perhaps she had just been missing all the clues? Stupid brain, she thinks.

"Yeah," Sadie says, moving forward and sitting down on the ground a few feet away from Caleb. "You weren't at practice, so I got worried." She hesitates, tucking her hair behind her ear. "Well, even more worried since I haven't heard from you all week."

"Sorry," Caleb says, looking toward Sadie now. "I feel terrible, but... a lot of unexpected stuff happened this week and I got overwhelmed."

Sadie looks directly into Caleb's eyes. "I stopped by your house and Lauren was there."

"Yeah," Caleb says. "She's definitely there. But for how long is the question."

"Is she okay?" Sadie asks. "I only talked with her for a couple minutes, but she seemed a little... off?"

Caleb smiles ruefully. "No, she's not okay. It's kind of the same story, you know? Like watching a movie over and over again. Except, in this case, it feels like we all have to pretend we don't know the ending."

Sadie scoots a little closer to Caleb. "I'm really sorry to hear that. That must be heartbreaking." Caleb nods but doesn't say anything. "What about Emily?"

Caleb puts a hand up in an exasperated gesture. "Yeah, that's the thing, isn't it?" He runs his hand through his hair, making it stick up. "Lauren and I got into an argument because she said she's taking Emily back when the school year ends. I was kind of going along with it for some stupid reason until I realized that, of course, Lauren is using again. And she is also planning to run back to some guy named Paolo." He pauses, staring out at the football field. "So now, I don't know what to do."

They sit in silence for a few moments and then Caleb says with a wry smile, "How did two punks like us end up here? Having to deal with real adult stuff." He shakes his head.

Sadie laughs. "Well, one punk," she says, pointing to herself, "and one wannabe punk," she points toward Caleb.

"Hey!" Caleb exclaims indignantly. "You don't remember the black eyeliner I wore when..." He trails off. Both of them find other things to look at so they don't have to look at each other.

"So, does that mean we're in this together?" Sadie says finally, breaking the awkward silence.

"What do you mean?" Caleb asks, eyebrows knitted.

"You said 'how did two punks end up here dealing with adult stuff?'" Sadie says. "Are we dealing with that stuff together or..." It's her turn to trail off.

"Oh." Caleb hesitates for a long time, rubbing his knee with the palm of his hand. "I... I don't know. Guess that's one more thing I don't know." He gives a little nervous laugh and then reaches out to rest his hand on Sadie's knee.

"You've always been the one, Sadie. Always. And even after everything, I still believe that. I never stopped loving you. And finding our way back to each other the way we have and getting to know Scarlett and seeing your parents last weekend and even getting to meet Preston the Peacock, a true legend by the way, all of it has been incredible." He stops again, staring into Sadie's eyes long enough that she begins to get anxious about what's coming next.

"But," he continues, "maybe I'm not supposed to end up with The One. Maybe that's just storybook stuff that doesn't work out in real life. I don't know."

Caleb removes his hand from Sadie's knee. She looks away, her eyes beginning to feel wet. "Why do you think that?" she asks softly, fighting to keep her voice composed.

"It's just," Caleb begins, looking up to the sky. "When things got difficult before, when we made mistakes or didn't understand each other or didn't make the right choices, we gave up... I gave up." He looks at Sadie again. "I could've found you after everything happened. Like, it's not *that* hard. I know how to use the internet and maps and stuff. I could've figured it out. I could've fought to make things right, but I didn't. I gave up. I just let you go and disappeared back into myself. And yes, I was young and confused, but now I'm old and confused and I'm still doing the same thing. Lauren shows up and boom!" Caleb punches his fist into his open palm. "I run away from you again. I can't live out another movie that I know what the ending is going to look like. Why should I expect anything to be different this time?"

"Because I'm here now," Sadie says, staring directly into Caleb's eyes. Her eyes are wide, urgent. "Here. Together. With you. I'm here now and this is the only place I want to be. And that's really saying something about my commitment because we are in Florida." They both smile. "And remember," Sadie continues, "when we were here before, all those years ago, we said we believed in forever. That we were in this together and we would be there to pick each other up when we stumbled under the weight of... well, everything. And I know a whole lot of shit went wrong between then and now, but I still believe that. I'm still in it for the long haul as long as you are there with me."

Caleb closes the distance between them, and they kiss deeply. Then, they sit side by side on the grass, their thighs touching, Sadie's head resting on Caleb's shoulder. They both wish they could stay there just like that forever, but they can't. They have adult things to tend to. People who are depending on them. They have other people they have to worry about. It's exhausting and it can certainly be a disaster at times, but that's love.

It's what they signed up for. It's all part of the deal.

CHAPTER 32

SCARLETT HAS ENDED up at Kaylee's house. She's not entirely sure how she got here, but there was some arrangement made between Paige, who picked her up from sword fighting club practice; her mom, who seems to be missing; and Kaylee's mom, who is present physically but never mentally as far as Scarlett is concerned. Being twelve years old is interesting, Sadie thinks, because you exist in that sweet spot where you finally realize that children are shuttled around from place to place like packages, but you're not yet old enough to take control of the delivery vehicle. Exciting times.

Kyra, Kaylee's mom, pokes her head into Kaylee's bedroom where the girls are hanging out. "Hey! What are you girls up to in here? Sharing some secrets? Do you mind if Mom joins in?" Kyra sounds like a high school cheerleader, which she almost certainly was at some point in the past. She still has the perfect hair, perfect teeth, and perfect body despite her constant complaints that she really needs to spend more time in the gym.

"Go away, Mom," Kaylee says, rolling her eyes. She is busy looking through her TikTok For You page which is populated almost entirely with, as far as Scarlett can tell, funny animal videos and young women talking about prioritizing me-time.

Kaylee's dad is at the golf course, as he typically is on the weekends, which is a relief to Scarlett. He's probably not a terrible person, but he is extremely obnoxious, loud, and seems to always take up a lot of space. Scarlett can picture him on the golf course cracking jokes with his equally unevolved bros, cracking open a can of beer, and bellowing loudly when he misses a shot. He actually might be a terrible person, now that Scarlett thinks about it a little more, but terrible people are everywhere, so they tend to blend in.

"I'm so excited for the last week of school." Kaylee tosses her phone onto the bed and sits down next to Scarlett. "It's going to be so much fun and then we're going to the beach for two whole weeks!" She looks at Scarlett expectantly.

"Nice," Scarlett says.

Kaylee sighs with a dreamy look in her eye. "Right? You never know, I might meet a boy there who will make me forget about Skylar."

"Who is Skylar?"

"Seriously?" Kaylee asks, completely incredulous. "I literally told you yesterday that he's been my boyfriend since three days ago!" She sighs. It is very difficult to be best friends with someone who doesn't pay attention to the important things in life.

"Oh, yeah," Scarlett says, feigning recognition. "What's his thing, again?"

"Hockey!"

"Like, roller hockey or..."

"No, real hockey! His mom drives him to the ice rink that's like an hour away." Kaylee says this with a hint of awe in her voice. "They must be really rich. And he is so short. You know I love the short ones!"

Scarlett shakes her head. Between hanging out with Kaylee and her mom, she seems to do that a lot these days. It kind of comes with the territory of being twelve years old. And always being the most mature person in the room. Kaylee opens the notes app on her phone and quickly types something. Scarlett looks at the screen out of the corner of her eye and she's pretty sure Kaylee has typed:

> what if Skylar was so small he could fit in my pocket?

She closes her eyes, wishing she hadn't looked. When she opens her eyes a moment later, there is a new notification on her phone. It's a message from her mom. She swipes it open, looks at it, and laughs quietly.

"What?" Kaylee asks, reflexively shielding her own phone with her hand.

"Nothing," Scarlett replies. "My mom just texted me."

"Anything good?"

"I wouldn't say good." Scarlett holds up her phone so Kaylee can see. Sadie has sent a screenshot of an article on the local newspaper's website with the headline "Local Couple's Favorite Peacock Has the internet Buzzing." Underneath the headline is a picture of Scarlett's grandparents and, of course, Preston the Peacock. Tom and Jess are standing together, Tom's arm wrapped around Jess's waist, both grinning at the camera. Preston is a few feet away, looking menacing, as if he's about to charge the cameraperson.

In the message accompanying the picture, Sadie says she found Caleb, everything is okay with him, and if she survives reading the article about Tom and Jess, she will be by to pick Scarlett up in about twenty minutes.

"So, everything is *okay* with Caleb?" Kaylee places a heavy emphasis on the "okay."

"That's what she said, yes," Scarlett replies. For some reason, she's not eager to get into all this with Kaylee right now even though they were responsible for the whole Caleb-Mom relationship in the first place.

Kaylee looks at Scarlett with a puzzled expression, like she's trying to make one of those Magic Eye pictures come into focus. "I wonder what okay means."

"I don't know. I guess he's definitely alive." Scarlett can't help turning into her mom, even if she doesn't realize when she's doing it yet.

"I bet they're kissing right now," Kaylee says gleefully.

"Ugh, gross, stop," Scarlett says, a disgusted look on her face.

"What?" Kaylee asks innocently. "That's what we wanted, right?"

"Well, yeah, I guess," Scarlett concedes, "but we don't have to talk about it. Tell me more about Skylar." Before the words even leave her mouth, she wants them back. She would snip her vocal cords with scissors if she could. Kaylee's eyes light up and Scarlett realizes it's going to be a long twenty minutes until her mom arrives.

...

Finally, Sadie does arrive. When Scarlett sees the

I'm here

text, she jumps up and races out of the room, pausing only momentarily to tell Kaylee goodbye. In the car, Scarlett and Sadie grunt greetings to each other. After sitting in silence for a few minutes, a Paramore song playing on the radio in the background, Sadie says, "Should we talk about the peacock first or Caleb?"

Scarlett considers this for a moment, looking out the window. They are passing through a part of town with clusters of newly constructed houses and townhomes, large oak trees, and generous walking paths. People love walking here. It is the defining characteristic of the neighborhood. And, since it's the weekend, many people are out walking their dogs or themselves, apparently enjoying the debilitating heat and humidity. "I don't think there's anything more to say about the peacock. Or at least nothing I want to hear."

"Agreed," Sadie says. "Did I tell you I looked into self-lobotomization when I first saw their Instagram?"

Scarlett snorts a laugh without turning away from the window. A man wearing a neon-yellow helmet and pedaling a reclining three-wheeled vehicle zips past on the walking path, heading in the opposite direction.

"And as far as Caleb goes, well, I found him."

Scarlett waits for Sadie to continue, but after about a minute she concludes that her mom has no intention of continuing. "And," she says impatiently.

"And... it's kind of complicated." Sadie sighs.

"It's always complicated, Mom," Scarlett says in a slightly exasperated tone. "When has it ever not been complicated?"

Sadie doesn't answer. She stares at the road, turns on her turn signal to switch lanes, and accelerates past a slow-moving truck that appears to have all the wires and cables on Earth twisted and balled up in the back. She knows that Scarlett is right, of course, so what is there to say?

"So, Caleb's sister, Lauren, showed up at the house last weekend," Sadie says finally. "After we went to your grandparents'. She's Emily's mom. I guess you probably know that? But she has some... problems. That's why Emily has been with Caleb."

Scarlett looks at Sadie now. "She's not going to take Emily, is she?" The strain is evident in her voice despite her best efforts to suppress it.

"Well, hopefully not," Sadie replies. "But Caleb is a little worried about it because they've been having some... well, some disagreements, I guess, about what's best for everyone."

Scarlett shakes her head and looks out the window again. Nothing is easy when you're twelve, she thinks. Especially since adults can't seem to sort out their own problems.

"I told Caleb I would help... that *we* would help however we could."

Scarlett isn't exactly sure what she might be able to do to help in this particular situation, but she doesn't say anything. Setting her mom up with a guy was one thing, but she has never claimed to be an expert on family law. As she considers her options, Sadie's phone begins to ring. It is connected to the car, so the name of the caller appears on the display screen on the dashboard. Caleb. Scarlett notices her mom's eyes flick toward the screen and then she squints a little, her eyebrows bunching up. In Scarlett's experience, unexpected phone calls are rarely good news.

...

This phone call is no exception.

CHAPTER 33

DRIVING HOME from the football field, Caleb's head is spinning. It's funny how everything seems to happen all at once. It would be nice, he thinks, if things came his way one at a time for a change. Like the beginning level of a video game. He would have the chance to slay one opponent before moving on to the next. Life isn't a video game, unfortunately. Or at least it's not a video game that he has control over. Caleb has always found the idea that life is one big simulation comforting. He can't remember where he first heard about the theory, but he was immediately drawn to it. He's not even sure if it's a theory, really, or just some off-the-wall idea cooked up on the internet, but as far as conspiracies go, he enjoys this one. When he looks back on his life and everything that's happened–his dad's death, everything with Sadie, the great parts and the disastrous, Lauren's troubles, his challenging relationship with his mom, and Emily's unwillingness to wear shoes pretty much ever–it's kind of nice to think that he had nothing to do with any of it. And, in fact, none of it was actually real. At least not in the way most people conceive of reality. If everything we experience in our lives is crafted and programmed by some supercomputer controlled by a more advanced species or higher power, then, wow, how freeing is that? Caleb guesses this is kind of what religious people must feel like every day.

On a whim, Caleb pulls into a Dunkin Donuts and orders two coffees and a half dozen donuts. He makes sure to order one donut with pink frosting and another donut with pink frosting and sprinkles because he remembers that Emily has extremely strong opinions about sprinkles and those opinions seem to change every two to three days. After he picks up his order at the window, he gets back on the road and heads toward home. He presses the buttons on the dashboard to switch between radio stations until he lands on an alternative station. It's playing a Pigeontoes song. Caleb shakes his head and smiles. Everything all at once.

...

Maybe it's just the iced coffee that was sweetened beyond belief, but Caleb is feeling a bit lighter as he nears his little yellow house. Everything going on with Lauren is tough to handle, of course, but he feels downright giddy that he made up with Sadie. The feeling of her lips on his lingers. Pleasant, like the warmth of the sun on a cool day. He taps the steering wheel in time with the beat of the song playing on the radio. There's a lot of work to be done, but he feels much more positive than he did a few hours ago. He knows it's a risk, but he's ready to make the leap with Sadie. It's comforting to have the one person who always understood him on his side again.

Caleb begins to sing along loudly to the punk pop song that's now playing. He spins the dial to turn the music up. And then, when he makes a left turn into his driveway, gunning it to beat the oncoming traffic, he stops singing. Lauren's car isn't in the driveway. Caleb checks his phone to make sure she hasn't called or texted. She hasn't.

It could be nothing. Maybe they just went to the park or the grocery store.

...

It could be nothing or... it could be everything.

...

Helen likes to keep to herself on the weekends. She likes to keep to herself most other times as well, but because she works in a high school and the lock on the door to the bookkeeper's office hasn't worked in more than seven years, despite her diligence in filing a new work order with the maintenance department first thing every Monday morning, she doesn't get much alone time during the work week. Helen likes everything about her job except for her co-workers and the students. She just doesn't understand why everyone always seems to have so much to say.

Her house in the quiet neighborhood near the elementary school that her husband Luke decided was the "perfect place to raise children" more than three decades ago is blissfully silent on this Saturday. She has just returned from her daily thirty-minute walk around the neighborhood that keeps her legs strong and her mind focused. The only sound in the house is the soft whirring of a ceiling fan, the clicking of jigsaw puzzle pieces as Helen deftly slides them into place on her dining room table, and the swooshing of Simon's tail on the ceramic tile floor. Simon is Helen's cat, and he is probably the living thing she likes most. Or at least tolerates most easily. He asks basically nothing of her except for food twice a day. He lives his life, and she lives hers. The way things should be.

The school year is winding down and Helen is looking forward to a more peaceful summer. The students won't be around, which is a huge improvement, but Sandra, the guidance counselor who has occupied the office next to Helen's for twenty-four years, will unfortunately still be there. The thing about Sandra is she loves to talk. She never stops as far as Helen can tell. And the worst part is she never has anything of value to say. Not once has she ever talked about the finer points of Excel macros, for example. Instead, she talks about what she did over the weekend, what she's planning to do next weekend, her feelings about various dessert items, and her stupid dogs who seem to have no common sense whatsoever. Helen can only remember one day in twenty-four years that Sandra didn't talk constantly. In fact, she only said four words all day long: *I'm here for you.*

That day more than two decades ago would have been one of the best workdays Helen had ever experienced if it hadn't occurred during the worst period of her entire life. The Monday after the Friday night when it happened, Helen showed up to work right on time at 7:05 a.m. She sat at her desk and worked. What else was she supposed to do? There was more paper back then and fewer computers, but the job was pretty much the same. She made sure the school's money was where it was supposed to be, and she fixed everyone else's mistakes. Unfortunately, there was one mistake she couldn't fix, and that mistake happened to be made by one of the three people in the world she cared about. The big happy idiot should've known better.

No one set foot in Helen's office all day that Monday. No one except for Sandra. She knocked softly and opened the door without hesitation at 7:15. She looked Helen squarely in the eyes, placed a small pot of colorful flowers on Helen's desk, and said, "I'm here for you." Helen took the pot of flowers home with her at the end of the day and tossed them straight in the trash. Flowers are of no use to anyone, but Helen has never forgotten Sandra's words that day. Or the quiet. She probably appreciated the quiet the most.

Helen's home is neat, clean, unsentimental, and most of all, quiet. There is only one photograph in the entire house. It sits unobtrusively on the bookshelf in the living room area. It seems like it's placed at random, but it isn't. It's directly in Helen's sightline from her chair at the dining room table where she sits working her puzzles most weekends and some weeknights. In the photo, Luke, Lauren, and Caleb are at the beach. Lauren, rail-thin and gangly, sits in the sand, eyes squinting against the sun. Luke stands beside Lauren, shirtless with a thick chest, strong arms, and a natural tan. He is lifting Caleb, who is small with a pudgy face, up into the air like he is about to toss him toward the ocean. Luke is laughing, of course. Helen can almost hear it. She actually didn't take the picture, one of Luke's friends did. She wasn't even there that day. Helen never liked the beach—it's much too salty, sandy, and disorganized—so she stayed home.

As Helen works her puzzle, a snowy mountain scene with 1500 pieces, she remembers how loud Luke always was. She used to chastise him all the time for it. His voice, his heavy footsteps, and most memorably, his laugh. So loud. Helen could hear that laugh even when she was at one end of the house and Luke was at the other. After the kids grew up and moved away, laughter in this house has been hard to find. At least until Emily appeared last year. No one else has noticed it, and Helen certainly hasn't mentioned it to anyone because they would probably dismiss it as the ravings of a batty old woman, but Emily has Luke's laugh. It's not the same laugh, obviously—Emily is a little girl after all—but Helen hears it. To her, it is unmistakable. She would know that laugh anywhere.

...

Thump, thump, thump. Caleb feels his heart thudding inside his chest as he steps out of his car. He walks toward the front door slowly, doing his best to stick with his normal routines and behaviors. There's probably no reason to panic. And if he starts walking fast or running or acting in the way a panicked person would act, who's to say those actions wouldn't actually cause the thing he's most worried about? With the butterfly flapping its wings and all that, how is it possible to know which comes first, the panic or the reason for panicking? Caleb opens the front door briskly and steps inside.

The house is quiet as expected. He knew with Lauren's car gone it was unlikely anyone would be here. Still, he calls out Lauren and Emily's names. He calls the names casually with the hint of a questioning inflection at the end, like a teacher calling the class roll.

Caleb's eyes scan the open living room, dining room, and kitchen area as he moves farther inside. Things appear to be mostly as they were when he left. Several of Emily's dolls and toys are strewn about on the rug in front of the TV. There's a cereal box sitting on the kitchen counter with the top flaps sticking up, and the mug Caleb was using this morning is still sitting on the dining table, filled halfway with milky lukewarm coffee with an oily sheen on the surface. And jutting out from under that coffee mug is a piece of white paper folded in half. Caleb has learned from watching many movies and TV shows that pieces of white paper left on tables in empty houses are never good.

...

This piece of white paper is no exception.

...

. . .

He lifts the mug slightly and plucks the paper out from under it. He unfolds the paper quickly now because there is no longer any reason for pretense. He reads the words that are written in a looping, frantic script. After reading the entire note through twice, he tosses it back on the table and pulls out his phone. He dials one number, and it goes straight to an automated voicemail box, indicating that the phone is likely turned off. His heart is racing now. Uncontrollable. Like it's caroming around inside his rib cage, darting back and forth like a suicidal squirrel racing in front a car in the morning when the light is soft and the air is wet.

Thumpthumpthumpthumpthumpthumpthump.

He pauses for a moment before dialing the one person in the world he wants to talk to. The one voice he needs to hear right now. He holds the phone up to his ear and waits.

...

Helen thinks she is making pretty nice progress. She has been working on the snowy white part, which is basically all of the puzzle, and she has managed to find and fit together seventeen pieces in just the five or six minutes she's been home after returning from her walk. After finding a particularly difficult piece that has eluded her for several days, she pauses and looks over toward the photograph on the bookcase. As she returns her attention to the puzzle, something in the hallway that leads to the back bedrooms catches her eye. One of the bedroom doors is open. Lauren's old room. Helen always keeps those doors closed and she's certain this door was closed when she left to go on her walk. Maybe Simon has figured out doorknobs, she thinks.

And then she hears something. It's a laugh. A laugh she would know anywhere.

She shakes her head. "Nonsense," she mutters softly. She refuses to turn into a batty old woman who hears things. She pets Simon with her foot and begins to scour the table for another white puzzle piece of a particular shape. Staying on task is important. It's what keeps Helen from remembering too much.

...

"Hey," Sadie says after tapping the screen on the dashboard to accept the call. "I've got you on speaker in the car here with Scarlett, we're driving home. What's up?"

Sadie doesn't usually talk so much and so fast when answering the phone, but she is attempting to remain breezy and nonchalant. If she acts like receiving an unexpected phone call is totally normal, maybe it will be.

"Hi, um..." Caleb hesitates.

He pauses for so long that Sadie begins to think the call has dropped. "Caleb?" she says. "Are you still there?"

"Uh, yeah... so, I got home, and Lauren and Emily were gone," Caleb says finally. "She left a note."

Sadie looks toward Scarlett who is clearly confused and alarmed. "Okay. What did the note say?"

There is a rustling of paper on the line. "It says, 'I'm sorry, but we had to leave. I just couldn't wait any longer. Please don't try to follow me. I'll let you know when we get home and that we're safe. Love, Lauren.'"

Sadie sighs and grips the steering wheel a little tighter. "Stay where you are." She tries to sound confident and self-assured. In addition to the panic washing over her, she also feels a small twinge of relief that Caleb has called her for help instead of pushing her away. "We'll head your way now and we'll figure out what to do. We've got this. Try not to worry." Sadie would like to have that not worrying part back, but it's hard not to utter empty words at times like these. And sometimes empty words are the most important kind.

Caleb says, "Okay, thanks," as if they are discussing a work assignment and Sadie has said she will have the report on his desk by the end of the day. They hang up and Sadie drives. Fast.

CHAPTER 34

A MOTHER SITS in her car in a gas station parking lot. She has dark circles under vacant, unfocused eyes. Her daughter is in the backseat talking incessantly about something, the mom isn't sure what. The sound of the tiny voice is giving her a headache. She powers on her cell phone and waits. When the phone loads, notifications begin to appear one after another. There are missed calls, several. And there is a single text message from a man named Paolo:

> Come home now. I won't take no for an answer.

She remembers those words: *I won't take no for an answer.* Even though they are words on a screen she can hear them. She can feel them. They make the hairs on the back of her neck stand up on end. Like a jolt of electricity has passed through her body. It's a remarkably clear and sunny day, the sky deep blue and vast like an ocean turned upside down, but she can hear a violent clap of thunder. It makes her jump in her seat.

"Are you okay, Mommy?" her daughter calls happily from the backseat. The mom doesn't answer. She turns the car on, maneuvers out of the gas station parking lot, and gets back on the road. She blinks hard four or five times, trying to clear her vision. She stares at the white line that runs along the side of the road. She focuses on it like she's never focused on anything before. She has to drive. She has to go.

What other choice does she have?

...

Life doesn't usually give second chances. Love is such a disaster. *Usually*.

...

When Sadie and Scarlett arrive at Caleb's house, they don't waste any time. Sadie gives the door a cursory knock but doesn't wait before going inside. Caleb is sitting at the table with his back to the door. He's clutching a mug of the old coffee in his hand, which he swirls absentmindedly as he looks at his phone. Lauren's note sits in the middle of the table, looking like a small paper tent.

"Hey," Sadie says tentatively, moving toward Caleb and resting a hand on his shoulder. He looks up at her with tired eyes. Scarlett lingers near the door, unsure where exactly she should go.

"Hey," Caleb says. "Thanks for coming. Hi, Scarlett, how was practice?"

Scarlett didn't expect to be brought into the conversation at all, and she certainly didn't anticipate this question at this particular moment. "Um, fine." She moves to take a seat on the couch.

"Good, that's good. Sorry I couldn't make it, but..." Caleb stops.

Sometimes empty words are the most important kind, but they can only go so far.

"Okay, Caleb," Sadie interrupts. "Let's focus here. I understand you're probably in shock or whatever, but we don't have time to waste." She takes her phone out of her pocket and moves it up and down subtly like she's checking its weight. "So, we know Lauren is probably headed... north? We need to call someone. The police or child welfare or something?"

"But Lauren is the mom," Caleb says. "It's not like she's kidnapping her. I don't have any legal rights here."

"Yes, but you said Lauren is using..."

"Yes... she said she was taking pills."

"Then she's likely impaired and that means Emily is in danger. And so is Lauren."

"I guess you're right," Caleb acknowledges.

Sadie and Caleb are both quiet now. They sit and stare at their phones or the walls as if there are clues lurking somewhere they need to find. Hiding in plain sight. As they sit and stand and wait, attempting to puzzle out the situation, Scarlett grows impatient. Adults can be so helpless sometimes, she thinks. She's just about to speak up in an attempt to get things moving when there's a knock on the door.

...

Thump, thump, thump.

...

A mom sits on the edge of a bed in a room that seems familiar yet completely foreign. Like it's a room she may have visited in a past life. The walls have been stripped bare, removed of all character, all feeling, but there are still faint rectangular outlines where posters used to hang. Her daughter sits on the floor next to the bed, tucked away in the corner, completely out of sight.

"Okay, remember," the mom says, trying her best not to let her voice crack. "I want you to be very quiet. Try not to let anyone find you until the timer on your iPad goes off. Just watch *Bluey* and wait. It'll be fun!"

"Okay, Mommy," her daughter says, seemingly unfazed.

The mom adjusts her daughter's headphones with a Minnie Mouse bow on top, double-checking that they are on properly and securely plugged into the tablet.

"I have to go, but I'll see you soon... I love you." The mom kisses her daughter softly on the cheek. She gets up and quickly walks out of the room without looking back, leaving the door open a few inches because she can't bear the thought of closing it. That would feel too final. She leaves the house, gets into her car, pulls out of the driveway, and waits on the side of the street a few houses down. She waits until a woman in well-worn tennis shoes walks up to the house and goes inside. Then, she drives away. Fast.

...

Helen has definitely heard something now. It's not just in her head or in her memories. It can't be. She's heard that laugh thousands of times over the past couple of decades, but it's never sounded this real before. She is really picking up some momentum on the puzzle and would prefer to keep going, but she feels compelled to seek out the source of the laughter. It's not easy to make herself get up, though.

Getting into a jigsaw puzzle groove is rare. Sure, anyone can have a few lucky finds in a row, but when the pieces start falling into place one after another, almost like they are moving on their own or perhaps a ghost is providing guidance from the great beyond, well, that kind of groove doesn't happen very often.

Helen didn't work puzzles as much in her younger days because there always seemed to be something she needed to do for the children or for Luke. But occasionally on a Saturday night after the kids were in bed, she would sit at this table and work a puzzle, both because she found it challenging and because it reminded her of her dad.

Helen's dad was a quiet man, nothing like Luke, but his heart was just as big. He worked from sunup to sundown as a construction worker and on his one day off per week, he loved to work puzzles. Young Helen would sit beside him and watch as his meaty, callused hands deftly moved the pieces into place. It didn't seem possible that hands that looked like his could be so nimble, but they were. They rarely talked during their puzzle sessions, but the quiet was comfortable, familiar, safe. Sometimes Helen's dad would get so engrossed in the task that Helen wondered if he even remembered she was there. But every time a puzzle was almost complete, her dad would clear his throat, rest his big hand on top of her small one just for a moment, and then get up and walk away, leaving the last piece for Helen to slot into place. Nothing felt quite so glorious. When she was eleven years old, Helen's dad died. A massive heart attack took him in his sleep. One moment he was there and the next he was gone. It's funny how that can happen.

Helen's dad left behind an unfinished jigsaw puzzle of a baseball field where two little league teams were playing and a little girl who promised herself she'd never love anyone so much again. She wouldn't allow herself to be hurt like that anymore.

On those occasional Saturday nights after the kids were in bed, Luke would sit beside Helen at the table while she worked her puzzle. It was much different working a puzzle with Luke. So much different. Luke was louder, there was never a moment of quiet. He tried to help find pieces, but he would quickly lose interest, becoming distracted by a college football game on the television. Sometimes he would slap his hand down on the table in excitement when a football player made what he considered to be a spectacular play. The pieces would jump and so would Helen. Luke was so loud. Helen would grimace and shush him. "You have to see this play, Sweetie," he would exclaim in an excited whisper, eyes wide, as eager as an eight-year-old in a chocolate shop. "Look!" Helen would dutifully watch the replay and make a little sound like "hmm." The plays never seemed that spectacular to Helen. The players were just doing what they were supposed to do, but she guessed that was more than she could say for most people. Luke would laugh and shake his head. Then he would stand behind Helen, wrap his strong arms around her, and kiss her gently on the top of the head. "What am I going to do with you?" he would say. Helen would smile shyly despite herself. Because nothing felt quite so wonderful as Luke's touch and his unabashed love.

Then Luke died. One moment he was there and the next he was gone. The Saturday night after the Friday when it happened, Helen sat down at this table to work a puzzle, because what else was she supposed to do? She didn't put the game on the TV. She sat in silence scolding herself for breaking the promise she made all those years ago. For letting herself love someone so much again. She should've known better. When she was nearly finished, she left the last piece of the puzzle undone. Just in case.

...

Is love ever *not* a disaster?

...

Finally, Helen gets up from the table. She doesn't move as quickly as she once did, but she's still pretty spry for a person her age. She already knows where she's going to look first. Truthfully, she knew where she was going to look before she even set foot inside her house after her walk. She knew from the moment she saw a car sitting on the side of the street a few houses down from hers. It's very difficult to slip anything past a mom. Helen was hopeful that if she sat back down, continued with her puzzle, and pretended everything was fine and normal then maybe, just maybe, it would be. Everything would work itself out without requiring her intervention. Then she could enjoy the rest of her peaceful, quiet Saturday.

...

Of course, best laid plans and all that.

...

Helen knows what she's going to find when she opens the door to Lauren's old room, but the reality of it, seeing it with her own eyes, is still a bit arresting. When she pushes the door with the palm of her hand, opening it all the way, she sees a pink Minnie Mouse bow protruding from behind the neatly made bed. Her granddaughter is under the bow, of course, her eyes fixed on the tablet resting in her lap. Emily is quiet at first, engrossed in whatever is happening on the screen, and then suddenly she erupts in a fit of laughter.

Helen feels a gentle chill pass through her. She is nothing if not a rational person, so she knew the laughter she heard would be coming from this little girl. She loves her granddaughter and she's happy she's safe, even if she is still mentally putting the pieces together, still figuring out what exactly is happening here. And she's certainly not disappointed. She gave up on disappointment years ago.

"Emily," Helen says in a loud voice so she will be heard through the headphones. "What are you doing here?"

Emily looks up, her eyes calm, apparently not at all perturbed by the unusual situation she finds herself in. "You found me!" she says enthusiastically, pulling the headphones off her ears. "Grandma, you have to see this, it's sooo funny!" Emily jumps up, hugs the tablet to her chest, and rolls across the bed, landing on her feet a couple steps away from Helen. She slides her finger across the screen to rewind the video, unplugs her headphones, and lets the show play. Australian cartoon dogs are playing some sort of strange game, talking in funny voices. Both child dogs and adult dogs are participating in this silliness. Maybe it's different with dogs, Helen thinks.

An adult dog makes a joke about a bodily function and Emily laughs uproariously. Her laughter echoes around the room, bouncing off the bare walls. That laugh. Helen nods and smiles politely and says something like "that's nice." She doesn't find the antics particularly funny, but to each their own.

"Oh, I forgot." Emily pauses the video again and looks up at Helen with concern in her eyes. "Mommy told me to wait until my timer went off to come out. It hasn't gone off yet. I hope it's okay that you found me."

Helen looks down at Emily and pats her on the back a bit awkwardly. "I'm sure it's fine," she says. "Do you want to help me work a puzzle?"

CHAPTER 35

T HUMP, *thump, thump.*

...

Everything all at once. That's what it feels like.

...

Sadie opens the door because she's the closest. Caleb has gotten up from his chair and he moves toward the door as well, so he is positioned just behind Sadie. Scarlett remains seated on the couch, but she looks toward the door because it is clearly the center of attention now. Standing on the front step are a small child and a small adult.

Caleb and Sadie's eyes take a moment to adjust to the bright light of the sun's glare. At first, the people outside are just dark silhouettes.

There is no time to wonder if maybe the silhouettes are optical illusions or ghosts or glitches in the simulation, however, because the smaller one barrels toward them, colliding with their legs, wrapping one arm around each of their waists to create a group hug that is filled with relief and joy and a little bit of awkward stumbling around and falling into each other because Emily has pulled both Caleb and Sadie off balance. Everyone laughs and begins to talk at once and it becomes too loud and chaotic for anyone to hear anything, so they pause and say things like "sorry, it's been a really long day." Helen and Scarlett both roll their eyes and shake their heads because even though they are very different people, they both think their family members can be downright embarrassing and overly emotional.

After a few minutes of noise and hugs and deep exhales, everything begins to settle into a new kind of normal. It's not the old normal, but considering that this group of people has never been under the same roof at one time, it doesn't feel as awkward as it might. Helen sits at the table with Caleb and Sadie while Scarlett sits on the floor with Emily playing a memory card game. Using as few words as possible and keeping her voice low so Emily won't hear, Helen tells Caleb what happened at her house. She knows that Sadie can hear her too, but that's not her problem. Helen explains to Caleb that she went for a walk and when she returned, she noticed a car that certainly looked like Lauren's lingering on the street not far away. She decides to skip the part about the roll she was on with the puzzle, because she knows non-puzzlers can't understand what it's like to enter that kind of flow state. Of course, there's not much else to tell. She found Emily in Lauren's old bedroom and here they are. She doesn't know why Lauren changed her mind after writing the note.

"Oh, I know!" Emily exclaims, leaping up from her spot on the floor and running over to the table. Apparently, Emily's ears are better than Helen suspected. Emily puts her hands on the table and presses herself up as if she's performing some sort of gymnastics maneuver. "We were at the gas station and Mommy said we were going home, but then I said we just came from home."

Emily smiles brightly, looking from Helen to Sadie and then to Caleb. No one responds, so Emily is more than happy to continue talking. "She brought me to Grandma's instead of here, but maybe it was just closer, I don't know."

Emily skips away, leaving the adults at the table amazed by how unfazed she seems. They know it won't always be so easy for her, but they are certainly willing to let her bask in the simplicity as long as possible. Everyone loves when things are simple. Of course, the reason Lauren brought Emily back wasn't quite as simple as Emily believes, but Caleb and Helen are happy to take it at face value. It's important to have a story that offers comfort, whether the story is truth or fiction.

...

Lauren's head is thick and her eyelids feel like they weigh a thousand pounds as she drives on a dark highway somewhere in north Florida. That she is still able to keep the car moving forward and mostly between the lines feels like a miracle. She's been honked at a few times by cars as they swerve dramatically around her, coasting out on the shoulder, tossing up bits of gravel and dirt as they pass. Those drivers are assholes, though. She raises a finger in the dark where no one can see and keeps driving, hugging the white line on the right side of the road the best she can, like a child clutching a favorite blanket.

Or maybe it's not a miracle that she's still driving, still breathing. Maybe it's a complete disaster. Maybe the miracle would be if her car were buried in the trees on the side of this godforsaken highway. Buried so deep that no one would find her for days, maybe weeks. Then it would all be over. The pain would be gone, and she would never disappoint anyone ever again. Never hurt anyone. Never make anyone die, disappear, disintegrate into nothing. All it would take is one turn of the steering wheel. One hard push on the gas pedal. It would be over in seconds.

I won't take no for an answer. The words she saw on her phone screen a few hours ago, the words that changed how her story ends, continue to reverberate in Lauren's head. The text came from Paolo this time, but she didn't hear it in his voice. She heard it in the voice of a teenaged boy. On that Friday night two decades ago, a boy who was a junior in high school and had electric blue eyes that were irresistible to a 15-year-old Lauren, said those words to her. They were huddled together under the bleachers at the football field. The game was over, and Lauren was ready to leave, but the boy had other ideas. When he grabbed her by the wrist, fixed her with a penetrating look, and said, "I won't take no for an answer," she felt helpless. He said it in a playful way with a small smirk on his lips, but Lauren saw something deeper behind the beautiful eyes and boyish face. She had to stay. What other choice did she have?

She grips the steering wheel tightly. Tighter than she's ever held onto anything in her life. Even tighter than she gripped her dad's wrist that night. She can still feel it in her hand. It was wet from the rain. Warm, almost hot. Electric. But still lifeless. And that's all that mattered. That's all that will ever matter. One turn of the wheel. One hard push on the gas pedal. It would be over in seconds.

Lauren blinks away tears she didn't even realize were there. She needs to see clearly now. She has to get this right.

She turns the wheel. She presses down on the pedal.

...

. . .

Caleb is lying on the floor next to Emily's bed. The room is dark and quiet, but dark and quiet in the way that a child's bedroom is dark and quiet. There is always some light and always some noise. Light and noise keep the monsters away. A small electric fan hums in the corner and two night-lights cast circles onto the ceiling. Ever since Emily arrived, almost a year ago now, Caleb has spent countless hours lying on this floor staring up at the shadows. Emily talks a lot when she's in bed; her mind always seems to be overflowing, and tonight is no exception. It has been a pretty eventful day.

"Caleb," Emily says. She peppers her nighttime monologues with Caleb's name to make sure he's paying attention.

"Yes," Caleb replies.

"When will I get to see Mommy again?"

Caleb pauses. He rolls over on his side and rests on his elbow with his head in the palm of his hand. "I'm not sure, Emily, but we will see her. Hopefully soon."

Emily doesn't respond. Caleb can hear her moving around in bed, likely adjusting the positioning of her stuffed animals. When Emily isn't talking, Caleb is never sure if she's thinking about what was just said or if she's already moved on. Kids can be confusing that way.

"You know what we can do?" Caleb continues. "Once we find out when we are going to see Mommy again, we can start a count-down. I used to love doing that when I was a kid."

"You mean count numbers?" Emily asks.

"Yes. Days or weeks or hours. Whatever we want to count. You know who taught me about that?" Caleb says this last part without thinking. He's never talked about his dad with Emily before and he's not sure why he decided that now is the right time.

"Who?" Emily asks.

"My dad," Caleb says quickly before he can change his mind.

"You have a dad? Where is he?"

"Well... he died."

"Oh."

"It was a long time ago. I was still a kid. Older than you are now, but just a few years older."

Emily is quiet for a few moments. "Are you sad?" she asks finally.

"Yes," Caleb replies. "Not all of the time now, but I still get sad sometimes. I miss him."

"Did you know that numbers just keep going?" Emily asks.

"What do you mean?" Caleb replies. He is used to Emily changing the subject seemingly at random, but this switch was a particularly unexpected one.

"I learned at school that numbers never end. They just keep going," Emily peeks over the side of the bed, looking down at Caleb. "Maybe people are like that, too."

"You mean people just keep going?" Caleb asks.

"Yes," Emily says. "They're... infinite?"

Emily stumbles over the word infinite, but she gets close enough that Caleb knows what she means.

"Hmm. You know what? I think you might be right about that," Caleb says. Emily rolls back away from the edge of the bed, out of sight. "Maybe people are infinite."

Emily doesn't say anything more. A minute or two later, Caleb hears her breathing grow heavier. He crawls toward the door, stands up, and slips out of the room, closing the door softly behind him.

...

Maybe people never end. They're like numbers. Infinite.

...

"You're still here?" Caleb asks quietly, sitting down at the dining table where Helen is still seated. She has her phone out but doesn't seem to be actually using it.

"I just wanted to make sure Emily got to sleep okay," Helen says. "I'll get out of your way now."

"No, no," Caleb says quickly. "Stay. I'm going to grab a glass of water. Do you want anything?"

Helen nods her head. She had been getting up to go, but she settles back down into the chair, her back straight, rigid. Caleb returns and sets two glasses down on the table and sits back down. They sit in silence for several minutes. They both tap their screens and press the buttons on the side to keep their hands busy.

Caleb takes a sip of water. "Some day, huh?"

"That seems to be the consensus, yes," Helen replies, looking up now, but not at Caleb.

"Are you doing okay?"

Helen gives a little sniff. "Of course, why wouldn't I be?"

"Oh, I don't know. Let's see... your daughter left your granddaughter at your house for you to find. And now, we don't know where your daughter is."

"We never know where she is," Helen says briskly. "I believe you told me that yourself."

Caleb sighs. He stands up from the table as if he has somewhere to go. He walks toward the kitchen but stops after a couple of steps. He doesn't turn back around before saying in a quiet voice, "I don't know if I'm ever going to be enough, Mom, but I'm trying." He stands still for a moment, then walks into the kitchen. He turns the faucet on and off a couple of times and moves a few dishes from one location to another.

"I'm here for you."

Four little words. Caleb freezes. He has a plate in one hand and a dish brush in the other, but he stops scrubbing. He places each item down carefully in the metal sink, and walks back toward the table, stopping at the kitchen counter and resting his arm on it.

"What did you say?"

"I said: I'm here for you," Helen says, looking squarely at Caleb now.

He runs a hand through his hair. "It just feels like I'm never going to be Dad no matter how hard I try. Whether it's with Emily or just with anything, you know? I just can't do the things that he did. He made everything seem so easy. I can never be him."

"Well, Caleb," Helen says in an even voice. "You shouldn't try to be. Luke was irreplaceable."

Caleb looks at his mom and she looks right back at him. It almost feels like they're locked in a staring contest. This is the first time Caleb has heard Helen say his dad's name in... he can't remember how long. He does his best to keep his face like a mask, expressionless. Helen is like a small animal, easily spooked, but instead of physical movement, what spooks Helen most easily is emotion.

"You're right," Caleb says slowly. "He was one-of-a-kind."

There's a long silence now and they both look away, searching for something, anything in the room to focus their attention on. Caleb is just about to turn away, to head back to the dishes.

"You are, too," Helen says.

Caleb nods, a small smile at the corners of his mouth. He turns and walks back into the kitchen.

...

Sadie is sitting on her bed with her back resting against the headboard when Caleb calls. It's late and she was just about to give up on this chaotic day and go to sleep, but she has been holding out hope that Caleb might at least text. She wants him to make the first move this time. She doesn't want to bother him after everything that happened with Lauren and Emily today.

Her heart flutters a little as she presses her phone's screen to accept the call and says, "Hey."

"Hey," Caleb says a little breathily. "Remember when we kissed earlier today?"

Sadie laughs, caught off guard by the lack of preamble, but she quickly regains her footing. "Was that today?"

"I think so?" Caleb says playfully. "It's all a bit fuzzy, really. Some other things happened afterwards, and it got all weird."

"Weird? Us? That doesn't seem right." They both laugh. "But yes, I do remember. It was very nice... I think we were at a Renaissance faire, right?"

"Exactly! Yes, God, I had forgotten that part. There was the horse, and I was thinking, please don't mess this up for me. I know Sadie gets hung up on smells and all that."

"Right?!? The old Sadie sniffer was about to cock block you again."

"I know. Disaster averted when that guy clopped away just in time. Also, was that a peacock reference?"

They both laugh, then a quiet settles across the line. They both know there are important things they could be talking about, but it's late and they are both sleepy. It has certainly been some day.

"So, I talked to my mom about some things a little bit ago after Emily finally went to sleep, and it actually went... pretty well?"

"That's great," Sadie says. "I know you both are going through–"

Caleb's phone buzzes and he removes it from his ear to check the screen. "Oh, sorry," he interrupts. "Someone's calling and it's a Jacksonville number. Um, maybe I should... take it?"

"Okay," Sadie says, and the line goes dead.

...

Unexpected phone calls are rarely good news.

CHAPTER 36

THE SECOND CALEB accepts this unexpected phone call, he stands up. He has no idea who is calling or why, or even why he answered an unknown number at 11:30 at night in the first place, but he does know he needs to be standing up instead of sitting. It just seems right.

"Hello?" he asks tentatively as he begins to pace back and forth at the foot of his bed. There is no response, and Caleb is about to hang up assuming it is an autodialed spam call when he hears someone's breath on the line. The breathing comes in small bursts. "Hello?" he says again. "Is anyone there?"

"Hey," a woman's voice says, and Caleb immediately knows who it is. "It's me."

...

Unexpected phone calls are rarely good news, but this call *is* an exception.

...

Lauren grips the steering wheel tightly and pulls it to the right. Then she steps on the brake pedal. She maneuvers her car off the highway onto the shoulder, making sure to pull as far away from the road as possible before putting the car in park. There aren't many cars on the road at this time of night, but she doesn't want to get rear-ended by a careless driver. That would be a death sentence. She remembers when her family was on summer vacation, she must've been twelve or thirteen at the time. Her dad was driving at night on a highway much like this one. Her mom was asleep in the front seat and Caleb was hunched over on the seat beside her, snoring softly. They drove past a car that was stopped on the side of the road, its hazard lights flashing.

Her dad looked into the rearview mirror and caught Lauren's eye. "Did you see that car?" he asked softly, then continued without waiting for an answer: "I almost had to swerve to make sure I didn't clip it. You're going to be driving soon, Lauren, so remember. If you ever have to stop on the side of a highway, make sure to pull off as far as you can. You just can't count on other drivers to be paying attention." He gave a little smile and a wink, looking into the rearview mirror at Lauren one last time before turning his eyes to the road.

It's funny what you remember when your survival instinct takes over.

Lauren turns on her hazard lights, picks up her phone, and turns it back on. She mostly ignores the deluge of messages and missed calls. There are at least thirty messages from Paolo, and she sees that some are in all capital letters, but she swipes left to delete the entire conversation. She opens a web browser, completes a quick search, closes the browser, and makes a phone call. Then she starts to drive again, letting the white stripe guide her to her next destination. Her dad also told her to get back on the road as soon as possible. It was safer to be moving than stopped. Keep moving forward. Don't give up. She wishes she could talk to him now. There probably hasn't been a day that she hasn't wished that.

...

"Hey," Caleb says into the phone. "Where are you?"

The line goes quiet again and Caleb thinks the call might've dropped. He removes the phone from his ear to see if the call is still connected.

"I'm in Jacksonville," Lauren says just as Caleb returns the phone to his ear. She sounds far away, like she's on the other side of the world instead of just one hundred fifty miles north. "I'm checking into a place."

Caleb closes his eyes. He feels a little bit of everything all at once: relief, sadness, joy. "That's good... I mean, that's great. "I'm so glad you're doing that and you're safe. We were worried sick."

"I know," Lauren says, her voice tinny and flat. "I'm sorry for... everything."

Neither of them says anything for a long while until finally Caleb jumps back in to fill the empty space with empty words. Sometimes empty words are the most important kind. They give us room to breathe. Caleb tells Lauren about the rest of Emily's day and assures her that she is fine. Better than fine, really. He makes a joke about Helen showing a glimmer of humanity and they both laugh like they used to before everything, sitting in the back seat of the car on the way home from school. He asks Lauren where she is, and she gives him the name of the facility and says she's calling from their phone, so this is the phone number to use if he needs to find her. Most of her life she hasn't wanted to be found, but now she does. She can't explain why, but sometimes life is like that. One moment you feel like one person and the next you feel like someone else entirely.

. . .

...

"Hey, sorry about that," Caleb says when Sadie answers his call. It's well past midnight now, but he had to call back. He needs to talk to someone. And there's really only ever been one someone he's wanted to talk to. He can't even begin to count how many times during the last decade he's wanted to hear Sadie's voice on the phone when things were difficult or confusing. Or when something important happened. He couldn't make that call for so long, but now he can.

"That's okay," Sadie says lightly. "Who was calling?"

"It was Lauren. Um, she's in Jacksonville and she's safe."

Sadie exhales. "That's great news. What is she doing there?"

Caleb explains what he knows and speculates about the things he's still unsure about. They talk about Emily and Scarlett and Caleb's mom and Sadie's parents and peacocks and anything they can think of to fill the space between them. It just feels good to be together like this. They've both changed so much, their lives have changed so much, but they're still good at being together. Even if the way they define together has also changed.

Two punks. Or, rather, one punk and one wannabe punk. Still trying to figure things out. Still wondering what comes next. That much will never change.

"Sadie," Caleb says after a long silence. He doesn't even know what time it is anymore, and his brain feels mushy, but there's one last thing he wants to say before the new day dawns.

"Yeah?"

"This is probably going to sound weird and I'm extremely punchy right now, but I've been wanting to say this since I saw you at that football field last fall. And hell, why not now, right?" Caleb pauses for a moment, gathering his thoughts. "Okay, here we go.

When I first saw you, it was like nothing I've ever felt before. I'm not a love-at-first-sight type of guy, but with you, it was... different. I believed it. I would say it was like I was struck by a bolt of lightning, but I won't say that for obvious reasons."

Sadie chuckles. "That's very understandable, yes."

"But that's what it was like," Caleb continues. "Truly."

There is a long silence and Caleb begins to worry that he's taken it too far. Dove in headfirst when he should've dipped a toe into the water to check the temperature. He's about to say something, because his instinct is to talk when things get awkward, but Sadie strikes first.

"I feel the same way," she says simply. "I think I always have. It was too much to deal with then and I panicked. Hopefully now that I'm old and wake up with back pain because I sneezed wrong the day before... maybe now I'm ready. Maybe now we're ready."

"I can't wait to find out," Caleb says.

EPILOGUE

3 Months Later

"How CAN I get Caleb to where I need him to be without him catching on? Help me, Scar!" Sadie is fixing dinner on a late August evening. The sizzling sound from the frying pan momentarily drowns out the whirring of the air conditioner as it struggles to fend off the relentless summer heat.

Scarlett looks up disinterestedly from her seat at the table where she is working on homework. "That's easy," she says flatly. "Tell him you're going to minigolf. He's a weirdo for that."

Sadie slaps the counter with her hand. "Scarlett, you're brilliant!"

Scarlett shakes her head and returns her attention to her work. Her mom is right in this case, but still, she's embarrassing, nonetheless.

There's a knock on the door and Paige barges in without waiting for anyone to respond. "Hey, m'ladies!" she shouts as she sweeps into the townhouse, making a dramatic gesture with one arm. "Get it? M'ladies. Just trying to capture the vibe for the big weekend!" She walks into the kitchen and peeks over Sadie's shoulder to see what's in the frying pan. "Wow, are you making risotto? Sadie, you've really come a long way since the Ramen Wars of 2009."

"Ramen Wars?" Sadie repeats, adding a cup of water to the sizzling pan.

Paige sits down at the table with Scarlett. "Yeah, I don't know what that means. You used to cook ramen a lot when we roomed together. And I haven't slept in like three nights, so I'm pretty delirious."

"That sounds rough," Sadie says. "Why did you have so many kids, again?"

"I ask myself that every day." Paige exhales dramatically, blowing a strand of curly hair out of her eyes. "Anyway, have you figured out the agenda for Saturday?"

"I think so," Sadie replies. "Scarlett suggested I tell Caleb we're all going to minigolf. I thought that was a pretty great idea."

"Oh, yeah," Paige says enthusiastically. "He's a huge weirdo for minigolf."

Scarlett snorts a laugh. "That's literally what I said."

"Great minds!" Paige reaches out a fist for a fist bump. Scarlett ignores her.

Paige lets her fist drop back to her side sadly. "Hopefully he won't be disappointed when he finds out there is actually no minigolf involved."

...

Caleb is counting down the days, the hours, and the minutes. Sadie has finally agreed to play minigolf with him again, and even better, it was actually her idea! Most years, when the long, hot August days begin to dwindle away and September looms on the horizon like a hulking thunderhead, Caleb begins to look backward. But this year is different. This year, Caleb is excited about what the future might hold. And he knows one thing is certain; his immediate future includes minigolf with his favorite people.

Overall, the summer was a good one. Like, *really* good. In fact, it was so good that even the daily thunderstorms didn't seem quite so menacing. Caleb and Sadie spent a lot of time together, as much as their schedules would allow. They stole away for quick iced coffee breaks when Emily was at day camp. Scarlett and Kaylee babysat Emily on Friday nights while Caleb and Sadie went to a concert and pretended to be young again. In other words, they drank too many beers or pomegranate-flavored cocktails and regretted it the next morning. More often, though, they simply went back to Sadie's house and made up for lost time.

Emily remains a handful, but Caleb feels like he is settling into his parenting groove with each passing day. He's not getting any better at parenting as far as he can tell, and he still spends an inordinate amount of time feeling befuddled or exasperated, but the difference is, he doesn't seem to care so much about his shortcomings anymore. And as far as parenting goes, that's probably about the best anyone can hope for. Lauren hasn't come back to visit yet, but they do talk to her on the phone and on FaceTime fairly regularly. She seems okay, Caleb thinks, but it's difficult to say for sure. One day at a time. Keep moving forward. There are still five days left until Saturday. Or about 120 hours. But who's counting?

...

It's been a long and winding road for Sadie, but it has finally led back here. To her parents' backyard of all places. Where she used to catch lizards when she was a little girl and sit forlornly in the rain when she was a teen, her clothes growing increasingly wet and heavy as her mood somehow lightened. Now, she is preparing for a pretty significant night. Well, it could be significant. It's always hard to tell how these things will turn out.

"Dad, can you grab the other end for me?" Sadie calls from her position on the top of a small ladder where she is trying to loop a strand of decorative white lights over the branch of an oak tree.

Tom has been milling around trying to feel useful for the better part of an hour. When you're a dad and your child is grown up, there's nothing more important than feeling useful. One day Sadie was little, and Tom could move the world for her, and the next she was gone. It's funny how that can happen with people, especially daughters. Once Sadie left, she never came back. Not really. She never needed Tom again. At least not like she did when she would run to him every time she scraped her knee on the pavement or couldn't find her favorite stuffed animal. He still remembers when she was five or six years old, at night when she was standing in front of the bathroom sink brushing her teeth, she would lean her head back against his stomach because she was too tired to stand on her own. She needed his body to help her stay upright. What he wouldn't give to feel needed like that again. So, when he hears his little girl call his name, he reacts much like a golden retriever would. He bounds over as if he's hoping Sadie will scratch him behind his ears and toss a tennis ball for him to chase.

"You've got it, Sadie!" Tom says eagerly, picking up the dangling string of lights and holding it up above his head. He doesn't know exactly what he's supposed to do, but he is determined to do something.

"Uh, thanks, Dad," Sadie says, looking down at Tom. She meant it to be sarcastic because whatever Tom is doing, it isn't super helpful, but when she looks down at him from the ladder, she sees something in his face that makes her pause. It's a hopeful look. Maybe she's just getting old and sentimental or maybe she is beginning to picture Scarlett growing up and leaving her behind, but for whatever reason, she shifts course and says brightly, "That's perfect. This is going to be a great night!"

Tom beams up at her like he's done so many times before, but Sadie can't help but feel like this smile is just a little wider. She's happy to do him this small favor. She really should stop taking her parents for granted, she thinks. She's lucky to have their unwavering support and she knows as well as anyone that people have a way of disappearing when you look away for just a moment too long.

"Great," Tom says. "I know Caleb is going to love this. How could he not?"

"I hope so." Sadie finishes up as best she can with the lights and climbs down from the ladder. "You don't think it's too much?"

"Oh, not at all," Tom says. "It can never be too much when it comes to love."

...

Right before Caleb was about to leave his little yellow home on the busy road, Sadie texted him and said she had a late change of plans and she needed Caleb to pick her and Scarlett up from Sadie's parents' house. So, now Caleb is driving toward Jess and Tom's place with Emily in the backseat. He is wearing a pastel orange polo shirt, his official minigolf shirt, and flat front khaki shorts. As he walked out of his house, Caleb thought he might've caught a hint of autumn in the air, but perhaps he was just imagining it. It's definitely not cool enough for long pants yet, but maybe within a month or two it will be. Hope springs eternal when Florida summers finally begin to wind down.

When Caleb makes the turn onto Jess and Tom's normally quiet street, he is surprised to find an unusual amount of traffic. There are vehicles parked along both sides of the road and several stacked up in

Jess and Tom's driveway. If all these people are going to minigolf, it's going to be quite an event! Caleb squeezes into an open spot and texts Sadie that he's here. When she doesn't respond right away, he and Emily get out and make their way up the driveway toward the house, Emily running ahead excitedly. The air smells of freshly cut grass and lingering rain. The sun has dropped behind the tree line and the light is soft, unobtrusive.

Sadie steps out from the side of the house and starts to walk toward Caleb. When Caleb sees her, his jaw drops. She is wearing a navy-blue sundress, her dark hair is down, and even in the twilight gloom, her blue eyes are piercing. It is quite the look for minigolf, Caleb thinks. He is so taken aback he barely notices that Scarlett is walking with her, a few steps behind. Emily, of course, notices and races up to Scarlett, wrapping her in a hug.

"Hey." Sadie walks up to Caleb and leans in to give him a peck on the cheek.

"Wow," Caleb says. "You look... amazing."

Sadie smiles. "Thanks. You look pretty okay yourself!"

"I feel a bit underdressed now." Caleb looks down at his shirt and runs a hand along his sleeve. "This is going to be quite the minigolf outing, I guess?"

"Yeah, about that... the minigolf was kind of a ruse."

"A ruse? You used minigolf as a ruse? I wore my minigolf polo shirt and everything!"

"Sorry." Sadie laughs. "It was Scarlett's idea."

"Hey!" Scarlett exclaims indignantly.

"Anyway," Sadie continues. "Come around to the back. I have something to show you. I think you're going to like it."

"Okay, if you say so," Caleb says, feigning skepticism.

Sadie takes Caleb's hand, and they walk around the house to the backyard. Caleb opens the wooden gate on the side of the house, holds it open for Sadie, and then steps through. When he looks out upon the medium-sized yard with the looming oak trees and small stone patio off the back of the house, his jaw drops again. It feels like he's stepped onto another planet. The first thing that catches his attention are the lights. Strings of white lights with round, clear bulbs float between the branches of the stately oak trees filling the entire yard with an ethereal glow.

The second thing that catches Caleb's attention is the people. Despite the shadows darkening their faces, Caleb immediately recognizes almost everyone. It seems like the whole sword fighting club is here. Tonya is talking loudly with Sadie's parents; she laughs and gives Tom a hearty slap on the back. The twins are skulking around the periphery, almost hiding in the pockets of darkness, eyeing a table laden with cubes of cheese, crackers, chips, and a huge platter piled high with strawberries, grapes, blueberries, and slices of watermelon.

Paige is here, too, her curly hair extra frizzy in the late-summer humidity. She raises a wine glass in salute to Sadie and Caleb as they look in her direction. She has her children with her and they are everywhere. Emily spots them; immediately intrigued seeing humans of her size and smaller, she trots in their direction to scope out the situation. Paige has even brought her husband, Matt, along. He has a big goofy grin on his face like he can't quite believe he's been included in all this.

One of the other guys from the sword fighting club named Brad is talking to... Caleb's mom? Brad is a mathematician and there's nothing he loves more than talking about arcane mathematical history. From the looks of things, he has found a willing audience in Helen.

Caleb chuckles to himself. What a group. And is that Blaise? It is. With the expensive-looking suit, heavily gelled hair, and dark sunglasses, it could be no one else. There is even a bar, Caleb notices, with a bartender and everything.

"Wait..." Caleb looks toward the small makeshift bar that is lined with bottles and cans. There is a very large man standing behind it. "Is that..."

"Harold?" Sadie says. "Sure is."

Caleb looks at Sadie now. "I have no idea what's happening. But this is really something."

"So, it turns out that Harold is an amateur bartender, or mixologist as he likes to call himself, and he is also a renowned biochemist."

"Are you serious?" Caleb asks incredulously.

"And that's his wife over there." Sadie gestures subtly toward a stunningly beautiful woman with long blond hair who is talking to Paige now.

Caleb can only say, "Wow."

"I know," Sadie continues. "And the crazy thing is she's super nice, too, so it's impossible to hate her."

They both laugh and stand quietly for a moment, hand in hand, taking it all in.

"So, what is this exactly?" Caleb asks finally.

"It's a party, of course."

"Right, I kind of gathered that, but... what is it for? What are we celebrating?"

"Life, Caleb. We're celebrating life."

Caleb looks at her solemnly. "Who are you? And what have you done with Sadie?"

Sadie laughs. "Wow, I can't believe I got through that with a straight face. Maybe I am growing as a person."

Caleb gives her hand a little squeeze and they begin to move around the yard, saying hello to everyone. Preston makes his arrival on the scene, and everyone is suitably starstruck. Jess calls everyone in for a group photo "for the Gram!" and everyone is happy to comply. Well, Scarlett isn't particularly happy about it, but she complies nonetheless.

After about an hour of mingling, food, and drinks, Sadie finds Caleb, who is deep in conversation with Blaise—well, Blaise is talking and waving his hands about and Caleb is half-heartedly listening, and tells him she has one last surprise.

"Okay," Sadie says, pulling Caleb away from Blaise. "I'm going to put this blindfold on you real quick." She holds up a black satiny blindfold.

"Uh...maybe we should save that for later." Caleb wiggles his eyebrows, and she slaps him on the arm.

"Just put it on."

Caleb slips the blindfold on, and Sadie adjusts it to make sure there are no gaps. She takes him by the hand and begins to guide him slowly toward the back of the yard.

...

Life doesn't usually give second chances. But...

...

Everything all at once. That's what it feels like.

...

Caleb can't see anything with the blindfold on, but the rest of his senses are heightened. He feels the grass crinkling under his feet, he smells a hint of honeysuckle in the clean, damp air, and he can taste the collective anticipation. He still doesn't know what's going on, but he knows it's important, meaningful, life-changing?

"Is a peacock going to attack me?" Caleb asks as he moves forward with slow shuffling steps, clutching Sadie's hand.

"Err, well, that's not part of the plan, but I can't make any guarantees."

"Preston would never attack anyone!" Jess calls out from some distance away.

"Well, except for our friend Don," Tom adds. "Preston did give him a little nip last week, but it only sent Don to urgent care, not the ER."

"Oh, right," Jess says. "But you know how Don is..."

"That's true," Tom says. "You remember Don, right, Sadie? Don Sanderson."

"Not now, guys!" Sadie grits forcefully through clenched teeth, waving a hand toward her parents. "Sorry," she says to Caleb. "It's fine, don't worry."

Everything is quiet now, so Caleb doesn't hear much of anything. Even the background chatter of people talking has dropped to a low hum. And then, he hears it. All of it.

Someone starts playing guitar and whoever is playing is not messing around. The music starts out fast and quickly escalates to ferocious. A man's voice begins to sing emphatically. Caleb recognizes it. How could he not?

"Is that...?" he begins, a small smile forming on his face.

"The Pigeontoes? Yes." Sadie reaches up and pulls the blindfold off Caleb, ruffling his hair in the process.

Caleb blinks a few times and looks around in disbelief. In the back of the yard there is a small stage that was hidden in the shadows before but is now illuminated with two spotlights that are poking up from the lawn. On the stage in the center of the spotlight stands a thin man with spiky black hair and tattoos snaking up and down his arms. He is cradling an electric guitar that is hooked up to a small amp and he is blazing through "All My Favorite Hearts are Broken," his voice raspy and fervent.

Caleb takes a moment to look around, widening his focus from Sadie and the stage to take it all in. The group has gathered around. Emily is off to one side, and she seems to be playing with Paige's kids and also the twins, Gavin and Garrett, who are down on all fours while the children climb on top of them and ride them like horses. Harold stands with his wife; her head is resting on his shoulder. Paige and Matt dance in a slightly R-rated fashion, and Helen and Brad remain deep in conversation despite the loud music. The other friends and family fill in the remaining space; over in the corner of the yard, almost behind the stage, Tom and Jess are standing–well, more like bouncing up and down on their toes to the beat of the music. Preston pecks at the grass obliviously beside them. Tom and Jess hold a sign between them that reads "Peacocks" and "Pigeons" with a big red heart in between. Not their best work, Caleb thinks. Scarlett stands even further away in the corner, pretending not to care about anything, even though she secretly likes the music and has a 2000s punk rock playlist in her music library.

Caleb leans into Sadie, speaking directly into her ear. "How did you manage this?"

"My old job came in handy for once," Sadie says. "I know a few people, pulled a few strings, offered The Pigeontoes' guy free drinks."

Caleb looks toward the stage. "Where is the rest of the band?"

"Well, it turns out several of the guys are dead Pigeontoes now. Kind of like the people in those old pictures."

"Ah!" Caleb exclaims. "There she is! My princess of darkness is back!" Sadie rolls her eyes, and he wraps an arm around her waist and pulls her in for a kiss. "I have to say, it does feel a little weird that there is no smoke in the air. If I'd known, I would've picked up some cigarettes."

"And... if you had cigarettes..." Sadie pauses for a moment. "How would that have added smoke to the air exactly?"

Caleb laughs and rests his head on Sadie's shoulder.

The music stops abruptly and The Pigeontoes' frontman says, "I've got one more song for all of you punks. Sadie," he pauses to find Sadie. "Can you help me out with this one?"

Caleb looks confused and he feels his heart pumping against his rib cage. *Thump, thump, thump.* Like a bass drum.

"What are you doing?" he asks Sadie, but she is already gone.

Sadie strides forward confidently and hops up onto the stage. She picks up an acoustic guitar that was leaning against a barstool and sits down, one foot on the bottom rung of the stool and one foot on the small stage. She nods toward the punk rocker, and they begin to play together.

Caleb knows what they are playing. He doesn't need to hear it. Time is a flat circle.

...

Love's a Disaster.

...

Caleb can't take his eyes off Sadie as she sings the song that started it all. Or ended it all, rather. It depends on how you look at it. Her fingers move across the fretboard effortlessly and her and Mr. Pigeon-toes' voices meld harmoniously. Caleb can't help but become lost in the music and he barely notices when the quiet bridge of the song approaches. Before he knows it, Sadie is standing in front of him, guitar abandoned on the stage behind her.

She takes his wrist in her hand and looks directly into his eyes. This time around, it is his turn to panic.

"Wait," he says.

Sadie reaches up and places a finger to his lips. She slides her hand down from Caleb's wrist and takes his hand in hers. She raises her other hand to signal Mr. Pigeontoe, and he begins to play again, softly now.

Sadie sings, "There's no need to ask her, I know I'm a bastard, My mind's racing faster, Love's a disaster!" Her eyes are wide, and her voice is calm and sweet.

"But not ours?" Caleb says. He doesn't shout it this time, there's no need to because the music has dropped now. And it's more of a question than a pronouncement. Time and age don't necessarily bring wisdom. More often than not, they bring uncertainty and doubt.

"Nope," Sadie says. "Our love is a disaster, too. And it probably always will be. But I'm more than okay with that. And with all that being said... will you marry me, Caleb?"

Sadie begins to drop to one knee, but before her knee even touches the grass, Caleb's arms are around her, pulling her towards him.

"Yes, my God, yes!" Caleb's eyes glistening as he stares into the eyes of the one woman who ever mattered. He leans in and kisses Sadie deeply. The small crowd whoops and cheers. Mr. Pigeontoe does a little riff on the guitar in celebration.

"Oh," Sadie says when they finish their embrace. "I got rings."

She holds up two simple unadorned bands that are solid black in color. Caleb's eyes light up even more.

"Sadie, these are so punk rock!" he says. "If only I had known to wear my black eyeliner."

They both laugh, holding each other close as the rest of the world melts away. At least for a moment.

...

The backyard is quiet now. There are only two people left in it. Everyone else has gone home or otherwise disappeared into the darkness. Mr. Pigeontoe and Blaise were the last to leave. They walked away together, Blaise had his arm slung around the aging punk rocker's shoulder and Caleb heard him say something about "synergistic crossover branding opportunities." Scarlett and Emily are inside watching a movie and being stuffed with food by Jess and Tom. Jess and Tom are infatuated by Emily. They don't think they've ever seen a more perfect first grader. Well, at least not in at least six years or so.

It is so quiet and still that Caleb can almost hear his heart beating. *Thump, thump, thump.* The strings of lights continue to bathe the abandoned grass in soft white light. There are a couple of plastic cups scattered across the lawn that Caleb thinks he'll need to pick up before he heads home. The hoot of an owl in the distance pierces the silence. Or maybe it's just a pigeon cooing. Caleb is never sure. There is so much he still doesn't know.

Caleb and Sadie sit side by side on a bench, their thighs touching. They've been sitting like this for a while now, both of them quietly sorting through memories in their minds.

"I don't mean to be ungrateful or, like, a nerd or whatever..." he says, breaking the silence.

"That ship has sailed, Lord Dagwyn," Sadie interrupts. "I mean the nerd part, of course."

Caleb shakes his head and smiles. "Yes, sorry, bad phrasing on my part. But what I was going to say was... you know it's September second, right? Not the third."

"I sure do," Sadie says confidently. "You're not the only one who is very experienced with using calendars."

"Okay," Caleb says, looking out across the yard. "I was just making sure..."

"We're taking control, Caleb. You've been chasing after that awful day for so long, and let's face it, you're never going to catch up to it. No one could. But now... now we have *this.*" Sadie raises her hands, spreads her arms wide, and gestures toward the yard. "We have a fresh start. A new date to look forward to and reflect back upon. Now, we can always remember the night that Sadie made a complete fool of herself singing 'Love's a Disaster' with Mr. Pigeontoe while finally... finally getting the boy for good!"

Caleb laughs and takes Sadie's hand in his. "I love you."

"I love you, too."

He slaps a hand down on his leg like he's ready to spring into action. "So, what should we do now?"

"Hmm, maybe we should head to the library and check out some instructional videos?"

Caleb smiles. "Always a solid choice."

"Unless you meant what should we do about a wedding or whatever," Sadie continues.

"Actually, I meant, like, what should we do with our lives in general now that we've clearly peaked."

"Oh, yeah, then I'll stick with my original library suggestion."

"Cool." Caleb reaches into his pocket to retrieve his phone. "I'll check the opening times for tomorrow."

"It's a date."

There's rustling from the bushes now and Preston emerges. He moves haughtily in their general direction, pausing to peck at the grass every few seconds. He encounters a red plastic cup on the ground, grabs it with his beak, and tosses it a few inches to the side. Then, as Caleb and Sadie watch in silence, Preston stops in front of them, and fans open his expansive tail. He stares at them for a moment with the two eyes on his head and the hundreds of eyes at the ends of his feathers. Caleb and Sadie stare back. After a few seconds, Preston folds up his tail and ambles away.

"Wow," Caleb says.

"Yeah, that was... weird," Sadie says. "Do you think it was some kind of sign?"

"A sign of what?"

"I don't know. Maybe it was from your dad or something?"

"You think my dad was reincarnated as a peacock?" Caleb asks, a touch of alarm in his voice.

"Not just any peacock." Sadie looks into Caleb's eyes with a blank expression. "An Insta-famous peacock."

"God, if that is my dad, I am going to be so annoyed. Even beyond the grave he is way more popular than I am. He has like two thousand times as many followers on Instagram."

Sadie laughs. She leans over and rests her head on Caleb's shoulder, and they sit in silence for a few moments. A light breeze kicks up, rattling the leaves of the oak trees.

"So, after the library, then what?" Sadie asks finally, breaking the silence.

"Hmm, I was thinking maybe we could get matching biking outfits and get really into cycling."

"Ha! The only way you'd catch me in one of those tight neon cycling get-ups is if you dress my corpse in it. You can wear yours and we'll match at my funeral."

Caleb begins to laugh and he can't stop. His laugh is infectious, and now Sadie is laughing too. They hold each other tightly, trying to keep the laughter at bay by force.

"We are such idiots," Caleb says after the tsunami of laughter has passed.

"We really are," Sadie agrees.

Caleb and Sadie sit on the bench a few moments longer until they hear a soft rumble of thunder far in the distance. They stand up and walk hand in hand toward the house. Together. They pass from the soft white light into the shadows. It's like one moment they're there, the next they're gone. It's funny how that can happen with people.

But love? Love rarely disappears so easily. Love's... pretty miraculous.

THE END

ACKNOWLEDGMENTS

For someone who loves reading the acknowledgments section in books (sometimes I even read them first), I somehow feel woefully unprepared to write one. But anyway, here we go.

First, thank you to anyone who has made it this far (or maybe you're reading this first...if so, I feel you)! It means the world to me that you have taken the time to read my silly book.

Thank you to Elizabeth Rands and the team at Bayou Rose Press for believing in this book. Your care and attention made the story so much better, and I am forever grateful for your support.

Thank you to my mostly online, far-flung writing friends, only a few of whom I have met in real life. Writing is such a weird pursuit and it's difficult to do it alone. I am so grateful that the internet exists, and it allowed me to find a community of funny, caring, and talented writer friends.

Thank you to Shannon Carpenter and Jared Bilski (The Dead Pigeons) for your thoughtful notes on this manuscript and for being hilarious and the most supportive guys on the planet.

Thank you to Lindsay Hameroff for your insightful notes on this manuscript and for always being ready to join me in griping about the ridiculousness of writing.

Thank you to Gary Almeter for having an uncanny knack for texting me with encouraging words when I need them most.

Thank you to the mysterious California Greg who goes by several names (you know who you are) for being my most reliable partner in complaining about pretty much anything.

Thank you to Burcu Ozcelik for being such a supportive friend even though we're so far apart.

And thank you to so many more writers and friends who have inspired and supported me in many ways through the years including Julie Vick, Liz Alterman, Kyrie Gray, and David Stanley. I'm sure I have missed other important people and for that, I apologize.

Thank you to my mom and dad, and my siblings, Lisa, Chrisie, and Clint, for always being my biggest supporters.

Thank you to Jacob, Bennett, and Olivia for giving me life every day. I couldn't do any of whatever it is I do without you.

Thank you to the rest of my enormous family. You are all incredible.

Thank you to my friends since forever including the AYGTS boys, Matt and Brad, and Wes who is always in my corner.

Thank you to Billie Joe Armstrong and Green Day both for obvious reasons and one not-so-obvious reason. About fifteen years ago, I was perusing Green Day fan message boards, as one does, and I came across a post from a guy saying that he had successfully proposed to his girlfriend in the pit at a Green Day concert during the song "Waiting." For whatever reason, that post stuck with me for decades. "Waiting" is a beautiful song with lyrics that are at least somewhat appropriate for a proposal, unlike the lyrics of "Love's a Disaster," but I always felt like that was such a bold and maybe crazy thing to do. There is just so much that could go wrong…

And most importantly, thank you to my wife Michelle for showing me what love can be. What love can do. How love can change a person's life for the better. How love can inspire a person to try to do more even when things feel dark and heavy. I love you!

ABOUT THE AUTHOR

Andrew Knott is a writer of essays, humor, and fiction based in the Orlando area. He is the author of the book *Fatherhood: Dispatches from the Early Years*, and the founding editor of Frazzled, a parenting humor publication. His writing has appeared in *McSweeney's Internet Tendency*, *The Washington Post*, and *Parents Magazine*, among others. *Love's a Disaster* is his first novel.

ABOUT THE PRESS

Bayou Rose Press is the romance imprint of Bayou Wolf Press, an independent publisher of quality fiction. If you enjoyed this book and would like to support us, the best thing you can do is leave a review on Amazon, Goodreads, or wherever you review books. If you'd like to learn more about our press, sign up for our newsletter, and stay informed on upcoming books, please visit www.bayouwolfpress.com.

www.ingramcontent.com/pod-product-compliance
Lightning Source LLC
Chambersburg PA
CBHW070622300726

48975CB00006B/1890